PRAISE FOR *DOORS OPEN*

'I read this in one sitting, on a sweltering hot beach in Greece; I kept meaning to do other things – find a beer, fetch a sunhat, check the BlackBerry – but somehow had to keep putting them off until I finished this chapter; and then the next; until I'd reached the end' *Guardian*

'*Doors Open* is a lot of fun. It's pacy, witty, full of action, twists and splendid dialogue. And Rebus does make a subtle appearance when an officer describes his police station as "a damn sight quieter since you-know-who retired"' *The Times*

'An immensely satisfying, bloody and constantly surprising story of middle-class amateurs mixing it with the big boys. And, as usual, Edinburgh – "a village masquerading as a city" – is a character in itself. So much so that "you-know-who" is hardly missed!' *Evening Standard*

'It convincingly shows that he can move with aplomb into another crime form, and tell a story that's typically at once gripping and full of subtle effects, without his depressive detective holding it together' *Sunday Times*

'It's different – and it's good' *Daily Mail*

'Ian Rankin can pull off an audacious criminal caper even without his trademark detective'
Scotland on Sunday

'You won't be able to turn the pages fast enough' *Red*

Born in the Kingdom of Fife in 1960, Ian Rankin graduated from the University of Edinburgh in 1982, and then spent three years writing novels when he was supposed to be working towards a PhD in Scottish Literature. His first Rebus novel, *Knots and Crosses*, was published in 1987, and the Rebus books are now translated into over thirty languages and are bestsellers worldwide.

Ian Rankin has been elected a Hawthornden Fellow, and is also a past winner of the Chandler-Fulbright Award. He is the recipient of four Crime Writers' Association Dagger Awards including the prestigious Diamond Dagger in 2005 and in 2009 was inducted into the CWA Hall of Fame. In 2004, Ian won America's celebrated Edgar Award for *Resurrection Men*. He has also been shortlisted for the Anthony Awards in the USA, and won Denmark's *Palle Rosenkrantz* Prize, the French *Grand Prix du Roman Noir* and the *Deutscher Krimipreis*. Ian Rankin is also the recipient of honorary degrees from the universities of Abertay, St Andrews, Edinburgh, Hull and the Open University.

A contributor to BBC2's *Newsnight Review*, he also presented his own TV series, *Ian Rankin's Evil Thoughts*. He has received the OBE for services to literature, opting to receive the prize in his home city of Edinburgh. He has also recently been appointed to the rank of Deputy Lieutenant of Edinburgh, where he lives with his partner and two sons. Visit his website at www.ianrankin.net

BY IAN RANKIN

The Inspector Rebus series

Knots and Crosses
Hide and Seek
Tooth and Nail
Strip Jack
The Black Book
Mortal Causes
Let It Bleed
Black and Blue
The Hanging Garden
Death Is Not the End (*novella*)
Dead Souls
Set in Darkness
The Falls
Resurrection Men
A Question of Blood
Fleshmarket Close
The Naming of the Dead
Exit Music

Other novels

The Flood
Watchman
Westwind
Doors Open
The Complaints

Writing as Jack Harvey

Witch Hunt
Bleeding Hearts
Blood Hunt

Short stories

A Good Hanging and Other
    Stories
Beggars Banquet

Non-fiction

Rebus's Scotland

Omnibus editions

Rebus: The Early Years
(Knots and Crosses,
Hide and Seek, Tooth and Nail)

Rebus: The St Leonard's Years
(Strip Jack, The Black Book,
Mortal Causes)

Rebus: The Lost Years
(Let It Bleed, Black and Blue,
The Hanging Garden)

Rebus: Capital Crimes
(Dead Souls, Set in Darkness,
The Falls)

All Ian Rankin's titles are available on audio.

Also available: *Jackie Leven Said*
by Ian Rankin and Jackie Leven.

IAN RANKIN

DOORS OPEN

An Orion paperback

First published in Great Britain in 2008
by Orion
This paperback edition published in 2009
by Orion Books Ltd,
Orion House, 5 Upper St Martin's Lane,
London WC2H 9EA

An Hachette UK company

Reissued 2011

A CIP catalogue record for this book
is available from the British Library.

Typeset by Deltatype Ltd, Birkenhead, Merseyside

Printed and bound in Great Britain by
Clays Ltd, St Ives plc

The Orion Publishing Group's policy is to use papers
that are natural, renewable and recyclable products and
made from wood grown in sustainable forests. The logging
and manufacturing processes are expected to conform to
the environmental regulations of the country of origin.

www.orionbooks.co.uk

Doors Open

The open door was only yards away, and beyond it lay the outside world, eerily unaffected by anything happening inside the abandoned snooker hall. Two thickset men had slumped bloodily to the floor. Four more figures were seated on chairs, hands tied behind them, ankles bound. A fifth was wriggling like a snake towards the doorway, straining with the effort. His girlfriend was yelling encouragement as the man called Hate stepped forward and slammed the door shut on all their hopes and dreams, hauling the chair and its occupant back to the original line.

'I'm going to kill you all,' the man spat, face smeared with his own blood. Mike Mackenzie didn't doubt him for a second. What else was someone called Hate going to do? Mike was staring at the door, reminded that this chain of events had begun – so innocently – with a party and with friends.

And with greed.

And desire.

But above all, with doors opening and closing.

A few weeks earlier

1

Mike saw it happen. There were two doors next to one another. One of them seemed to be permanently ajar by about an inch, except when someone pushed at its neighbour. As each liveried waiter brought trays of canapés into the saleroom, the effect was the same. One door would swing open, and the other would slowly close. It said a lot about the quality of the paintings, Mike thought, that he was paying more attention to a pair of doors. But he knew he was wrong: it was saying nothing about the actual artworks on display, and *everything* about him.

Mike Mackenzie was thirty-seven years old, rich and bored. According to the business pages of various newspapers, he remained a 'self-made software mogul', except that he was no longer a mogul of anything. His company had been sold outright to a venture capital consortium. Rumour had it that he was a burn-out, and maybe he was. He'd started the software business fresh from university with a friend called Gerry Pearson. Gerry had been the real brains of the operation, a genius programmer, but shy with it, so that Mike quickly became the public face of the company. After the sale, they'd split the proceeds fifty–fifty and Gerry then surprised Mike by announcing that

5

he was off to start a new life in Sydney. His emails from Australia extolled the virtues of nightclubs, city life and surfing (and not, for once, the computer kind). He would also send Mike JPEGs and mobile-phone snaps of the ladies he encountered along the way. The quiet, reserved Gerry of old had disappeared, replaced by a rambunctious playboy – which didn't stop Mike from feeling like a bit of a fraud. He knew that without Gerry, he'd have failed to make the grade in his chosen field.

Building the business had been exciting and nerve-racking – existing on three or four hours' sleep a night, often in hotel rooms far away from home, while Gerry preferred to pore over circuit boards and programming issues back in Edinburgh. Ironing the glitches out of their best-known software application had given both of them a buzz that had lasted for weeks. But as for the money ... well, the money had come flooding in, bringing with it lawyers and accountants, advisers and planners, assistants, diary secretaries, media interest, social invites from bankers and portfolio managers ... and not much else. Mike had grown tired of supercars (the Lambo had lasted barely a fortnight; the Ferrari not much longer – he drove a second-hand Maserati these days, bought on impulse from the small ads). Tired, too, of jet travel, five-star suites, gadgets and gizmos. His penthouse apartment had featured in a style magazine, much being made of its view – the city skyline, all chimneypots and church spires until you reached the volcanic plug on top of which sat Edinburgh Castle. But occasional visitors could tell that Mike hadn't made much of an effort to adjust his life to fit his new surroundings: the sofa was the same one he'd brought from his previous home; ditto the dining table and chairs. Old magazines and newspapers sat in piles either side of the fireplace, and there was little evidence that the vast flat-screen television with its surround-sound speakers ever got much use. Instead, guests would fix their attention on the paintings.

Art, one of Mike's advisers had advised, was a canny investment. He'd then gone on to suggest the name of a broker who would ensure that Mike bought wisely; 'wisely and well' had been his exact words. But Mike learned that this would mean buying paintings he didn't necessarily like by feted artists whose coffers he didn't really feel like filling. It would also mean being prepared to part with paintings he might admire, solely to comply with the fluctuations of the market. Instead of which, he had gone his own way, attending his first sale and finding a seat right at the front – surprised that a few chairs were still vacant while people seemed content to stand in a crush at the back of the room. Of course, he had soon learned the reason – those at the back had a clear view of all the bidders, and could revise their own bids accordingly. As his friend Allan confided afterwards, Mike had paid about three grand too much for a Bossun still life because a dealer had spotted him as a tyro and had toyed with him, edging the price upwards in the knowledge that the arm at the front of the room would be hoisted again.

'But why the hell would he do that?' Mike had asked, appalled.

'He's probably got a few Bossuns tucked away in storage,' Allan had explained. 'If prices for the artist look like they're on the way up, he'll get more interest when he dusts them off.'

'But if I'd pulled out, he'd've been stuck with the one I bought.'

To which Allan had just shrugged and given a smile.

Allan was somewhere in the saleroom right now, catalogue open as he perused potential purchases. Not that he could afford much – not on a banking salary. But he had a passion for art and a good eye, and would become wistful on the day of the actual auction as he watched paintings he coveted being bought by people he didn't know. Those paintings, he'd told Mike, might disappear from public view for a generation or more.

'Worst case, they're bought as investments and placed in a vault for safe keeping – no more meaning to their buyer than compound interest.'

'You're saying I shouldn't buy anything?'

'Not as an investment – you should buy whatever *pleases* you ...'

As a result of which, the walls of Mike's apartment were replete with art from the nineteenth and twentieth centuries – most of it Scottish. He had eclectic tastes, so that cubism sat alongside pastoral, portraiture beside collage. For the most part, Allan approved. The two had first met a year ago at a party at the bank's investment arm HQ on George Street. The First Caledonian Bank – 'First Caly' as it was more usually called – owned an impressive corporate art collection. Large Fairbairn abstracts flanked the entrance lobby, with a Coulton triptych behind the reception desk. First Caly employed its own curator, whose job it was to discover new talent – often from degree shows – then sell when the price was right and replenish the collection. Mike had mistaken Allan for the curator, and they'd struck up a conversation.

'Allan Cruikshank,' Allan had said, shaking Mike's hand. 'And of course I already know who *you* are.'

'Sorry about the mix-up,' Mike had apologised with an embarrassed grin. 'It's just that we seem to be the only people interested in what's on the walls ...'

Allan Cruikshank was in his late forties and, as he put it, 'expensively divorced', with two teenage sons and a daughter in her twenties. He dealt with HNWs – High Net Worth individuals – but had assured Mike that he wasn't angling for business. Instead, in the absence of the curator, he'd shown Mike as much of the collection as was open for general viewing.

'MD's office will be locked. He's got a Wilkie and a couple of Raeburns ...'

In the weeks after the party, they'd exchanged emails, gone out for drinks a few times, and become friends. Mike had come to the viewing this evening only because Allan had persuaded him that it might be fun. But so far he had seen nothing to whet his jaded appetite, other than a charcoal study by one of the major Scottish Colourists – and he already had three at home much the same, probably torn from the self-same sketchbook.

'You look bored,' Allan said with a smile. He held his dog-eared catalogue in one hand, and a drained champagne

9

flute in the other. Tiny flakes of pastry on his striped tie showed that he had sampled the canapés.

'I *am* bored.'

'No gold-digging blondes sidling up to you with offers you'd be hard pressed to refuse?'

'Not so far.'

'Well, this *is* Edinburgh after all; more chance of being asked to make up a four for bridge ...' Allan looked around him. 'Busy old night, all the same. Usual mix of freeloaders, dealers and the privileged.'

'And which are we?'

'We're art lovers, Michael – pure and simple.'

'So is there anything you'll be bidding on come auction day?'

'Probably not.' Allan gave a sigh, staring into the depths of his parched glass. 'The next lot of school fees are still on my desk, awaiting my chequebook. And I know what you're going to say: plenty of good schools in the city without needing to pay for one. You yourself attended a rough-hewn comprehensive and it didn't do you any harm, but this is *tradition* we're talking about. Three generations, all schooled at the same fusty establishment. My father would curdle in his grave if I put the boys elsewhere.'

'I'm sure Margot would have something to say about it, too.'

At the mention of his ex-wife, Allan gave an exaggerated shudder. Mike smiled, playing his part. He knew better than to offer financial assistance – he'd made that mistake once before. A banker, a man whose daily dealings

10

involved some of the wealthiest individuals in Scotland, couldn't be seen to accept handouts.

'You should get Margot to pay her share,' Mike teased. 'You're always saying she earns as much as you do.'

'And used that purchasing power to good effect when she chose her lawyers.' Another tray of undercooked pastry was coming past. Mike shook his head while Allan asked if the fizz could be pointed in their direction. 'Not that it's worth the effort,' he muttered to Mike. 'Ersatz, if you ask me. That's why they've wrapped those white cotton napkins around the bottles. Means we can't read the label.' He took another look around the chatter-filled room. 'Have you pressed the flesh with Laura yet?'

'A glance and a smile,' Mike replied. 'She seems popular tonight.'

'The winter auction was the first one she'd fronted,' Allan reminded him, 'and it didn't exactly catch fire. She needs to woo potential buyers.'

'And we don't fit the bill?'

'With due respect, Mike, you're fairly transparent – you lack what gamblers would call the "poker face". That little glance you say you exchanged probably told her all she needed to know. When you see a painting you like, you stand in front of it for minutes on end, and then you go up on your tiptoes when you've made up your mind to buy it.' Allan attempted the movement, rocking on his heels and his toes, while holding out his glass towards the arriving champagne.

'You're good at reading people, aren't you?' Mike said with a laugh.

11

'Comes with the job. A lot of HNWs want you to know what they're thinking without them having to spell it out.'

'So what am I thinking now?' Mike held a hand over his own glass and the waiter gave a little bow before moving on.

Allan made a show of screwing shut his eyes in thought. 'You're thinking you can do without my smart-arsed remarks,' he said, opening his eyes again. 'You're wishing you could stand in front of our charming hostess for minutes on end – tiptoes or no tiptoes.' He paused. 'And you're just about to suggest a bar where we can get ourselves a *real* drink.'

'That's uncanny,' Mike pretended to admit.

'What's more,' Allan added, raising his glass in a toast, 'one of your wishes is about to be granted …'

Yes, because Mike had seen her, too: Laura Stanton, squeezing her way through the throng, heading straight towards them. Almost six feet tall in her heels, auburn hair pulled back into a simple ponytail. She wore a sleeveless knee-length black dress, cut low to show the opal pendant hanging at her throat.

'Laura,' Allan drawled, pecking her on both cheeks. 'Congratulations, you've put together quite a sale.'

'Better tell your employers at First Caly – I've got at least two brokers in the room scouting on behalf of rival banks. Everyone seems to want something for the boardroom.' She had already turned her attention towards Mike. 'Hello, you,' she said, leaning forward for another exchange of kisses. 'I get the feeling nothing's quite caught your fancy tonight.'

'Not strictly true,' Mike corrected her, causing her cheeks to redden.

'Where did you find the Matthewson?' Allan was asking. 'We've one from the same series outside the lifts on the fourth floor.'

'It's from an estate in Perthshire. Owner wants to buy some adjacent land so developers can't spoil the view.' She turned towards him. 'Would First Caly be interested ...?'

Allan offered little more than a shrug and the puffing out of his cheeks.

'Which is the Matthewson?' Mike asked.

'The snowy landscape,' Laura explained, pointing towards the far wall. 'Ornate gilt frame ... not really your thing, Mike.'

'Nor mine,' Allan felt compelled to add. 'Highland cattle and sheep huddled together for warmth beneath trees with no leaves.'

'Funny thing about Matthewson,' Laura added for Mike's benefit, 'is that they fetch more if you can see the faces of the animals.' It was the sort of titbit she knew would interest him, and he nodded his appreciation.

'Any sniffs from overseas?' Allan was asking.

Laura gave a thoughtful pout, measuring her response. 'Russian market is strong ... same goes for China and India. I reckon we'll have plenty of telephone bidders come sale day.'

'But no pre-emptives?'

Laura pretended to swipe at Allan with her catalogue. 'Now you're just fishing,' she chided him.

'Incidentally,' Mike began, 'I've hung the Monboddo.'

'Where?' she asked.

'Just inside the front door.' The Albert Monboddo still life had been his only purchase at the winter auction. 'You said you'd come see it,' he reminded her.

'I'll email you.' Her eyes narrowed a little. 'But meantime, feel free to quash a rumour I've been hearing.'

'Uh-oh,' Allan said, snorting into his glass.

'What rumour?'

'That you've been cosying up to the city's other, less likeable auction houses.'

'Where did you hear that?' Mike asked her.

'Small world,' she replied. 'And gossipy with it.'

'I've not bought anything,' Mike said defensively.

'Poor swine's actually blushing,' Allan added.

'You don't want me visiting the Monboddo,' Laura went on, 'and having to turn on my heel because there's half of Christie's and Sotheby's hanging next to it. Well, do you?'

But before Mike could answer, a meaty hand landed on his shoulder. He turned his head and was staring into the dark, piercing eyes of Robert Gissing. The older man's huge dome of a head gleamed with sweat. His tweed tie was askew, his blue linen jacket creased and stretched beyond saving. All the same, he carried real presence, and his booming voice took no prisoners.

'I see the playboys have arrived, just in time to save me from this awful hooch!' He wafted his empty champagne

14

flute like a conductor's baton. His eyes fixed on Laura. 'I don't blame you, my dear, it is your job after all ...'

'Actually, it's Hugh who orders in the catering.'

Gissing shook his head theatrically. 'I'm talking about the paintings, child! Don't know why I come to these tragic affairs.'

'The free booze?' Allan pretended to guess, but Gissing ignored him.

'Dozens and dozens of works, representing the best each artist could muster ... a story behind each brush stroke, each carefully considered placement of object or subject ...' Gissing had pinched his thumb and forefinger together, as though holding a tiny brush. 'They belong to us all, part of our collective consciousness, our nation's narrative ... our history.' He was in his element now. Mike caught Laura's eye and offered a wink: they'd both heard the speech – or variations on its central theme – plenty of times in the past. 'They don't belong in boardrooms,' Gissing went on, 'where only a security pass will get you into the building. Nor do they belong in some insurance company's vault or a captain of industry's hunting lodge ...'

'Or a self-made millionaire's apartment,' Allan teased, but Gissing wagged a finger as fat as a sausage at him.

'You lot at First Caly are the worst offenders – overpaying for undeveloped young talent that then gets too big for its boots!' He paused for breath, and slapped a hand down on Mike's shoulder again. 'But I won't hear a word said against young Michael here.' Mike flinched as Gissing's grip tightened. 'Especially as he's just about to buy me a pint-pot of whisky.'

15

'I'll leave you boys to it,' Laura said, fanning out the fingers of her free hand as she waved goodbye. 'Sale's a week today ... make sure it's in your diaries.' There was, it seemed to Mike, a final smile just for him as she moved away.

'The Shining Star?' Gissing was offering. It took Mike a moment to realise he was talking about the wine bar along the street.

2

It was a low-ceilinged, windowless basement with mahogany slats on the walls and brown leather furnishings. In the past, Gissing had complained that it felt like being in a well-upholstered coffin.

After private viewings and the auctions themselves, it had become their custom to drop into the Shining Star for what Gissing called 'post-match analysis'. Tonight, the place was half full – students by the look of it, albeit of the well-heeled variety.

'Living in Daddy's Stockbridge pied-à-terre,' Gissing muttered.

'But still *your* bread and butter,' Allan teased him.

They found an empty booth and waited for the staff to take their order – whisky for Gissing and Mike, the house champagne for Allan.

'Need a glass of the real McCoy to wash away the memory,' he explained.

'I mean it, you know,' Gissing was saying, rubbing his hands together as if soaping them. 'About all those paintings in purdah ... meant every bloody word.'

'We know,' Allan told him. 'But you're preaching to the converted.'

Robert Gissing was head of the city's College of Art, but not for much longer. Retirement was only a month or two away – at the end of the summer term. It seemed, however, that he was determined to argue his various points to the very last.

'I can't believe it's what the artists themselves would have wanted,' Gissing persisted.

'In the past,' Mike felt obliged to ask, 'didn't they all crave patrons?'

'Those same patrons often loaned out important works,' Gissing shot back, 'to the national collections and elsewhere.'

'First Caly does the same,' Mike argued, looking to Allan for support.

'That's true,' Allan agreed. 'We send paintings all over the place.'

'But it's not the same,' Gissing growled. 'It's all about commerce these days, when it should be about taking pleasure in the works themselves.' He balled one hand into a fist, thumping the table for effect.

'Steady there,' Mike said. 'Staff'll think we're impatient.' He noticed that Allan's gaze was fixed on the bar. 'Good-looking waitress?' he guessed, starting to turn his head.

'Don't!' Allan warned, lowering his voice and leaning across the table, as if for a huddle. 'Three men at the bar, necking a bottle of what looks suspiciously like Roederer Cristal ...'

'Art dealers?'

Allan was shaking his head. 'I think one of them's Chib Calloway.'

18

'The gangster?' Gissing's words coincided with the end of a music track, seeming even louder in the sudden silence, and as he craned his neck to look, the man called Calloway caught the movement and stared back at the trio. His bulbous shaved head rested on huge hunched shoulders. He wore a black leather jacket and a distended black T-shirt. The champagne glass looked like it was being choked by his fist.

Allan had opened his catalogue on the table and was pretending to skim through it. 'Nice going,' he muttered.

'I was at the same school as him,' Mike added quietly. 'Not that he'll remember ...'

'Probably not the time to remind him,' Allan cautioned as their drinks arrived.

Calloway was a known face in the city: protection, strip bars, maybe drugs, too. Their waitress added a warning look of her own as she moved off, but it was too late: a hulking figure was moving towards the booth. Chib Calloway rested his knuckles against the table and leaned across it, casting a shadow over the three men seated there.

'Are my ears burning?' he asked. No one answered, though Mike returned the gangster's stare. Calloway, only half a year older than Mike, had not worn well. His skin had an oily look to it, and his face was chipped and dented, evidence of past battles fought. 'Gone all quiet, hasn't it?' he went on, lifting the catalogue and examining its cover. He opened it at random, examining an early masterpiece by Bossun. 'Seventy-five to a hundred? For some wattle and daub?' He tossed the catalogue back on

19

to the table. 'Now that, my friends, is what I call daylight robbery. I wouldn't pay seventy-five pence for it, never mind K.' He met Mike's stare for a moment, but, as the silence persisted, decided there was little else to detain him. He was chuckling to himself as he went back to the bar, chuckling as he finished his drink and headed out into the night with his scowling colleagues.

Mike watched as the waiting staff's shoulders relaxed and they scooped up the ice bucket and glasses. Allan's eyes were on the door. He waited a further few seconds before speaking.

'We could've taken them.'

But his hand wasn't at its steadiest as he lifted the champagne to his mouth. 'Rumour has it,' he added from above the rim of his glass, 'our chum Calloway pulled off the First Caly heist back in ninety-seven.'

'He should be retired then,' Mike offered.

'Not every retiree is as canny with their cash as you, Mike.'

Gissing had drained his whisky and was waving towards the bar that a further offering was required. 'Maybe we could get him to help us,' he said as he gestured.

'Help us?' Allan echoed.

'Another raid on First Caly,' the professor explained into his empty glass. 'We'd be freedom fighters, Allan, fighting for a cause.'

'And what cause might that be?' Mike couldn't help asking. He was working hard at controlling his breathing, bringing his heartbeat back to something like normal. In the years – around twenty of them – since he'd last seen

Calloway, the man had changed substantially. These days he glowed with menace and a sense of his own invulnerability.

'Repatriation of some of those poor imprisoned works of art.' Gissing was grinning as the whisky arrived. 'The infidels have held on to them for long enough. Time we took our revenge.'

'I like your thinking,' Mike said with a smile.

'Why pick on First Caly?' Allan complained. 'Plenty of other villains out there.'

'And not all of them as public as Mr Calloway,' Gissing agreed. 'You say you were at school with him, Mike?'

'Same year,' Mike answered, nodding slowly. 'He was the kid everyone wanted to know.'

'To know or to be?'

Mike looked at Allan. 'Maybe you're right. Be nice to feel that sense of power.'

'Power through fear isn't worth the candle,' Gissing grumbled. As the waitress swapped his glass for its replacement, he asked her if Calloway was a regular.

'Now and then,' she said. She sounded South African to Mike.

'Big tipper?' he asked her.

She didn't like the question. 'Look, I just work here ...'

'We're not cops or anything,' Mike assured her. 'Just curious.'

'Pays not to be,' she confided, turning on her heel.

'Tidy body,' Allan said appraisingly, once she was out of earshot.

'Almost as tidy as our own dear Laura Stanton,' Gissing

added, winking in Mike's direction. By way of response, Mike said he was heading outside for a cigarette.

'Can I bum one off you?' Allan asked as usual.

'And leave an old man on his own?' Gissing pretended to complain, opening the catalogue at its first page. 'Go on then, off with the pair of you – see if I care ...'

Mike and Allan pushed open the door and climbed the five steps leading from the basement bar to the pavement. It had only just grown dark, and the roadway was busy with midweek taxis seeking work.

'Pound to a penny,' Allan said, 'when we go back inside he'll be bending someone's ear.'

Mike lit both their cigarettes and inhaled deeply. He was down to four or five a day, but couldn't quite give them up completely. As far as he knew, Allan only smoked when around smokers – *obliging* smokers. Looking up and down the street, Mike saw no sign of Calloway and his cohorts. Plenty of other bars they could be in. He remembered the bike sheds at school – there really had been bike sheds, though they were only used for improvised kickabouts. Behind them, the smokers gathered at break and lunchtime, Chib – having earned the nickname even at that early stage in his career – chief among them, breaking open a pack of ten or twenty and selling singles at inflated prices, plus another few pence for a light. Mike hadn't smoked back then. Instead, he would hang around on the periphery, hoping for some sort of welcome into the brotherhood – an invitation that had never come.

'Town's quiet tonight,' Allan said, flicking ash into the air. 'Tourists must be lying low. I always wonder what they think of the place. I mean, it's home to us; hard to see it with anyone else's perspective.'

'Thing is, Allan, it's home to the likes of Chib Calloway, too. Two Edinburghs sharing a single nervous system.'

Allan wagged a finger. 'You're thinking of that programme on Channel 4 last night ... the Siamese twins.'

'I caught a bit of it.'

'You're like me – too much TV. We'll be in our dotage and wondering why we didn't do more with our lives.'

'Thanks for that.'

'You know what I mean, though – if I had your money I'd be helming a yacht in the Caribbean, landing my helicopter on the roof of that hotel in Dubai ...'

'You're saying I'm wasting away?' Mike was thinking of Gerry Pearson, of emails with embedded photos of speedboats and jet skis ...

'I'm saying you should grab what you can with both hands – and that includes the blessed Laura. If you nip back to the auction house, she'll still be there. Ask her out on a date.'

'*Another* date,' Mike corrected him. 'And look what happened last time.'

'You give up too easily.' Allan was shaking his head slowly. 'It amazes me you ever made any money in business.'

'I did, though, didn't I?'

'No doubt about it. But ...'

'But what?'

'I just get the feeling you're still not comfortable with it.'

'I don't like flaunting it, if that's what you mean. Rubbing my success in other people's faces.'

Allan looked as though he had more to say, but natural caution won him over and he only nodded. Their attention was distracted by sudden music, pulsing from a car as it cruised towards them. It was a gloss-black BMW, looked like an M5. Thin Lizzy on the hi-fi – 'The Boys are Back in Town' – and Chib Calloway in the passenger seat, singing along. The window was down, and his eyes met Mike's again. He made the shape of a pistol with his fingers, thumb curving itself into a trigger, drawing a bead on the two smokers. And then he was gone. Mike noticed that Allan had been watching.

'Still reckon we could've taken them?' he asked.

'No bother,' Allan replied, flicking the unsmoked half of his cigarette into the road.

That night, Mike ate alone.

Gissing had suggested dinner, but Allan had said there was work waiting at home. Mike, too, made his excuses, then hoped he wouldn't bump into the professor later on in the restaurant. Thing was, he quite liked eating without company. He'd picked up a paper from a late-opening newsagent's. Walking towards Haymarket, he'd decided on Indian. Restaurants didn't much cater for readers – the lights were usually too low – but he was able to find a table with a wall lamp behind it. In the paper, he read that it was crunch time for Indian restaurants – rice shortages leading to price hikes; tighter immigration meaning fewer chefs were entering the country. When he mentioned this to the waiter, the young man just smiled and shrugged.

The restaurant was pretty full, and Mike's table was too close to a party of five drunks. Their suit jackets were draped over the backs of their chairs. Ties had been loosened or undone altogether. An office night out, Mike guessed, maybe celebrating a satisfactory deal. He knew how those nights could go. People he'd worked with, they'd often commented on how he never seemed to get quite drunk enough, never seemed completely elated whenever a major contract was concluded. He could have told them: *I like to stay in control*. Could have added a postscript; *these days*. The men were on to coffee and brandies by the time his food arrived, meaning that they were getting ready to leave as he asked for his bill. Rising to his feet, he saw that one of the men was losing his balance as he shrugged his arms into his coat. With the diner threatening to back into Mike's table, Mike held a hand out to steady him. The bleary head turned towards him.

'What you up to then?' the man slurred.

'Just stopping you falling over.'

Another of the group had decided to step in. 'Did you touch him?' he asked Mike. Then, to his friend: 'He lay a finger on you, Rab?'

But Rab was concentrating on staying upright, and had nothing further to say on the subject.

'I was trying to help,' Mike argued. The men were gathering round him in a semicircle. He knew how easily these things could turn tribal – five against the world.

'Well, help yourself right now and piss off,' Rab's friend snapped.

25

'Before you find your face on the wrong end of a bottling,' one of the others piped up. The waiters were looking on anxiously. One had pushed open the nearby swing door to alert the kitchen.

'Fine.' With his hands held up in a conciliatory gesture, Mike headed for the street. Once outside, he moved briskly along the pavement, glancing back. If they were going to come after him, he wanted a bit of distance. Distance meant time to think, to assess the situation. Risk versus return. He was fifty yards away before the men emerged. They were arm in arm, pointing across the street towards their next destination: another pub.

Probably forgotten about you already, Mike told himself. He knew that he would remember the encounter in the restaurant. In the next few weeks and months there'd be flashbacks, and he would consider alternative scenarios that would leave him the last man standing, the drunks sprawled at his feet. Aged thirteen, he'd got into a fight with a kid in his class and come off second best. For the rest of his school career, he had plotted elaborate revenge scenarios – without ever carrying them out.

The worlds he moved in these days, there was no need to watch your back. The people were polite and civilised; they had manners and breeding. For all Allan's bravado at the Shining Star, Mike doubted the banker had been in a punch-up in his whole adult life. Walking in the direction of Murrayfield, he thought about student days. He'd found himself in a few bar brawls. Another time, he'd tangled with a potential suitor over a girlfriend ... Christ, he couldn't even remember her name! Then there was the night he'd been walking back to his digs with friends and some drunks had lobbed a metal rubbish bin at them. He'd never forget the fight afterwards. It had travelled from the street into an adjacent tenement and out of the back door into a garden, until a woman had screamed from her window that she was calling the police. Mike had emerged with bruised knuckles and a black eye. His opponent had gone down and stayed down.

He wondered how Chib Calloway would have reacted to the situation in the restaurant. But then Calloway travelled with back-up – the two men in the bar with him weren't just there for the conversation. One of Mike's colleagues had joked once that he should maybe think about a body-guard, 'now that you're so publicly rich'. He'd meant the publication the previous Sunday of a newspaper list placing him in the top five Most Eligible Men in Scotland.

'Nobody needs a bodyguard in Edinburgh,' Mike had answered.

And yet, pausing at a cash machine to take out some money, he looked to right and left, assessing the level of threat. A beggar sat against the shop window next to the bank, head bowed. He looked cold and lonely. Allan had accused Mike once of being a loner – Mike couldn't disagree; didn't mean he was lonely. Tossing a pound coin into the beggar's cup, he headed in the direction of home, some late-night music and his collection of paintings. He thought of the professor's words – *those poor imprisoned works of art* – and then of Allan's – *grab what you can with both hands* … A pub door swung on its hinges, expelling a drinker into the night. Mike dodged the stumbling man and kept on walking.

As one door closes, another one opens ...

3

So far, it had been another bad day for Chib Calloway.

The problem with surveillance was, even if you knew you were being watched, you couldn't always know who the watchers were. Chib owed a bit of money ... all right, a *lot* of money. He owed other things, too, and had been keeping his head down, answering only one or two of his dozen mobile phones, the ones whose numbers only kith, kin and close associates knew. He'd had two meetings scheduled for lunchtime, but had cancelled both. He'd apologised by phone without bothering to explain why. If it got out that he was being tailed, his reputation would dip further. Instead, he'd drunk a couple of cups of coffee at Cento Tre on George Street. It was a pretty upmarket spot – a bank at one time. A lot of Edinburgh's banks had been turned into bars and restaurants. With cash machines everywhere, banks weren't needed. The machines had brought with them a variety of scams, of course: card numbers skimmed, the cards themselves cloned; devices attached to the machine that could transfer the necessary info to a microchip ... There were some petrol stations you didn't dare use. They sold your details on. Chib was careful that way. The gangs with the cash machine know-how all seemed to originate overseas – Albania, Croatia, Hungary. When Chib had looked into it as a possible business proposition, he'd been informed that it was something of a closed shop – which rankled, especially when the gangs then targeted Edinburgh.

It was a small city, population of under half a million. Not big enough to attract the major players, which meant a lot of the available territory belonged to Chib. He had understandings with a number of the bar and club owners. The past several years, there'd been no need for a turf war. Chib had served his apprenticeship in turf wars, building up a solid rep as a soldier. He'd worked as a bouncer for Billy McGeehan at his pool hall and at a couple of his pubs in Leith, just Saturday-night stuff, regulars becoming rowdy as the evening dragged, strangers getting uppity with the locals.

In his early teens, he had thought himself a fair foot-baller, but a trial with Hearts had been a washout. He was reckoned too big, too awkward.

'Switch to rugby, son,' had been the scout's advice.

Rugby! As if …

He'd tried boxing as a means of keeping fit, but couldn't seem to control himself – got in the ring and wanted to lash out with his feet, his knees, his elbows, thrash the opponent to the floor and keep on thrashing.

'Switch to wrestling, son,' had been the advice that time round. But then Billy McGeehan had come to him with another proposal, one that suited Chib fine: he could sign on, pretend to be looking for work, and do some cash-in-hand at weekends – enough to see him through to the next government hand-out. Slowly, Billy had taken him into his confidence, which meant that when Chib switched allegiances and started working for Lenny Corkery instead, he'd taken a fund of knowledge with him. During the war that followed, Billy had decided to up sticks to Florida, signing over the pool halls and pubs, leaving Lenny Corkery king of the hill and Chib his trusted lieutenant.

But then Lenny had dropped dead on the eleventh fairway at Muirfield, and Chib had made his move. He'd been thinking about it for a while anyway, and Lenny's men hadn't made any complaint – not to his face, at any rate.

'A smooth succession is always best for business,' one of the club owners had commented.

Smooth for the first few years, anyway ...

Trouble had been brewing for a while. Not his own fault, not entirely: the cops getting lucky with a shipment of coke and eccies, just after the money had changed hands, meaning a double whammy with Chib on its receiving end. This was unfortunate, as he already owed on a shipment of grass that had come into the country by way of a Norwegian trawler. The suppliers, a Hell's Angels chapter from a town with an unpronounceable name, had given him ninety days to settle.

That was a hundred and twenty days ago.

And counting.

He could have gone to Glasgow, secured a loan from one of the heavyweights there, but that would have meant word getting around. It would involve loss of face. Any sign of weakness, there'd be vultures hovering ... and worse.

He'd demolished those two cups of Italian coffee without tasting them, but knew from his heartbeat that they'd been extra-strength. Johnno and Glenn had accompanied him, all three of them squeezed into a booth by the window, while good-looking women took the other tables, not giving them the time of day. Stuck-up bitches. He knew the type: shopping at Harvey Nicks; cocktails at the Shining Star later on; and a lettuce leaf to sustain them between times. Their husbands and boyfriends would work in banking or as lawyers – bloodsuckers, in other words. Big houses in the Grange, skiing holidays, dinner parties. It was an Edinburgh he'd hardly been aware of while growing up. As a young man, his Saturdays had been about football (if Hearts were at home and a rumble with the away fans seemed probable), or the pub. Maybe chasing skirt along Rose Street or attempting chat-ups in the St James Centre. George Street, all boutiques and jewellery windows with no prices, had seemed alien to him – and still did. Which didn't stop him coming here: why shouldn't he? He had the same cash in his pockets as anyone else. He wore Nicole Farhi polo tops and DKNY coats. Shoes from Kurt Geiger, socks by Paul Smith ... He was as good as any other bastard. Better than the bulk of them. He lived in the *real* world.

'Warts and fucking all.'

'What's that, boss?' Glenn asked, making Chib realise he'd spoken the words aloud. Chib ignored him and asked a passing waitress for the bill, then turned his attention back to his two foot-soldiers. Glenn had already been outside on a recce, reporting back that there was no one loitering in the vicinity.

'What about office windows?' Chib had asked.

'I checked.'

'In one of the shops maybe, pretending to browse?'

'I already said.' Glenn had bristled. 'If there's anyone out there, they're better than good.'

'They don't have to be better than good,' Chib had snapped back. 'Just better than *you*.' Then he'd gone back to gnawing his bottom lip, the way he sometimes did when he was thinking. Until, having paid the bill, he'd come to a decision.

'Okay then ... the two of you can eff off.'

'Boss?' Johnno this time, trying to work out if he'd heard right.

Chib didn't say anything, but the way he saw it was, if it was the Angels or someone like them, they'd be more likely to make their move if he was alone. And if it was the cops ... well, he wasn't sure. But at least he'd know, one way or the other. It was a plan. It was *something*.

The look on Glenn's face, however, told him this didn't mean it was necessarily better than nothing ...

Chib's idea was to hit the shopping crowds on Princes Street. Cars weren't allowed down there, so any tail would have to come after him on foot. He could then climb the steep flight of steps at the side of the Mound and head for the quieter streets of the Old Town, streets where anyone following on foot would be easy to spot.

It was a plan.

But not much better than nothing, as he soon learned. He'd told Glenn and Johnno to stay with the car, he would call them when he needed them. Then he'd headed down Frederick Street, crossing to the quieter side of Princes Street, the side with no shops. The Castle loomed above him. He could make out the tiny shapes of tourists as they leaned over the battlements. He hadn't been inside the Castle for years; seemed to remember a school trip there, but he'd sneaked away after twenty minutes and headed into town. A couple of years back, he'd been cornered in a bar by someone he knew. The man had confided a carefully thought-out scheme to steal the Scottish Crown Jewels, but Chib had given him a slap across the jaw for his trouble.

'Castle's not just for tourists,' he'd explained to the hapless drunk. 'It's a working bloody garrison. How you going to sneak the jewels past that lot, eh?'

He crossed the foot of the Mound at the traffic lights and walked towards the steps. Kept stopping, casting glances back – no sign of anyone. Bloody hell, though ... Peering up the incline, he realised just how steep the steps actually were. He wasn't used to walking. The shoppers and tourists on Princes Street hadn't helped his blood pressure. He'd broken into a sweat just dodging the buses as he crossed the road. What was the point of banning cars when the place just became a racetrack for taxi-cabs and double-deckers? He knew he couldn't face climbing those steps, so stood his ground for a moment instead, weighing up alternatives. He could take a detour into Princes Street Gardens – couldn't stomach the thought of Princes Street itself again. There was a big Greek-style

34

building in front of him; two of them, actually, one behind the other. Art galleries: he knew that much. One of them, they'd wrapped its pillars last year to make them look like soup cans. Something to do with an exhibition. Chib remembered the three guys in the bar. He'd gone over to their table knowing a fifteen-second glare would put the frighteners on them, and it had. That catalogue they'd been perusing – full of paintings. Now here he was outside the National Gallery of Scotland. Yeah, why not? Sort of like a sign from above. Plus, if anyone followed him inside, he'd know for sure. As he walked up to the door, it was held open for him by one of the staff. Chib hesitated, hand in pocket.

'How much?' he asked.

'No charge, sir,' the guard answered. He even gave a little bow.

Ransome watched as the door swung shut behind Chib Calloway.

'Now I really *have* seen everything,' he muttered to himself, reaching into his coat for his phone. Ransome was a detective inspector with Lothian and Borders Police. His colleague, Detective Sergeant Ben Brewster, was in an unmarked car, parked somewhere between the Mound and George Street. Brewster picked up straight away.

'He's gone into the National Gallery,' Ransome explained.

'Meeting someone?' Brewster's voice was tinny; it sounded like he was being beamed down from a space station somewhere.

35

'Dunno, Ben. Looked to me like he was considering the Playfair Steps, but then thought better of it.'

'Know which I'd choose.' Brewster was chuckling.

'Can't say I was looking forward to hauling myself up them,' Ransome agreed.

'Reckon he's spotted you?'

'Not a chance. Where are you?'

'Double-parked on Hanover Street and not making many friends. Are you going to follow him inside?'

'I don't know. More chance of him clocking me indoors than out.'

'Well, he knows *some*one's watching him – so why ditch the two stooges?'

'That's a good question, Ben.' Ransome was checking his watch. Not that he needed to – a blast to his right was followed by a puff of smoke from the Castle's ramparts: the one o'clock gun. He peered down into the Gardens. There was an exit from the gallery down there ... no way he could cover both doors. 'Stay put,' he said into his phone. 'I'm going to give it five or ten minutes.'

'Your call,' Brewster said.

'My call,' Ransome agreed. He slipped the phone back into his pocket and gripped the railings with both hands. It all looked so orderly down in the Gardens. A train was rumbling along the railway track, making for Waverley Station. Again, all very calm and orderly – Edinburgh was that kind of city. You could live your whole life and never get any inkling of what else was going on, even when it was living next door to you. He turned his attention towards the Castle. It appeared to him sometimes like

36

a stern parent, frowning on any impropriety below. If you looked at a map of the city, you were struck by the contrast between the New Town to the north and the Old Town to the south. The first was planned and geometric and rational, the second higgledy-piggledy and seemingly chaotic, buildings erected wherever space permitted. Story was, back in the old days they kept adding floors to the tenements until they started collapsing in on themselves. Ransome liked the feel of the Old Town even today, but he had always dreamed of living in one of the New Town's elegant Georgian terraces. That was why he took a weekly lottery ticket – only chance he was ever going to get on a CID salary.

Chib Calloway, on the other hand, could easily afford the New Town life, but chose instead to live on a ticky-tack estate on the western outskirts of the city, only a couple of miles from where he'd grown up. There was, it seemed to Ransome, no accounting for taste.

The detective didn't think Chib would linger in the gallery – to someone like him, surely art had to act like kryptonite. He would emerge either from the main door, or from the one in the Gardens. Ransome knew he had to make a decision. But then again ... how much did it matter in the great scheme of things? The meetings Chib had arranged – the ones Ransome knew about – were no longer going to happen. No evidence would be gathered; several more hours of Ransome's life wasted as a result. Ransome was in his early thirties, ambitious and alive to possibilities. Chib Calloway would be a trophy, no doubt about that. Not, perhaps, as much of a trophy as four or five years ago, but back then Ransome had been a lowly detective constable and unable to direct (or even suggest to his superiors) a long-term surveillance operation. Now, though, he had inside info, and that could mean the difference between failure and success. One of Ransome's first CID cases had been a push against Calloway, but in court the gangster's expensive lawyer had picked apart the evidence – to the cost of the youngest member of the team of investigators.

Detective Constable Ransome … you're sure that's your correct title? Only, I've known plain constables with more apparent ability. The advocate smug and ruddy-cheeked in his wig; and Chib Calloway braying in the dock, wagging a finger at Ransome as the young detective sloped from the witness box. Afterwards, his team leader had tried telling him it didn't matter. But it had; it did; all the way down the passing years.

The time felt right to him … right here, right now. Everything he knew, everything he suspected, led to one imminent prospect: Chib Calloway's life was about to implode.

It might well be messy, might happen without any interference from Ransome himself, but that didn't mean he couldn't be there to enjoy it.

Nor did it mean he couldn't take the credit …

Chib Calloway waited in the foyer for a couple of minutes, but the only other arrivals were a middle-aged couple with Australian accents and leathery skin. He pretended to be studying a floor plan of the building, then gave a twitch of the mouth, signalling to the guards that he was quite satisfied with arrangements. Taking a deep breath, he walked inside.

It was quiet in the gallery. Bloody big rooms, too, echoing with coughs and whispers. He saw the Aussies again, plus some overseas students who were being taken round by a guide. No way they were locals – too tanned, too fashion-conscious. They shuffled slowly, near-silently past the huge canvases, looking bored. Not too many guards in here. Chib craned his neck, seeking out the all-seeing CCTV cameras. They were just where he thought they'd be. No wires trailing from the paintings, though, meaning no alarms. Some of them looked fixed to the walls by screws, but by no means all of them. Even if they were, thirty seconds with a Stanley knife and you'd have what you came for ... most of it, anyway. The canvas, if not the frame. Half a dozen pensioners in uniforms – no problem at all.

Chib sat himself down on an upholstered bench in the middle of one of the rooms and felt his heart rate begin to slow. He pretended to be interested in the painting opposite, a landscape with mountains and temples and sunbeams. There were a few figures in the foreground, dressed in flowing white robes. He'd no idea what any of it was supposed to mean. One of the foreign students – a bronzed, Spanish-looking lad – blocked his view for a moment before moving to the side to check out the information panel on the wall, oblivious to Chib's glare: *hey, pal, this is my painting, my city, my country ...*

Another man walked into the room: older than the

student and better dressed. A black woollen overcoat fell to just above his feet. His shoes were black, glossy and unscuffed. He carried a folded newspaper and looked like he was just killing time, cheeks puffed out. Chib gave him the stare all the same, and decided he knew the face from somewhere. His stomach clenched – was this whoever'd been tailing him? Didn't look like a villain, but then he didn't look much like a cop either. Where had Chib seen him before? The visitor had given the painting the briefest of glances, and was heading away, brushing past the student. He was already out of the room by the time Chib placed him.

Chib got to his feet and made to follow.

4

Mike Mackenzie had recognised the gangster straight away, hoping it wasn't too obvious when he exited the room pronto. This collection wasn't really his thing anyway; he'd only come into town to do a bit of shopping: shirts to start with (not that he'd found any he liked). Then some eau de cologne and a slight detour into Thistle Street and Joseph Bonnar's jewellery shop. Joe specialised in nice antique pieces, and Mike had gone there with Laura in mind. He'd been thinking of that opal around her neck, imagining her wearing something different, something unusual.

Something bought by him.

But though Joe was a master of his craft – Mike had a pocket watch back home to prove it – he hadn't managed to work his charms this time. Mainly because it had suddenly dawned on Mike: *what the hell am I doing?* Would Laura thank him for the gesture? What exactly would she read into it? Did she even like amethysts and rubies and sapphires?

'Call again, Mr Mackenzie,' Bonnar had said, opening the door for him. 'It's been too long.'

So: no shirts and no jewellery. One o'clock had found

him on Princes Street, not quite hungry enough for lunch and within a stone's throw of the National Gallery. His mind felt clogged; hard to say why he'd been drawn to the place. There were some nice pieces – he'd be the first to acknowledge as much – but it was all a bit stuffy and reverential. 'Art is good for you,' the collection seemed to be saying. 'Here, have some.'

The past few days, he'd been mulling over Professor Gissing's argument about art as collateral. He wondered what percentage of the world's art was actually kept in bank vaults and the like. Like unread books and unplayed music, did it matter that art went unseen? In a generation's time, it would still be there, awaiting rediscovery. And was he himself any better? He'd visited regional galleries and viewed their collections, knowing he had better examples of some of the artists hanging on his walls at home. Wasn't each home and living room a private gallery of sorts?

Help some of those poor imprisoned paintings to escape.

Not from public galleries, of course, but from wall safes and bank vaults and the unvisited rooms and corridors of all those corporate buyers. First Caledonian Bank, for example, had a portfolio running into the tens of millions – most of the usual suspects (they even boasted an early Bacon), plus the cream of new talent, snapped up at all those annual degree shows around the UK by the bank's portfolio curator. Other companies in Edinburgh owned their own hauls and were sitting tight on them, the way a miser would sit on a mattress filled with cash.

Mike was wondering: maybe if *he* made a gesture.

Opened a gallery and placed his own collection there ... could he persuade others to join him? Talk to First Caly and all the other big players. Make a thing of it. Maybe that was why he'd felt drawn to the National Gallery – the perfect place to do a little more thinking on the subject. The last person he'd expected to see was Chib Calloway. And now, turning around, here was Calloway stalking towards him, smile fixed but eyes hard and unblinking.

'You keeping tabs on me?' the gangster growled.

'Wouldn't have taken you for a patron of the arts,' was all Mike could think of by way of an answer.

'Free country, isn't it?' Calloway bristled.

Mike flinched. 'Sorry, that came out all wrong. My name's Mike Mackenzie, by the way.' The two men shook hands.

'Charlie Calloway.'

'But most people call you Chib, right?'

'You know who I am, then?' Calloway considered for a moment and then nodded slowly. 'I remember now – your pals couldn't look at me, but you held eye contact throughout.'

'And you pretended to shoot me as you drove away.'

Calloway offered a grudging smile. 'Least it wasn't the real thing, eh?'

'So what brings you here today, Mr Calloway?'

'I was just remembering that book of paintings, the one you lot were poring over in the bar. I take it you know about art, Mike?'

'I'm learning.'

'So ... this one we're standing beside ...' Calloway took

a step back. 'Guy on a horse, so far as I can see. Not a bad likeness.' He stuffed his hands in his pockets. 'How much would it fetch?'

'Unlikely it would ever come to auction.' Mike gave a shrug. 'Couple of million?' he guessed.

'Hell's teeth.' Calloway moved along to the next painting. 'And this one here?'

'Well, that's a Rembrandt ... tens of millions.'

'Tens!'

Mike looked around. A couple of the liveried custodians were beginning to take an interest. He gave them his most winning smile and started to move away in the opposite direction, Calloway catching him up only after a few more seconds of staring at the Rembrandt self-portrait.

'It's not really about the money, though, is it?' Mike heard himself say, even though he knew only a part of him really believed that.

'Isn't it?'

'What would you rather look at – a work of art, or a framed selection of banknotes?'

Calloway had retrieved one of his hands from its pocket, and he was now rubbing the underside of his chin. 'I'll tell you what, Mike – ten million in cash wouldn't be on the wall long enough to find out.'

They shared a laugh and Calloway ran his free hand across the top of his head. Mike began to wonder about the other hand – the one in the pocket. Was it holding a gun? A knife? Had Calloway come in here with something other than browsing in mind?

'So what *is* it all about then,' the gangster was asking, 'if not the money?'

'Money plays a big part,' Mike was forced to admit. He glanced at his watch. 'Look, there's a café downstairs … do you fancy a quick coffee?'

'I've had a stomachful,' Calloway said with a shake of the head. 'Might manage a cup of tea, though.'

'My treat, Mr Calloway.'

'Call me Chib.'

So they headed down the winding staircase, Calloway enquiring about prices, Mike explaining that he'd only been interested in art for a year or two and wasn't exactly an expert. One thing he didn't want Calloway to know was that he had a collection of his own, a collection some would doubtless term 'extensive'. But as they queued at the service counter, Calloway asked him what he did for a living.

'Software design,' Mike said, deciding that he would elaborate as little as possible.

'Cut-throat business, is it?'

'It's high pressure, if that's what you mean.'

Calloway gave a twitch of the mouth, then got into a discussion with the girl behind the counter about which of the many teas on offer – Lapsang, green, gunpowder or orange pekoe – tasted most like actual tea. After which, they took their table, with its views on to Princes Street Gardens and the Scott Monument.

'Ever been to the top of the Monument?' Mike asked.

'Mum took me up there when I was a kid. Scared me stupid. That's probably why, a few years back, I dragged

45

Donny Devlin up there and threatened to sling him off – owed me money, you see.' Calloway had his nose in the teapot. 'Smells a bit weird, this.' But he poured some all the same, while Mike stirred his own cappuccino, wondering how to respond to such a warped confession. The gangster didn't seem to realise that he'd said anything at all out of the ordinary. The memory of his mother had segued seamlessly into a momentary depiction of horror. Mike couldn't tell if Calloway had set out to shock him; maybe it wasn't even true – the Scott Monument was a stupidly public place for such a scene. Allan Cruikshank had hinted that Calloway had engineered the First Caly heist. Difficult now to envisage him as a criminal mastermind ...

'Anyone ever tried breaking into this place?' Calloway asked at last, studying his surroundings.

'Not that I know of.'

Calloway wrinkled his nose. 'Paintings are too bloody big anyway – where would you stash them?'

'A warehouse, maybe?' Mike suggested. 'Art gets stolen all the time – a couple of men in workmen's uniforms walked out of the Burrell collection with a tapestry a few years back.'

'Really?' This seemed to tickle the gangster. Mike cleared his throat.

'We were at the same school, you and me – same year, actually.'

'Is that a fact? Can't say I remember you.'

'I was never on your radar, but I recall that you more or less ran the place, even told the teachers what they could and couldn't do.'

Calloway shook his head, but seemed flattered none-theless. 'I'm sure you're exaggerating. Mind you, I was a tearaway back then.' His eyes lost focus, and Mike knew he was thinking back to those days. 'A solitary O-Grade, I ended up with – metalwork or something.'

'One project, we made screwdrivers,' Mike reminded him. 'You put yours to good use ...'

'Persuading the nippers to hand over their cash,' Chib agreed. 'You've got a good memory. So how did you get into computers?'

'I stayed on for Highers, then college after that.'

'Our paths diverged,' Chib said, nodding to himself. Then he stretched his arms out. 'Yet here we are, meeting up after all these years, proper grown-ups and no damage done.'

'Speaking of damage ... what happened to Donny Devlin?'

Chib's eyes narrowed. 'What's it to you?'

'Nothing at all ... just curious.'

Chib pondered for a moment before replying. 'He got out of the city. Paid me back first, mind. D'you keep up with anyone from the old days?'

'Nobody,' Mike admitted. 'Took a look at Friends Reunited once, but there wasn't anyone I particularly missed.'

'Sounds like you were a loner.'

'I spent a lot of time in the library.'

'Might explain why I don't remember you – I only went there the one time, took out *The Godfather*.'

'Was that for recreational purposes or for training?'

Chib's face darkened again, but only for a second. Then he burst out laughing, acknowledging the joke.

And so the conversation continued – fluidly; light-heartedly – neither man aware of the figure who twice passed by the window.

The figure of Detective Inspector Ransome.

5

Mike was standing at the very back of the saleroom, just inside the doorway. Laura Stanton had taken her place at the lectern and was checking that her microphone was working. She was flanked by plasma screens on which images of the lots would be shown, while the genuine articles were placed on an easel or pointed to (if they happened to be hanging on one of the walls) by a team of well-rehearsed staff. Mike could tell that Laura was nervous. This was, after all, only her second sale, and so far her performance had been judged 'solid' at best. No real treasures had been unearthed, no records smashed. As Allan Cruikshank had observed, the art market could go that way for months or even years at a stretch. This was Edinburgh, after all – not London or New York. The focus was on Scottish works.

'You're not going to be offered a Freud or a Bacon,' Allan had said. Mike could see him now, seated two rows from the back, not in the market to buy anything, just keen for a final glance at each painting before it vanished into private hands or some corporate portfolio. From where Mike stood, he could take in the whole room. There was whispered anticipation. Catalogues were browsed one last

time. Staff from the auction house were seated at their telephones, ready to hook up with distant bidders. It intrigued
Mike: who were those people on the other end of the line?
Were they Hong Kong-based financiers? Manhattan Celts
with a penchant for Highland scenes of kilted shepherds?
Rock stars or movie actors? He imagined them being given
manicures or massages as they yelled their bids into the
receiver, or pushing weights in their home gym, or seated
aboard private jets. Somehow he always imagined them as
being more glamorous than anyone who actually took the
trouble to attend an auction. He'd asked Laura once for
some gen on the telephone bidders but she'd just tapped
the side of her nose, letting him know there were secrets
she couldn't share.

He knew probably half the people on view: dealers for
the most part, who would then try to sell the paintings
on. Plus the curious, dressed drably as though they'd
only stumbled indoors for want of anything better to
do with their time. Maybe some of them had a couple
of paintings tucked away at home, a legacy from some
long-dead aunt, and now wondered how much the artist
was fetching. There were two or three people like Mike
himself – genuine collectors who could afford pretty well
anything that might come up. There were also a few faces
new to him. And seated right at the front – in Newcomers'
Row – but with no paddle (and therefore only satisfying
his curiosity), Chib Calloway. Mike had spotted him the
moment he'd walked into the room, but had managed (so
far) to go unnoticed. He realised that the two men leaning
against the wall to Calloway's left were the same ones from

a week ago in the Shining Star. When Mike had bumped into Calloway in the National Gallery, the gangster hadn't seemed to need his henchmen. Mike wondered what had changed. Maybe it was because he wanted to be noticed, wanted the people around him to know he was the sort of man who could boast protection. A very public show of his importance.

The gavel came down to signal that the auction was underway. The first five lots came and went in a blur, fetching the bottom end of estimate. A figure filled the doorway and Mike gave a nod of greeting. With retirement looming, Robert Gissing seemed to have more time on his hands for previews and auctions. He was giving the room an all-encompassing, beetle-browed glower. While Allan might regret the whisking away of so many paintings, Gissing had been known to rise to a state of apoplexy in salerooms, storming out, his voice booming down the corridor: *works of genuine genius! Sold into servitude and wrenched from the gaze of the deserving!* Mike hoped he wasn't going to cause a scene today – Laura had quite enough on her plate as it was. He noted that Gissing, too, had failed to collect a bidding paddle, and began to wonder just how many people in the room were interested in actually buying something. The next two lots failed to reach their reserve, adding to Mike's fears. He knew that some of the dealers would get together beforehand to express their individual interests, making pacts to ensure they didn't get into bidding wars. This tended to keep prices down unless there were collectors in the room or on the ends of those telephones.

Mike thought he could see the blood rising up Laura's neck, colouring her cheeks. She gave a little cough and paused between lots, taking a few sips of water and scanning the room for signs of interest. There was little enough atmosphere, and oxygen seemed to have been sucked from the place. Mike could smell the dust from antiquated picture frames, mixed with tweed and floor polish. He tried to guess at the secret life of each painting, at the journey they had made from imagination to sketchbook, sketchbook to easel. Finished, framed, displayed and sold. Passing from owner to owner, handed down as an heirloom, perhaps, or dismissed as worthless until rescued from a junk shop and restored to glory. Whenever he bought a painting, he made sure to spend time examining its rear end for clues – chalked measurements calculated by the artist on the frame; a label from the gallery where the first sale had been made. He would check the catalogues, tracing the line of ownership. His latest purchase, the Monboddo still life, had been painted during a trip to the French Riviera and brought back to Britain, shown as part of a group exhibition in a townhouse in Mayfair, but only sold a few months later by a small gallery in Glasgow. That first purchaser had been the scion of a tobacco family. Much of this information had come from Robert Gissing, who had written more than one monograph on Monboddo. Daring a glance in Gissing's direction, Mike saw that the arms were folded, the face stern.

But something was happening at the front of the saleroom. Calloway had raised a hand to make a bid on something, and Laura was asking if he had a paddle.

'Do I look like I'm in a canoe?' Calloway responded, bringing laughter from those around him. Laura apologised that she could accept bids only from those who had registered at the reception desk, and explained that there was still time if the gentleman wanted to ...

'Never mind,' Calloway said, waving the offer away.

This seemed to relax the room, and things perked up even more with the next lot. One of the Matthewsons: sheep in a snowdrift, late nineteenth century. Laura had mentioned at the preview that there was interest in it, and now two telephone bidders were going head to head, focusing the attention of the room on the members of staff who held the receivers. The price kept cranking up and up until it was double the top estimate. The gavel eventually came down at eighty-five thousand, which would do no harm at all to Laura's bottom line. This seemed to give her a renewed confidence and she made a well-received joke, which in turn brought a little more life to the room as well as a delayed guffaw from Chib Calloway. Mike flicked through the next few pages of the catalogue and saw nothing tempting. He squeezed past the crush of dealers next to him and shook hands with Gissing.

'Isn't that,' Gissing muttered with a nod towards the front of the room, 'the rogue we had the run-in with at the wine bar?'

'You can't always judge a book by its cover, Robert,' Mike whispered into the professor's ear. 'Any chance of a word later?'

'Why not now,' Gissing shot back, 'before my blood pressure gets the better of me ...'

At the far end of the hallway were some stairs leading upwards to floors where antique furnishings, books and jewellery were displayed. Mike stopped at the foot of the staircase.

'Well?' Gissing prompted.

'Enjoying the sale?'

'As little as usual.'

Mike nodded slowly, but couldn't think how to start the real conversation. Gissing smiled indulgently.

'It's been preying on your mind, Michael,' he drawled. 'What I said to you that night in the wine bar. I could see that you understood straight away, understood the absolute validity of what I was proposing.'

'Not a serious proposal, though, surely. I mean, you can't just go around stealing art. For a start, First Caly wouldn't be too thrilled at the idea … And what would Allan say?'

'Maybe we should ask him.' Gissing sounded serious.

'Look,' Mike argued, 'I agree it's a nice thought – I like the idea of planning some sort of … heist.' Gissing, listening intently, had folded his arms again.

'It's been preying on *my* mind, too,' he said eventually. 'For some considerable time – as you say, a nice little exercise for the grey cells. It occurred to me early on that First Caly wouldn't do, their security's too good. But what if there were a way to emancipate a certain number of paintings without them even being noted as missing?'

'From a bank vault?'

Gissing shook his head. 'Nothing so onerous.' He patted

54

his distended stomach. 'Do I look like I could break into a bank?'

Mike gave a little laugh. 'This is all hypothetical, right?'

'If you say so.'

'Okay, then enlighten me – where are we stealing these paintings from?'

Gissing paused a moment, running his tongue along his bottom lip. 'The National Gallery,' he said at last.

Mike stared at him for a few seconds, then gave a snort. 'Yeah, right, absolutely.' He was remembering his encounter with Calloway: *anyone ever tried breaking into this place?*

'No need for sarcasm, Michael,' Gissing was saying.

'So we just waltz in and then out again, and no one's any the wiser?'

'That's pretty much the size of it. I can explain over a drink, if you're interested.'

The two men stared one another out. Mike was the first to blink. 'You've been mulling this over for how long?'

'Probably a year or more. I'd like to take something with me when I retire, Mike. Something no one else in the world has got.'

'Rembrandt? Titian? El Greco …?'

Gissing just shrugged. Mike saw Allan emerging from the saleroom and waved him over.

'Maybe that Bossun you bought wasn't such a bad punt,' Allan informed him with a sigh. 'One's just gone for thirty-eight K. This time last year he was lucky to break twenty …' He looked from one man to the other. 'What's up with you two? You look like kids who've been caught with their hands in the sweetie jar.'

'We were just going to have a drink,' Gissing said. 'And maybe a little chat.'

'What about?'

'Robert here,' Mike began to explain, 'has been stating his intention to lift some paintings from the national collection without their absence being noticed. A little retirement gift to himself.'

'Beats a gold watch,' Allan agreed.

'Thing is, I think he might actually be serious.'

Allan focused his attention on Gissing, who offered a shrug.

'Drink first, talk later,' the professor said.

Detective Inspector Ransome watched the three men leave the auctioneer's and head just half a block along the street to a basement wine bar called the Shining Star. He recognised one of them – the one he'd seen a few days back, drinking coffee with Chib Calloway in the National Gallery's café. First a gallery and now an auction house. Ransome had checked the notice in the window: the sale had commenced at 10 a.m. Calloway had arrived twenty minutes early, buying a catalogue from the receptionist and being pointed in the direction of the actual saleroom. What the hell was he up to? He'd brought Glenn and Johnno with him, as if some deal might be about to go down. Johnno had come out for a cigarette about fifteen minutes in, looking bored, checking for texts and calls on his mobile. No chance of him spotting Ransome, who was standing eighty feet away behind one of the pillars outside the concert hall.

But with no clue what was going on.

He was on his own today. Ben Brewster was back at the station, working through a heaped in-tray. Ransome's own desk wasn't exactly empty, but the phone call tipping him off could not be ignored. And now he had two for the price of one: Calloway, and the handsome, well-dressed man. He was torn between going to the wine bar, maybe overhearing something, and staying put. He wished now he'd dragged Brewster out with him.

It was another half-hour before the auction house started to empty. Ransome watched from behind his pillar as Calloway emerged, flanked by Johnno and Glenn, Johnno lighting up at the first opportunity. But Calloway seemed to change his mind and darted back inside again, leaving the two goons to roll their eyes. Couldn't be easy, working for a nutter like Calloway. Johnno and Glenn both had form. They'd served time at Saughton Prison and further afield – casual violence; threats; intimidation. Johnno was the less predictable, the one likely to reach for the switch marked 'berserk'; Glenn had at least a bit of sense about him. Did as he was ordered, but otherwise kept pretty quiet.

It was a couple of minutes before Calloway re-emerged. He was talking to a woman Ransome recognised. Calloway gestured along the street, suggesting a drink maybe, but she was shaking her head, trying to be polite. She accepted his handshake and headed back indoors. Johnno patted his boss on the back, as if to say: worth a try. Calloway didn't seem to like that, snapped some remark back at him. Then the three men started making their way towards – well, well, well – the selfsame wine bar. Decision time again, and this time Ransome didn't hesitate. He crossed the road and threshold both, smiling in the direction of the receptionist as he followed Laura Stanton into the deserted saleroom.

Not quite deserted, actually: chairs were being stacked by staff in brown overalls. Telephones were being unplugged from wall sockets. A lectern was being dismantled, plasma screens taken down. Someone had handed Laura a sheet of numbers, with a total circled in red at the foot of the page. Her face was difficult to read.

'Hiya, Stanton,' Ransome said. It took her a moment to place him, then a tired but genuine smile appeared.

'Ransome, long time no see.'

The two had been in the same year at college, shared a mutual friend so tended to be at the same parties, the same nights out. They'd lost touch for over a decade, until a reunion had taken them to their alma mater. A few more reunions had followed, though they'd last bumped into one another months back at a jazz concert in the Queen's Hall. Laura stepped forward now and pecked him on both cheeks.

'What brings you here?' she asked.

Ransome was making a show of studying the room and its contents. 'I remember you saying you worked for an auction house … didn't realise you actually run the show.'

'You're way off the mark.' But she sounded flattered all the same.

'If I'd arrived a bit earlier, would I have caught you in full flow?'

'More of a constant trickle.' She glanced at the sheet of numbers. 'Markedly up on the winter sale, though, which is encouraging ...'

'I'm not interrupting?' Ransome tried to sound concerned.

'No, it's fine.'

'Only, I was passing and I thought I saw you enjoying a tête-à-tête with Chib Calloway.'

'Who?'

He met her stare. 'You know, the gorilla with the shaved head. Was he shopping for anything in particular?'

She knew who he meant now. 'Didn't seem to have much of a clue. He was asking at the end, how did all the bidding work?' Her face tightened. 'Is he in some sort of trouble?'

'Since the day he climbed out of the cot. You've never heard of Chib Calloway?'

'I'm assuming he's not some distant relation of Cab?'

The detective reckoned this deserved a smile, but it was gone by the time he spoke. 'Streak of violence a mile wide. Fingers in many and sundry dirty pies.'

'Is he trying to launder money?'

Ransome's eyes narrowed. 'What makes you ask?'

She gave a shrug. 'I know it happens ... I mean, I've heard of it happening elsewhere, other auction houses. Not here, though, God forbid ...' Her voice drifted away.

'It's something I might look into.' Ransome rubbed the underside of his jaw. 'I've half a feeling one of his "associates" brought him here today.'

'There were two of them,' Laura started to correct him, but Ransome shook his head.

'I'm not talking about the performing monkeys – they're called Johnno Sparkes and Glenn Burns. They provide muscle for Calloway when he doesn't feel like doing his own dirty work. No, I mean the tall fellow, wears a suit well, brown hair combed back from his forehead and over his ears. He left here with a big bear of a man in green corduroy and another guy, skinny, short black hair and glasses.'

She smiled at the description. 'The Three Musketeers – that's how I always think of them, they seem to get along so well, even though they're different.'

Ransome nodded as though this made perfect sense to him. 'Thing about the Three Musketeers, though ...'

'What?'

'As I recall, there were four of them.' Having said which, he took out his notebook and asked Laura for their names.

'Wasn't one of them Porthos?' she teased. But the detective, her old drinking chum from college, was past jokes and attempts at humour. Anxiety flashed in Laura's eyes. 'There's no way any of them would have anything to do with a character like that,' she said defensively.

'Meaning there's no reason you shouldn't give me their names.'

'They're potential clients, Ransome. There's *every* reason I shouldn't tell you anything.'

'Christ, Laura, you're not a priest or a clap-doctor.' Ransome gave a heavy sigh. 'I'm a detective, remember. I could stop them in the street if I liked and make them tell me. I could haul them down to the station.' He gave this a moment to sink in. 'And I'm sure you're right – they've got nothing to do with Calloway. But this is me being nice, trying to be as inconspicuous as possible. If you give me their names, I can do a quick background check without them ever knowing. Much better all round, don't you think?'

Laura considered this. 'I suppose so,' she eventually conceded, winning a conciliatory smile from Ransome.

'We're agreed then?' he checked. 'This is going to be kept between us?' As she nodded, he stood with pen poised against his notebook, and at the same time asked her how she'd been keeping of late …

6

Gissing seemed in no hurry to tell his story. He was swill-
ing the malt around in its glass, nosing it now and then
as if reluctant to take that first fragrant sip. It was too
early in the day for Mike, and Allan was due back at the
office, having lied about meeting a client for coffee. He
was stirring the froth that covered his cappuccino and
making regular checks of his watch and mobile phone.

'Well?' Mike said, for the third or fourth time. His
own drink was a double espresso. It had come with a
little almond biscuit, which he'd placed to one side. The
Shining Star was near empty – just a couple of women
taking a break from their shopping. They were at the other
end of the room, well out of earshot, purchases at their
feet. Electronic music was playing through the speakers,
but kept just audible.

Gissing reached across and placed his fingers around
the biscuit, proceeding to dunk it in the whisky. He started
sucking on it, eyes gleaming with humour.

'I'd better get back,' Allan started to say, shifting in his
seat. They were at the same booth as a week ago. Same
waitress, too, though she hadn't seemed to remember
them.

Gissing took Allan's hint. 'It's actually pretty simple,' he began, a few crumbs flying from the corners of his mouth. 'But you head off if you like, Allan, while I tell Mike here how to steal a painting without really trying.'

Allan decided he could manage a few more minutes. Gissing, having finished the biscuit, tipped the glass to his mouth and drained it with a satisfied smack.

'We're listening,' Mike told the professor.

'All the galleries and museums in this fair city of ours ...' Gissing leaned over the table, resting his elbows on its surface. 'They don't have room to display even a tenth of their collections. Not even a *tenth*.' He paused to let this sink in.

'With you so far,' Mike commented drily.

'And those sad artefacts sit unloved in the dark ... they sit there for *years*, Michael, and no one ever sees them.' Gissing started to count on his fingers. 'Paintings, drawings, etchings, jewellery, statuary, vases, pottery, carpets, books – from the Bronze Age onwards. Hundreds of thousands of items.'

'And you're saying we can walk off with a few of them?'

Gissing lowered his voice still further. 'They're stored in a huge warehouse on the waterfront at Granton. I've been there on several occasions, and the place is a bloody treasure trove!'

'An itemised, inventoried treasure trove?' Allan speculated.

'I've known stuff get wrongly shelved – it can take months to track a piece down.'

'And it's a warehouse?' Mike watched Gissing nod. 'With guards, CCTV, maybe a few German Shepherds and some razor wire ...?'

'It's secure enough,' Gissing admitted.

Mike smiled – he was enjoying this little game. The old man seemed to be enjoying it, too, and even Allan was looking intrigued.

'So what do we do?' Allan asked. 'Dress up as commandos and storm the compound?'

It was Gissing's turn to smile. 'I think we can deploy a soupçon more subtlety, Allan, dear boy.'

Mike leaned back and folded his arms. 'Okay, you're the one who knows this place – how would someone get in? And even if they did, how come nothing would be noticed as having walked out with them afterwards?'

'Two excellent questions,' Gissing appeared to concede. 'To answer the first – they would walk in through the front door. More than that, they would have been *invited*.'

'And the second?'

Gissing held his hands out, palms showing. 'Nothing would *be* missing.'

'The one thing "missing" from all of this is any notion of reality,' Allan complained. Gissing looked at him.

'Tell me, Allan, does First Caledonian ever take part in Doors Open Day?'

'Sure we do.'

'And what can you tell me about it?'

Allan shrugged. 'It's exactly what it sounds like – one day a year, a lot of institutions open their doors to the general public so they can take a look around. Last year, I went to the observatory ... year before that I think it was Freemasons' Hall.'

'Very good,' Gissing said, as if to a prize pupil. Then, to Mike: 'You've heard of it, too?'

'Vaguely,' Mike conceded.

'Well, the Granton warehouse is another participant – I'm assured they'll be throwing their doors open again to the masses at the end of this month ...'

'Okay,' Mike said, 'so we can just walk in as members of the public. Walking out again might be the problem.'

'That's true,' Gissing agreed. 'And I'm afraid such things as guardrooms and CCTV are outwith my area of expertise. But here's the rub – nothing's going to be missing. Everything will appear to be just the way it was.'

'See, you've lost me again,' Allan said, fiddling with his watch strap and starting to text his secretary.

'There's a painter ...' Gissing began, breaking off as a shadow loomed over the three of them.

'Getting to be a regular occurrence,' Chib Calloway said to the silenced table. When he stretched out a hand for Mike to shake, Allan visibly flinched, as though a punch were about to be thrown. 'Has Mike here told you we were at the same school?' Calloway had slapped a hand down on Mike's shoulder. 'We did some catching up the other day – didn't see you at the sale, Mike ...'

'I was standing at the back.'

'Should've come and said howdy – might've saved me making a prick of myself by heading up shit creek without the necessary paddle.' The gangster laughed at his own joke. 'What's your poison, gents? This one's on me.'

'We're fine,' Gissing snapped. 'Just trying to have a *private* conversation.'

Calloway returned the stare. 'That's not very friendly now, is it?'

'We're fine, Chib,' Mike said, trying to defuse whatever was threatening to start. 'Robert's just ... well, he was in the middle of telling me something.'

'So it's sort of a business meeting?' Calloway nodded slowly to himself and straightened up. 'Well, head over to the bar when you're finished, Mike. I want to pick your brains about the auction. I did try asking that tasty auctioneer, but she was too busy counting the shekels ...' He turned to go, but then paused. 'And I hope the business you're discussing is all above board – walls have ears, remember.'

He returned to the bar and his two bodyguards.

'Mike,' Allan said warningly, 'suddenly you and him are buddies?'

'Never mind about Chib,' Mike replied quietly, eyes on Robert Gissing. 'Tell me more about this painter.'

'Before I do ...' Gissing reached into his jacket pocket for a folded sheet of paper. 'Here's something I thought you might like.' Mike opened it up while Gissing spoke. It was a page torn from a catalogue. 'Last year at the National?' Gissing was reminding him. 'The Monboddo exhibition – that's where Allan introduced us, if you remember.'

'I remember you bending my ear about Monboddo's strengths and weaknesses.' Mike stopped talking as he realised what he was holding.

'This was your favourite, wasn't it?' Gissing was saying.

Mike just nodded. It was a portrait of the artist's wife, painted with such passion and tenderness ... and looking uncannily like Laura Stanton. (Someone else he'd met for the first time that night.) Mike had thought he might never lay eyes on it again.

'This is in that warehouse?' he asked.

'Indeed it is. Went straight back there after the retrospective. What does it measure? No more than eighteen inches by twelve, yet they can't find regular room for it on their walls. And such an exquisite piece. You start to see what I mean, Michael? We'd be freeing them, not stealing them. We'd be doing it out of love.'

'I really do have to get going,' Allan said, getting to his feet. 'Mike ... Calloway's part of your past, remember, and probably best kept there.' He glanced in the direction of the bar.

'I can look after myself, Allan.'

'I've a parting gift for you, too,' Gissing interrupted. Another page from a different catalogue was handed over. Allan Cruikshank's mouth fell open.

'Better than any of the Coultons in your own bank's portfolio,' Gissing said, reading Allan's mind. 'I know you're a massive fan – and there are half a dozen others to choose from, if these don't suit.'

Seeming still in a daze, Allan found himself taking his seat again.

'Now,' Gissing continued, satisfied with this reaction, 'the painter I was going to tell you about ... a young fellow of my acquaintance. He goes by the name of Westwater...'

7

Hugh Westwater – 'Westie' to those who knew him well enough – was sitting comfortably amid the chaos of his top-floor tenement flat, smoking yet another joint. The bay-windowed living room had become his studio, grubby bedsheets draped over the old sofa and chair that Westie had claimed from a skip. Canvases rested against the skirting boards, newspaper cuttings and magazine photos were taped to the walls. Greasy pizza cartons and beer cans littered the floor, some of the cans torn in half to provide makeshift ashtrays. Wonder was, Westie thought, 'they' still let you smoke in the comfort of your own home. These days you couldn't smoke in pubs, clubs or restaurants, or at your place of work or even in some bus shelters. When the Rolling Stones had played a stadium gig in Glasgow and Keith had lit one up onstage, 'they' had considered prosecution.

Westie always thought of the authorities as 'they'.

One of his first portfolio pieces had been a manifesto, printed in black against a glossy blood-red backing.

They Are Out To Get You

They Know What You Do

They See You As Trouble ...

At the very bottom of the canvas, the printing had switched to white-on-red for Westie's coda: But I Am Better At Art Than Them.

His tutor had only just agreed, scoring him a 'narrow pass'. The tutor was a big fan of Warhol, so Westie's next piece had been calculation itself: a stylised Irn-Bru bottle against a custard-yellow background. The mark had been more favourable, sealing (though he couldn't know it then, of course) Westie's fate.

He was in his final year now and had almost completed the portfolio for his degree show. It had struck him only recently that there was something odd about the whole notion of a degree show: if you studied politics or philosophy, you didn't attach your essays to the walls for strangers to read. If you were going to be a vet, you didn't have the general public watching as you put some poor animal to the knife or stuck your arm up its backside. But every art and design college in the land expected its students to parade their shortcomings to the world. Was it attempted humiliation? Preparation for the harsh realities of life as an artist in twenty-first-century philistine Britain? The space for Westie's showcase had already been allocated – deep in the bowels of the college building on Lauriston Place, next to a sculptor who worked with straw and a 'video installationist' whose main claim to fame was a looped stop-motion animation of a slowly lactating breast.

'I know my place,' was all Westie had said.

Influenced (retrospectively) by Banksy, and spurred on by his experience with the Warholesque Irn-Bru bottle,

Westie's stock in trade was pastiche. He would copy in minute detail a Constable landscape, say, but then add just the tiniest idiosyncrasy – a crushed beer can or a used condom (almost his signature, according to the other students) or a scrap of wind-tossed rubbish such as a Tesco bag or crisp packet. A Stubbs portrait of a proud stallion might feature a jet fighter in the distant sky. In Westie's version of Raeburn's *The Reverend Walker Skating*, the only perceptible difference was that the man of the cloth now found himself sporting a black eye and stitches to a cut on his left cheek. One of his tutors had gone on at length about 'anachronism in art', seeming to think it a good thing, but others had accused him of simple copying – 'which is by no means the same as art, merely capable draughtsmanship'.

All Westie knew was that he had a marketable-sounding nickname and only a few more weeks to go before the end of term. Which meant he should either be applying for postgraduate places or else looking for gainful employment. But he'd been up half the night working on a graffiti project: stencils of the muffled face of the artist Banksy with the words 'Money In The Banksy' and some dollar bills painted above and below. The stencils were anonymous. He was hoping the local media would pick up on the story and make 'the Scottish Banksy' a fixture in the public imagination. It hadn't happened yet. His girlfriend Alice wanted him to become a 'graphic artist', meaning comic books. She worked front-of-house at an artsy cinema on Lothian Road and reckoned the way for Westie to become a top Hollywood director was for him to start drawing cartoons. He would then move into promo videos for indie rock bands and from there to the movies. The only problem with this – as he'd pointed out to her several times – was that he had no interest whatsoever in film directing … *she* was the one who wanted it.

'But you're the one with the talent,' she'd responded, stamping a foot. That gesture said quite a lot about Alice – an only child raised by doting middle-class parents who had praised her in everything she'd ever attempted. Piano lessons were going to turn her into the Vanessa Mae of the keyboard; her songwriting would see her sharing a stage with Joni Mitchell or at the very least K.T. Tunstall. She'd thought herself a prodigy as a painter, until her teacher at the fee-paying high school put her right. Having dropped out of university (Film and Media Studies with Creative Writing), she was pinning her scant hopes on Westie. The flat was hers – no way he could have afforded the rent. It was owned by her parents, who dropped by sometimes and never failed to be unimpressed by their daughter's choice of live-in boyfriend. He'd overheard them one time asking her a heartfelt question – 'Are you quite sure, dear?' – knowing they were talking about *him*, their golden child's bit of rough. He'd wanted to barge in, trumpet his working-class credentials – the Fife coalfields; Kirkcaldy High. Nothing given to him on a plate. But he'd known how it would sound to their ears …

Cretins.

Another time, he'd told Alice about a screen academy that was setting up in the city – she could do it part-time, learning all about film-making. Her excitement had lasted until a trawl of the internet had revealed the potential financial outlay.

'Mummy and Daddy will be happy to pay,' Westie had suggested, and she'd blown up at him, accusing him of accusing *her* of being a leech, of bleeding her poor parents dry. Another stamp of the foot and she'd bounded out of the room, slamming the door after her and causing one of his drying canvases to fall from its easel on to the floor. He'd managed to calm her down eventually with tea and a cuddle in the flat's cramped kitchen.

'I only need to work for another ten years and I'll have savings enough,' she had sniffled.

'Maybe I can bump up my prices at the degree show,' Westie had offered. But they both knew this wasn't exactly feasible – he was probably going to sell next to nothing. No matter how good his draughtsmanship, in terms of actual artistry he was still that same 'narrow pass', at least in the eyes of the people whose marks counted most. The head of department – old Prof Gissing – had never been a fan. Westie had looked up Gissing himself once and had found that the grumpy old sod had pretty well stopped painting in the 1970s, meaning all he'd done these past thirty years was write articles and give boring lectures. Yet people like him, they were the ones who'd give the thumbs-up or thumbs-down to Westie's whole future as an artist. Westie, the son of a postman and a shop assistant, sometimes felt that there was a conspiracy afoot to stop the lower orders being recognised as any sort of creative force.

Having finished the joint, Westie, arms folded, took

a stroll around the room. Alice didn't come in here very much any more. She stuck to the kitchen and bedroom. The mess irritated her, yet she was reluctant to tidy up in case it interfered with his creativity. She'd explained about a poet she'd been friendly with at college whose flatmates had done this big spring-clean of his bedroom one time and surprised him with it. He'd tried to be grateful but hadn't been able to write poetry in there for weeks afterwards. Westie had considered this, then had asked just exactly how 'friendly' the two had been.

Cue another lovers' tiff.

When the doorbell sounded, he realised he'd been practically asleep, staring out of the window at the passing traffic for at least a few minutes. Bed was one answer, but Alice would be expecting him to have achieved something with the day. The doorbell rang again and he considered who it might be. Did he owe money? Would Alice's parents want a quiet word, maybe slip him a few quid to clear out? Someone rattling a tin for charity or needing to know his political leanings? Last thing he needed in his life was these constant interruptions. He was meant to be working ... putting the finishing touches ... surfing the junkyards and bric-a-brac merchants for cheap gilt frames into which to place his Stubbs, his Constable, his Raeburn ...

Instead of which, he found himself opening the door to one of those people whose marks counted most: Professor Robert Gissing, in the flesh, and apologising for the intrusion.

'Looked for you in the studios, and then in your allocated exhibition space ...'

73

'I keep most of my paintings here, tend to work on them at night.'

'Hence the bleary expression, eh?' Gissing was smiling. 'Would it be all right with you, Mr Westwater, if we were to come inside for a moment? Rest assured, it won't take long.'

'We' because there were two other men with him. Gissing introduced them as 'two friends', but didn't mention names, and Westie didn't recognise their faces. Dealers, perhaps, or maybe collectors, here to make pre-emptive bids on the contents of his degree show? He didn't think so, but he led the way into the living room. Gissing had taken charge and was gesturing for them all to be seated. One of the 'friends' made to remove the covering sheet from the sofa.

'I wouldn't if I were you,' Westie warned him. 'Got it from a skip ... a few interesting stains.'

'And the aroma of turps,' the visitor decided.

'To cover the more interesting smells.'

Gissing was sniffing the air. 'It's not turpentine I'm detecting, Mr Westwater, it's something much more akin to our old friend *Cannabis sativa*.'

'Guilty as charged,' Westie said. 'Helps my brain to get moving.'

The three visitors nodded slowly, and silence descended. Westie interrupted with a cough. 'I'd offer tea or something,' he apologised, 'but we're all out of milk.'

Gissing waved this aside, then rubbed his hands together, making eye contact with the classier-looking of the two strangers. It was this man who eventually spoke.

'What we'd like to do,' he said, 'is help you buy yourself a new sofa – and maybe a few other bits and pieces besides.' He hadn't sat down, and was inspecting some of Westie's work instead. The accent was local and hadn't travelled too far from the tenements.

'You're in the market for a painting?' Westie shifted a little. 'I didn't think the professor was my biggest fan.'

'I can see you have a talent,' Gissing objected with a thin smile. 'And I'm enough of a "fan" to ensure that you pass the course with distinction. You know what that would mean – a real chance of being accepted for something in the postgraduate line.'

'Is this some sort of ... what do you call it ...?'

'Faustian pact?' Gissing offered. 'Not a bit of it.'

'Though there *would* be that cash incentive,' the stranger reminded him.

'As head of the College of Art,' Gissing added, 'I've taken a look at your file, Westie. Each year you've applied for every bursary and hardship grant going.'

'And been turned down for all of them,' the student reminded him.

'So what's your debt up to now? Five figures, I'm guessing ... Fresh start, clean slate – that's what's on offer here.'

'Well, I'd be happy to show you some of my work ...'

'I'm looking at your work, Mr Westwater,' the talkative stranger said.

'Everyone calls me Westie.'

The man nodded. 'I'm pretty impressed.' He had picked up the Stubbs horse. Its coat shone like a freshly peeled chestnut. 'You've an eye for colour. Besides which, we already have it on the professor's authority that you know what you're doing when it comes to copies. But we wouldn't be buying off the peg, Westie ...'

'A commission?' Westie was almost bouncing on the spot, even though he still didn't feel comfortable. Why didn't the other stranger say anything? He just kept checking his phone for text messages.

'A *secret* commission,' Gissing was correcting him. 'No questions asked.'

But now the talkative stranger was looking at the professor. 'Thing is, Robert, I can see that Westie here's not stupid – he's suspicious, and rightly so. We can hardly keep the project a secret from him, can we? He'll find out eventually.' He was homing in on Westie now, still holding the Stubbs in one hand as he walked to within a foot of the student. But when he spoke, Gissing still seemed his target. 'We need Westie to be part of it, and that means trusting him.' He smiled for the young man's benefit. 'The professor tells me you have an anarchic streak – you like to poke fun at the art establishment. Is that right?'

Westie didn't know which answer would serve him best, so he just shrugged instead. The man who had yet to talk made a show of clearing his throat. He had finished with his phone and was holding up a used stencil, which had been teased out from below the sofa.

'I've seen these around town,' he said – posh Edinburgh tones – keeping his voice low as if fearing being told off.

The other stranger examined the stencil, and his smile broadened. 'You want to be the next Banksy?'

'There was a story in the papers,' the second stranger said. 'Police seemed *very* keen to talk to the artist responsible ...'

'That's the anti-establishment stance I was talking about.' The first stranger faced Westie again and waited for him to say something. This time, Westie decided to oblige.

'So you want me to copy a painting?' he blurted out.

'Half a dozen, actually,' Gissing corrected him. 'All of them from the national collection.'

'And it's to be done without anyone knowing?' Westie's eyes were widening. Was he stoned and imagining this whole thing? 'They've been stolen, is that it? And the gallery doesn't want any of the public to get an inkling ...'

'I told you he was smart.' The visitor was leaning the Stubbs back against the skirting board. 'Now then, Westie, if we've whetted your appetite, maybe we can take you to the professor's office and show you just exactly what we're after ...'

8

The four of them sat at individual desks in Robert Gissing's room. He still gave occasional tutorials, hence the chairs with writing surfaces attached. His secretary had left for the day – at Gissing's request. Mike and Allan had eventually introduced themselves to Westie by their first names, having decided that it would be too cumbersome to use aliases. After all, it wasn't as though Gissing could use one, and if Westie went to the police with the professor's name, it wouldn't take a Columbo or a Frost to connect Mike and Allan with him.

Mike wasn't sure why Allan had said so little back in Westie's flat – cold feet, perhaps, or maybe it was because Mike had already stated his intention to bankroll the operation. Stood to reason they'd need funds, and Mike was the one with cash to spare. For a start, he was sure Westie would need paying – payment for his silence, as well as his expertise.

At this stage, of course, it was still a game they were playing. Making the copies didn't mean they had to take the scheme any further. Allan had seemed to accept this, but maybe also thought that Mike, being willing to pay for the privilege, should be the one to do the talking.

'Whatever I end up forking out, I might still be getting a masterpiece on the cheap,' Mike had assured him.

'Not that we're doing this for the money,' Gissing had growled.

The professor's room was chaotic. He had already cleared some of his bookshelves into boxes in preparation for retirement. There was a stack of mail on his desk, along with a computer and an old golfball-style typewriter. More books were heaped either side of the desk, and piles of art magazines were threatening to topple. The walls were cluttered with prints by Giotto, Rubens, Goya and Brueghel the Elder – these were the ones Mike recognised. There was a dusty CD player on one shelf and half a dozen classical titles. Von Karajan seemed to be the conductor of choice.

The blinds had been closed, leaving the room in semi-darkness. A screen had been pulled down from the ceiling immediately in front of the bookcases, so that Gissing could show them a wide selection of slides from the collection of the National Galleries, everything from Old Masters to Cubism and beyond. On the way over, Mike had explained a little more of the plan to Westie, who had slapped his knees, laughing with glee. Maybe it was just the dope kicking in.

'If I can help, count me in,' he'd said between gulps of air.

'Don't be too hasty,' Mike had cautioned. 'You need to think things through.'

'After which, if you still want in,' Gissing had added, 'you'll have to start taking it a bit more seriously.'

Now, as they looked at the slides, Westie slurped cola from a vending machine can. He sat forward in his chair, both knees pumping.

'I could do that,' was his refrain as the slides came and went.

Gissing, Allan and Mike had already pored over the slides, all of them showing items held in the overflow warehouse. Where possible, Gissing had found reproductions on paper to accompany them. These sat on the various desks, but Mike and Allan felt no need to study them further – they had already chosen a couple of favourites apiece, as had Gissing himself. But they needed to be confident that the young artist would cope with the different styles and periods.

'Now, how would you begin here?' Gissing asked, not for the first time. Westie's mouth twitched and he began drawing shapes in the air as he explained.

'Monboddo's actually pretty straightforward if you've studied the Scottish Colourists – nice big flat brush, laying the oil on in thick swirls. He'll go over one colour with another, and then another after that so you're left with hints of what was there before. Bit like pouring cream on to coffee where you can still glimpse the black through the white. He's after harmony rather than contrast.'

'That sounds like a quote,' Gissing commented.

Westie nodded. 'It's George Leslie Hunter – from your lecture on Bergson.'

'Would you need special brushes, then?' Mike interrupted.

'Depends how thorough you want me to be.'

'You need to defeat the naked eye, the gifted amateur ...'

'But not the forensic specialist?' Westie checked.

'That's not an immediate concern,' Gissing reassured him.

'It would be nice if we had access to the right papers and ages of canvas ... brand-new canvas looks just that – brand new.'

'But you have ways ...?'

Westie gave a grin and a wink at Mike's question. 'Look, if an expert comes along, they'll spot the difference in a few minutes. Even an exact copy isn't an *exact* copy.'

'A point well made,' Gissing muttered, rubbing a hand over his forehead.

'Yet some forgers get away with it for years,' Mike offered.

Westie shrugged his agreement. 'But these days, with carbon dating and Christ alone knows what else waiting in the wings ... don't tell me you've not watched an episode of *CSI*?'

'The thing we need to keep reminding ourselves, gentlemen,' Gissing said, removing the hand from his forehead, 'is that nothing is going to be missing, meaning there's no reason for any of these boffins to become involved.'

Westie chuckled, not for the first time. 'Got to say it again, Professor – it's mad but brilliant.'

Mike was forced to agree: walk into the warehouse on Doors Open Day and replace the real paintings with Westie's carefully crafted copies. It sounded simple, but he knew it would be anything but. There was a lot of planning still ahead of them ...

And plenty of time to pull out.

'We're like the A-Team for unloved artworks,' Westie was saying. He had calmed a little – only one knee was pumping as he drained the can of cola – but was no longer concentrating on the slideshow. He turned in his chair to face Mike. 'Look, none of this is really going to happen, right? It's like Radiohead might say – a nice dream. No disrespect, but you three are what I'd call establishment guys of a certain age and cut. You're suits and ties and corduroy, nights at the theatre and supper afterwards.' He leaned back in his chair and crossed one busy leg over the other, concentrating on the wagging motion of a paint-spattered trainer. 'You're not master criminal material, and no way can you pull off something like this without a bit more firepower.'

Secretly, Mike had been thinking the selfsame thing, but he didn't let it show. 'That's our problem, not yours,' he said instead. Westie nodded slowly.

'But here's your other problem ... I want in.'

'In?' Allan echoed, his first contribution for some considerable time. Westie switched his attention to him.

'I don't just want to be the grafter who churns out a few copies for you. I'm on the team. You want six paintings, why not make it seven?' He folded his arms as if it was a done deal.

'You understand,' Mike asked slowly, 'that if you take a painting, you're as deep in this as any of the rest of us – you're not just a paid employee any longer?'

'Understood.'

'And we're not selling the paintings on – they can never,

82

ever hit the open market?' Westie was still nodding. 'And if it ever got out that we'd ...'

'I'm not going to grass you up – isn't that actually another incentive? With me on board, I've got as much to lose as anyone.' Westie opened his arms to reinforce the point. 'I totally agree with the whole crazed concept. It's just that I want to be more than a brush for hire.'

'In return for which, we hand you a painting?' Mike asked.

'I'll earn my painting, Mikey-boy. I'll also earn all that cash you're going to pay me.'

'We've not talked sums yet,' Allan ventured, ever the banker.

Westie pursed his lips and leaned forward again in his chair. 'I'm not greedy,' he stated. 'I only want enough to see a friend of mine through film school ...'

When Westie left, there was silence in Gissing's office for a couple of minutes. The professor kept the slideshow coming, seemingly for his own amusement, while Mike stared at the torn page from the catalogue showing Monboddo's portrait of his wife. Allan Cruikshank was the first to speak.

'All getting a bit serious, isn't it?'

'Something we'd do well to remember,' Gissing muttered. He switched off the projector and got up to open the blinds. 'Worst-case scenario we'd all go to prison, lives and reputations in tatters.'

'For the sake of a few paintings,' Allan said quietly.

'You getting cold feet, Allan?' Mike asked him.

Allan thought for a moment before shaking his head. He'd removed his spectacles and was polishing them with a handkerchief.

'We need to be sure in our own minds,' Gissing added, '*why* we're prepared to go through with it.'

'That's easy,' Allan said, replacing his glasses. 'I want something at home my employers could never have.'

'Or your ex-wife's boyfriend, come to that,' Mike teased.

Gissing gave an indulgent smile. 'When I retire to Spain, my two go with me. I could be happy all day just staring at them ...'

Mike studied his two friends but said nothing himself. He didn't think they'd want to hear him say he was just bored to high heaven and looking to be challenged for the first time in a long time. And then, of course, there was Monboddo's wife to consider ...

'Young Westie has a point,' he said at last. 'Even with four of us, it's going to be far from easy.' He looked at Gissing. 'Have you had a chance to draw up the plan?'

Gissing nodded and reached into his desk drawer. The three men stood over the sheet of paper, holding its corners flat against the table as Gissing unrolled it. As a professor and a noted art historian, Gissing had visited the warehouse dozens of times in the past. Problem was, this made him a known face – dangerous for him to be part of any actual heist. On the other hand, he had drawn a beautifully rendered plan of the site, complete with guardroom, security cameras and panic buttons.

'You did this from memory?' Mike asked, duly impressed.

'And in such a short time,' Allan added.

'I told you, I've been mulling this over for quite a while. But be warned – they may have made some changes to the layout since my last visit.'

'But the measurements are accurate?' Mike was studying the route from the loading bay to the guardroom. Gissing had marked it with a thick red dotted line.

'Fairly accurate, I'd say.'

'And you'll do another recce before we hit the place?' Allan added.

Gissing nodded. 'After which, I'll be useful to you only as the getaway driver.'

'Better watch a few episodes of *Top Gear*, then,' Mike said with a smile.

'Prof,' Allan asked, 'you've been to Doors Open Day before, right?'

Gissing started running his finger along a line marked in blue. It started at the main gate to the compound and continued through a door into the warehouse itself. 'This is the route I'm hoping they'll take – can't really see any alternative. The tour is limited to a dozen visitors every hour, on the hour. Tour itself only takes about forty minutes, leaving them twenty to prepare for the next lot of arrivals. Names are on a list at the gatehouse. One guard stays there, the other three are inside, usually drinking tea in the guardroom and watching their CCTV screens. Staff from the Museums and Galleries Department conduct the actual tour.'

'And they don't do background checks on visitors?'

Gissing shook his head. 'Not last year, at any rate.'

'So fake names won't be rumbled?' Mike persisted.

Gissing just shrugged. 'They ask for a contact phone number, but in my experience there's never any contacting.'

Mike's eyes caught Allan's and he knew what his friend was thinking – *we need more bodies*. Mike was thinking much the same thing. The problem was ...

Whose?

At the end of the meeting, Allan hopped into a cab, heading back to the office, his phone already pressed to his ear. Mike preferred to walk. Standing with Allan on the pavement outside the art college, he had touched him lightly on the forearm.

'Sure you're ready to go through with this?'

'Are any of us?' Allan asked in return. 'I like all the *Ocean's 11* stuff – the prof's detailed plan of attack. It makes me think we really could pull this off ... if we wanted to.'

'Do we want to?'

'You seem keen enough.' Allan studied Mike, then gave a twitch of the mouth. 'Not sure about Westie, though. How far can we trust him?'

Mike nodded his agreement. 'We'll keep an eye on him.'

'Christ, listen to you.' Allan was laughing. 'You sound more *Reservoir Dogs* than George Clooney.'

Mike offered a smile. 'It *could* work, though, couldn't it?'

Allan thought this over for a moment. 'Only if we can get the guards scared and keep them scared. We have to convince them we really are the mean team ... think we can manage that?'

'I'll practise my snarling.'

'And how will they see it, behind the mask you'd be wearing?'

'Good point,' Mike conceded. 'There's a lot we need to think about.'

'There is,' Allan agreed, stretching out an arm to wave down an approaching cab. 'The prof's done the ground-work and you're fronting the cash ...' Allan stared at Mike. 'Not exactly sure what the pair of you think *I* can offer.' He pulled open the cab's back door.

'You're our details guy, Allan. Stuff like the masks – just keep mulling over all the potential flaws and glitches and you'll be earning your stripes.'

Allan gave a mock salute as he closed the door behind him.

Mike watched the cab pull away, then crossed the road and headed down Chalmers Street, towards the Meadows. This had all been farmland once, but was now playing fields, edged with trees. Cyclists were out in force – students, he assumed, on their way to and from lectures. There were a few geriatric joggers, too, and he wondered if he should make an attempt to get fit. Would it help cow the guards if he added some muscle to his upper body? Probably not. Not as much, certainly, as a big fat handgun. Or maybe a machete of some kind, or a hatchet. There would be shops in the city where such items could be bought. Not real guns, of course, but replicas. Some of the tourist shops sold claymores and even Japanese-style swords. Passing a couple of dog-walkers, he had a little smile to himself. Probably no one in the history of the Meadows had ever been thinking such thoughts as these.

'You're a regular little gangster, Mike,' he told himself. But he knew he wasn't. All the same ...

He knew a man who was.

Alice Rule was late getting home from the cinema. She was trying to set up a Sunday-evening film club and had been finalising the mailshot. European arthouse of the 1950s and '60s; she knew there was an audience for it, just wasn't sure she could attract enough of them. On Sunday afternoons the cinema ran a quiz in the bar. That was popular, and she wanted to capitalise on it, wanted to see those people stick around for a meal and an actual film. She'd run a short season of Hitchcock's early work, the stuff he'd done in Britain. It had broken even, and she'd handed out questionnaires on the door, asking for suggestions. French New Wave ... Antonioni ... Alexander Mackendrick ... Hong Kong cinema ... Plenty for her to think about.

As she climbed the stairs to her top-floor flat, she wondered what sort of day Westie had had. He'd said he would be sourcing picture frames, plus putting the finishing touches to some of his portfolio. She just hoped he hadn't been sitting on the sofa rolling spliffs all day.

It would be nice, she thought, to walk into the flat and smell supper cooking, but she knew better than to expect anything like that. Eggs on toast was the sum total of Westie's painfully proletarian style; or meals out, meals she ended up paying for.

As she unlocked the door and stepped into the hall, she caught no aroma of fresh paint, never mind fresh cooking. Westie's coat, however, was in a heap next to his shoes, evidence that he had been out somewhere. As she walked into the living room (refusing, even after all these months, to bow to pressure and call it 'the studio'), glancing around in vain for signs of frames purchased, there was a loud popping sound, followed by a spume of foam from the neck of the champagne bottle Westie was holding.

'And what exactly are we celebrating?' Alice asked, aware that it would have been *her* salary paying for the bubbly. She had shrugged herself out of her jacket and was placing her shoulder bag on the floor. Westie was pouring the champagne into two wine glasses. It didn't look as if they'd been rinsed too thoroughly from the previous night.

'Some men came to see me,' he explained, handing her a filled glass.

'Men?'

'Businessmen.' Westie clinked glasses and took a huge gulp, swallowing and stifling a belch. 'They want a few of my originals for their offices.' He started to do a little dance, and Alice, her drink untouched, wondered just how much he'd been smoking.

'Their offices?' she echoed.

'That's right.'

'What company? How did they hear about you?'

Westie proffered a huge wink, which told her he'd already had a few drinks to go with the dope. 'It's all very hush-hush,' he confided in a stage whisper.

'Hush-hush?'

'They're offering enough money for you to do that film course.' Westie nodded slowly, making sure she knew he wasn't joking.

'You mean thousands?' Alice couldn't manage to keep the disbelief out of her voice. 'For some of your paintings? What's the catch, Westie?'

He looked crestfallen. 'Why should there be a catch? They're canny investors, Alice, the kind who like to ride a wave just before it explodes on to the shore.' To paint this picture more fully, he started making sounds approximating to just such an event. Then he tapped Alice's glass, encouraging her to drink. 'I need to get started, though. It's a big job – seven paintings.'

'From scratch?'

'They're not buying off the peg, Alice. It's a *commission*.'

Alice was looking for somewhere to sit, but not one single surface appealed. 'Your portfolio,' she argued. 'You need to finish your degree show ...'

But Westie was shaking his head. 'Don't you worry about that – it's all in hand.' And he had a little chuckle to himself.

'Are you sure about this?' Alice asked. She experimented

with a small sip of the champagne. It was chilled to perfection and sharp-tasting – the real thing.

Westie held his glass out towards her, and this time she did the clinking. *All very hush-hush* … She had to smile at that. Westie was terrible at keeping secrets. He would always blurt out the identity of her birthday and Christmas gifts before she had a chance to unwrap them. When he'd snogged a girl at a party once, a party Alice had missed because of work, he'd admitted everything to her over breakfast the next morning. She didn't think he could lie to her, even if his life depended on it. She doubted she'd have any trouble finding out what the story really was.

Especially when she was so intrigued.

9

The last thing Chib Calloway ever expected to see squatting on his parked Beamer was a six-foot-three Hell's Angel in a tailored double-breasted suit. The man wore polished black brogues on his feet and a crisp white shirt with a mauve silk tie. His long brown hair was tied back into a presentable ponytail, and he sported just the single studded earring (though with lobes pierced for plenty more). He had removed any other facial jewellery and was clean-shaven, cheeks glowing. When he raised his head there was a giveaway blue dotted line across his throat – a prison tattoo. As he scratched his hands down his face, Chib noted more tattoos on both sets of knuckles – HATE on the right, HATE on the left. Blue ink again, home-made. The guy sported laughter lines around his eyes, but the eyes themselves glowed with milky-blue malevolence.

Now this is more like it, Chib thought to himself. *This I understand ... sort of.*

It wasn't the most genteel part of town, nearer Granton than Leith and not yet part of any regeneration scheme. Leith itself had changed. There were more Michelin restaurants there than in the city centre. It made Chib wonder what the *Trainspotting* tours made of the place. The guy who did those tours, Chib had tried persuading him that he should feature one of Chib's pool halls. Chib also owned a couple of neighbourhood bars, and had just been into one of them to do the weekly check. He was realistic enough to know that the staff would be skimming, but needed them to know that he knew. That way nobody got too greedy. And if temptation proved too much, leading to takings below the norm, Chib would get out the photos of Donny Devlin and tell the staff, 'This is what I do to *friends* who cheat me. So consider what I'll do to you if that cash doesn't magic its way back into my till by next week.'

Exiting the bar, happy enough with its turnover, Chib had started gnawing his top lip. The place was run almost *too* well. The manager had come to Chib from a big pub-grub chain in the south; said he missed Edinburgh and wanted to come home. Overqualified for the job, but never complaining. It was making Chib wonder. Could the guy be a plant, some kind of grass or CID undercover thing? Johnno and Glenn had checked him out as best they could, but that didn't mean much. They were with Chib now as he crossed the road towards his car, flanking him in the approved manner. Across the street was a park – not much of a park, just playing fields for football, criss-crossed with paths and a few benches where teenagers could gather of an evening to scare their elders. Twenty-odd years ago, that would have been Chib, swigging cheap booze and blasting the ciggies, shouting and cursing, eyes on the lookout for intruders, strangers, victims … Top of the world and wanting the world to acknowledge the fact.

'Hell's going on?'

Johnno had been the first to spot the Hell's Angel. Chib's car was a 5-Series BMW, solid but not too showy. There was a Bentley GT in the garage back home, never used for business. The stranger had parked himself on the Beamer's bonnet, sitting there cross-legged in his suit, hands rubbing up and down his cheeks as he watched the three men approach. Though he wore shoes, his ankles were sockless. There were tattoos there, too. Chib clicked his fingers and Glenn reached a hand into the front of his jacket, even though there was nothing there. The stranger couldn't know that, of course, but he still grinned at the gesture, seeming to dismiss it. His eyes bored into Chib's.

'Better not have scratched the paint,' Chib warned the man. 'Respray could end up costing you an arm and a leg.'

The man eased himself off the bonnet and stood with his hands either side of him, fists bunched.

HATE and HATE.

'You were not expecting me, Mr Calloway?' The accent was foreign. Stood to reason. 'I represent some people, Mr Calloway, people you should know better than to disappoint.'

By which he meant the Norwegians, the biker gang from Haugesund. Chib had known there'd be some trouble there.

'You owe your friends for a shipment, Mr Calloway, and you have not been forthcoming.'

Johnno had taken half a step forward, but Chib swiped

94

a hand against his shoulder. 'I've already told them the money's on its way,' he rasped.

'Repeatedly so, Mr Calloway, but it is hardly a sustainable bargaining position, is it?'

'Chewed a bloody dictionary,' Glenn snorted, Johnno adding a low chuckle.

The Hell's Angel turned his face towards Glenn. 'You mean because I speak your native language better than you yourself do?'

'You don't just come barging up to Mr Calloway!' Glenn barked back. 'You show him some respect!'

'The same respect he has displayed towards my clients?' The question sounded genuine.

'You're not part of the gang, then?' Chib interrupted.

'I am a collector of monies due, Mr Calloway.'

'For a percentage?'

The man shook his head slowly. 'I work for a straight fee, half of it in advance.'

'Do you always collect the other half?'

'So far.'

'First time for everything,' Johnno spat, while Glenn pointed out some marks on the BMW's bonnet. The man ignored the pair of them: he had eyes only for Chib Calloway.

'Tell them,' Chib said, 'the money's coming. I've never let them down before and, frankly, I'm insulted they've sent you.' He looked the stranger up and down. 'A grocer's boy running their errands for them.' Chib decided a wagged finger might even be in order. 'You report back to them, and we'll talk again next week.'

'That won't be necessary, Mr Calloway.'

Chib's eyes narrowed. 'Why not?'

The man offered a sliver of a smile. 'Because by next week they'll have had their money paid in full.'

Johnno's face broke into a snarl and he lunged forward, but the man sidestepped him neatly and grabbed his wrist, twisting until Johnno buckled in pain. Chib noticed that there were spectators: the manager from the bar had been told by a couple of pavement smokers to come look. Kids bunking off school had stopped their BMX wheelies to follow the entertainment. Glenn was ready to wade in but Chib stopped him. He'd never liked playing to an audience. Not since schooldays …

'Let him go,' he said quietly.

The stranger held Chib's gaze for a few more seconds and then pushed Johnno's arm away. Johnno was left sitting on the roadway, rubbing at his injury. The look the stranger was giving Chib said it all: Johnno and Glenn were as much use as infants in a playground when the artillery comes calling.

'I'll be sticking around,' the man was saying. 'I need to hear from you today; tomorrow at the latest. After that, the talking will all be over – do you understand?'

Johnno took a petulant swipe with one foot, trying to make contact with the stranger's shins. The man ignored him and handed Chib a folded scrap of paper. It was a row of digits: a mobile phone number. When Chib looked up, he was walking away, making to cross the park.

'Hey!' Chib called out to him. 'What's your name, big man?'

96

The stranger paused for a moment. 'People have a habit of calling me Hate,' he called back over his shoulder, striding past the serried ranks of BMXs.

'That figures,' Chib muttered to himself. Glenn had helped Johnno to his feet.

'Dead man walking!' Johnno yelled. 'Next time I see you – that's a promise, pal!' He jabbed a finger in Hate's general direction. Glenn was patting him on the back, trying to calm him down. Johnno's eyes were on his employer. 'We need to take him out, Chib. See him taken care of ... send a message to anyone and everyone.'

'Reckon you're up to the job, Johnno?' Chib asked. 'I wouldn't say you looked rusty back there, but I've known scrapyards with merchandise in better nick – and that's *after* the compactor's had a go at them.'

'We could follow him,' Glenn was saying. 'Find out where he's staying, what his real name is ...'

Chib nodded thoughtfully. 'Knowledge *is* power, Glenn. Reckon you could track him without him noticing?'

'We can give it a go,' Glenn offered. But the giant was three quarters of the way across the playing field. No way they could go after him on foot without him knowing about it: there was no cover.

'Make some calls instead,' Chib suggested by way of an alternative. 'Bed and breakfasts to start with. Say you're from the tourist office and some Norwegian bloke's gone and dropped some money.'

Glenn was nodding. 'I want to get his money back to him.'

'And put out his description among the dossers and the

97

jakeys – that lot have got eyes in the backs of their heads and would pimp their granny for a bottle of Buckie.'

Glenn was studying his employer. 'Can I take it you're not planning on paying up?'

'Let's see,' was all Chib Calloway said, unlocking the car with his remote.

10

'I don't like this,' Mike Mackenzie was saying.

He was in Robert Gissing's office, the door locked and the plan of the warehouse spread across the desk, weighted down at its corners with oversized art books. Gissing had paid another visit to the warehouse and had amended the plan accordingly.

'You turned up there unannounced,' Mike stated. 'Might make them suspicious come the heist.'

The professor patted Mike on the back. 'I never thought of that, Michael. You're quite right, and I'll be sure to check with you first in future. But to put your mind at rest, I do the same thing once or twice a year, and I don't think my presence was much noticed. They're too busy finding space for all the new arrivals.'

By which he meant the extensive overflow from the Royal Museum. The place was getting a major overhaul, and a good part of its collection needed shifting elsewhere for the duration. As Gissing had explained, it might make their job harder on the day. Items could have been moved to make space. But he didn't think the paintings would be relocated – he'd made the trip to assure himself of that.

Mike was studying the plan. 'Gatehouse,' he recited.

'CCTV cameras. Guardroom. Staff acting as guides, plus everyone on the tour. If you're sitting in the getaway van, that only leaves three of us to cope with it all.'

'And at least one of you will need to be collecting the actual paintings.'

Mike nodded slowly, then began shaking his head instead. 'We'll never manage.'

'Cold feet, young Michael?'

'Just want to make sure we're covering all the angles.'

Gissing seemed to accept this. 'Maybe it's Allan whose feet are getting chilled ...'

Allan hadn't been able to make the meeting. Mike had called it at short notice, and Allan had apologised by text: there were things at work he couldn't get out of. Mike tapped the plan a final couple of times and then walked over to one of the chairs, sitting down on it heavily, running both hands through his hair while he looked around the room. The office was emptier than before – some of the boxes of books had gone. Pictures were missing from the walls.

'Allan's fine. He wants you to make a copy of the plan so he can study it at home.'

'I'll arrange it, but meantime, put my mind at rest ...'

'What?'

'Something's worrying you.'

'It just seemed so straightforward, back at the start,' Mike admitted with a sigh.

'Most plans do, when you first think of them,' Gissing offered.

'Bottom line, Robert – we've been through this a dozen

times ...' A dozen late-night phone calls; Mike pacing his living room, deep in thought. 'You *know* it comes down to the same thing – we need more hands.'

Gissing folded his arms and rested his backside against the edge of his desk. He was keeping his voice down, aware of his secretary outside the locked door. He'd warned Mike – not too many more meetings, or she'd start to have suspicions of her own. 'Remember,' he said now, 'the old adage about too many cooks?'

Mike just shrugged. 'The only other alternative is, this stays on the drawing board – a nice dream, just as Westie said, never to be realised.'

'I was under the impression, Michael, that that's pretty much been your attitude throughout: a little challenge to keep the grey cells active. Or has the pull of Lady Monboddo finally become too strong to resist?'

'I'm every bit as serious about this as you are, Professor.'

'That's good to hear, because, with your help or without it, I intend going ahead with the plan.'

Mike ignored this. His thoughts were elsewhere. 'One other thing,' he said. 'The switch – we can't do it in the warehouse itself. We'll be in there maybe twenty minutes ... no way we can walk away apparently empty-handed.'

'Not even if we've raised the alarm ourselves?'

Mike shook his head determinedly. Gissing's plan had been, swap the real paintings for Westie's copies. Once that was done, hit an alarm and make a run for it, pretending the thieves had been spooked into leaving before they could take anything.

'When the CID arrive, first thing they're going to won-der is: what were we up to in those twenty minutes? How come we didn't just grab something and run when we tripped the alarm?'

'Then maybe we should take something ...'

Mike shook his head again. 'Better yet, we take *every-thing* – the originals and the copies. We only get frightened afterwards and abandon the van, with one lot of paintings in the back. Everyone will be so relieved to get the stuff back, they'll not be thinking about anything else.'

Gissing's eyes grew unfocused and Mike knew he was running it through his mind. Then he smiled.

'You really have been doing some thinking, Michael. And maybe you've struck on something.'

'But it does throw up another problem – we need a van we can jettison, meaning it can't be traced back to us. Any good at a spot of hot-wiring, Professor?'

'What do you think?'

'Me neither, and I doubt either Allan or Westie has the necessary skills. So now we can add a van to the shopping list, alongside some weaponry and a few spare bodies.' Mike got up from his seat, so he was facing Gissing at eye level as he went on. 'What we really need is someone who knows about heists ... someone Allan mentioned right at the start of this project. The raid on First Caly, remember?'

Gissing's eyes widened in disbelief. 'We'd be mad to let him near this!' he gasped.

Mike had moved a step closer. 'Think about it, Robert:

102

Calloway has the know-how and the manpower. He can find us that van *and* the necessary firearms.'

'I believe the gangland terminology is "shooters".'

Mike gave a conciliatory smile. 'I mean, if there's anyone else who springs to mind ... anyone equally qualified ... Because if we bring in any more amateurs like us, how do we know we can trust them?'

'Are you telling me you think Chib Calloway is a man to be trusted?'

'He's got more to lose than any of us. With a record like his, the law would come down on him like Carl Andre's bricks.'

'A fitting enough analogy,' Gissing conceded, folding his arms. 'But why would friend Calloway be willing to offer us any form of assistance?'

Mike shrugged. 'Maybe he won't, but at least I can sound him out on it. Maybe I'll persuade him it's good for art. Calloway's getting the bug, and I know from experience what that can do to a man.'

Gissing had walked back around to his own side of the desk. 'I'm not sure, Michael,' he said, slumping into his chair. 'I'm just not convinced that he won't try to push us aside.'

'Well, we can always call it off,' Mike offered. 'At this stage, there's no damage done – except to my bank balance if Westie demands some sort of compensation.'

Gissing smiled at this. 'Maybe you're right, my boy. The more I think about it, the clearer it becomes that Calloway would bring certain ... *qualities* to the project.' His eyes met Mike's. 'How exactly would you pitch it to him?'

'I think Calloway's a man who understands the value of a wad of notes,' was all Mike could think of to say.

'Then you have my blessing to talk to him.'

Which left Mike to wonder at his own powers of persuasion. Except that, really, the professor hadn't needed much persuading at all.

'Good for art?' Chib Calloway echoed, laughing out loud. 'I'll tell you, Mike, I've been needing a bit of light relief all day, so bless you for that. That's cheered me up no end ...'

They were seated in Chib's BMW. The two had exchanged phone numbers after their drink together at the Shining Star, and Mike had called Chib as soon as he'd left Gissing's office. The meet had been arranged for two. Chib had picked Mike up from outside the Last Drop pub in the Grassmarket, Johnno and Glenn in the back, eyes open for anyone following.

'Safer this way,' Chib had explained from the driver's seat, before introducing Mike to the two henchmen. Mike had met them that day in the Shining Star, but Chib had been too busy with questions about art auctions to be bothered with names. Mike nodded a greeting and then asked if there was some trouble. 'No trouble,' he'd been assured. All the same, Chib had taken right turns and lefts and more rights, doubling back on himself so that at one point they ended up passing the Last Drop again.

'Know why it's called that?' Chib had asked.

'Isn't it where they used to hang criminals?' Mike had answered.

'Meaning people like yours truly. The town would turn out in force to watch, make a sort of party of the whole thing. Wasn't just thieves and muggers, either – they hanged you if you were a Covenanter or a witch. They'd slaughter anyone in those days.'

'Things have moved on.'

'Bet you'd still get a crowd for an execution, though …'

Eventually, a voice from the back seat had declared that they were 'clear', which was when Chib had pulled the car to a stop and ordered his men out. They'd put up a bit of resistance until their boss handed over a twenty-pound note for a cab and told them to meet him 'at the snooker hall'.

'Sure about this?' Johnno had said with a glare. He kept rubbing his wrist, as if he'd sprained it. Probably, Mike reckoned, after belting someone.

'I'm sure,' Chib had said.

'But what if the Viking …?'

Chib had ignored this and raced off, leaving Johnno and Glenn on the pavement. Mike hadn't felt able to ask who or what 'the Viking' might be. Instead, Chib had turned to him with a question of his own. 'So what's on your mind, Mike?'

And Mike had told him, starting at the beginning, almost as if it was some story he'd heard somewhere. *There's this collection of artworks in the city and not many people know about it … and there's a way, apparently, to get hold of some of these paintings without anyone twigging …*

To the man's credit, it hadn't taken Chib long to work things out.

By that time, they were sitting in a car park halfway round Arthur's Seat in Holyrood Park. Mike seldom ventured up here: it was a place for dog-walkers and tourists. You rounded a bend and were met by incredible windswept panoramas of the city. But at other moments you felt surrounded by wilderness, the humped shape of Arthur's Seat itself fooling you into imagining you were miles from civilisation. Yet Edinburgh surrounded you, the chimneypots, church spires and housing schemes just out of view.

'Good for art,' Chib said again, shaking his head. But then he sniffed and rubbed a finger across his nostrils and asked Mike to reprise the story. Only this time Chib had questions, concerns and ideas of his own. The ideas were too elaborate, but Mike listened patiently, his heart racing. He'd experienced a frisson from the moment he'd stepped into the car – actually, even before that. Waiting outside the pub as office workers and visitors hurried past, he'd wondered what they would say if he blurted out the identity of the man he was waiting for and the reason for their meeting.

I'm putting together a team …

I'm leading a gang …

The heist of the century …

And then the car had pulled up. He'd felt uneasy with those two gorillas hulking in the back, couldn't help thinking of all the other people who, down the years, had taken a ride with Chib Calloway and his men, many of them fearful or plain petrified, some never seen again. But what Mike had felt chiefly was exhilaration. There was something feral about Chib. Mike's first week in high school, the weakest newcomers had been selected and given a half-hearted kicking by the older boys. But Chib had been there, too, already accepted by his elders, his reputation preceding him. It hadn't bothered Mike – better to be picked on than ignored completely. But afterwards, that was just what Chib had done – ignored him. And a couple of years later he was gone from the school, expelled after a headbutt on his chemistry teacher, leaving behind only the legend. There had still been bullies and gangs, but nothing like Chib. By the fourth year, Mike had been the one laying into the new kids . . .

Afterwards, Mike had studied at college, found himself a flat on the edge of the New Town. And, a few brawls apart, he'd succeeded in leaving his upbringing far behind – parents dead, his only sister living in Canada. It interested him that Chib wasn't merely about anger and the need to be the alpha male. There was intelligence in those piercing eyes, and a hunger for something – knowledge, perhaps. Maybe the gangster was beginning to realise just how narrow his world had become.

And just maybe, Mike conceded, the same thing was happening to *him*.

He watched as, without saying anything more, Chib got out of the car and walked to the edge of the car park, from where he could stare out across a nearby pond. Mike decided to follow, getting a cigarette lit as he exited the car. His hands were trembling, but only just. There was a small island in the middle of the pond, a swan nesting while its mate swam in protective circles. A woman had brought her toddler along so they could toss chunks of bread to a nearby cacophony of ducks, coots and moorhens. But it was the swans that interested Chib. He'd slipped his hands into his pockets as he watched them. Mike wished he knew what the man was thinking. Maybe he wanted the same sense of poise and certainty, the same equilibrium. Mike made the offer of a cigarette from his packet, but Chib shook his head. It was another minute or so before he spoke.

'You lied to me, Mike, back in that gallery. Said you were in computers. I suppose it's sort of true, but you didn't want me to know all of it. Mr Success Story. Mr Millions in the Bank. A tenner to a kid in an internet café and I had more gen on you than I knew what to do with.' He glanced towards Mike. 'Scared I'd come calling on you one cold dark night, hand stretched out for a sub?'

Mike gave a shrug. 'I didn't want to look like I was showing off.'

'We Scots are bad that way,' Chib eventually acknowledged. 'You ever been back to the school? Have they not invited you to hand out the prizes, inspire the kids with a few words of wisdom?'

'No.'

'Your old college gave you an honorary degree, though – was it the cash they were after?'

'One day, I suppose,' Mike conceded.

'Kid says you're not signed up to any of those sites that put you in touch with old pals.'

'Like I told you, that's because I don't have any old pals.'

'No, me neither ...' Chib leaned forward to spit on to the surface of the pond. 'Doubt most of the folk I was at school with would give me the time of day. They organised some anniversary do last year for kids in our year – did you get an invite to that?'

'I think so.'

'You should've gone. Rented a Roller for the night and a couple of nice-looking escorts ... rubbed all their noses in it.'

'You could've done that, too,' Mike offered, causing Chib to smile.

'Don't go thinking it didn't cross my mind, but in the end ... Well, fuck it.' He made a little writhing motion, as though a cold wind were blowing. Then he turned his body so he was face to face with Mike. The hands stayed in their pockets. Mike was reminded of their meeting at the gallery and his fear that the gangster carried a gun or a knife. He doubted it now. But Calloway had worries in his life – maybe to do with 'the Viking'. And Mike had given him something to take his mind off them – a fresh challenge. 'You'll need to be tooled up, Mike, you do realise that? You're going to have to put the fear of God into everybody, make them think you'll do whatever it takes.'

'But the gun doesn't need to be real, right?'

Chib shook his head. 'Just needs to *look* real – if that's what you want.'

'That's all we'll need.'

'Better be sure of that – just takes one of the guards to be ex-military ... you poke an airgun in his face and he's going to know it.'

'Replicas, then.'

'Even better is the real thing with the firing pin out.'

'You're the expert, Chib.'

'Damned right I am.' He was silent for a few more moments. 'Four additional crew, I reckon. One apiece for the gatehouse and guardroom and two to keep the visitors quiet. That leaves the three of you clear to do the actual finding and fetching.'

'Quicker we're in and out, the better for all concerned.'

'Still can't see it, though, Mike – you and the old professor guy and that poofy-looking pal of yours? More I think about it, more I'm convinced it's a wind-up.'

'You don't think it'll work?'

'Actually, it sounds all right. It's the planners rather than the plan I'm thinking of ...'

'Needn't concern you, Chib. If it falls apart, it's *our* problem – you'll still get your fee, and so will the four crew. Have you got anyone in mind?'

'You want them young,' Chib stated. 'Means they're hungry, on top of which there's all that testosterone ... makes them even scarier.'

'How much will they want?'

But Chib shook his head. 'Guns and bodies aren't a problem. Crew don't even need to be told who they're working for – a word from me'll be enough. All they'll see is a warehouse, won't know what's being taken.'

'They will if they're in the back of the van. Speaking of which ...'

'Getting a van's easy enough – maybe with faked

number plates. Something plain, something like a Transit. Nobody looks twice at blacked-out windows in the back of one of those ...'

'Fair enough. So, really, we're back to your fee ...'

'How does a hundred and fifty thou sound?'

Mike's Adam's apple bobbed as he swallowed. 'Bit on the high side, actually,' he was able to say eventually. 'Are you in some sort of trouble?'

Chib barked out a laugh and slid a hand from his pocket so he could slap Mike on the arm with it. 'Tell you what,' he offered. 'I'd be willing to take a painting off your hands, so long as it was worth that sort of money.'

'What?'

'Auctions don't make much sense to me, Mike. You're planning on lifting seven paintings ... seems to me one extra won't make much difference.'

'You'd never be able to sell it ... not on the open market.'

'I'm not planning on selling it.'

'If one forgery's identified,' Mike persisted, 'the others won't be far behind.'

Chib's face hardened. 'That's my price, Mike. Unless you want to stump up the cash equivalent.'

Mike thought hard. 'Our forger's pushed as it is,' was all he could manage.

'Then we push him harder.' Chib had leaned in towards Mike. Although the gangster was a good couple of inches shorter than him, Mike felt he was being towered over. The city he knew was no longer visible and the temperature had dropped. The bird-feeders had disappeared. No cars

111

passed, no other humans within hailing distance. 'Have we got a deal?' Chib was intoning. 'Or do I start to get narked again that you lied to me back in that gallery?'

One of the ducks had vanished beneath the surface of the pond. Mike was beginning to understand how it felt ...

The oversized envelope had been left at reception by a courier. Allan opened it in his office, relieved afterwards that he hadn't delegated the task to his secretary – a scale photocopy of Gissing's drawing of the compound.

'You silly bugger, Robert,' Allan muttered. No forewarning; no sense of danger. And now a receipt on file at the courier company – urgent delivery of documents from Professor R. Gissing, Edinburgh College of Art, to Mr A. Cruikshank, HNW Relationship Manager, First Caledonian Bank. Allan shook his head slowly. The beginnings of a paper trail now existed where none had been necessary. Despite which, he was glad to have the plans. He would lock them in his briefcase and take them home with him at day's end. He would close his curtains and make sure his front door was bolted. And only then would he spread them out on the table, pouring himself a glass of Rioja and commencing to study them.

Determined to prove himself.

Determined to pay his way.

He might even push the glass to one side, keeping a clear head for later, when a night-time drive down to Granton's industrial estates and warehouses might be in order.

11

Chib was having dinner that evening with a woman who ran an escort agency. A couple of years back, he had offered to help her with the business, an offer she'd turned down out of hand. All the same, Chib had grown to like her. She was tougher than most of the men he knew, tougher certainly than Glenn and Johnno, the latter still nursing his wrist along with his wounded pride. The morning visit from the Viking seemed a lifetime ago. Chib was supposed to be talking to him tonight, tomorrow at the latest. He had the slip of paper in his pocket, but what was he supposed to say?

Chib and this woman, it wasn't serious between them. Just dinner now and then, maybe a film or a show. They swapped news and gossip, rumours and anecdotes. Sometimes, he even let her pick up the tab. His wife had died a few years back from lung cancer. It was a terrible way to go – his own mum had been the same. He used to say to Liz, long before they were married, that he didn't want kids, didn't want them going through what he'd had to go through with his mum. His dad hadn't been much use either, hitting the bottle and falling asleep in his clothes every night. *Cheery bugger, aren't you?* had been Liz's response the first time he'd told her. It'd made him angry that she made light of it, but he hadn't done anything about it – that was how much he'd loved her.

Tonight's venue was a newish restaurant in one of Leith's gentrified sections. Chib remembered Leith when it had been all about the docks and the hard men, drinking dens with knocking shops upstairs and tattoo parlours along the street with wraps of speed under the counter for those in the know. There was still that side to it, but a lot of the dockside had been spruced up, style bars opening, bonded warehouses turned into flats. Chib often wondered what happened to the old-timers when these makeovers took place. All across the city, neighbourhoods were changing. Where Chib lived, there hadn't been any houses at all until ten or twelve years back. Now it had its own railway station. Sometimes it was hard to keep up.

He'd been chewing over Mike's crazy scheme the remainder of the afternoon, to the extent that he'd lost three frames of snooker in a row, Johnno teasing him that there must be a woman behind it. There was a smell in the snooker hall; Chib wasn't sure he'd registered it before. It was nasty and vinegary and it caught in his nostrils. Old men's sweat and desperation; bad diet and wasted time. Nothing like that here – the chef had his first Michelin star, so Chib had been told. Seafood was cooking, and the staff were busy dicing vegetables in the kitchen – there was a window between them and the tables, so you could follow every move. Chib liked that. Back as a child, the owner of his local chip shop used to hawk into the fryer to test how hot the fat was. The thought of it now made Chib's stomach turn.

He was early for his assignation, and had driven there himself in the Bentley. He didn't like bringing Johnno and Glenn, even when they stayed with the car or ate at a distant table. They always made jokes next day about whether his 'lady friend' snored and how did she like her eggs at breakfast ... When he'd told them they weren't needed, they'd been quick to warn him again about the Viking. Questions had been asked in town, feelers were out, but no one had reported any sightings of him. Could turn up at any moment ...

'Sure you don't want us around, boss?'

'Positive.'

Seated at his corner table – with an uninterrupted view of the entrance area – Chib noticed that he'd been studying the art on the walls. Not even reproductions of anything worthwhile, just splotches bought as a job lot to cover the pale yellow plasterwork. He'd been reading up on the subject ever since visiting the auction house. A bookshop in town had suggested various 'primary texts' – the very words the assistant had used. 'Primary' to Chib meant junior school, so he'd started to argue that he wasn't thick, thank you very much, until the assistant had explained what she meant, her voice shaking. After which, they'd got along fine. Now 'primary' got him thinking back to high school ... funny he didn't remember Mike. Recognised the type, though: still wanted the hard kids to notice him, even twenty-odd years on. The scheme wasn't really that daft – he'd encountered plenty worse, and a good number of those had come off. If anything went wrong this time round, well, Chib wouldn't be there to take any of the rap. The kids he talked into helping, they'd know better than to blab – better to spend a bit of time behind bars than have to face a grassed-up Chib Calloway. Mike and his pals might well want to cooperate with the filth, but that wouldn't get them very far – Chib would stay at one remove. And nobody would ever be able to lay their hands on the painting ...

The valuable painting ... Christ, yes! Of course!

He reached into his pocket and took out one of his mobile phones, along with the slip of paper. Punched in the numbers and waited. He saw his friend walk in, and offered her a wave. She was being fussed over as usual by the maître d', her coat removed. Now and then, a wealthy visitor to one of the city's better restaurants might be tempted to pick the brain of the maître d'. They'd want to know where they could find a girl for the night, just someone to spend a bit of time with ... And the maître d' would know just the place – very nice girls; all very discreet. After which he'd pocket a tip from the customer, and another next day, this time from Chib's friend. She was pressing her hand to the maître d' right now, and Chib didn't doubt that there was a twenty or maybe even a fifty there ... His call was picked up and he moistened his lips with his tongue.

'Is that you, Hate?'

'Calloway?'

'The one and only. I can't help thinking we got off to a bad start, and I want to make it up to you.'

'I'm listening.'

'Well, while I'm putting the funds together for your employers, how about a peace offering? Something you could place under the heading of collateral. Thing is, it's going to take a few more days to organise – maybe as long as a week – so I need you to persuade your employers that it'll be worth waiting for.'

'You're playing games with me.'

'Believe me, I'm not. I'm talking about something the mafia does all the time.'

'You wish to put the head of a racehorse in my bed? Is that why you are working so hard to locate my place of residence?'

Shit, this guy is good …

'I think I can do better than that, Hate – a whole lot better.'

'I'm listening, Mr Calloway …'

By the time Chib's dinner guest reached the table, the offer had been made, the phone switched off for the rest of the evening. Chib stood up to kiss her perfumed cheek.

'You,' he said, 'look especially stunning tonight.'

'And you look …' She considered for a moment. 'Smug's the word that comes to mind. Like a cat that's just got the cream.'

'And who's to say I haven't?' Chib teased, sitting down again and grabbing at his napkin before one of the waiting staff could unfurl it and start laying it across his groin.

He hated that. Really hated it.

The phone was ringing as Mike emerged from the shower.

By the time he'd towelled himself dry – noting in the bathroom mirror that he needed to refresh his gym membership – the ringing had stopped. No message left, but he recognised the number. Robert Gissing, calling from home. Mike slid his feet into flip-flops and his body into a towelling robe, then pushed the buttons on his phone, exiting the bathroom and making for the balcony.

'What's up, Robert?' he asked when the call was answered.

'I was just curious – is friend Calloway on board?'

'I think so.'

'And how much exactly is that going to cost us?'

'He wants a painting.' Mike held his breath, knowing what was coming.

'But the man's a bloody infidel! Wouldn't know good art if it bit him on the arse!'

'Nevertheless ...' Mike listened as Gissing's breathing grew less ragged. 'I suppose it all depends on whether there's enough time for Westie to come up with another fake.'

'Well, I'll leave that negotiation in your capable hands, Michael.' Gissing still sounded irritated. 'You seem to have the measure of students and criminals both.'

'I'm not sure about that.' Mike gave a little laugh, but was pleased all the same.

'And besides,' the professor was saying, 'I've been thinking that Calloway may prove more useful to us than we first thought ...'

'How so?' The night air was chilled; Mike retreated back inside, sliding shut the door.

'There's a curator at the National Gallery,' Gissing was beginning to explain. 'And Charles Calloway may be the very chap to deal with him ...'

'Deal with him?' Mike's eyes narrowed; he wondered if he'd misheard.

'Deal with him,' Professor Gissing confirmed.

12

It occurred to Allan Cruikshank that the reason he made a good banker was that he was intrinsically boring. He had barely taken a risk in his life. This meant he was cautious and prudent, and therefore good at not losing his clients' money. But banking had also made him cynical. It was a truism that those who already had money would find it easy to increase their wealth, and they never seemed very grateful for Allan's work on their (often unmerited) behalf. Some of the High Net Worth individuals on his books owned three or four homes, yachts, racehorses, private islands and innumerable works of art. Yet they seemed to appreciate very little, being too busy amassing yet more. He found them dull and blinkered, and wondered if they thought of him the same way. Then there were his fellow account executives at First Caledonian Bank, some of whom hardly registered his existence. The chief executive had met him a dozen times, yet never seemed to remember him from one occasion to the next. With a drink in one hand and a canapé in the other, he would regale Allan time and again with the same anecdote, while Allan smiled and tried not to scream out, *You've told me that before, you fuckwit!* He had perfected the art of looking interested, and could gasp in surprise at any and every predictable punchline.

I want something he *can't have*, Allan would think to himself. *I want something none of my feckless clients could ever own.*

I want those two Coultons.

But he didn't want to go to jail.

These past few nights, he had been waking in a sweat, adrenaline shuddering through him. He would sit in his dressing gown at the dining table, poring over the plan. How many years would he serve for his part in the scheme? How would his kids react to a father banged up at Her Majesty's pleasure? Would it all be worthwhile for just a couple of desirable paintings – paintings he could never show to anyone, never boast about to clients, colleagues, boss? Then again, his ex-wife, Margot, had chided him for years that he was dull. His conversation was dull, his cooking was dull, his dress sense was dull.

And his lovemaking, too.

When she'd moved out, he'd realised he loved her. But by then she had found herself a new man, a younger model who wore black lambswool polo necks and a smug, seemingly permanent half-smile. This hadn't stopped Allan calling her every few days for a catch-up, suggesting lunch at various trendy bistros. She seemed already to have been wined and dined in each of them.

Well, there was one thing Allan could do that Mr Lambswool couldn't: pull off the perfect crime. Which was why, despite the sweats and the bad dreams, he was determined to go ahead with the heist. Hell, his kids might actually like him a little better, even supposing he went to jail – notoriety beat anonymity in most teenagers' eyes.

'You're sure?' Mike asked him for the umpteenth time as they climbed the stairs to Westie's third-floor flat.

'Positive,' Allan replied, hoping he sounded convincing. Mike had stressed that his job was to study the fine detail, but every time he made a suggestion or spotted a potential problem, it seemed Mike had been there before him. With Chib Calloway on board, bringing muscle and firepower, Mike had explained that Allan could jump ship if he was anything but one hundred per cent behind the project.

'You won't be losing face or anything,' he'd said.

'Mike,' Allan had replied, 'are you sure it's not *you* that wants me out?'

To which Mike had shaken his head, maintaining eye contact but saying nothing.

They had reached Westie's landing and stood for a moment outside the door, catching their breath. Then Mike gave a slow nod before pressing the bell. Westie, however, looked more nervous than either of his visitors, something Mike was quick to point out as the student led them inside.

'Your fault,' Westie snapped back. 'Know how much sleep I've had this past week? I'm running on caffeine, cigarettes and the odd Bloody Mary.'

'Tabasco or Worcester sauce?' Mike asked. Westie just glared at him. They were in the living room by now. It smelt of fresh paint, varnish, wood. Westie was using old wood where possible for the stretchers – no need for frames, they'd be swapping them on the day. Where old wood hadn't been available, he was staining new pine with several coats of instant coffee.

'Works a treat,' he explained, as Mike picked up one of the frames and sniffed it.

'Fairtrade, I hope,' he commented. Westie ignored him. He actually seemed prouder of the stretchers than of the copied paintings themselves, but as Allan studied them, he could see that they were marvellous, and this was the very word he uttered, Mike making a noise of agreement while Westie preened. Gissing had provided reproductions of the paintings, and these were pinned to the walls of the makeshift studio. They'd been torn from books and catalogues. There were also close-up photographs showing sections of individual paintings – courtesy of the College of Art's own library. Printed information sheets – some sourced from internet sites – detailed each artist's working methods and, where possible, the exact colours and producers of the paint used. There were tubes of oils everywhere, some squeezed dry. Squares of plywood and cardboard had been used as palettes. Brushes sat in jars of turps. Others had been discarded, stiffened beyond repair. Westie was dressed in a crusty T-shirt and a pair of baggy knee-length shorts. It was hard to tell what colour either item of clothing had been at the start of its career.

'Told you I could do it,' he was saying. But as he made to light a fresh cigarette from the butt of an old one, he gave a hacking cough and pushed the greasy hair back from his eyes.

'You need a lie-down,' Allan told him.

'Try stopping me,' Westie snorted.

'Plenty of time for that once the job's done,' Mike cautioned. 'How many are ready?'

'See for yourself.' Westie stretched out an arm towards the relevant canvases. 'Five down, two to go.'

'Three,' Mike corrected him.

Westie glowered. 'We said seven – two apiece for you lot and one for me.'

'Another partner has come on board.'

'Can't start changing the goalposts now.'

'Yes, we can. Our new partner is insistent.'

The two of them began to argue, Westie pushing for more cash. But Mike stood his ground as Allan watched in silent appraisal. His friend had changed, had grown into the role he was now playing – deal-maker, tough guy, criminal. Maybe he'd been spending too much time with Chib Calloway, but Allan thought it went further: quite simply, Mike was enjoying himself for the first time in an age. The electricity that coursed through Allan's body was coursing through Mike's, too, but to very different effect.

Mike was ready for anything.

A tall man, he'd always affected a slightly round-shouldered posture, as though embarrassed by his size. But now he was more comfortable in his skin, shoulders back, spine stiffened. He made eye contact more readily and spoke slowly but with growing authority. This was what he must have been like in business, Allan thought. This was how he got to the top. Which meant that selling the company had brought Mike wheelbarrows of cash, but only at the cost of his vigour. The problem was, Allan liked this new Mike just that little bit less. In the past, they had gossiped like fishwives, telling jokes and sharing anecdotes. Now it seemed the heist was their only currency. And what about afterwards? Was it likely to galvanise their friendship or drive a wedge into it? Allan was almost afraid to ask. So he watched and listened and wondered about Chib Calloway. He'd argued against the gangster's involvement, until giving in to the combined will of Mike and the professor. Still, he knew it was a mistake. As a move, it was anything but cautious.

The men Calloway provided would be *his*. He could make them do whatever he liked. But would they do whatever Mike or Allan or Gissing told them to do? And what was to stop Calloway ripping them all off afterwards? They could hardly run to the authorities to complain. Mike had nodded throughout, then had argued his own corner. Did Allan want to go find some guns? Steal a van? Talk a few hooligans into helping them out? Doors Open Day was less than a week away. Calloway was the only realistic option they had.

We could buy a van second-hand ... fake names and paying cash ... and do we really need weapons ...?

Defeated by a show of hands, two against one. So much for his role as the 'details guy'.

The five completed forgeries sat on their individual easels. Paint glistened on several. Allan didn't doubt they'd be tacky to the touch – oil took a while to dry. Days, he seemed to remember. And would they retain that newly painted smell? Mike had come here today because he wanted to make sure Westie hadn't been tempted to add any flourishes – no drinks cans or aeroplanes tucked away in a corner of the canvas. When he started peering at each painting in turn, Allan did the same.

'These look good, Westie,' Mike said at last. The student accepted the reiterated praise with a bow, and Allan knew then that he would complete the necessary eighth canvas – Mike was in charge, and the bow acknowledged this. Allan watched as Mike pulled five folded sheets of paper from his pocket. Gissing had cherry-picked them. They were valuable but obscure and should prove relatively easy to copy.

'Your choice,' Mike allowed, handing the pictures to Westie. 'Whichever one's going to be easiest and quickest.'

'He's not fussy then, our new "partner"?' Westie started sifting the short-list. 'He'll take whatever we give him, yeah?'

'You're a fast learner, Westie – now choose.'

Westie held up one of the pictures. 'This one.'

Nodding, Mike turned towards Allan. 'What do you think?'

The question caught Allan unawares. 'Think?' he echoed.

'About these.' Mike jabbed a hand towards the easels.

'They look fine. Be even better once they're framed. But are they really going to fool an expert?'

'Depends on the expert,' Mike answered. He was studying Monboddo's portrait of his wife. It wasn't quite finished yet – the background needed to be filled in – but from a distance of only a few feet Allan was hard pressed to tell it apart from the original. He remembered the exhibition and Mike's reluctance to move on from the painting to the dozens of others in the show. Allan had made two circuits of the room before Mike could be tempted away. It looked like the same thing might be happening today, but then Allan caught movement out of the corner of his eye – someone was standing in the doorway.

'What the ...?'

'Smile for the birdie.' It was the voice of a young woman. She was holding a video camera up in front of her, training it directly at them. Westie gave a little wave.

'Who's this?' Mike was asking.

It was the woman herself who answered. '"This" is Alice.' She was still holding the camera in front of her at head height as she walked slowly into the room. 'And one of you is Mike, the other Allan. Thing is, though, you know Westie's full name, where he lives ... and he knows almost nothing about you.'

Mike's attention was on Westie. 'Is there anything you've *not* told your girlfriend here?'

'Why would he keep a secret from me?' She was lowering the camera as she approached Mike. She wore a short black skirt and thick black leggings. Her T-shirt had a photo of Al Pacino on it from the movie *Scarface*. 'Are you Mike or Allan?'

'This is Mike,' Westie said. He had the good grace to look embarrassed by the stunt Alice was pulling. All the same, Allan got the feeling he'd known about it in advance. No surprise in his face; no questioning in his voice.

Alice had transferred the camera to her left hand so she could reach out with the right, but Mike was not in the mood for social niceties. She quickly realised this and tried Allan instead.

'Allan – right?' she asked.

'Right,' Allan said, shaking the proffered hand. No point making an unnecessary enemy, something he tried to communicate to Mike with a look. Mike, however, was concentrating on Alice. She was making a show of perusing the paintings, giving the artist a peck on the cheek as she passed him. 'So, so talented,' she murmured. She stroked the cheek she'd just kissed and then turned towards Mike again.

'Is that thing still on?' he asked.

'But pointed floorwards,' she felt it necessary to say.

'Still picking up our voices, though,' Mike shot back. Alice studied him for a couple of seconds, then smiled and switched the camera off. She waved it in front of her face.

'Call it insurance – our way of making sure we're all in this together. If Westie gets dumped on at any point, from any height, this ends up at the local CID. You have to appreciate that I'm just looking out for his best interests ...'

Allan was wagging a finger at her. 'I know you,' he stated quietly. 'I've seen you at the Filmhouse.'

She acknowledged this truth with a twitch of the mouth, but was not to be deflected. Her eyes remained fixed on Mike. 'Westie says you offered him a cash payment. As you can see, he's earning every penny. But just now I overheard you trying to squeeze another painting out of him without adding anything to the price. Hardly sounds fair, does it?'

'What do you want?'

'I want what's best for Westie. It sounds insane to me, but he says he's keen to go along on the raid itself. He's also getting a painting – one we both happen to like very much, so that's all right ...'

'I sense a "but".'

'But,' she obliged, 'something up front would seem to be in order ... we were thinking a grand.'

Mike made a show of patting his pockets. 'I don't seem to have that sort of cash on me.'

'You could always write a cheque.' She paused for effect. 'But then that would mean us knowing your surname, Mr Mike.' Her smile was full of mischief, the tip of her tongue rubbing itself against her top lip. Mike's face had hardened and he'd slipped his hands into his pockets. Allan sensed the right hand curl into a fist, and he was grateful the guns had not yet been delivered. When his friend spoke, it was in an ominous monotone.

'I can get you the money, but I'll need something in exchange.'

'This?' Alice guessed, waving the camera. Mike nodded slowly. 'It's a nice piece of kit,' she teased, pretending to examine it. 'Not sure I could bear to part with it.'

'For five hundred pounds, I think you can.'

'A grand,' she corrected him. Mike had his hand stretched out, palm upwards. 'You want it *now*?' She raised an eyebrow. 'Before we've even seen the colour of your money?'

'Can't leave it with you, Alice.' Mike's voice still lacked all emotion. 'You could copy the footage, download it – anything.'

'But handing it over would mean trusting you.'

'Then make your decision.' Mike was brushing something invisible from his tailored jacket. 'Just so long as you know – you're part of this now, and that means all our futures are linked.'

'Like worry beads,' Alice offered.

'Or dominoes – only takes one to fall the wrong way ...'

Her smile was more expansive this time. The camera was placed in Mike's waiting palm.

'One goes, they all go,' Alice was saying.

'That's right.' Mike slipped the camera into his pocket, and although his eyes were still boring into Alice's, Allan couldn't help thinking that the whole exchange could just as easily have been aimed at *him*.

13

'Your boss,' Detective Inspector Ransome said, 'is getting good at losing us.'

He was seated in a coffee shop on the High Street, just up from the Parliament building, talking into his mobile phone. The man he was talking to was seated three tables away. They held eye contact and their phones to their faces, but couldn't risk an actual meeting.

'That's because he won't let me drive,' Glenn Burns said into the mouthpiece. 'Or Johnno, come to that.'

'You think he's suspicious?'

'If I thought he was on to me, I'd have packed my passport and fake beard by now.'

'He's the one who'll be going away, Glenn,' Ransome stated with confidence. 'Leaving his little empire going begging.'

'And you just let me take over? How do I know you won't try shafting me, same as you're doing to him?'

'We've been through this before, Glenn,' Ransome said with a grin of reassurance. 'I *will* try shafting you – but you'll be top dog, not just a spear-carrier. And you'll be wise to me.'

'Plus you'll owe me one.'

'That, too, of course.' Ransome broke off eye contact long enough to lift the oversized mug of coffee to his lips. The liquid was scalding and tasted mainly of frothed milk.

'Is that the latte?' Glenn asked into the phone.

Ransome nodded. 'What've you got?'

'Hot chocolate with whipped cream.'

'Sounds disgusting.' Ransome wiped the foam from his top lip. 'So what's your employer up to, Glenn?'

'Dunno.'

'Thanks for sharing ...'

'No need to get sarky,' Glenn said huffily. 'He's up to something, though.'

'You just said he wasn't.'

'What I said was, I don't know *what* he's up to.'

'But there is something?'

Glenn nodded. The door opened with a tinkling of its bell and both men looked round, checking the new arrival, in case it was someone they should avoid. But it was just another young mum pushing a buggy.

'They should ban nippers from places like this,' Glenn was commenting, staring at the table of mothers and infants that was greeting this latest arrival. One of the kids was griping, and didn't look like stopping any time soon.

'I agree,' Ransome said, 'and I'd stop students coming in, too.' He glanced over to where a solitary teenager, coffee long finished, had spread laptop and coursework over a table intended for four. The laptop was sucking electricity from a socket nearby. 'But then the place would be half empty,' the detective relented, 'and we'd stick out all the more.'

'Suppose so,' Glenn agreed.

'So that's the important issues of the day taken care of ... maybe we can get back to your employer?'

'He's keeping me and Johnno out of it.' Glenn sounded aggrieved, and Ransome knew now why the man had asked for a meet: he had some steam to blow off. 'But a couple of the pubs we've been to, he's been asking about kids.'

'Kids?'

Glenn saw that he'd been misunderstood. 'Tearaways, soccer casuals ... not kiddie kids.' With a nod towards the table of young mums.

'So give me some names.'

Glenn shook his head. 'No idea.'

'What does he want them for?'

'Dunno. It all started when he bumped into this guy he was at school with. I mean, he *tells* me they were at school but I can't see it – the other bloke's a class apart, if you get my meaning. Chib and him went for a drive a few days ago, and when Chib came back he was starting to think about putting together this posse of kids.'

'Reckon you're being put out to pasture, Glenn?'

Even at a distance, Ransome felt the power of the big man's stare. 'Nobody's putting me out of the game, Mr Ransome.'

'All the same, if he's putting together a "posse", there's got to be something they're after.'

'Something or someone ...' Glenn let his words hang in the air between them.

'You're talking about a hit?' Ransome's eyes widened. 'Who could he be planning to whack?'

'Well, there's this big tattooed guy, foreigner, comes from Iceland or somewhere. He's in town to collect a back payment on some merchandise. Problem is, your lot grabbed our goods. Hell's Angels still want paying.'

'And Chib's unwilling to cough up?'

'Four or five schemies with pool cues might be his way of thinking.' Glenn paused again. 'I doubt they'd cause this guy too many problems though, not unless they were seriously tooled up. And even if they were, there'd be others where Hate comes from.'

Ransome thought he'd misheard. 'Hate?' he repeated.

'That's what he calls himself.'

Ransome jotted down Glenn's description of the man, then flicked back through his notebook a few pages. He'd run a check on all three of the names Laura Stanton had given him: Mike Mackenzie, Allan Cruikshank, Robert Gissing. He'd drawn a blank with Cruikshank, though she'd said he worked at First Caly. Gissing had done a bit of painting a while back, and had also written lots of boring-sounding tomes about art. Mackenzie ... well, Mackenzie was some sort of computer fat-cat.

'What does Chib's old school pal look like?' Ransome asked into his phone. Glenn's description fitted Mackenzie like a glove.

'We were in a wine bar when Chib bumped into him. Dunno what happened after that, but suddenly they're pals.'

134

Ransome tapped his pen against the notepad. 'Could mean something or nothing,' he admitted.

'Yeah,' Glenn agreed.

'So what's the deal with Hate? Is he just scratching his arse while he waits for the cash?'

'We've been looking for him. Bastard must be camping under the stars on Arthur's Seat or something – nobody in town seems to have seen him, and trust me, he's a hard man to miss.'

'Is Chib bricking it?'

'He thinks he's got something up his sleeve.'

'And what's that?'

'He's keeping it to himself.'

'Maybe this hit he's planning.'

'Maybe.'

Ransome sighed. 'Christ on a bike, Glenn – you're supposed to be my guy on the *inside*!'

'Fuck you, too, Mr Ransome. Last thing I need right now is any more grief from *you*.'

The detective made a show of incredulity. 'You think this is grief, Glenn? I've not got started yet. I'm still in the home team changing room with my kitbag zipped up. Grief's what I'm saving for the moment I'm placing the cuffs on Chib Calloway's wrists. But I don't want to grow old in the process – and neither do you.'

'Point taken.' Glenn glanced at the front of his phone and Ransome knew he was checking the time. 'Got to go. I'm supposed to be collecting from a pub at the top of Abbeyhill.'

'Careful not to skim too much before you hand it over

to our friend.' There was silence on the other end of the phone. Skimming was a sore point with Glenn. It was how he'd ended up where he was. Walked into one of his boss's bars one day to check the takings; walked out again twenty minutes later carrying a bag but with one side of his jacket weighted more heavily than before. Ransome stepping out in front of him and squeezing the jacket pocket, feeling the weight of coins there, the tightly banded banknotes. Tutting and shaking his head.

And to think I had you down as the brains of the operation, Glenn ... Still, gives us a chance to have a little chat ...

Glenn risked a full-blown glower at the detective as he stood up and shoved his phone into his pocket. Then he stomped out of the coffee shop, barging past a couple of female tourists in the doorway. One of them carried a map, and had been about to ask Glenn something, but the look on his face had changed her mind. Ransome had a little smile to himself as he lifted his mug to his mouth.

'Ever handled a gun before, Mike?'

'Not since I was a kid. They tended to be made of plastic and fired caps ...' Mike felt the heft of the handgun. It had a dark sheen to it, and an oily smell.

'It's a Browning,' Chib explained. 'Best of the bunch, so I hope you like it.'

They were in the workshop of an MOT garage in Gorgie, not far from where they'd both grown up, walking distance to their old school. There was a rusty-looking Sierra sitting in the only bay, cranked up above the examination pit. Wheel hubs and tyres were scattered around the place, corroded exhausts, headlamps with wires curling from them. A couple of venerable topless calendars on the wall above the workbench. The mechanics had clocked off for the night. The forecourt had been in darkness as Mike walked across it. He'd felt it as he approached the door – last chance to back out with a few shreds of dignity intact. Moment he went in and accepted a gun, that was it.

Chib had been waiting for him, arms folded and a smile scratched across his face. *Knew you'd be game*, the look seemed to say.

The other guns were in a flimsy-looking cardboard box that had once contained forty bags of prawn cocktail crisps. While Mike got used to the feel of the Browning, Chib brought out the sawn-off shotgun.

'Bit rusty,' he commented, 'but good for the fear factor.' He pointed it at Mike and chuckled. Mike pointed the Browning back at him. Chib cocked the gun and angled it upwards before pressing the trigger. There was a damp-sounding click. 'Decommissioned, as promised. Normally they'd cost you a double ton a day.'

'I'm good for it,' Mike stated.

'Oh, I know you are, Mike. Makes me wonder what this is all about ... I'm guessing you can afford to buy near as dammit anything that takes your fancy.'

'But what if it's not for sale?'

'Like that, is it?' Chib was watching Mike switch hands with the Browning. 'Tuck it in the back of your waistband, see how it feels.'

Mike did as he was told. 'I can tell it's there.'

137

'Me, too – that's a problem. Might want to think about a longer jacket, and something a good bit more roomy. There's a couple of starting pistols. They've got blanks in them, just in case you need to make some noise. Plus a replica of your Browning and some old piece of junk from the Falklands or Iraq or somewhere.'

'It's a revolver,' Mike said, lifting the gun in his right hand. 'I didn't know the army still used them.'

Chib just shrugged. 'The student and your pal Allan should get some practice in. They've got to look comfortable when they go crashing through that door.'

Mike nodded. 'And the rest of the crew?'

'My lads will have handled shooters before, don't worry about them.'

Mike placed the revolver back in the box, keeping the Browning tucked in against the small of his back. He tried the shotgun next. It felt awkwardly heavy and lacked balance. He shook his head and handed it back. 'When do we meet your "lads"?'

'On the day itself. They'll be primed, and they'll be under orders to do everything you tell them to.'

Mike nodded. 'And the van?'

'Nicked this very evening. It's safely garaged – fake number plates are probably being installed as we speak.'

'Not here, though?'

Chib shook his head. 'I've got a few places like this dotted around the city. So if you ever need an MOT on a dodgy motor ...'

Mike managed a smile. 'I'll bear it in mind. You need to tell your crew that there'll be disguises to wear. And we don't want them toting any flashy jewellery, anything that could get them recognised.'

'Listen to the resident expert,' Chib said with another low chuckle. 'Is that us, then? All set?'

Mike nodded slowly. 'Day after tomorrow. I just hope the paint's dry on the fakes.' Chib's phone sounded and the gangster lifted it from his pocket, checking the number on the screen.

'Got to take this,' he said by way of apology, turning away from Mike as he answered. 'I was beginning to think you'd gone AWOL ...' Mike pretended to be checking the guns again as he listened. 'He's going to go for it?' Chib was saying, head angled downwards, as if studying his shoes. 'That's good ... Definitely no funny business, believe me ... just good honest collateral ... Two or three days tops ... Cheers, then.' He ended the call and turned back towards Mike with a wide smile.

'Collateral?' Mike echoed. Chib just shook his head.

'Is that us, then?' he repeated, keen to wrap things up.

'I suppose so ...' But then Mike gave a little wince. 'No, not quite, actually – there's something I forgot ...'

'Spit it out.'

Mike slipped his hands into his pockets, as though wishing to make the request seem more casual.

'There's this mugging victim ...'

Chib's eyes widened slightly, and then narrowed as if in comprehension. 'You want me to find out who did it, have them made an example of?'

139

'Not exactly.' Mike paused for effect. 'You see, this particular mugging hasn't actually happened yet.'

Chib's eyes narrowed again. 'I don't get it,' he conceded.

'Keep listening,' Mike advised, 'and you soon will ...'

14

'Chib was disappointed,' Mike said, 'when I told him the National Collection doesn't stretch to a Vettriano.'

Gissing snorted into his drink. The two men were seated in an anonymous bar near the railway station. It was a no-nonsense place, meant for drinkers only: no TV or jukebox and only crisps to stave off any hunger pangs. Not having indulged in the best part of a decade, Mike had found himself ordering two packets of prawn cocktail, thinking of the box of guns that was hidden, for want of a better place, in the boot of his car. Three old-timers were seated on stools at the bar itself and had ignored Mike completely as he ordered the drinks and snacks. Gissing had chosen the table furthest from the door. He wrinkled his nose at the crisps and stuck to alternating between sips of malt and gulps of IPA.

'Vettriano isn't universally admired,' he commented, wiping foam from around his mouth.

'Popular, though,' Mike countered, knowing full well the professor's views on the subject. Gissing decided not to rise to the bait.

'So what exactly is our gangland friend settling for?'

'An Utterson.'

141

'*Dusk on Rannoch Moor*?'

'That's the one. Westie didn't think he'd have any trouble painting it.'

'You showed a picture of it to Calloway?'

'I did.'

'And he liked it?'

'He asked what it was worth.'

Gissing rolled his eyes. 'Well, good riddance to it, I suppose.' He took another swallow of beer, and Mike realised how nervous the professor was, while Mike himself was growing calmer with each passing hour. From the internet, he had printed off an aerial map of the streets around the warehouse, charting the best route for the van. He'd arranged with Chib where to pick up the four extra crew, and where to drop them afterwards. The crew would take the guns and dispose of them. Looking at Gissing, he felt glad the old boy wouldn't be storming the warehouse, firearm at the ready: the hand reaching for the whisky glass was trembling.

'It'll be fine,' Mike assured him.

'My dear chap, of course it will. You don't think I'm having doubts?'

'A lot could still go wrong.'

'You'll handle it, Mike.' The professor gave a tired smile. 'You seem to have developed a taste for all of this.'

'Maybe a little,' Mike conceded. 'But it was *your* idea, remember.'

'Still, I won't be sorry when it's done and dusted, while I have the sneaking suspicion you just might be.'

'So long as we don't end up in jail. Christ, imagine it

142

– with Chib Calloway as our disgruntled cellmate.'

Gissing raised a hand, palm out. 'As the Americans might say, let's not even go there.'

They shared a smile and concentrated on their drinks. Just one more day to go. Mike knew he'd have to fill tomorrow with activity, so that he didn't start to fret. They'd gone over the plan on paper, rehearsed the details a dozen times. Allan had been through it with a fine-tooth comb. They knew what they had to do, and how much time would be available. But there were factors they couldn't determine. Mike wondered if that was why he felt so calm: a case of *que sera sera*. As a businessman, he'd always liked to be in charge, knowing what would happen, in control of the various sequences of events. But when he'd picked up that Browning, he'd felt a thrill of electricity. The weight of it, the machine-tooled detail. It was a work of art in itself. He'd loved playing with guns as a kid; had a huge collection of plastic soldiers, cowboys and Indians. Hell, give him a banana and he'd have been aiming it at the nearest target. An aunt had brought him back a boomerang from Australia – same thing: point, aim with one eye closed, then make that plosive sound of the bullet and its trajectory.

He remembered Chib, aiming a nonexistent pistol from the passenger seat of the 5-Series. And back at the garage, hoisting the sawn-off. Shifting against the back of his chair, he could feel the Browning tucked into his waist-band. It was rash to carry it – what if anyone glimpsed it and reported him? – but he couldn't help himself. He only had it until Saturday afternoon. He thought back to the

Indian restaurant and wondered how those drunken suits would have reacted if he'd pulled a gun on them. Not in the restaurant itself – too many witnesses. But outside, waiting in the shadows for them to come reeling out …

When the door to the bar opened, Mike swivelled his eyes. Caution mingled with mistrust … but it was just another drinker. A scant week or two back, he would have paid no heed – the world ended at the length of his stretched arms – but this was different. He wondered how he could go back to his old self again, seated in his flat's spare bedroom, the one he kept all his computer stuff in, staring at the monitor or checking the shelves for signs of his relevance – the business initiative awards and framed citations (Outstanding Achiever; Creative Spirit; Scottish Entrepreneur …). What did any of it mean?

The drinker had joined his friends at the bar. The door was swinging shut again, reminding Mike of that day at the auction house.

When one door opens, another closes …

And vice versa, obviously.

'We're really going to do it, aren't we?' Gissing had punched his right fist into his left palm and was rubbing the one against the other.

'Oh, yes,' Mike confirmed. 'No getting away from it now.'

'Getting away *from* it may not be the problem. We need to focus on getting away *with* it. And what happens afterwards, Michael?'

'We're freedom fighters, remember … afterwards, we get to feel good.' Mike shrugged; he had nothing else to offer as yet. The professor was silent for a few moments. Then he sighed, staring into the remains of his beer.

'Cézanne's *Boy in a Red Vest* was stolen, you know – not so long ago. From a museum in Switzerland. They reckon it was taken to order. Someone has it on their wall at home.'

'I heard about it. Interpol reckon six billion dollars' worth gets stolen each year ... know how much of it they recover? Not much.' Mike saw the enquiring look on Gissing's face. 'I've done my research, Robert. Few clicks of the mouse and there it was – fourth largest criminal enterprise in the world after drugs, arms-running and money-laundering. Which is good news for us – means that if and when our little undertaking is discovered, the police will be focusing on criminal gangs.'

'And we're not one of those?'

'Not the way the local plod would understand it.'

'You see yourself more as Thomas Crown,' Gissing teased. 'Does that make Laura your Faye Dunaway?'

'I'm a long way short of Steve McQueen, Prof – or Pierce Brosnan, come to that ...'

They had another little laugh to themselves.

'"The still watches of the night",' Gissing eventually said.

'Sounds like a quote.'

'A Victorian cat burglar called Adam Worth – some say he's the basis for Moriarty. He once stole a Gainsborough and said it was so he could worship it in "the still watches of the night".'

'I hope he worshipped it in daylight, too.'

Gissing nodded, deep in thought.

'Another?' Mike offered.

Gissing shook his head. 'Early night for me,' he said. 'What was Allan's excuse this time?'

'Dinner with a client. Wasn't sure how long it would go on. But he's cleared his diary for tomorrow.'

'Well, that's something, I suppose.' Gissing rose slowly to his feet, then noticed there was a trickle of whisky remaining, so drained it and exhaled noisily. 'I'll see you in the morning, Michael. Try to get some rest.'

'Do you need me to run you home?'

Gissing waved the offer aside and made for the door. Mike waited a couple of minutes, then emptied his own glass and nodded goodbye to the barman as he exited. His car was on a single yellow line fifty yards along the road. There was no sign of the professor. This was a street of galleries. Mike peered through the window of the nearest, but couldn't make out anything other than vague shapes on the walls. He looked to left and right, but saw nothing to trouble him. Unlocked his car and slid into the driver's seat. He decided to take the long route home, the one that would lead him past Allan's flat. It was just off Leith Walk, in an undistinguished part of the New Town. Nice flat, though, and never any trouble in the vicinity, due in no small part to the police station directly opposite. Mike kept his indicators on as he stopped adjacent to two patrol cars. They were parked kerbside, locked and empty. Allan's flat was two floors up. The lights were on behind the curtains. Didn't mean he was home, of course – could be for security. Didn't mean he'd lied about the dinner. Didn't mean he was becoming a liability.

Not yet.

The problem was in the detail. Mike had asked Allan to look for chinks in the plan's armour, meaning he spent all his time on negatives – what could go wrong – rather than getting any sort of buzz from the adventure. Allan had been to Granton, driving past the warehouse, skirting its perimeter, noting movements and personnel, then had reported back with news of several dozen potential problems and setbacks. And, it seemed to Mike, had begun believing the task to be altogether more fraught than was manageable, while Mike himself felt the opposite. Even Chib Calloway – Chib Calloway! – was bending to his will. He rubbed his spine against the driver's seat, feeling the gun in his waistband. With a well-lit police station not fifteen feet away.

In charge.

In control.

Senses heightened.

Mike switched off his flashers and let the Maserati rumble down the hill into the heart of the New Town.

15

They met at Mike's flat in Murrayfield. Gissing spent the first few minutes studying the works of art that lined the walls, while Allan wanted to see Mike's den, asking questions about the spec of his computer and commenting on the display of awards.

Mike knew what they were doing: deferring the inevitable. He busied himself making coffee, Miles Davis providing the soundtrack. The flat was fitted with a centralised music system, meaning anything on his iPod could be piped into any or all of the rooms. The speakers were in the ceilings, but a couple of them had stopped functioning. Same went for the display panel on the living room wall. That was the problem with a 'smart home': the smarter it got, the more could go wrong. One of the recessed lights in the kitchen needed replacing, too, but it was a halogen thing and fiddly to install. Mike would sometimes joke that when the last bulb fizzled out, he'd have to find somewhere else to live.

He took the tray into the living room and placed it on the dining table next to the cardboard box.

'Everything's ready,' he said.

His guests accepted their drinks with silent nods, trying

not to show any interest in the box or its contents. Gissing had brought a list with him: fake names of the seven individuals booked on to tomorrow's tour.

'How long ago did you book the tour?' Mike asked.

'It tends to fill up pretty quick,' Gissing commented.

'How long?' Mike persisted.

The professor shrugged. 'Three ... four weeks back.'

'Before we started planning this?'

Gissing acknowledged as much with a twitch of his mouth. 'I told you, Mike, I've been thinking about this for a long time. I did the same thing last year: reserved a block of names for the tour.'

'You bottled out?' Allan guessed.

'Didn't know who might be willing to help.' The professor slurped some coffee. 'I hardly knew you back then, Allan ...'

'And you'd yet to meet me,' Mike added.

Gissing nodded slowly. 'It's one thing to have an idea, another to carry it to fruition.' He toasted Mike with the coffee mug.

'We're not there yet,' Mike warned. 'How did you make the bookings?'

'By phone.'

'But without using your own name?'

'Fake names throughout. They asked for contact details, as I knew they would, so I used the phone numbers of some Indian and Chinese restaurants. They won't need to phone unless the tour is being cancelled.'

'And it's not going to be cancelled this year?'

Gissing shook his head. 'I had my secretary call them

yesterday to see if there was any chance of adding a student to one of the tours. She was informed that all the tours are full, meaning they're going ahead.'

Mike thought for a moment. 'Okay,' he said, trying to sound reassured. He then opened the box and lifted out the first of the guns. He placed it on the surface of the table, and another followed it, followed by a third and a fourth. 'Take your pick. Whatever's left goes to Chib's men.'

'And the sawn-off?' Allan had spotted it, still resting in the box, barrel pointed upwards.

'That's for them, too.'

Gissing was weighing up one of the starting pistols. 'Believe it or not, I used to shoot as a lad. My school had cadet training. Sometimes we were allowed live ammo.'

'Not tomorrow,' Mike said.

'Heavier than it looks,' Allan commented, picking up another of the guns. He studied it. 'I thought you were supposed to file off the serial number.'

'They're untraceable,' Mike assured him.

'According to your friend Chib,' Allan countered. He was taking aim at the window, one eye squeezed shut. 'Thing is, if we go in there waving these around, the guards might get spooked, start lashing out ...'

'Chib's men are there to lash back.'

'But say one of them rushes me,' Allan persisted. 'Do I pull the trigger and shout "Bang!"?'

'Just improvise,' Gissing growled.

'The starting pistols fire blanks,' Mike explained. 'The noise should be enough to freeze anyone in their tracks.'

Gissing picked up the revolver. 'This one's genuine, isn't it?'

'Ex-Falklands or Gulf War,' Mike confirmed. 'You know a bit, don't you?'

'Actually, I think that's my knowledge of these things pretty well exhausted. How about you, Michael? Any preference?'

Mike reached around into the waistband of his denims. He was wearing a loose shirt, and the Browning emerged in one fluid movement.

'Jesus, Mike,' Allan said, 'you make that look almost *too* practised.'

Mike smiled. 'I had it on me last night in that pub.'

'Did you now?' Gissing said. 'I'd no idea.'

'I bet service would have improved if you'd whipped it out,' Allan added.

'Once you're happy with your choice,' Mike went on, nodding towards the guns, 'I want you to keep it with you, try to get comfortable handling it.'

'Not that I should have any reason to use mine,' Gissing stated.

'Not if you're outside in the van, no ... but we don't know what the situation's going to be like in the compound. Just needs one extra guard to be patrolling the perimeter and we've got a problem. *That's* why you'll be carrying it.' He pointed towards Gissing's gun.

'Understood,' the professor said with a nod.

'That was my idea, by the way,' Allan added. 'Compound's a huge area, which makes it vulnerable.'

'Good to see you're pulling your weight,' Gissing

responded. 'When you cried off last night, I admit I started having doubts ...'

'That reminds me,' Mike interrupted, 'how did your dinner go?'

'Fine,' Allan replied, just a little too quickly, his eyes everywhere but on his friend.

Gissing and Mike shared a look. The professor was passing his chosen gun from hand to hand. He tried fitting it into the inside pocket of his tweed jacket but it threatened to fall out. 'Maybe I'll wear something with bigger pockets tomorrow.'

'Whatever you wear, it's got to be disposable,' Mike reminded him. 'No favourite shirts or coats. Whole lot's going to have to be got rid of.'

'Right,' Allan said. He'd pushed his own gun into the front of his trousers. 'Going to do my groin an injury if I try sitting down,' he complained. He shifted the gun round to the small of his back. 'That works,' he decided.

'Then we're all set, aren't we?' Mike waited for his two friends to nod their agreement. There was a slight niggle at the back of his mind. Seven false names for the tour ... booked weeks ago by Gissing. So the old man had known they would need back-up. He said as much to Gissing.

'That's not what I was thinking,' the professor corrected him. 'My rationale was, the more "ghosts" I could load on to the tour, the fewer actual participants I'd have to deal with on the day. There happened to be seven spaces left, so I gave seven names. End of story.'

Mike turned his attention to Allan – his 'details guy'. Allan gave a twitch of the mouth, then cleared his throat.

'The one thing I still don't like,' he said, 'is Westie's girlfriend.'

'Agreed,' Gissing growled. 'I might have a word with our young friend about that particular little stunt.'

'Not until he's finished his work,' Mike advised. 'We need him focused.'

'We *all* need to be focused,' Allan added.

'Which may mean missing the occasional dinner party,' Gissing chided.

'You want me to change my routine?'

'Allan's got a point,' Mike interrupted. 'On the surface, it has to be business as usual.' At which moment, Allan's mobile sounded. It was a text message, and he started to check it. Mike felt like swiping the phone from his friend's grasp, but doubted it would do much for team spirit.

Gissing, noting Mike's conflict of feelings, gave a lop-sided smile and mouthed the words 'business as usual', before pointing the revolver at the phone and pretending to shoot it to smithereens.

Mike had suggested they take his Quattroporte, but Allan had pointed out that it was the sort of car that got noticed, so they travelled in his Audi instead, Gissing in the front passenger seat, Mike in the back but leaning forward so that his face was level with the front seats. Gissing had proposed sitting in the back until Allan reminded him that he'd be driving tomorrow. Better if he got used to the view from the front.

'You really *have* thought of everything,' Gissing said.

153

'Probably not,' Mike warned him. 'Hence this morning's recce.'

There was no fast route to anywhere. Chunks of the city centre were being turned into tramlines, meaning road-works, tailbacks, and temporary traffic lights. Classic FM on the radio – ostensibly to calm the nerves. Gissing asked if this was the same route they'd be taking tomorrow.

'Depends on whether you want to rendezvous at mine,' Mike said, 'or make your own way to the pick-up point.'

'And where's that?' Allan asked.

'Gracemount – we're headed there now. I don't know exactly where the van's going to be – Chib's going to text that to me first thing in the morning.'

'So we don't get to try the van out beforehand?' Gissing sounded sceptical. 'Isn't that risky?'

'That's exactly what *I* said,' Allan chipped in.

'Chib assures me it'll do the job,' Mike stressed.

'He's an expert, is he?'

Mike stared at the professor. 'So far, I'd have to say yes, he is – certainly compared to us.'

'Then I'll have to take your word for it.'

Mike reached into his pocket and brought out a couple of sheets of paper, folded in four. 'I printed this from the internet – best route from the Gracemount area to Westie's flat, and from there to Granton.' He handed them over to the professor. 'Saturday, so there'll be no rush hour to speak of, but I've factored out Leith Walk.'

'Because of the tram works.' Allan was nodding appreciatively.

'I didn't even know where Gracemount *was*,' Gissing

154

muttered, staring at the map and accompanying instructions.

'That's why we're headed there now,' Mike explained. He'd already decided that Gracemount Drive, just beyond the school, would be their starting point for today's adventure. When they arrived, Allan asked Gissing if he wanted to swap places, but received a grizzled shake of the head.

'Easier for me to learn the route if I'm a passenger.'

'Which begs the question,' Allan commented, 'you need to be in the van while we're in the warehouse, but do you need to do any of the actual driving?'

'You think I'm not capable?' Gissing had turned to fix Allan with a glare. 'I used to drive an MG sports car in my younger years.'

'What happened to it?' Mike asked with a smile.

'I didn't think it ... *seemly* for a man in his sixties. One of the other staff members bought himself a Porsche at fifty-five, and that's when I decided the MG had to go.'

'Because the Porsche trumped your car?' Allan guessed.

'Not at all,' Gissing barked. 'But I could see for the first time how bloody ridiculous a man of advancing years looks in a sports car.'

'My Quattroporte's a sports car,' Mike reminded him.

'And you're just the right age for it,' Gissing stated.

'I think,' Allan informed Mike, 'the professor wants to drive the van.'

'Then he has my blessing,' Mike conceded.

Gissing just gave a loud sniff and went back to his studying.

From the school, they headed back into town towards Westie's flat – they'd be picking up him and his paintings tomorrow – sat for a minute outside his tenement block, and then, when a warden started taking an interest, signalled back into traffic and made for The Mound and the New Town.

'What are you going to do when you retire?' Allan asked the professor.

'Sell up and ship out,' Gissing replied. 'With the money I get from the house, I can buy a cottage somewhere on the west coast, fill it with books and art, and enjoy the scenery.'

'Won't you miss Edinburgh?'

'I'll be too busy enjoying walks along the beach.'

'Got somewhere in mind?' Mike asked.

'I'll put the homestead on the market first, see how much cash it'll give me to play with.'

'They're going to miss you at the college,' Allan said. Gissing's silence did not dispute the fact.

Mike cleared his throat. 'You sure about the west coast? A while back, I thought you said you'd be heading for Spain.'

'Man's entitled to change his mind,' Gissing barked. 'Anywhere except this bloody city ...'

Soon they were on Inverleith Row, passing the Botanic Gardens, and then Ferry Road, glimpsing the Firth of Forth in front of them. As they headed along Starbank Road, Allan asked if Mike was sure this would be the quickest route in the morning.

'Maybe not the quickest, but definitely the easiest.'

Google Earth had given Mike an aerial printout of the area around the warehouse. The trading estate would be near deserted at weekends, but was busy with lorries and vans this Friday as lunchtime approached. The drivers, Mike guessed, would be thinking about a trip to the pub after work, and maybe the football or shopping tomorrow and a lie-in on Sunday. He got the sudden and outrageous notion that maybe there was another would-be heist crew out there, who had figured out what Gissing had figured out and were making their own plans. But as they drove at a measured pace past the gatehouse, the cars parked kerbside were empty, awaiting their owners at workday's end. The only van was selling hot food to a small, orderly queue. The men smoked and joked and shuffled their feet. Mike had a craving for a cigarette – only his second of the day. Allan pulled the Audi into the nearest available space and stopped the engine. Mike asked him to turn the key again so the electrics were working, then slid down the back window and lit a cigarette. Allan took one and slid his own window down.

'Can we stretch our legs or are you worried CCTV might snap us?' Mike asked.

'I'm not sure,' Allan conceded. 'There are cameras ...' He gestured in their direction. 'But they're pointed at gates and inner compounds. I doubt any are picking us up, but all the same ...'

'You've been here before?' Gissing asked.

'More than once, I'm guessing,' Mike offered, before opening his door and getting out. After a moment's thought, Allan followed, but Gissing stayed where he

157

was. Mike leaned down and spoke to him through the window.

'Not joining us?'

'You forget, Michael – I'm a weel-kent face in these parts. If one of the security men should decide he needs a burger or a bacon roll, I might be recognised.'

Mike nodded his agreement. While smoking, Allan was pretending not to be studying the building they'd just passed. 'Looks anonymous enough, doesn't it?' he commented.

There were certainly no signs posted, nothing to alert passers-by to the multimillion-pound contents of the grey concrete warehouse. The guard in the gatehouse was reading a newspaper and snacking on a chocolate bar. The fence was high and in good repair, topped with razor wire. But then the same could be said of all the other compounds in the vicinity, one of which advertised itself as a double-glazing showroom. A sign on the fence warned of twenty-four-hour security and guard dogs. Mike caught Allan's eye.

'Guard dogs?'

'On the night shift only. A bloke in a van does the rounds.'

Mike nodded and concentrated on his cigarette again.

'Feeling peckish?' he asked Allan.

'Do we really want Greasy Joe to be able to give CID our description?'

Mike shrugged his acceptance of this. All the same, he had sudden hunger pangs. How exquisite to walk over there and strike up a conversation, pistol tucked into waistband and criminal intent in one's mind. It was almost unbearable, irresistible.

And outrageously stupid.

Another car – a Rover – had pulled into a gap four cars ahead of the Audi. The man who emerged was overweight and wearing a pinstripe suit which, like its owner, had seen better days. He locked up and was heading for the van, which meant passing the two smokers. He offered a nod of greeting, and kept going, but then paused and turned around.

'Nice motor, chief.'

'Thanks,' Allan replied.

As the suit headed towards the snack van, Allan could see that the men in the queue were interested in the car now, too. He flicked his half-finished cigarette into the gutter. 'Thank Christ we didn't bring the Maserati,' he commented. Having said which, he got back in behind the steering wheel. Mike stood his ground, however, finishing the length of his own cigarette before stubbing it underfoot. Only then did he slide on to the Audi's back seat.

'Reckon the mobile chippie will be there on a Saturday?' he asked.

'Doubtful,' Allan reasoned, starting the engine. 'Not enough workers around here at the weekend to make it worth his while.' He moved off and turned the first available corner, then braked again. 'This is the spot for tomorrow,' he said.

'We can see the gates, but the guard can't see us,' Gissing confirmed.

'So we can watch the punters come and go,' Mike added.

Allan executed a three-point turn and paused again at the chosen location, facing the warehouse now, making sure his instinct was right. Any cameras trained on the roadway? None. The route was a dead end, meaning no passing traffic. At the same time, they had a clear view of anyone entering or leaving the compound. It was about as perfect as they were going to get.

'So you're parked here, Robert,' he intoned. 'We go in, and you give it a couple of minutes, then start moving.'

Mike took up the commentary. 'One of Chib's lads will be in the gatehouse by then. He'll lift the barrier for you.'

'And I reverse up to the loading bay,' Gissing recited.

'After which?' Mike tested him.

'I wait,' came the response.

'And if we don't start coming out within the quarter-hour?'

'I drive off and leave you to your fates.' Gissing gave a cold smile. 'But do I need to pick up the gatehouse felon or do I abandon him, too?'

'That'll be your call,' Mike decided. 'Everybody happy with things as they stand?'

'I have a couple of concerns,' Allan piped up from the driving seat. 'Chib's guys are going to come to this cold.'

'So long as *we* know what we're doing, that shouldn't be a problem. It actually works in our favour if they don't know too much.' Mike paused. 'Next concern, please.'

'Why isn't Westie with us? He'll be here tomorrow, too.'

160

'He's got his hands full finishing the Utterson copy,' Mike said. 'But I'll go over it with him later, don't worry.'

Allan was nodding, apparently satisfied, but Mike held eye contact with him in the rearview mirror, until he was happy that his friend really was reassured.

'I still can't believe we're giving that bloody thug a painting,' Gissing muttered.

'Well, we are,' Mike snapped back, 'so get over it.' There was silence after that, the three men staring at the warehouse, their thoughts kept to themselves. 'Okay,' Mike said eventually. 'The only thing now is the getaway car. I was planning to leave the Maserati on Marine Drive, but I'm not so sure ...'

'The Audi's a safer bet,' Allan agreed. 'It won't pick up half the attention.'

'And you're willing to risk leaving it on Marine Drive for a few hours?'

'I don't see why not.'

'I'm assuming it's not going to die on us?'

'It's only just been serviced.' Allan rubbed his hands down the steering wheel as if to assuage his car's feelings.

'Why don't we just rent some cars?' Gissing asked.

'Best not to,' Mike cautioned. 'Means leaving a paper trail.'

'Is that what your friend Calloway told you?'

Mike ignored this. Instead, he had another question for Allan. 'Your boot's big enough to take the paintings?'

'Check for yourself.'

'Do you want to park it overnight or first thing in the morning?'

'Early morning,' Allan decided. 'Forecast's for rain, so even the dog-walkers may be dissuaded.'

'I'll meet you there, then. We can do breakfast at my place and then head to Gracemount.'

'Is it best if I meet up with you at Gracemount?' Gissing asked.

'Up to you, Professor,' Mike told him.

'I'll probably do that then – I'll order a mini-cab.'

'In which case, pay cash,' Allan interjected. 'Don't use an account or anything that would leave one of those paper trails we've been talking about.'

'In fact,' Mike added, 'best take a bus into town and then transfer to a cab.'

'Bloody hell,' Gissing grumbled, 'you both sound like the real thing.'

'That's because we are the real thing,' Allan reminded him. 'Now fasten your seatbelts, gentlemen. It's a short hop to Marine Drive, but I don't want us getting pulled over by the traffic cops ...'

16

Westie was a wreck, but he was enjoying the challenge. He'd complained to Alice about the lack of food in the fridge and booze in the cupboard. She'd reminded him that the nearest shop was only a two-minute walk.

'Do I look like I can afford two minutes?' he'd screamed at her.

'If you stopped rolling joints every quarter-hour, you could take the whole sodding afternoon off,' she'd snapped back.

'I'm doing this for *you*, remember.'

'Yeah, sure ...'

With which, she had flounced out of the studio, kicking an empty pizza box out of her way. But the box had rattled, meaning it wasn't quite empty. Two crusts with a trace of tomato paste on each – a feast, under the circumstances. Westie worked with music in the background – Bob Marley, John Zorn, Jacques Brel, P.J. Harvey. The Brel had been turned into an accidental drinks coaster at a party a while back, as a result of which it skipped on some tracks; not that Westie minded – he didn't speak French anyway. The singer's passion was what he wanted. Passion, elegance and striving.

'Same wavelength,' he cooed to himself, picking up yet another paintbrush, grinding its hardened bristles against the edge of the easel. Then he had a smile to himself as he remembered his little secret. If he looked closely, he would see it staring back at him. Westie placed a finger to his lips.

'Sshhh,' he said.

And with a quiet chuckle, he popped the last morsel of pizza crust into his mouth, lit what remained of his previous spliff, and got back into the swing.

Ransome was reminded of the old cliché: things were quiet; too quiet.

He'd tried tracking down the man called Hate, with no luck whatsoever. Nor had Glenn fared any better, despite every ne'er-do-well in the city having been alerted to the search. Hate had to be staying somewhere outside Edinburgh, which was why Ransome had widened the net to West and East Lothian and even over the Forth Bridge to Fife Constabulary – all to no effect.

Plenty of campsites and caravan parks, but so far Ransome had drawn a blank there, too. He'd then decided to start at the other end, so to speak. There had been a slight frisson in contacting Interpol – he was ashamed to admit it, but it was true nevertheless. Full description ... possible Hell's Angel affiliation ... Scandinavian. How much more did they need?

Well, a name for a start, one of his email respondents had joked. As a last resort, Ransome had contacted a mate at the Scottish Criminal Records Office, though he doubted Hate would have form in the UK.

'I share your scepticism,' the mate had said, 'but I can run it through a few databases here and there.'

Ransome had also gone into the Shining Star and asked staff there about Chib Calloway and Michael Mackenzie. Mackenzie they barely knew, and Calloway they were unwilling to discuss.

'Never causes us any trouble,' the manager had opined.

'He will,' Ransome had warned her. Liked the line so much, he'd repeated it to Ben Brewster back at the station. Ben had given a half-hearted laugh, his eyes on the paper-work piling up on his colleague's desk.

'I'll get round to it,' Ransome had chided him.

But Calloway was consuming too many of his waking hours, along with some of his sleep. In his dreams, he was chasing the gangster on foot through the streets of a sprawling city. His prey seemed to know the place better than him, and would lead him a merry dance through hotels and office blocks and factories. At one point, Ransome had been chatting up a good-looking woman in a hallway, while slowly becoming aware that Calloway had squeezed himself into a cupboard right next to them and was eavesdropping on the seduction.

Jesus, he needed a drink. He'd tried calling Laura to see if she might be free after work. So far he'd left three messages. He was seated at his desk in the CID unit at Torphichen Place and finding it hard to breathe. It was as if all the oxygen was being sucked from the place. He'd been to the toilets, splashed water on his face. Too much coffee, he told himself. Too much stress. His wife Sandra had been studying cookery at night school – Thai, Chinese, Kashmiri, fusion. The nightly assaults of spiced concoctions previously unknown to him were playing havoc with Ransome's digestion. Not that he could say as much to Sandra's face. He kept a supply of Rennies in his desk drawer, but the indigestion tablets could do nothing about the pungent sweats he broke into occasionally.

If only he could open one of the windows ...

His request for 24/7 surveillance on Calloway had been met by his bosses with a hoot of derision. Cutbacks were biting – where was the money for overtime going to come from? CID was short-handed as it was. Ransome had taken it on the chin and walked out of the room with his pride intact. He'd even driven out one night to the newish housing scheme where Calloway lived. Car in the driveway; lights on in the living room; no sign of either Johnno or Glenn.

Glenn ... someone else who owed him a text, a phone call, a message.

Glenn the Gullible, who would be easy meat for CID once Calloway was behind bars. Always supposing Johnno let him climb on to their old boss's throne unopposed. Glenn might be the clever one, but Johnno could boast a wide streak of viciousness. With Calloway gone, he was bound to fancy his own chances. Who would Chib's old team be the more willing to follow – brain or brawn? Didn't much matter to Ransome. The whole set-up was coming crashing down.

At going-home time, Brewster suggested a quick one.

But a quick one was never quick. For a start, they couldn't drink anywhere near the station – too strong a chance they'd be sharing the place with people they didn't want to meet, villains fresh out of the holding cells, scowls with a grudge. So that meant a jaunt, and Ransome didn't feel much like a jaunt with his colleague.

'Doing anything at the weekend?' he asked instead, trying to sound interested.

'It's Doors Open tomorrow – I'm taking the girls to St Bernard's Well.'

'And what's that when it's at home?'

'It's down by the Water of Leith ... used to be some sort of health spa. Kept under lock and key these days.'

'I meant, what's Doors Open?'

'Doors Open Day. People get to go into lots of buildings, ones they're normally barred from. Masonic lodges and banks and stuff. I think Leith cop shop's throwing open its doors.'

'Sounds a riot.'

'It's fun. Ellie says it'll be good for the girls, too.'

'Well, good luck with that.' Ransome knew that Brewster had two daughters just shy of adolescence and a wife who, like Sandra, always got her way. The girls were being educated privately, which kept funds tight elsewhere. As good a reason as any never to have kids ... not that Sandra had shown much interest in that department ... Ransome sat at his desk until the office had emptied. He liked the CID suite when it was deserted and silent. Staring at his screen, however, he realised he couldn't think of a single thing he wanted to do. There was the paperwork to be got through, but it could wait. Maybe he'd come in tomorrow or Sunday – a couple of hours would clear the backlog and give Brewster something to think about on Monday morning.

An hour and a half later, Ransome had been home, eaten lamb Peshwari, changed clothes, and was seated in his local on Balgreen Road. There was a darts match, and normally he would have pitched in, but not tonight. Teams were wanted for a pub quiz, but he steered shy of that commitment, too. He was thinking about Chib Calloway and all his money ... and Michael Mackenzie and all *his* money. Sure enough, they'd been at school together – a check of the records had confirmed as much. And it could well be true, as Glenn said, that they'd just bumped into one another. But Glenn could be pulling a flanker; or Chib could have lied to Glenn. Mackenzie had made a mint from computers. Calloway *had* to want him for something – either to fleece him or to bully him into paying protection.

Or there was some skill Calloway needed, and Mackenzie was privy to it. Hacking came to mind. It was a stone-cold fact that these days to rob a bank like First Caly you didn't need to ram-raid it or pick the locks – you just had to chip away at its digital defences. And that could be done from anywhere ...

He held out another hour before phoning the station, asked if anything had been happening. He did this some evenings – and on days off, too. He'd call the central switchboard at Bilston, or the comms room at Torphichen Place.

'It's Ransome here.'

Usually that was all he had to say. They knew him well enough by now and would reel off the details. Cars nicked or torched, break-ins, fights, domestics. Dealers busted, flashers collared, shoplifters hunted down. Friday nights were second only to Saturday in the number and variety of offences. Tonight was no different. 'Still on the lookout for a few stolen cars and vans,' Ransome was informed. 'Two drunks ejected from a stag do on Lothian Road and taking umbrage. And one poor old chap mugged down by the canal.'

Ransome wasn't surprised: like a lot of Edinburgh, the canal was more dangerous than it looked. Probably kids from Polwarth or Dalry.

'What was he doing down there?' he asked.

'Nothing suspicious, far as we can tell. He lives in the new flats by the old Arnold Clark showroom.'

Just bad luck then – wrong place, wrong time. 'Anything else?' he asked.

'Couple of shoplifters earlier on today, and a hit-and-run in Shandon. Teenagers smoking dope in the Meadows – give it till later, there'll be the usual booze casualties and fights.'

Ransome gave a sigh and put away his phone. He'd promised Sandra he wouldn't be late, even though Friday had always been his night out. But looking around him, he wondered why he bothered. The darts players were going through the motions. The quiz hadn't found enough bodies to make up the requisite teams. Nobody was playing the bandit. Ever since the smoking ban, the place had been dying on its feet.

'Too quiet,' Ransome muttered to himself, finishing his pint and deciding enough was enough.

Mike was sitting on his balcony, smoking a cigarette, when the phone rang. He answered and there was a lengthy pause filled with static hiss. Then a voice he recognised.

'Michael, you old bugger, how's tricks?'

Mike smiled to himself and sat back down. The past few days, whenever his phone had started ringing he'd assumed the worst: Westie had exploded or Allan had gone running to the police for absolution. But this was just his old business partner, calling for a gloat.

'Where are you?' Mike asked.

'Sydney, of course.'

'What time is it?'

'Tomorrow. Bit of a breeze out here on the deck, but balmy with it. What are you up to?'

Mike considered all the possible answers open to him. 'Not much,' he eventually said. 'I've got half a cigarette left to smoke and then I was thinking about bed.'

'You're a desperate man, Michael. Isn't it Friday night over there? Shouldn't you be out making merry and draining the spuds? I could ship you over one of the girls I know here ...'

'I bet you could. So what have you been up to? Make me jealous ...'

'Just the usual – parties, more parties, sun, sand and surf. Chartering a boat later on today.'

'Sounds awful.'

There was laughter on the line. 'Yeah, well, you always did prefer the quiet life – behind the scenes, I mean.'

'So did you, Gerry. What happened?'

'Life happened, mate.' It was the answer he always gave. 'Maybe it'll happen to you some day.'

'In Edinburgh?'

'Good point – you need to drag your sorry carcass down here. How many times do I have to ask?'

'It's on my list, Gerry.' And why not? What exactly was keeping him in Scotland? Then again, what was waiting for him elsewhere? 'How's your portfolio doing?'

'Moved out of property just in time.' Mike could hear his friend exhale noisily. 'Minerals and gold, plus a smattering of new technologies.'

'You should get back into the game, Gerry. The world needs brains like yours.'

'Pickled, you mean?' Mike heard a female voice. Gerry covered the mouthpiece with his hand as he answered it.

'Who is she?' Mike asked.

'Just someone I met.'

'It's considered courteous to get a first name at the very least.'

'Harsh, Michael.' There was a pause. 'But fair.' Followed by an explosion of laughter from the other side of the world. 'Suppose I better go see how I can keep her happy.'

'You do that.'

'Come visit, Mike – just picture the fun we'd have.'

'Night, Gerry.'

'Morning, cobber.'

Their usual sign-off routine. Mike was still smiling as he placed the phone on his lap. He took a deep breath and stared out across the city, a jagged silhouette dotted with points of light.

What happened?

Life happened ...

Wasn't that the truth of it? He knew he could have told Gerry about the heist, probably *would* tell him about it some day, if it turned out a success. Or even if it didn't, come to that. Gerry would whoop and slap his thighs and shake his head in wonder, same as he had when Mike had walked into the office with news of the cash offer for their company from the consortium.

Shouldn't you be out making merry?

Who with, now that his friends had become 'business associates'? What would Chib Calloway be up to? Bars and nightclubs, wine, women and song? Fine and dandy, but Mike needed a clear head for the morning, needed to rehearse each and every step one final time. At what point would there be no turning back? Hadn't that point already been reached?

What happened?

'A door opened,' he told himself, flicking the cigarette butt out into the night sky.

17

Saturday was Doors Open Day in Edinburgh.

There was a light drizzle and a chill breeze, but that wouldn't deter the sightseers. For some locals, Doors Open had become as welcome a part of their year as the various festivals. They would plan an all-day itinerary, perhaps taking in the Castle or Freemasons' Hall, the observatory or the city's main mosque. Sometimes sandwiches and a flask of tea would be packed. The bulk of the buildings earmarked for public inspection stood in the city centre, all of it dubbed a UNESCO World Heritage Site. Others lay further afield, and included a power station and the sewage works.

Not forgetting the seafront warehouse at Granton where the national galleries and museums stored their overflow. Much of Granton had yet to succumb to the modernisation evident in neighbouring Leith. Potholed roads led past trading estates and abandoned factory units. The grey North Sea could be glimpsed now and again behind some of these fences and buildings, reminding visitors that Edinburgh had yet to make the most of its largely coastal location.

Likewise, the warehouse served as a reminder that the

city's museums and public galleries, while arguably making the most of their collections, were forced by circumstances to hide the bulk of their holdings.

'Which is what happens,' Professor Gissing muttered, 'when a culture gets greedy.'

He was seated behind the steering wheel of the stolen van. His disguise comprised sunglasses, a flat tweed cap, and a check shirt.

'No corduroy today, Robert?' Allan Cruikshank had joked nervously when they'd rendezvoused in Gracemount. Allan himself was now wearing a brown wig beneath his blue baseball cap, and had forsaken his business suit for a pair of baggy denims and a shapeless sweatshirt. The rest of the team sat in the back of the van: Mike Mackenzie, Westie, plus the four young tearaways supplied by Chib Calloway. The teenagers had decided that the only disguise they would endure was a baseball cap with the brim tugged low over the eyes, and a Burberry-style scarf to cover the lower half of the face. All anyone had heard from them so far were grunts and guttural mutterings. No names, no pack drill.

Which was just fine by Mike. He glanced at his watch again. They were parked on the side road with the view of the gatehouse. Fifteen minutes had passed since the previous tour had made its way out of the warehouse, Allan counting twelve individuals. Forty minutes they'd been inside. Twenty-minute gaps between tours, meaning the next group would start gathering in around five minutes' time. Limited to twelve names, pre-booked. This time round, seven of those names would be fake. Seated

174

in the front of the van, Gissing and Allan had a much better view of the arrivals and departures. No one would contemplate coming here on foot – too far from any form of public transport. A couple of cabs had arrived to pick up prosperous-looking couples, leading Mike to wonder again what the odds were of anyone he knew turning up. The prof would stay with the van, but Mike and Allan would be in the warehouse. Most of the people who bothered with Doors Open were mildly curious, attracted by the notion of passing through doors normally kept locked to the public. But this was an extension of the National Gallery – chances were, it would be art-lovers who made the trek ... the very sorts of people Mike and Allan knew from the various exhibitions and auctions they attended.

Gissing had been warned – 'You don't step out of the van except in the direst straits.' But now Mike was wishing the raid could be carried out without the need for either Allan or himself saying anything. Or Westie, come to that – art-lovers usually visited all the college degree shows, and voices could be identified as readily as faces. There was a thin trickle of sweat running down Mike's spine. All these factors they hadn't taken into account – if Chib's crew had been briefed sooner, *they* could have been the ones doing all the talking. So far, all they'd been doing was listening, and Mike was afraid that the conversation between Gissing and Allan had given too many clues. They'd talked about building projects in the city and the financing of same, Allan sounding too knowledgeable. Then Gissing had started rattling on about the various art and antiquity holdings, showing he knew a fair bit about the topic. How hard would it be for the teenagers to put two and two together? If they were arrested at any point in the future, might they try cutting a deal by telling what they knew? Was the fear of Chib Calloway enough to keep them silent in the long term?

One bonus: the chippie van was locked tight for the weekend – one potential witness out of the running ...

'That's the first two arriving now,' Allan piped up.

Mike's heart was pumping; he could hear the blood singing in his ears. He saw that Westie had clamped his hands between his knees, as if to stop them shaking. He'd done well, though. The van's first stop had been his flat, where they'd loaded the fakes into the back, Gissing giving each of the eight a final once-over before declaring them 'first class', adding that this was also the mark Westie could be confident of getting for his degree show. This had probably been meant to relax the student, but it had the opposite effect on Mike – Chib's lot, seated in the van as the paintings were loaded and inspected, now knew they had a student in their midst, and probably someone who taught him, too. Westie had declared himself 'shattered' by the experience, and he really didn't look too good: pale and pasty and with eyelids drooping towards sleep. Mike had the feeling only caffeine was keeping him going. Last thing they needed was one of the team nodding off or losing his concentration during the actual heist.

Heist: the very word made Mike's nerve endings jangle.

But here they were, ready and waiting.

'Two more,' Allan said. 'Only one to come ...'

There had been no sign of Alice in Westie's flat. Mike had come across with the money she'd asked for, confirming that it was by way of an advance rather than extra cash, and had then driven his Maserati forwards and backwards over the video camera until it was flattened. He'd been sure to scatter its constituent parts around the city, leaving nothing to chance. But who was he kidding? There were plenty of loose ends already, with more to come. He stared down at the pile of unframed paintings on the floor of the van. As they were leaving Westie's, he'd pleaded that no one accidentally put a foot through one of them.

'You'll have me to answer to if you do,' Westie had snapped, at which Chib's crew had just smiled to themselves. The morning had gone well so far. Mike had rendezvoused with Allan on Marine Drive at seven, leaving the Audi and travelling back to the penthouse in the Maserati. They'd toyed with their bacon sandwiches, but managed orange juice and coffee before donning their disguises – Mike had burst out laughing when Allan had walked into the living room wearing the wig, and with contact lenses in place of spectacles.

'Got it in a junk shop,' Allan had said of the wig. 'Feels a bit itchy ...'

At Gracemount, Gissing had been waiting, looking agitated and failing to blend in with his surroundings as he paced up and down. Mike had parked the Maserati, hoping no one would take a shine – or a dislike – to it. Five minutes later the van had arrived, with its crew of four but no sign of Calloway. Mike had exhaled in relief.

He'd half expected the gangster to want to come along for the ride. He'd tried a bit of chat with the teenagers, hoping maybe to break the ice, until told that 'Mr Calloway' had said they should do what they were told but otherwise keep their 'gubs' shut.

'Nae offence,' one of them had added, before clambering into the back of the van. Since when it had been grunts and gutturals and a steady stream of nicotine. Which, now Mike came to think of it, was illegal, smoking having been banned in all Scottish workplaces – vans included.

Tut-tut, he thought to himself. Breaking the law. He rubbed a hand across his face. Like everyone else he was wearing latex gloves, bought from a chemist's shop in Bruntsfield.

'That's the last one going in now,' Allan suddenly piped up, voice half an octave higher than previously.

'Two-minute countdown,' Mike stated, lifting his watch to his eyes. Normally he wore a Cartier; other times he carried the antique pocket watch from Bonnar's. But Allan had suggested something not quite so showy. It had cost less than a tenner from the same chemist's shop as the gloves, but still seemed to work, though the second hand was now appearing to crawl around the dial. Could the battery be dying on him?

'Ninety seconds …'

He was trusting Allan's head count. Didn't want any other visitors arriving after them …

'Sixty …'

No backing out now. He found himself glancing in Westie's direction. Westie was staring back at him, grim-faced or maybe just zonked. His disguise: sunglasses and a woolly hat. The sunglasses were just going on now.

'Thirty ...'

'Awright, lads, nae fuck-ups,' one of Chib's kids was telling the rest of them. Nods and yet more grunts. Adjusting their baseball caps and scarves. Even Gissing was nodding his agreement, hands welded to the steering wheel.

'Coast clear?' Mike asked, hoping his voice sounded okay.

'Clear,' Allan confirmed.

Mike took a deep breath but couldn't bring himself to bark the command. Gissing, half turning, seemed to sense this and did it for him.

'Go!'

The van doors opened with a creak, seven of them moving briskly, turning the corner, coming into the gatehouse guard's line of sight. Should have staggered it, Mike thought – we look like a gang. One of Chib's crew was at the front, doing everything but breaking into a jog. Mike had visualised their walk as something like the start of *Reservoir Dogs* – calm, collected, going to work. But his knees were only just locking. The guard didn't seem too concerned, however. He had risen from his comfy little chair, sliding open his window and reaching for his clipboard. There was a peaked cap he usually wore, but not today.

'You're late,' he started chiding them. 'If I can just have your names ...'

Turning his head at the sound of his door being opened; brought up short by the sight of the sawn-off appearing from under a jacket; bundled back on to his chair by one of Chib's lads. The rest of them didn't pause, kept walking down the path towards the warehouse door. It was to the side of the main loading bay. One of the museum's vans was parked up, but there was space to squeeze a new arrival next to it. Mike could hear a motorised click behind him and knew it would be the barrier starting to rise.

'This is it,' he said, hand gripping the door handle.

'Let's do it then,' he was told.

He pushed open the door and stepped inside. It was just as expected – a warehouse. Plenty of shelving; lots of items smothered in hessian and bubble wrap. Guardroom to the right. The five on-time visitors were being addressed by a member of the gallery's staff – maybe it was his van outside. He wore a suit and tie and had a name badge on his lapel. One of Chib's crew was already heading for the guardroom. He walked straight in before lifting out his gun. There were two guards inside, seated at a bank of CCTV screens. Mike watched through the window as their hands went up, eyes fixed on the firearm.

Drawing his own gun, Mike realised it was his turn to speak. Probably only ten or fifteen seconds had passed since he'd opened the door, but it felt like minutes. He had rehearsed the words, rehearsed the voice he would use – gruffer than his own, an instant snarl. Harking back to his roots.

'Up against that wall, all of you!'

The visitors hesitated, thinking maybe some tasteless practical joke was being played. The staff member had begun to remonstrate, but one of Chib's remaining two boys stuck the revolver's barrel against his ear.

'D'you want your brains splattering the bastardin' floor?'

The curator didn't think so. He lifted his hands in surrender and started backing towards the wall, the tour party following his lead.

Mike realised that Allan and Westie were already on the move, striding into the warehouse proper. Mike walked into the guardroom, ignoring the hostage situation, and removed from an already open wall-mounted box the keys he would need. He had memorised the numbers, helped by Professor Gissing, who had also explained that the box was normally kept locked. *But not for Doors Open.*

There was a split second where one of the numbers escaped him, but he remembered it. Christ, Mike, he told himself, how hard can it be? Only three bloody numbers ...

Three vaults. Well, not really 'vaults' – Gissing had explained that they were more like walk-in cupboards, but with metal walls. Exiting the guardroom, Mike gave a nod, and the visitors and their guide were marched inside. It would be snug in there. The surveillance cameras were being switched off, the blinds closed. No one would see what was happening – less chance of disguises being noted, physical descriptions tucked away for future reference.

It took Mike longer than expected to find Westie. He thought he knew the layout, but they had reckoned without the additional overflow from the museum on Chambers Street. Some of the pieces were huge, and necessitated detours. Westie rolled his eyes when he saw him. Mike didn't bother apologising, just tossed him the key, then went in search of Allan. He tried to stay focused – difficult when surrounded by so many treasures. Shelf upon shelf of artefacts, only a few of which were identifiable. Celtic, Mayan, Greek, Roman ... no telling just how many cultures and periods were represented. He passed a penny-farthing bicycle and a vast swaddled shape that could have been an elephant. You could spend weeks in here, just as Gissing said, and not have exhausted your sense of wonder. Mike had a sudden thought: this was his first and last visit ... he would never be able to come here again. Indeed, it was doubtful the place would ever again open its doors to the general public ...

Allan was grinning through a sheen of sweat, and had removed his wig to claw his fingers through his hair.

'So far so good?' he asked. Mike felt that the wrong answer would turn his friend to dust. He nodded and handed over the key, while Allan replaced the wig.

'Did you spot anyone you know in the tour group?' Mike remembered to ask.

Allan shook his head, dislodging the hairpiece again. 'Wasn't really paying attention,' he apologised.

'Same here,' Mike confided, turning in search of his own vault.

It was number 37. The key had a little tag to that effect. Gissing had warned him that the strongrooms were not sequential. To one side of the warehouse lay the even numbers, with the odd numbers on the opposite wall. Crossing the floor at a gap in the shelves, Mike worked his way down the numbered row, tucking his pistol back into his waistband. There were no other guards; no stray visitors. Plenty of cameras, but hopefully turned off. What if Chib's crew missed one? Allan with his wig off, clawing at his scalp. Too late to be worrying about that. Vault 37. He turned his key in the lock and pulled the heavy door open. It creaked on its hinges only slightly. There was an overhead light inside, just as Gissing had promised. Framed canvases – dozens of them. He knew which numbers he was looking for. The paintings were stored side-on, cocooned in two layers – bubble wrap and cloth – with labels hanging from them. He slid out both paintings and tucked one under each arm before heading back the way he'd come. Lord alone knew what he was leaving behind. Given time, maybe he would have chosen differently. He could feel the Monboddo – it was the smaller of the two. If he had to sprint, he knew which one he'd drop first ...

All was quiet behind the closed door of the guardroom. He hoped Chib's lads were behaving themselves. One of them had opened the loading bay doors, bringing natural light into the warehouse and the taste of fresh air and freedom. Mike could see that the van was waiting. Gissing had backed it into position and the rear doors were already standing open. Gissing was now in the back of the van. He looked relieved at Mike's arrival, causing Mike to wonder if there was a problem with Allan and Westie. Where the hell were they? He handed Gissing the first painting – a Cadell – which the professor unwrapped while Mike lifted its duplicate from the van floor. Gissing eased the canvas away from its frame. His hands were practised and it took

183

him only half a minute. Wooden wedges had been used to take up any slack, and he removed these first, his fingers strong and seemingly steady.

Mike held his breath as the original frame was then placed around Westie's forgery. It was a perfect fit, and he let out a little hiss of satisfaction. Gissing pushed the wooden pieces back into place, and examined the back of the original canvas, seeking identifying marks on both it and its stretcher. They couldn't hope to copy any he found, not with any great skill. They had only so much time. But Gissing pronounced it 'clean'. As he had predicted, the markings and labels tended to appear on the frame rather than the actual artwork. This was another reason why they'd opted for smaller canvases: less chance of cross-bracing, which meant one surface fewer that could hold identifying details …

'Get it wrapped,' Gissing growled, already starting work on the second masterpiece – the Monboddo portrait. Mike heard a noise and turned round to see Allan and Westie emerging from the warehouse, toting three paintings apiece. How could he have been so stupid? *That* was why they'd taken longer than him! Three each to his two.

'No trouble?' he asked, voice fluttering slightly.

'No trouble,' Allan confirmed, sweat dripping from his chin. Mike entertained a wild thought: could forensics take DNA from sweat? He didn't think now was the time to ask. Westie was already starting work unwrapping one of his own canvases. Like Gissing, he knew exactly what he was doing; knew, too, that time was against them. No telling how early the next party of visitors might be. Mike glanced around the side of the van towards the gatehouse. There was no sign of the guard – he must be crouched on the floor. In his place sat Chib's kid, and he was wearing the peaked cap – a nice touch, but Mike doubted it would fool anyone close up, not with the scarf still in place across the bottom half of the teenager's face.

Back at the van, Mike saw that Gissing was breathing hard. He still had his wits about him, however, and reminded them to make sure the labels were showing when they reswaddled their copies.

'They've got to look just the same as they were …'

'We know,' Westie complained, adding: 'I still say we could be doing this elsewhere.'

Mike had heard the argument before, but had sided with Allan first time round: no alarm would be raised until they were off the premises. *That* was when time really started to be against them. Best to make the switch now, meaning a cleaner and faster getaway later, when the cops were on to them.

'Three down,' Allan intoned, watching Westie and Gissing at work. Mike checked his watch again. Twelve minutes since they'd first walked into the warehouse. It was going like clockwork. No … better than that – it was going like digital. He found himself forcing a smile, and gave Allan a pat on the back.

'Bit early for that,' Gissing snarled, wiping perspiration from his eyes. 'Back inside, the pair of you, and do the final check.'

Final check: vault doors left wide open and keys in locks. There *would* be trace evidence – Westie had said as much; knew it from all the cop shows he watched with Alice. A stray hair, maybe, or fibres from their clothing, faint prints from their shoes. But the less they left the better. Standing together in the middle of the warehouse, Mike and Allan shared a nod. Then Allan made for the van again while Mike opened the door to the guardroom. A gun was aimed straight at him, lowered once its owner recognised him. Mike held up three fingers, meaning three minutes. The 'hostages' were crouched on the floor, hands on their heads and eyes screwed shut. The CCTV screens were blank.

Back at the van, Allan was in the passenger seat, wiping his face with a handkerchief. Westie was wrapping another painting. Gissing was holding a hand to his chest, but nodded to let Mike know he was all right really.

'Just a bit breathless.'

'Sit back,' Mike told him. 'I'll drive.' He got into the driving seat and checked the key was in the ignition.

'How are we?' he asked Allan.

'It would be nice to leave right now.'

Mike heard a noise and peered into the rearview mirror: three figures emerging, jumping in the back. The van doors creaked shut and Mike gunned the engine. Something was handed to him from the back – a key.

'Locked them all in the guardhouse,' he was told.

'That's great,' Mike said, dropping the key into the van's ashtray. 'But unless you took away their mobile phones, it's not going to slow things down.'

The van juddered towards the gatehouse. 'Not too fast,' Gissing warned. He was right: last thing they wanted right

186

now was to announce themselves to passing traffic or a cruising patrol car. Mike paused long enough at the gate-house to pick up the final member. The kid had brought the peaked cap with him, causing his friends to laugh.

'That stays in the van,' Mike warned them.

Allan was making a show of studying him. 'Mr Professional,' he purred.

'Get going!' one of the crew yelled from the back. In the wing mirror, Mike could see the guard emerging from his lair. He stepped on the accelerator.

'Should've thumped him,' somebody was saying.

'Couldn't do it,' came the reply. 'Guy's a Hearts fan. Calendar, fanzine, the works.'

'He got the number plate,' Allan commented.

'Much good it'll do him.' Mike turned towards Westie. '*That's* why we did it this way round.'

Westie just sniffed, saying nothing. They drove in silence after that, listening for sirens.

'Should've brought a CB,' one of the kids eventually piped up. 'Could've tuned it to the pigs' frequency.'

Mike and Allan shared a look – something else they hadn't thought of. Mike's senses seemed heightened to an incredible degree. The sound of the rutted tarmac under the van's wheels was amplified; his nose was picking up the aroma of hops from a distant brewery. There was a tin-gling in his blood and a tang of adrenalin in his mouth.

This, he thought, *is how it feels to be alive*. It was as if his nervous system had been fitted with a supercharger.

Allan's Audi was where they'd left it. There were no other vehicles to be seen except an antiquated Rover, its sills eaten by rust. The rain had grown heavier, dissuading the dog-walkers. The unframed paintings were transferred to the Audi's capacious boot. One of Chib's lads went to close the van doors, but Mike told him to leave them open.

'We were in a hurry, remember?' he explained.

The Rover was for the four teenagers. Its ignition key was tucked in beneath one of the front wheels. Mike held out a hand for shaking, but the four young men just stared at it. Then one of them asked for the guns. These were handed over – Mike's with great reluctance – and placed in the Rover's boot. Before they drove off, he checked that the peaked cap had been left, as ordered, in the van.

Allan gave a half-hearted wave. 'Lovely bunch of lads,' he commented, watching the car roar off. Gissing was already in the Audi, and Westie with him.

'Let's go,' Gissing said.

'Hang on,' Mike said, heading back to the van. He lifted out one of the bundles and dropped it on the roadway. Back in the Audi, Gissing asked for an explanation.

'The robbers panicked and fled,' Mike obliged. 'Just as they were starting the transfer. Adds a touch of drama, don't you think?'

Westie was punching numbers into a mobile phone. He'd asked to be the one to make the call. The phone was a gift from Calloway. It had been in the box with the guns. Chib had promised it was untraceable and warned it only had about two minutes' credit on it. Westie took a deep breath and gave an exaggerated wink to all around him. Then he started speaking.

'Is that the police?' His voice had reverted to its working-class Fife roots. 'Listen, I've just seen the strangest bloody thing down by Marine Drive ... some guys at the back of a white van, looked like they were dumping bodies or something. I think I spooked them, but I got the number plate ...'

He reeled it off, ended the call and gave a little bow from the waist.

'Dumping bodies?' Mike echoed.

'You're not the only one who can improvise.' Westie wound down his window and flung the mobile into a roadside ditch.

'Hey, guys,' Allan said. 'Can we take these bloody things off now?' He meant the latex gloves.

Mike nodded his agreement. They were safe. They were on their way. They'd done it.

They'd done it!

Seven unframed paintings sat arranged on the two sofas and two easy chairs in Mike's living room. The three men stood gazing at them, champagne flutes in their hands. They had got rid of their disguises and had used Mike's bathroom to freshen up, sluicing off sweat and dust and the smell from the gloves. Allan was still scratching his scalp intermittently, fearing 'beasties' might have relocated there from the hairpiece. The Maserati had not been vandalised during its short stay in Gracemount, but fingerprints on the windows showed where kids had been peering in at its interior. They'd dropped Westie at his flat, reminding him yet again to keep his chosen painting hidden. He'd asked Mike about the rest of his money.

'It'll be in your account today or tomorrow,' Mike had assured him.

Westie had actually seemed reluctant to get out of the car, smiling and telling everyone how well it had gone.

'Strikes me I should have held out for two,' he'd grumbled.

'Don't go getting gold fever, young man,' Gissing had growled.

Westie had raised his hands as if in surrender. 'I was

making a joke … trying for a bit of light relief. The looks on your faces, you'd think we were standing graveside.'

'Get some sleep,' Mike had told him. 'And spend a quiet Sunday with Alice – no splurging, remember.'

'No splurging,' Westie had echoed, eventually opening his door and getting out, his painting tucked beneath his arm.

'I like your two better,' Allan was now telling Gissing as the two of them studied the mini-exhibition.

'Tough,' the professor answered with a thin smile.

'What about Calloway's Utterson?' Allan asked.

'I'll see it gets to its new owner,' Mike stated.

'But can we trust him?' Allan countered. He pressed a finger to one of his eyelids, trying to still the pulse that had started there. 'Robert talked about gold fever … isn't Calloway the most likely to start wanting what we've got?'

'He'll be fine,' Mike tried reassuring his friend. 'You can leave him to me.'

'He knows the painting has to be kept secret?' Allan persisted.

'He knows,' Mike said, adding an edge to his voice. He reached down to the coffee table and picked up the TV remote, switched on the plasma screen and started flicking through the channels, looking for news.

'May be a bit early,' Allan said, rubbing at his reddened eyes. Although he loathed them, he was wearing disposable contact lenses – part of his disguise. Mike ignored him. Really, he wanted them all gone, so he could concentrate on the portrait of Monboddo's wife. He'd only held it for a few moments. Gissing was making a circuit of the room. He'd hardly looked at his own picks, and was instead studying some of Mike's saleroom purchases.

'I've just had a thought,' Allan said. 'What if somebody got there first? To Marine Drive, I mean ... What if they walked off with an armful of Westie's beautiful forgeries?'

'Then the cops'll pick them up and think they've got their thief,' Mike answered.

'True,' Allan seemed to agree. His flute was empty but Mike had decided one bottle of champagne was enough – there was the journey home to consider, at least as far as Allan was concerned. The professor would need a lift, too, at some point – no way Mike was calling him a taxi, not when the passenger would be carrying an expensive-looking painting under his arm ...

The words BREAKING NEWS had begun scrolling along the foot of the screen. Above the newsreader's shoulder there was an old photo of Edinburgh Castle. This changed into a map of the city, zeroing in on the Granton area.

'Here we go,' Mike muttered to himself. 'Now the fun and games really begin.' He started to turn up the volume, but a mobile phone was ringing. It was Gissing's, so Mike switched the TV to mute instead. When Gissing offered him a smile, Mike nodded back. They knew who it would be ... at least, they knew who they *hoped* it would be. Gissing placed a finger to his lips in warning, then answered the call.

'Professor Robert Gissing,' he intoned by way of

introduction. Then, after a few seconds: 'Yes, I'm watching it now on my TV at home ... absolutely shocking. Did they take anything?' A slightly longer pause, during which he made eye contact only with the window and the darkening view beyond it. 'I see ... But how can I help? Jimmy Allison's your man for ...' Gissing's flow was interrupted. He made a show of raising an eyebrow as he listened. 'How awful! Nobody's safe on the streets these days, Alasdair.'

Confirmation, as far as Mike was concerned, that Gissing was in conversation with the head of the National Galleries of Scotland, Alasdair Noone.

'Yes, of course,' Gissing was saying now. 'Soon as I can, Alasdair. No, I'll make my own way there ... Half an hour?'

Mike did a swift calculation – yes, from the professor's home to Marine Drive was just about feasible in thirty minutes.

'Oh, did you?' Gissing glanced in Mike's direction. 'Well, I've been having some problems with it. Or maybe I had the TV up too loud. Sorry about that. Yes, yes, I'm on my way, Alasdair. Bye.'

Gissing ended the call and his eyes met Mike's again.

'He tried your landline,' Mike guessed. 'You didn't answer, so he called your mobile. But then you went and told him you were at home ...'

'He won't make anything of it,' Gissing assured him.

'But the police might,' Allan commented. 'Tiny details, inconsistencies ...'

'He's got enough on his plate,' Gissing persisted. 'I'd lay

a hundred pounds it's already forgotten.' He looked at his watch. 'Well, I'd better be on my way.'

'Give it a few minutes,' Mike warned him. 'It's only fifteen minutes by taxi to Marine Drive from here.'

'Good point,' the professor conceded.

'And you need to relax a little.'

'Maybe a small whisky ...'

'Don't want them smelling hooch on their expert's breath – I'll fetch you some water.' Mike walked into the kitchen, Allan following close on his heels.

'It's going to be all right, isn't it?' Allan asked, placing his empty flute on the spotless worktop. Mike didn't think it was the last time he would hear this question from his friend.

'So far, there hasn't been a hitch. That's down to good planning. The rest is all about holding our nerve.' Mike offered a wink and poured the water into a tall glass, which he carried back into the living room. Gissing was popping two square tablets from their foil packaging.

'Heartburn,' he explained, accepting the drink.

'Did Alasdair say how Mr Allison was doing?' Mike enquired.

Gissing chomped down on both tablets. 'He's out of hospital but there's concussion and bruising.' He glared at Mike. 'I think maybe your friend went a wee bit far.'

'Just far enough to stop his services being called for,' Mike answered. 'When you're finished at Marine Drive, get a cab to bring you here and either Allan or me will run you home.' His own mobile was sounding. Not a call as such: a text message from Chib Calloway.

HERD MY BOIZ DID GUD! NEED COLLATERAL ASAP. R U NEAR A TV?

Mike decided to ignore it. Collateral: the very word Chib had used when taking that phone call. *Good honest collateral* ... The news had shifted to the aftermath of some flooding in England. The journalist at the scene said something about the locals fearing they'd 'got in too deep'. Gissing was popping a third tablet, hands unsteady, while Allan rubbed at the pulse in his eyelid and hopped from one foot to the other like a hyperactive kid.

In too deep? Nobody knew the half of it ...

19

DI Ransome was seated at his desk in the empty CID
suite when he heard the news. The radio had been providing him with background music and blather. It was
some local station, mixing golden oldies with traffic and
weather. Ransome had been in the office for a solid two
hours, clearing an inch from his in-tray. He was due to
appear in court three times over the next two weeks, and
needed to bone up on his evidence. The amount of time
cops – uniform and CID – wasted in the city's sheriff and
high courts was a scandal, and often, at the last minute,
some plea deal was done, meaning they didn't have to go
into the witness box anyway. One officer he knew had
earned himself an Open University degree, doing most of
his studying and essay-writing while seated outside various courtrooms waiting to say his piece.

Ransome was spending an idle minute wondering what
subject he would study, given the chance, when the radio
DJ announced a 'break-in at an industrial site in Granton'.
Ransome had started to tune out until he heard the words
'valuable artworks'. What the hell were those doing in
a warehouse in Granton of all places? Holdings belonging to several city-based museums … staff and visitors

threatened with guns ... not known as yet which items are missing ...

Artworks and guns.

Guns and artworks.

Ransome phoned Laura at the auction house, but there was no answer. Same story with her mobile. Cursing under his breath, he headed out to the car park. It took him only twenty minutes to reach Marine Drive. It was one of the things he liked about the city: nowhere was more than half an hour from anywhere else. Felt more like a village sometimes, which was why his mind was already turning. A warehouse heist, artworks stolen ... and Edinburgh's premier gangster having so recently started showing an interest in paintings. He remembered Calloway that day in the National Gallery, drinking tea with his old school pal Michael Mackenzie. Mackenzie the computer wizard, the art collector. They made an odd couple and no mistake ...

The white Transit had been cordoned off with blue-and-white-striped crime-scene tape. Uniformed officers were diverting what traffic there was away from the immediate vicinity. A forensics team was busy at work, dusting surfaces, taking photos. A detective inspector called Hendricks seemed to be calling the shots, causing Ransome to wince a little as he got out of his car. He considered Hendricks a serious rival in the promotion stakes – same sort of age; good track record; personable and presenting himself well to public and top brass alike. He'd been in the same intake as Ransome at Tulliallan Police College, more years ago now than Ransome cared to calculate. There had been a special challenge for all new recruits – raising money for charity. Despite Ransome's best endeavours, Hendricks had won by a country mile, hosting a sportsmen's dinner in Stirling and attracting a couple of high-profile footballers to the event as speakers. Only later did Ransome discover that Hendricks' uncle was chairman of a Premier League club. Strings had obviously been pulled ...

There was never any animosity between the two men – Ransome knew better than to get on his rival's wrong side. In public, there were displays of professional courtesy and even occasional collaboration. Besides, with Ransome stationed at West End and Hendricks across town at Gayfield Square, they met only infrequently. Ransome wondered now whether Hendricks had been on call or had barged his way on to the inquiry. He was dressed in a sharp suit with a new-looking shirt and tie. Maybe he'd been doing the same as Ransome – working unpaid hours behind his desk in the hope of snaring something interesting.

A TV crew was already *in situ*, along with radio and print journalists. Dog-walkers had come up from the beach to spectate. The media were in a sort of scrum, comparing notes. One of them recognised Ransome and came bounding over, asking if there was anything he could add to the story. Ransome just shook his head. High-profile case ... and it just *had* to fall into Hendricks' lap.

'Ransome? What are you doing here?' Hendricks was trying to make the query sound matey. He'd slipped his hands into his trouser pockets and was coming towards Ransome with a spring in his step. Neat hair, trimmed moustache, but the slip-on shoes looked cheap. Ransome consoled himself with that.

'I'm nosy, Gavin. You know me. How are things at Gayfield Square?'

'A damn sight quieter since you-know-who retired. Look, good to see you and all that, but I'd better ...' He gestured with his thumb over his shoulder. Busy man, lots to do.

Important man.

Ransome nodded his understanding. 'Don't mind me, Gavin.'

'Just don't get in the way, okay?' Adding a little laugh at the end, as though he meant it as a joke when in fact he was being deadly serious. Which left Ransome bristling and trying to think of a comeback as Hendricks moved away again. He took a couple of steps closer to the action. The van doors were wide open, and one of the paintings lay on the ground. It had come loose from its wrapping, and Ransome could make out an ornate gold-coloured frame. He kept staring at it as one of the scene-of-crime officers took a few more snaps.

'I hear tell,' the SOCO commented, 'it's by someone called Utterson.'

'Never heard of him.'

'It's signed in the bottom corner. One of the reporters says it's worth a couple of hundred grand. My house didn't cost half that.'

From what little Ransome could see, it was a bleak country landscape, maybe thirty inches by twenty. He'd seen better stuff on the walls of his local pub. 'Who's that Hendricks is talking to?' he asked.

The SOCO looked over towards where Hendricks was in close conversation with a short, bald, worried-looking man. He shrugged and shook his head, so Ransome wandered back towards the reporter who'd recognised him and asked the same question.

'You're not in the loop, then?' the reporter teased. Ransome just stared him out. 'He's head of the National Galleries,' the man eventually admitted. 'And the guy just turning up ...' Ransome followed the direction of the pointed finger. A black cab had drawn up, its passenger emerging. 'He runs the city's museums. And that's one you owe me, Inspector.'

Ransome ignored this, focusing instead on the new arrival. He was taller and a bit calmer or more resolute than the galleries boss, whose hand he shook before giving a consoling pat on the shoulder. Ransome edged forward until he was within eavesdropping range.

'We think they must have been making the transfer,' Hendricks was explaining for the benefit of the newcomer. 'A member of the public phoned it in – he probably disturbed them, they lost their bottle and fled the scene in a hurry.'

'Luckily for you, Alasdair,' the museums boss told his colleague with another apparently sympathetic pat. Alasdair seemed to resent this and shuffled half a yard further away from his tormentor.

'We can't be sure yet if everything's been recovered,' Alasdair said, rubbing a hand across his forehead.

'Witnesses say there were only about three or four of them doing the actual taking,' Hendricks offered. 'The others were holding the hostages. Whole thing was over in ten or fifteen minutes. They can't have got away with much ...'

'Full inventory needed?' the museums boss was asking Alasdair. 'Wasn't one about to happen anyway?'

'You're not off the hook, Donald,' Alasdair snapped back. 'They could have walked off with *anything*. Most of the paintings are kept in the vaults, but the majority of *your* stuff is just lying there on the open shelves – especially with the influx from the Chambers Street refit.'

The look on Donald's face seemed to cheer Alasdair up a little. It was as if a load had been lifted.

Not just colleagues, Ransome thought to himself, but rivals, too ...

'It's a good point, sir,' Hendricks was telling Donald. 'The sooner we get that inventory under way the better. Meantime, can I ask how many people knew about the warehouse and its contents?'

'The whole bloody city,' the man called Donald grumbled. 'This is Doors Open Day, remember? Only day of the year they could just waltz in and take whatever they liked.' He stabbed a finger towards the contents of the van. 'But mostly paintings, from what I can see – vaults or no vaults.'

It looked as though Alasdair was about to remonstrate, but their attention was diverted by the diesel chugging of yet another taxi as it arrived on the scene.

'Ah,' said Alasdair, 'here comes our resident expert.'

He strode towards the cab and yanked open its back door. Handshakes were exchanged, after which he led the distinguished-looking gentleman towards the small group. In the interim, Hendricks had noticed Ransome again and given him the benefit of a practised glower. But Ransome didn't think his colleague would want to cause a scene – not in front of the Edinburgh establishment (Donald was even wearing a New Club tie) – so he held his ground.

'Our chief curator was the victim of a street attack near his home last night,' Alasdair was explaining. 'But we're grateful that Professor Gissing, head of the College of Art and no mean expert himself, has made his services available.'

'Thought you'd retired, Robert,' Donald was saying, shaking hands. Gissing said nothing by way of reply, but allowed himself to be introduced to DI Hendricks. As the conversation continued, Gissing seemed to realise he was the object of scrutiny from beyond the immediate circle. He gave a surreptitious glance in Ransome's direction, Ransome turning away a moment too late.

'I was sorry to hear about Jimmy,' the professor was saying. Ransome remembered hearing about the mugging – guy down by the canal. Turned out the victim was an art expert. Well, well, well. And now here was Gissing ... Professor Robert Gissing ... friend to Michael Mackenzie ... one of Laura's 'Three Musketeers'. He'd been at the auction house the same day as Calloway. And all of them had ended up in the wine bar just along the street.

Oh, it was a small city, all right, was Edinburgh. Staring

at Hendricks' back, Ransome knew he was going to keep it all to himself, all the various connections and coincidences, the personalities, permutations and probabilities. Alasdair was explaining to Gissing that they needed to verify the identities and authenticity of the abandoned paintings and also ensure they were undamaged.

'But we'll need to dust them for prints, too,' Hendricks was saying. 'The thieves may have got careless.'

'Not a chance,' the friendly SOCO next to Ransome muttered for his benefit. 'That van's as clean as a whistle.'

'Have you ID'd it yet?' Ransome asked in an undertone. The SOCO shook his head.

'It'll have been stolen to order, though, you mark my words – probably changed the plates and all …'

Ransome nodded in agreement, his gaze fixing once again on Professor Gissing. The man's arms were folded as he listened to Hendricks. Might just have been concentrating, but to Ransome the body language was all about defensiveness. Maybe they'd fail to find any fingerprints – he'd seldom known the SOCOs to be wrong – but something was whispering a name into his ear.

The name of Charles 'Chib' Calloway …

20

'Not too many snooker halls left,' Calloway was telling Mike Mackenzie. 'I mean *proper* ones, full-sized slate tables. Know how much they weigh? You need to check that your floor can stand up to them.' The gangster was switching on some of the lights in the cavernous yet musty-smelling room. Mike could make out six tables, but none of them in the best of health. Two were covered with gashed and stained dust sheets while the remaining four had suffered nicks, rips and rudimentary repairs to their green baize. A game seemed to have been abandoned on one of them, Mike rolling the pink ball towards the centre pocket.

'Why's this one shut on a Saturday evening?' he asked.

'Overheads,' Chib explained. 'Costs me more to run than I get back. I could always put pool tables in instead, maybe a few slot machines ...' He wrinkled his pugnacious face. 'But I'll probably end up selling it. Some developer can turn it into apartments or one of those huge super-pubs.'

'Why not do it yourself?'

'With my reputation?' Chib gave a cold chuckle. 'What do you reckon the chances are of me getting planning permission, never mind a licence?'

'You could bribe a few councillors.'

Chib had picked up a cue, but found it wanting. It rattled when he replaced it in the rack. 'Maybe a few years back, Mike. Things have changed.'

'Or set up a front company, so no one knows you're the one in charge ...'

Chib gave another chuckle, warmer this time. 'Listen to yourself, Michael – maybe we should swap places, eh? You seem to be thinking more like a criminal every day.'

'Maybe that's because I *am* a criminal.'

'So you are,' Chib agreed with a slow nod. 'And how does it feel?'

Mike shrugged. 'Ask me again further down the line.'

Chib had made a circuit of the table. He now gestured towards the package under Mike's arm. Mike laid it flat on the dusty green baize and carefully undid the brown paper. He had wrapped it himself, hoping to make it look less like one of the works recovered from Marine Drive, just in case he was pulled over and asked to open his boot. Chib had sent two more texts before Mike had decided to get their transaction out of the way, leaving Allan in the penthouse awaiting Gissing's return.

'An extremely good example,' he told the gangster, 'of late-period Utterson.'

'I'd still rather have had something by Jack the Vee.' But Chib took his time studying the painting, running a finger along the edges of the canvas. 'Not very big, is it? They look bigger when they're framed.'

'They do,' Mike agreed. 'Speaking of which ...'

'I know, I know – I can't go taking it into a shop, tell

them I want a nice new surround for it. And I can't put it up anywhere it might be noticed.' He affected a disappointed sigh. 'Hardly worth the effort.' Then he smiled and looked at Mike, eyes twinkling. 'My youngsters were okay? Did as they were told?'

'They were great.'

'The shooters?'

'Worked a treat. We handed them all back afterwards.'

'I know.' Chib paused for a moment, folding his arms. 'Had half a mind you might hang on to yours – seemed to be forming quite an attachment to it. I've still got it if you want it.'

'Tempting,' Mike confessed. 'But better all round if they just disappear.'

'Agreed. So nobody got hurt, eh?'

'It was a piece of cake.' Mike found himself laughing as he ran a hand through his hair. 'If I could do it again, I'd grab twice as much.'

'Getting a taste, eh, Mikey?'

'We couldn't have done it without you.'

Chib picked up his Utterson and pretended to study it. 'I still say you could just have swapped the paintings – no need for the stunt with the van.'

'How would it have looked if we'd gone into that warehouse and come out again without anything being missing? This way, they think they've got back what was taken and that means they'll be relieved rather than suspicious.'

'Thinking more like a criminal every day,' Chib repeated. 'So what happens now?'

'They've got the professor at the scene. He'll be in the process of verifying that the recovered paintings are the originals.'

'And they'll take his word for it, just like that?'

'They've no reason to doubt him. Besides which, he's the only expert they've got.'

'If I'd known how gullible these sods were, I'd have done something like this long ago.'

'You didn't know someone like Westie, though – the plan depended on him, and it was the prof's idea to bring him in.'

'Will Gissing's nerve hold, do you think?' Chib placed the painting back on the green baize.

'He'll be fine.'

Chib seemed to ponder this. 'You did well, Mike. Makes me wish we'd teamed up years back.'

'The actual plan was Gissing's, remember.'

Chib ignored this. 'What about your other mate?'

'Allan?' Mike watched Chib nod. 'Allan's fine.'

'Sure about that? See, the thing is this – we're connected now, aren't we? And out of the whole lot of us, the only one I trust is me.' He stabbed a finger towards himself and then Mike. 'I need to be sure none of you lot will start blabbing if the cops come asking.'

'Won't happen,' Mike stated.

'I don't even know this Westie, but in my experience students are always bad news.'

'Thing is, he doesn't know anything about *you*.'

'So where does he think the shooters and my lads came from? Out of thin fucking air?'

'He doesn't seem to be the inquisitive sort.' Mike decided that Chib need not know about Alice. 'You don't ...'

'What?'

'The Utterson – I just thought you'd be more excited.'

There was a sound at the door. A thin smile spread across Chib Calloway's face. 'Now I'm excited,' he said. Then he sniffed and rubbed his nose. 'Seeing how you've developed a taste, Mike, I thought you should be part of this.'

Mike started to get a bad feeling. 'Part of what?'

But Chib was ignoring him and heading for the door. He unlocked it and in stepped a very tall ponytailed and tattooed man, incongruous in a powder-blue suit and shoes with no socks. Chib led this new arrival over to the table, where Mike was pulling his shoulders back, trying for a bit more height and heft.

'This is Mr Hate,' Chib was saying by way of introduction. 'Hate, I'd like you to meet the friend I was telling you about – you could even call him an associate of mine – Mike Mackenzie.'

The way Chib said his name told Mike something was going on. The man called Hate meantime ignored him altogether, giving Mike the chance to study him more closely. There was a dotted line across his throat, and when he rested his meaty hands against the edge of the snooker table, Mike saw that the word HATE had been tattooed along both sets of knuckles.

'This is the collateral?' Hate was saying, ignoring any niceties.

'This is it,' Chib agreed.

'And I am supposed to believe it is worth how much?' The accent was Scandinavian, but Mike couldn't place it more exactly.

'Mike here is the expert in that department,' Chib was saying. Mike's eyes bored into his, but Chib was far from being fazed.

'It is a piece of shit,' the giant concluded.

'A piece of shit worth around two hundred K on the open market,' Mike stated.

Hate gave a snort and picked up the Utterson – none too gently. Mike feared the stretcher might snap. The big man turned it over, examining it.

Collateral, Mike was thinking. He'd suspected as much, and this had to be the 'Viking' Johnno had mentioned that day in the car. Calloway had no interest in the painting. Not really. Instead, he was about to hand it over to this monster, a monster who now had Mike's name and would forever link him to the painting. If it turned out not to be worth the figure quoted, would things turn nasty? He knew now that this was why Chib had made sure Hate knew his name ... why the gangster had wanted Mike here when the deal went down. *We're connected now.* Hadn't Chib said so himself? And if flak was coming, Chib wanted Mike as his human shield.

Mike Mackenzie, what the hell have you got yourself into?

Hate meantime was sniffing the surface of the painting – actually sniffing it!

'Doesn't smell so old,' he commented.

'None of that,' Chib chided him with a wag of the finger. 'You think I'd try to pull a cheap stunt? Get someone to verify it if you don't believe me – Mike here knows some-one at the College of Art.

Christ, now he's trying to drop the professor in it, too!

Mike held up a warning hand. 'The painting is stolen – I'm sure you know that already. Watch tonight's news if you need persuading. But the only way anyone – *anyone* – will find out is if it starts to be seen by people.'

'So I am supposed to trust you?' Hate's eyes were milky blue, the pupils tiny shards of darkness.

'You could go online,' Mike found himself suggesting. 'Check other works by the artist – he's pretty famous. Find out what they've been fetching recently at auction. Samuel Utterson – there've been exhibitions, books about him ...'

Hate looked from one man to the other. 'Two hundred thousand pounds,' he intoned slowly.

'Don't go getting any ideas,' Chib said, wagging his finger again and forcing out a short laugh. 'It's just tem-porary security – the cash is coming.'

Hate fixed him with a gaze. 'You've still got your men out looking for me, haven't you? Otherwise you'd be a fool. But they won't find me, Mr Calloway. And if they did, they'd soon wish they hadn't.'

'Understood,' Chib said.

Hate turned his attention back to the painting he was still grasping, and Mike feared he was about to punch a hole through it. But he placed it back on the table instead – actually with a reasonable attempt at gentleness, which told Mike the man was at least halfway convinced – and started to wrap the brown paper around it.

'So we're cool?' Chib asked. It was only because of the relief evident in his voice that Mike realised how nervous the gangster had been ever since Hate's arrival.

'That is something I will need to ask my client.' Hate was tucking the package beneath his arm.

'No way I can let you walk out of here if we don't have an understanding.' Chib's relief, it seemed to Mike, had quickly turned to bravado.

Hate just stared him out. 'Then you'll have to stop me,' he offered, heading for the door. Chib looked around him, his eyes alighting on the rack of snooker cues. But when he glanced in Mike's direction, Mike gave a shake of the head before calling out a question towards the giant's back.

'Why English?'

The man stopped and half turned his head.

'Your tattoos – the word "Hate",' Mike explained. 'Why English?'

The only reply was a shrug of the shoulders before the door was yanked open and slammed shut again. Mike waited for the echo to die, then nodded towards the snooker cues.

'Maybe if they'd been nine-millimetre.'

'I wouldn't trust a nine-mil to stop that fucker.' Chib rubbed a hand down his face.

'In your line of work, you do meet the most congenial people.'

'Not much worse than the ones you meet in any other business.'

'That may be true,' Mike conceded, and both men

211

laughed, releasing the tension in the room. 'By the way,' Mike added, 'whatever it is – I don't want to know.'

'Clever sod like you, Mike, my guess is you've already worked it out. I owe some money on a deal – the Utterson buys me time.'

'I know it happens with the mafia and Old Masters.'

'Well, now it happens in Edinburgh, too. You want a drink?' There was a bar area in one corner. Chib unlocked one of the cupboards and pulled out a half-empty bottle of whisky and two tumblers. Mike brushed dust from a stool with the palm of his hand before sitting down.

'In a funny way,' he offered, 'it actually makes sense.'

Chib drained his glass and exhaled. 'What does?'

'If the painting's not in your hands, the police haven't a chance of finding it in your possession.'

'That's true – maybe they'll try running Hate in instead.' Chib gave a snort and poured himself another. 'Sure you don't want to swap professions?'

'I don't have a profession.'

'That's right – you're a man of leisure. Unless you fancy "gentleman thief" on your passport instead.'

'This was strictly a one-shot deal, Chib.' Mike's mobile was vibrating. He lifted it from his pocket and checked the screen – it was Robert Gissing.

'The prof,' he explained to Chib, answering the call. 'How did it go, Robert?'

'I'm only just finishing up.' Gissing was keeping his voice low – obviously there were people in the vicinity.

'Remember,' Mike said, 'when you order a cab, make sure you give your home address as the destination – just in case anyone's listening. Once you're on your way, you can tell the driver you're headed to mine instead.'

'I'm not a fool, Mike!'

'What's wrong?' Mike had sensed something in the professor's voice. The whisky froze halfway to Chib Calloway's mouth.

'Are you with our friend?' Gissing was asking.

'As arranged. He's happy with the goods.'

'Never mind that – I'm sending you a snap. Bloody amazing things, these camera phones. I think I got it without him knowing.'

'Got what?' Mike asked, eyes narrowing.

'The photo – your phone *does* accept photos?'

'What's this all about, Robert?'

'I just want to know if we've got a problem.' Chib was by Mike's side now, listening in. He smelled faintly of sweat beneath the aftershave and the whisky. 'I didn't like the way he was looking at me,' Gissing was saying. 'Get back to me in five.'

The call ended. Mike stared at his phone's blank screen.

'Is that meant to be a dig at me?' Chib asked.

'What?'

'"I didn't like the way he ..."'

'Hell, no. It's just that he has something he wants us to see.'

'Don't tell me the paint's still wet on your student pal's efforts.'

Mike's phone trilled: a photo was coming through. Chib peered at the screen as Mike held it in the space between them. The professor had a quality mobile – he'd used it to take pictures for a recent photography exhibition at the college. Highest possible resolution ... zoom ... the works. Mike's own phone was the latest model, too, with a nice big screen. The photo itself appeared in three horizontal chunks of download. It showed the profile of a man, taken from the waist up. He'd been shot from some distance and using the full extent of the zoom, meaning the picture was slightly blurred. All the same, Chib let out a hiss of air.

'That's Ransome,' he growled. 'He's CID, been chasing me all across town since way back.'

'Is he the one you thought was following you the day we went to Arthur's Seat?' Mike watched Chib Calloway nod slowly. 'Well, he's now showing an unhealthy interest in Professor Gissing.' Mike gnawed at his bottom lip for the best part of a minute, while Chib explained that Ransome had tailed him on and off for a while ... reason he always took evasive action when driving anywhere in the city ... thought by now maybe the detective had given up the fight, been a while since Chib had clocked him ... but then again ...

'I knew he was trying to tail me that day we bumped into one another at the gallery.'

'So he might have seen us there?' Mike asked, not really expecting an answer. 'That's more than a little worrying.' He stared at Ransome's picture for a while longer, then called Gissing back.

'Houston,' he began by saying, 'we do indeed have a problem.'

*

The man who called himself Hate had brought a laptop with him on his trip to Scotland. In fact, he never travelled anywhere without it, though he was careful to keep nothing on its hard drive that the police of any country he visited might find interesting. With the painting by Samuel Utterson – the possibly worthless painting – stowed in the rental car's boot, he fired up the laptop and got to work, accessing the internet and running a search on the artist. If he failed to be convinced, he might visit a bookshop or library, seeking further information. The man back in the snooker hall – Mackenzie, if that was his real name – had warned that the painting was stolen. Well, that wasn't Hate's problem, was it? His problems only started if it turned out to be worth less than Calloway owed. Hate needed to know, and that might well mean asking someone. In fact, it would mean showing them the painting … which could bring further potential problems.

Hate had already texted his client with news that he had taken receipt of the Utterson. Like him, they'd never heard of the artist. Again, not an insurmountable problem – money was money. A search of the BBC's regional news site showed that a warehouse belonging to the National Galleries of Scotland had been broken into earlier that day. But 'a number of paintings' had been recovered afterwards. It was not known if anything was still missing. Hate tugged at his ear lobe as he considered his options. He could feel the little hole where one of his earrings usually rested. When off duty, he preferred denims and a T-shirt, but knew that the suit unnerved people – or rather, the combination of the suit and the man inside

215

it unnerved people. Hate couldn't wait to get home. He disliked Edinburgh. It was all surface, a kind of street con – showing visitors one thing while easing the cash from their wallets without being noticed. All the same, at least the galleries and museums were free of charge. Hate had visited a number of them, looking at paintings. He'd hoped the exercise might pay off, hoped it would help him spot a fake. But all that seemed to happen was, members of staff followed him round, as if they couldn't quite believe what they were seeing. Perhaps they were expecting him to take a knife or razor to one of their precious canvases. Calloway, the first time he'd mentioned the possibility of collateral to Hate, hadn't said where the painting would come from. Hadn't mentioned an artist's name. Hate didn't recall Utterson from any of the galleries he'd visited, but he knew now from the internet that the man was collect-able. Sotheby's, Christie's, Bonham's – they had all sold examples of his work in the past couple of years. The high-est price paid at auction had been three hundred thousand pounds, so maybe the man called Mackenzie hadn't been exaggerating. On a whim, Hate decided to run a search on Mackenzie's name, too.

And found almost as many hits as for Samuel Utterson himself.

One of which took Hate to a magazine's website and photos of Mackenzie's penthouse apartment. There looked to be some nice paintings on the walls. And it was the same guy, no doubt about it – there was a small photo of him – a man of wealth and taste, as Hate's favourite song might have put it. Hate tugged on his ear lobe again. He was going to have to rethink his opinion of Charles 'Chib' Calloway. The man might be a boor, an oaf, an ugly, low-life specimen.

But he had a good class of associate.

Laura was at a dinner party in Heriot Row. The host had just sold two paintings at Laura's auction, but neither had achieved the top end of estimate. As a result, Laura had been expecting to have her ear bent, but thankfully all anyone could talk about was the heist – its audacity, its stupidity, and how close a call it had been. She had thought about asking Mike Mackenzie to be her date for the evening, but had been unable to summon up quite enough courage. As a result, the host and hostess had placed her next to a lawyer whose divorce, as it turned out, was still a fresh and painful wound, to be anaesthetised only with alcohol. The call on her mobile had come as blessed relief towards the end of the pudding course. She'd mumbled an apology for not having had the foresight to turn the thing off, then had plucked it from her shoulder bag, stared at the screen, and told the room that she had to take it. Walking briskly into the hallway, she'd expelled breath noisily before holding the phone to her ear.

'What can I do for you, Ransome?'

'Not interrupting anything, I hope?'

'Actually you are – a dinner party.'

'I'm hurt I didn't make the guest list …'

'I'm not hosting.'

'I could still have chaperoned …'

She let out another sigh for his benefit. 'Is it anything important, Ransome?'

'Just wanted to pick your brains. It's to do with the Granton warehouse. I'm guessing you'll have heard.'

Laura raised an eyebrow. 'You're working on that?' She had to step aside as one of the liveried waitresses – hired for the evening from an agency – wheeled a cheese trolley towards the dining room.

'I'm not alone,' Ransome was saying. 'Your friend Professor Gissing is lending a hand, too.'

'He's hardly my friend ...'

'But he *is* some sort of authority?'

'Depends on the period.' Laura saw the hostess's head peer around the doorway and nodded to let her know she was nearly finished. 'I've got to go, Ransome.'

'Could we meet later for a drink?'

'Not tonight.'

'Other plans, eh? Who's the lucky man?'

'Bye, Ransome,' Laura replied, ending the call. She entered the room again and made another apology. The lawyer got up to help her into her chair.

'Nothing untoward?' he asked solicitously, face reddened with drink.

'No,' she reassured him. Who the hell said 'untoward' these days? Well, Robert Gissing almost certainly did. She wondered about Ransome's call. Was Gissing really the best-qualified man for the job of checking the paintings? She doubted it. She remembered the last time she'd seen him, in the doorway during her auction. Mike had made his way towards him and the two men had then left,

218

Allan Cruikshank following soon after. It was Allan who'd introduced her to Mike, the evening of the Monboddo retrospective opening party. She seemed to remember he'd introduced Mike to Gissing that night, too. She'd been talking to Mike, enjoying his company. And, by his body language, he'd seemed to be enjoying hers. But then Allan had brought the professor over, and Gissing had begun the job of monopolising the conversation, droning on about 'the importance of taste and discrimination'. Eventually, Laura had moved to another part of the gallery, connecting with other people she knew, but still feeling Mike's eyes on her from time to time.

You're only a couple of months out of a two-year relationship, she'd told herself. *Don't you dare give in to the rebound* ...

'A piece of brie, Laura?' the hostess was asking, knife hovering over the cheese trolley. 'And quince or grapes with that?'

'I'm fine, thanks,' Laura said, aware that the lawyer's eyes were lingering on the swell of her chest as he poured her more wine.

'You used to have a Monboddo, didn't you?' another guest was asking the host.

'Sold it a decade back,' she was informed. 'School fees ... ' The host gave a shrug of the shoulders.

'The raiders tried to get away with a Monboddo,' the guest explained to the table. 'Portrait of the artist's wife.' She turned to Laura. 'Do you know the one I mean?'

Laura nodded. She knew it all right, and remembered the last time she'd seen it.

And who'd seemed most interested in it ...

That night, Westie and Alice ate at their favourite Chinese restaurant, then headed for a couple of bars and a night-club, where they could dance off some of their excitement. The DeRasse abstract had been given pride of place in Westie's studio, on an easel recently vacated by one of the fakes. Westie had even proposed a wild notion to Alice – he would display the DeRasse as part of his portfolio at the art college, passing it off as one of his copies.

'And Gissing will see it and kick your arse to Iceland and back,' Alice had shrieked, laughing along with him.

Dancing, dancing, dancing into Sunday.

While Ransome lay awake in bed, staring at the ceiling, careful not to disturb his wife by moving about too much, even though his nerves were jangling, his heart pounding. The late supper of spiced vegetable couscous lay like a slab in his stomach.

Allan was awake, too. His eyes were still sore from the lenses, his scalp itchy despite a shower and half a bottle of shampoo. He stood by the window in his darkened living room, staring out across a patch of grass towards Gayfield Square police station. A couple of TV crews had come and gone, the reporters illuminated as they said their pieces to camera. Every time a patrol car arrived, Allan expected to see somebody he knew – Westie or Mike or the profes-sor – being led from it in handcuffs. He wanted to tell someone – Margot, maybe, or one of the kids. Or just pick up the telephone, press buttons at random, and blurt it all out to the first stranger who answered.

But instead he kept vigil by the window.

Robert Gissing had a busy night ahead, but took time to inspect his paintings. Nice additions to his little collection. He'd been driven home by Allan, and hadn't said much during the journey. The detective, DI Ransome, worried him. Michael, however, had warned him to say nothing to Allan, confirming Gissing's fears. If anyone were to unravel, it would be Allan Cruikshank.

And it might happen at any moment – hence the busy night ahead. Not that Gissing minded. Sleep could be left till later. Afterwards, he would have nothing but time. He even spoke the words out loud – 'Nothing but time.' And smiled to himself, knowing this to be anything but the truth …

21

Edinburgh was Sunday-morning quiet: the rhythmed toll-
ing of church bells; a warming sun; denizens and visitors
alike spreading out their newspapers across café tables.
Nice day for a drive, though not many people would have
chosen Granton as their destination. Gulls shrieked all
along the waterfront, feasting on fast-food leftovers from
the previous night. In the near distance, another new
development of high-rises was creeping skywards, surrounded by wasteland and gasometers.

Not for the first time, Ransome wondered why the
National Gallery of Scotland had sited its overflow warehouse here. He didn't even know why one was necessary
– couldn't the various paintings and statues have been
loaned to needy collections across the land? Surely there
had to be room in the likes of Dundee, Aberdeen and
Inverness. Wouldn't Kirkcaldy have welcomed a few
sketches or the bust of some historical personage? He could
almost see Kirkcaldy through the haze that lay across the
becalmed Firth of Forth, yesterday's rain a memory. There
was a fresh guard manning the gates of the warehouse,
his colleague having been excused duties, the better to
answer police questions.

Questions such as: how much did they pay you? 'They' being the robbers. Ransome knew what Hendricks would be thinking: inside job. The gang had known the building's layout, how many guards there would be and where those guards would be posted. The CCTV cameras had been shut down, only certain vaults targeted. It all smacked of an inside job, and that was how Hendricks and his crew would be treating it.

Ransome suspected he knew better, which was why he'd come to Granton this morning, parking next to a locked-down snack van. The van would be manned on weekdays, meaning the proprietor or his customers might have seen something. Any gang worth its salt would have recced the site. On the late-night TV news there had been speculation about the timing of the robbery. It wasn't just that it coincided with Doors Open Day – it also took place at a time when the warehouse was playing host to new arrivals from the closed-for-renovation National Museum. Coincidence? The reporter didn't think so. He'd spoken straight to camera from a vantage point directly in front of the gatehouse. Ransome headed the same way. His ID was checked thoroughly by the liveried guard, his details logged. He walked down towards the loading bay, hands in pockets, scrutinising the ground for anything the forensic team might have missed. Only then did he open the door marked PRIVATE – STAFF ONLY and step inside.

The investigators were looking busy. Museum and gallery curators were commencing a full inventory. Although this was not Ransome's inquiry, he'd phoned a pal at Hendricks' station. The pal had given him what info he had. Witnesses reckoned the gang had been inside the building for no longer than twenty minutes, even though 'it felt like hours'. Twenty minutes was, to Ransome's mind, slick. Even so, they'd left having taken only eight paintings. Fair enough, those eight added up to well over a million quid, insurance-wise, but still it didn't make sense. He knew what Hendricks would be thinking: stolen to order, wealthy and unscrupulous collectors willing to pay for something they couldn't otherwise have. Experts would be asked for their opinion – like the ones on the TV last night. They'd mentioned the use of art as mafia collateral, discussed cases where famous paintings had been linked to gangland bosses and billionaire aficionados. Some thieves in the past had tried pulling off heists just to show they could.

Once he'd had enough of the TV (having tiptoed downstairs from the bedroom), Ransome had called Laura Stanton again on her mobile. She'd complained she'd been asleep, Ransome realising midnight had come and gone. He'd apologised, then asked if she had company in bed.

'You've got a one-track mind, Ransome.'

'That's what makes me such a good copper. So ... do you have any names for me?'

'Names?'

'Art-lovers who might put a gang together.'

'This is *Edinburgh*, Ransome.'

He'd agreed that this much was true. He'd then thrown Robert Gissing's name into the pot and asked if she could give him any more background.

'Why?'

'Just wondering how much of an expert he is.'

'Expert enough,' she'd told him, yawning.

'You didn't seem so sure earlier ...'

'I'm sure now.'

'Funny, though, isn't it – the gallery's own expert getting himself mugged the night before he's needed?'

'What are you getting at, Ransome?'

'Just keep me posted, will you, Laura?'

He'd hung up, and gone back to sipping his tea – Rooibos, Sandra's idea. Good for the digestion, apparently ...

Standing in the warehouse now, mouth dry and stomach unsettled, he watched the curators. They wore thin white cotton gloves. They all seemed to be wearing them, didn't matter if they were dressed in suit and tie or blue overalls. The cops meantime wore latex, if they wore anything. Alasdair Noone was there, still fraught after the best part of a day. He looked like he'd got by on about fifteen minutes' sleep. His museums counterpart, Donald Farmer, was present, too, but altogether calmer. Seemed to Ransome that nothing from the museum overflow had been touched, as intimated by Farmer on TV the previous night. The look on the man's face had bordered on smug then, and bordered on smug now. There were guards standing on sentry duty inside the loading bay doors, as clear a case as Ransome had ever seen of shutting the stable door – and typical of Hendricks, who had almost certainly ordered it. It would look good if the brass came calling – they liked things busy but controlled. There was, as yet, no sign of Hendricks himself. Ransome doubted he was having a lie-in. Maybe he was in the guardroom, or conducting interviews back at the station. Ransome didn't take any chances, and made his way quickly into one of the aisles between the high, groaning shelves. Last thing he wanted was his colleague-cum-adversary challenging him as to what the hell he was doing here. Any lie would do, of course, but Ransome doubted Hendricks would swallow any of them.

I'm walking all over your case, he said to himself. *And when it's done and dusted, I'll be right and you'll be wrong ... and I'll be the one staring promotion in the face.*

The three unlocked vaults were still open, or had been reopened this morning to allow the forensic team further access. There were plenty of paintings left inside. The ones the gang had taken would be allowed home only after their examination was complete. They'd already been declared unharmed and genuine – verifications made by Professor Robert Gissing – but they would still be checked for fingerprints and fibres. The journalist on TV last night had talked of the 'relief felt by the arts community here in Scotland, and doubtless further afield as well'. Fine, but why abandon the van? Media speculation had been brief – the gang had been disturbed and had panicked. They'd been unloading the paintings, probably transferring them to another vehicle. A member of the public had become suspicious and had called it in. (Ransome had already asked his pal at Hendricks' station for news of the caller's identity – seemed no name had been given, and the caller's number had yet to be traced.) The alarm, of course, had already been raised by the guard at the gatehouse – he'd provided a description of the van along with its licence number. (Stolen a couple of days previously from a street in Broxburn.) The licence plate was fake but the owner, a painter-and-decorator, had ID'd the van, annoyed to find that the tools of his trade had been ditched somewhere along the way.

So: a successful heist, followed by a botched transfer and the abandonment of the treasure. To Hendricks, this all made sense … but not to Ransome. Abandoning the van? Yes, maybe. But why not take at least a few of the paintings? The reckoning was that between six and ten men must have been involved, and only eight paintings recovered, the largest measuring five feet by four, even framed. Why leave them? After all that meticulous planning and the perfect execution … Were these the sorts of men likely to be spooked by a passing motorist or dog-walker? They were toting guns, for Christ's sake – what could they possibly have had to fear?

The more Ransome thought about it – and he didn't think he'd managed much more sleep than Alasdair Noone over the past twenty-odd hours – the less sense it made. His conclusions were simple: maybe it was an inside job and maybe not, but there'd been no cause for panic on the part of the thieves.

So here he was, giving up his Sunday morning to examine the scene and possibly ask a few questions and glean a few more facts of his own. He looked into all three unlocked vaults. The paintings were stored in racks, sideways on, with brown cardboard tags, which identified them only by numbers. Another reason for the inside job theory – if the art had been stolen to order, someone had known what they were getting. Who would have access to the numbering system, besides the staff? His pal back at Hendricks' station hadn't been able to answer that. The same SOCO Ransome had spoken to at Marine Drive yesterday had just finished running some sort of torch over the floor in one of the vaults.

'Anything?' Ransome asked.

'A few fibres … half a footprint. Probably won't mean much.'

'They'll have dumped the clothing?' Ransome speculated.

The SOCO nodded. 'So far, the only strands of hair we've found are synthetic.'

'Wigs?' Ransome reasoned, receiving another dispirited nod.

'I've got a caseload piling up while I waste my time here.'

'Haven't we all?' Ransome turned away and headed back towards the guardroom. During the heist, the guards and visitors had been herded inside and made to crouch on the floor. They hadn't seen anything useful, so far as Ransome was aware. Nor had they heard anything. Their captors had communicated by means of grunts. One thing the curator in charge of the tour had pointed out – the men who'd held them had seemed younger than the ones doing the actual thieving. Glenn's words came back to Ransome: *four or five schemies with pool cues* … Glenn had been thinking of the lads as a gang to intimidate Hate. But maybe he'd been wrong. The younger thieves hadn't worn much by way of disguise either – just baseball caps pulled low and scarves muffling mouth and nose. Ransome couldn't see anyone in the guardroom, so stepped inside. There were TV screens, working again now and showing interior and exterior views of the warehouse. Coverage of the gatehouse was hopeless – the camera was trained on the vehicle barrier. You could make out half the gatehouse but nothing of the pedestrian walkway beyond it. He knew that Hendricks had already complained to the galleries boss about this. Ransome sat himself down at the desk and peered through the window into the warehouse proper. You couldn't see the relevant vaults from here in any case. The warehouse and its contents were sitting targets – amazing no one had thought to turn the place over sooner ...

There was a knock at the open door. Ransome turned his head sharply, fully expecting to see his nemesis, but it was someone else – someone he recognised. Professor Robert Gissing.

'Oh,' the academic began, clearly flustered. 'I was looking for DI Hendricks ...'

Ransome was on his feet, taking a step forwards. 'He's not here,' he ventured, offering his hand. 'I'm a colleague, DI Ransome.'

'Yes, I saw you at Marine Drive.'

'Did you?'

'What about Alasdair Noone?' Gissing was staring down at his shoes.

'He's around somewhere.'

'Thank you.' Eyes still directed floorwards. 'I'd better have a word with him.'

But Ransome wasn't about to let him go without a fight. 'Professor?'

Gissing hesitated. 'Yes?' Eventually raising his eyes to meet the detective's gaze.

Ransome was right in his face now. Gissing was a good inch and a half taller than him, but that meant nothing. 'Just wondered if I could have your take on things, sir. Bungled robbery – someone on the inside – is that your reading of it?'

Gissing folded his arms – defensive again – then gave a pout and looked thoughtful. 'I dare say more fanciful scenarios exist – I've seen them in today's newspapers. But my job's not to make wild guesses, Inspector.'

'That's right, sir. Your job was to verify the paintings – but you did that yesterday ... so what brings you here this morning?'

Gissing straightened his back. 'My attendance was requested by Alasdair Noone. He seems to think I may be able to pinpoint any gaps in the holdings of nineteenth- and twentieth-century Scottish art.'

'Because that's what the thieves took?'

'Indeed.'

'Pretty specialised market, would you say, sir?'

'Hardly – there are collectors from Canada to Shanghai.'

'Your field of expertise, though?'

'I suppose so, yes.'

'Well, I'd better let you get on – inventory's well under way already.'

For the first time, Gissing seemed to notice the activity going on around them.

'Due to happen in a few weeks anyway, wasn't it?' Ransome added. 'Robbery just speeded it up.'

'Look, Inspector, I'm not sure how any of this can be of benefit to your investigation.'

'Oh, it's not my investigation, Professor Gissing – I'm just curious, that's all.' Ransome paused, watching Gissing try to take this in. 'Shame about Mr Allison, wasn't it?'

The question threw the academic.

'Him being the *resident* expert and all,' Ransome pressed on. 'Do you know him, sir? I believe he's pretty badly shaken ...'

'Terrible business,' Gissing seemed to agree.

'Still, silver linings and all that, eh?'

'I'm not sure I get your meaning.'

Ransome gave a shrug. 'I'm just saying, it's lucky you were on hand to step into the breach, so to speak.'

'Yes, well ...' Gissing, having nothing to add, was again about to leave.

'See much of Chib Calloway these days?'

Gissing kept his back to the detective for several seconds, then half turned his head. 'Sorry – what was that name again?'

Ransome just smiled and winked.

22

The two paintings were still propped up on one of the sofas in Mike Mackenzie's penthouse. So far today Mike hadn't been able to spend as much time as he would have liked with Lady Monboddo. He'd had to surf the web, checking the level of interest – national and international – in the heist. Either the National Galleries had been 'spectacularly lucky' or else the robbers had been 'spectacularly inept'.

'Cack-handed, they called it in my day,' Allan Cruikshank had offered when he arrived at the flat. He'd also warned that Mike should be thinking of a hiding place for the two paintings.

'What have you done with yours?' Mike asked in return.

'Under the desk in my study.'

'Reckon there's a chance the cops will miss them if they come looking?'

'What the hell else can I do? Stick them in the bank for safe keeping?'

Mike just shrugged. Allan was looking awful. He kept wandering over to the window and staring down towards the car park, as if fearing the imminent arrival of blue flashing lights. The pair of them had stepped out on to the balcony for a cigarette, Mike trying to push away the thought that his friend might be about to jump, but glad all the same when they retreated indoors. Mike had made peppermint tea, which Allan said he couldn't remember asking for. He held the mug cupped in both hands.

'Help you relax,' Mike offered.

'Relax?' Allan hooted, rolling his eyes.

'How much sleep did you get last night?'

'Not much,' Allan conceded. 'Tell me, have you ever read any Edgar Allan Poe? "The Tell-Tale Heart"?'

'We just have to hold our nerve, Allan. A few days of fuss and it'll all die down – you'll see.'

'How can you say that?' A splash of tea had spilled on to the wooden floor, but Allan seemed not to have noticed. '*We* still know what we did!'

'Why not shout a bit louder? I'm sure the neighbours will be thrilled.'

Allan's eyes widened. He removed one hand from the mug so he could clamp it over his mouth. Mike didn't bother saying he'd been exaggerating for effect – the flat was pretty well soundproofed. When he'd first moved in, he'd cranked up the hi-fi then gone downstairs to ask the couple – he a restaurateur; she an interior designer – if they could hear it.

'I'm sorry,' Allan was muttering now from behind his fingers. He went to sit down, but his eyes fell on the paintings again. 'You really should hide those,' he advised, voice quavering.

'If anyone asks, they're copies,' Mike explained sooth-ingly. 'You could do the same – stick them on a wall where

233

you can see them ... maybe the Coultons will calm you down where mere mortals like myself can't.'

'They're better than any of the ones First Caly has,' Allan intoned.

'Yes, they are,' Mike agreed. 'Look, the whole point of this exercise – *if* you cast your mind back – was the pleasure of owning a masterpiece or two. The professor's already convinced everyone they've got their paintings back. Today at the warehouse, he'll reinforce that – nothing missing, everything accounted for. After that, the media interest will disappear in a puff of smoke.'

'I wish *I* could disappear in a puff of smoke.' Allan bounded to his feet again and made for the window. 'What about this cop you mentioned?'

'I wish to God I hadn't,' Mike muttered to himself. Having told Gissing not to say anything, he'd decided Allan actually did need to know about Ransome. They were a team, after all, and they were still mates. You didn't keep stuff hidden from your mates. But when Mike had called him to explain, Allan had said he was coming straight over.

'He's already on our trail,' Allan persisted.

'He's got nothing. Even if he thinks something fishy's going on, how's he going to prove it?'

But Allan was not to be consoled. 'What if I give mine back? Or just abandon them somewhere?'

'Good thinking ...' Mike bore down on his friend. 'Then they'll know the ones they found in the van are copies and start wondering why the esteemed professor didn't say anything.'

Allan gritted his teeth in frustration. 'You take them, then. I'll give them to you. I can't get to sleep with them in the house!'

Mike considered his options, and placed a hand on Allan's shoulder. 'Okay, how about this – we'll bring them here, and I'll look after them for a few days ... maybe even a week or two, just until you start to feel good about them.'

Allan thought for a moment, and then nodded slowly.

'As long as we're agreed,' Mike persisted. 'I'm holding them *for* you, not taking them *from* you. Is it a deal?' He waited until Allan started nodding again. 'And we don't tell anyone else,' he added. 'It's our little secret.'

Mike did not want *anyone* knowing that Allan was getting the shakes – least of all Chib Calloway. He was hoping it was just shock, meaning it would wear off. On those occasions when he'd been able to study the portrait of Monboddo's wife, he'd been unable not to see another face there – not Laura's this time, but the man called Hate. Something told Mike that even if he were never again to be in the same room as him, he'd still be haunted by the face and figure.

The face, the figure, and those hellish tattoos.

It was, of course, no business of Mike's whom Chib chose to give his painting to, but it was dangerous. At the heist's conception, there had only been the three friends – Mike, Allan and Gissing. Westie had been added as a necessity, but now Westie's girlfriend was a player, too. And Chib ... Chib had been Mike's idea. It would be his fault if things started to go wrong. Chib, Chib's four lads, and now Hate. And who knew where Hate would lead …

'What's on your mind?' Allan was asking.

'Nothing,' Mike stated. *I'm lying to him. And keeping things from him, too …*

'I'd never blurt anything out, Mike … you know that, right? I mean, we're mates, always will be. That's the truth of it.'

'Of course it is.'

Allan attempted something like a grin. His face was pasty, coated with perspiration. 'You're so in control, Mike. Always got the answers up here.' He tapped the side of his head. 'You got a real buzz out of yesterday, didn't you?'

'I did,' Mike confessed with a smile. But meeting the debt-collector had been another, very different kind of buzz, one that told Mike he was rubbing shoulders with the big boys in the playground now.

Playing with the bullies.

They wouldn't play fair, wouldn't let sentiment or emotion or friendship get in the way.

Allan had slumped back into his chair, sloshing more tea. *Mates … always will be*. Well, you never could tell.

'Let's go fetch your paintings,' Mike offered. 'That way you can rest easy.'

'Some sleep would be nice,' Allan agreed. 'How come we haven't heard from Robert?'

'Not easy for him to phone from the warehouse,' Mike counselled, even though he, too, wanted to know what was happening there. He checked his watch. 'You sure it's okay if we go pick up the paintings just now?'

'Why wouldn't it be?'

'It's Sunday, Allan. I want to be sure you're not breaking any arrangements – don't you see your boys on a Sunday?'

'Margot's taken them to London to see some show.'

Mike nodded his satisfaction with this. It was a relief that Allan wouldn't have to try making small talk with his sons during a Princes Street shopping trip or a restaurant meal.

'Anything else you normally do on a Sunday?' he asked. 'Got to keep our routines as normal as possible.'

'You and me sometimes go for a drink,' Allan reminded him.

'So we do ... mind if we skip that tonight?'

'Fine by me. I feel better for talking, though. I'm glad you invited me over.' Allan was looking around the room. 'Now what did I do with my jacket ...?'

'You're wearing it,' Mike informed him.

When Westie, still hungover from the night before, checked at the cash machine, the money was in his account. Paid in full for services rendered: eight good likenesses and true ... well, nine, actually, but who was counting? What mattered was that his work was busily fooling the art world into thinking the heist had failed.

'Bloody beautiful,' he said out loud, staring at the amount on the screen for a few seconds more. He printed out a mini-statement, then, just because he could, he withdrew two hundred pounds and marched with it into the café, where Alice was sitting in front of a stack of papers. They hadn't got to bed till dawn and she was still bleary.

'Front page of most of them,' she informed him. 'Well, the broadsheets anyway. Some actress with new, improved udders beat you on a couple of the tabloids.'

'Tell the whole caff,' he warned, handing her the cash machine statement. She squealed and reached across the table to kiss him. When he drew back and lifted his cappuccino, she noticed the bank notes fanned out on top of one of the newspapers. She gave another little squeal, louder this time, and jumped to her feet to hug him. Coffee splashed across one of the front pages, but neither of them minded. In fact, none of the other customers took a blind bit of notice – too wrapped up in Sunday supplements or college textbooks, or sending messages on their phones, or listening through earphones to the latest sounds. The café was fairly new, sited beside the Meadows where the old infirmary was being turned into expensive flats. Handy for the art college, but neither Alice nor Westie was a regular. He'd picked it for that reason – and because there was a bank close by.

Alice had seated herself again. She was dabbing at the spilt coffee with a paper napkin. 'Know what it feels like?' she asked. 'A Tarantino film – early Tarantino – we're the young lovers who've escaped with the cash!' Having said which, she scooped up the notes and folded them into the pocket of her zip-up.

Westie couldn't help grinning, even though he'd wanted the money for himself. Still, there was plenty more where it had come from. But he had a further warning for her.

'We don't go splurging too much – remember, that's to finance you through film school. Just promise me you won't turn any of this story into your first screenplay.'

'Third or fourth, maybe,' she agreed. The pair of them were still laughing as their waitress – was she Polish? – brought the focaccia toastie Alice had ordered. Afterwards, just prior to taking her first huge bite out of the sandwich, Alice commented that for once they could afford to leave a tip. Westie winked at her, then settled back to read about his exploits. He wasn't hungry – still had paint fumes and varnish in his lungs. But he'd be happy to sit there for a while, swapping papers, ordering yet more coffee, noting the gradations in light, the lengthening shadows, as afternoon segued into evening ...

Which was exactly what he was doing when he noticed that Alice had stopped reading and was gazing out of the window. He doubted she was seeing the same world he was. She was using the edge of her pinkie nail to prise slivers of dough from between her teeth.

'Penny for them,' he offered.

She gave a shrug, seemed to be considering her response, then turned to face him, leaning her elbows on the tabletop, chin resting between her cupped palms.

'I was just wondering,' she began, as though musing aloud for no one's benefit but her own, 'why they all got two paintings apiece and we only got the one.'

'The guy who provided the muscle only got one,' he corrected her.

'But he wasn't *there*, was he? He wasn't at the warehouse, risking arrest. And look at the work you put in ...

239

all those days and nights ... nobody worked harder than you, Westie.'

'I got paid, though, didn't I?'

She nodded slowly. 'That's sort of what I'm getting at. The cash was to pay for the work you did, but then you did more. You went on the raid, helped switch all those frames – you told me yourself, Professor Gissing was taking forever to do it, and nearly having a coronary in the process. It was all down to *you*, Westie, and you came good.' She reached out to him with one hand, clasping his own in hers. There were still streaks of colour on his knuckles – traces of reds, blues, whites and greens. Monboddo's wife had taken the longest; so many folds in the material of her dress ... Alice's chin was no longer supported by either hand. She was stabbing a finger against one of the newspapers. 'Says here some of the artists would fetch high six figures. *High* six figures ... and we end up with one lousy DeRasse.'

Westie was stung. 'One of our favourite artists,' he reminded her. Influenced by Mondrian, through a prism of sixties counterculture. Alice just made a face, and it was one Westie recognised: she was not going to be convinced.

'It just seems so unfair, Westie – that's all I'm saying.'

'Well, it's a bit late now to do anything about it,' he argued, before draining his latest cup. Her eyes met his above its rim, and he felt skewered by them.

'Is it really, though?' she said. 'Is it really too late?'

Westie lowered the cup slowly back into its saucer.

*

240

Mike was alone in his flat. He'd put some music on, without really caring what it was. Allan's Coultons were on a chair next to the fireplace – Mike had never really been a fan of the man's abstracts. Great whooshes of colour and little doodles that were 'symbolic, like cartouches' according to Allan. Mike had poured himself a malt and was savouring it as he studied Monboddo's wife. Light seemed to pour from the canvas. He put down his tumbler and picked up the portrait, pressing his lips to those of the gently smiling woman. Close up, the surface of the paint was criss-crossed with hairline fractures. Too bad: he could hardly call in a restorer. Monboddo hadn't signed the work; he seldom signed his name to anything. The show Mike had been at, the one where he'd first set eyes on the painting he was holding right now, plenty of the work on display had been given the wrong provenance until scholarship had improved. Even so, a few of the works were 'attributed to' or 'school of'. But not the wife. The wife was one hundred per cent genuine. Her name … He went to a shelf and took down a biography of the artist. Her name was Beatrice. The painting bore the title *A Reflective Pose*, but the sitter was definitely Beatrice – she appeared in at least four other works by Monboddo. The biographer stated his belief that the artist had painted her in as flattering a light as possible, 'probably to make up for some transgression notably more heinous than the norm'.

Transgression.

Heinous.

Mike's stomach did a little flip and he decided he'd had

enough whisky. Gissing still hadn't called. But then they'd sort of agreed – contact was to be kept to a minimum. Let the dust settle. Mike placed the Monboddo back on the sofa and reached for his mobile anyway – couldn't do any harm to send the prof a text. Keep it short and offhand, just the sort of casual enquiry any friend might send – How are you? Let's have a drink soon. Any news your end? He turned the phone over in his hand, and almost dropped it when it buzzed. Incoming message. It was from Gissing. Mike felt his hand starting to shake as he pressed the tiny button to accept the text.

Subject of photo is probing. Let's give him nothing to work with.

It was nicely vague – even though Mike knew what it meant, few others would. Calloway had put a name to the cop in the photo. DI Ransome. Ransome was working the heist, and there was a history between Calloway and him. It was far from perfect, but they could ride it. Of course they could.

What the hell else could they do?

Mike found that he had refilled his tumbler without meaning to. He went into the kitchen and poured it down the sink. Last thing he needed was a hangover. Well ... actually there were a lot of things he needed less than a hangover. In fact, right now, it wouldn't even make his top five. Having rinsed the glass and left it to drain, he walked back into the living area and flopped on to the sofa, so that he sat flanked by his two paintings. He hadn't given the other one much thought. It was an early Cadell, a beach scene. Westie had been dismissive: plenty

242

of impasto and sharp angles. *Could do it in my sleep*. Mike wanted to call Gissing, wanted to hear him say reassuring things. Wanted to share with him the story of Calloway's 'collateral'. A text message wasn't going to cover any of it. He turned the phone over and over again in his hand. Took a deep breath. Punched in the professor's number and listened to the ring tone. Gissing would have caller ID – had to know who was calling. But nobody was answering. It went to the messaging service, a pleasantly robotic female voice, but Mike decided to ring off instead.

Tomorrow: it could wait till tomorrow. He'd go surf the net one final time for news, then call it a night.

He carried Beatrice with him under his arm ...

23

'How did you get this address?'

Monday morning. Mike hadn't eaten breakfast yet, and here he was opening his door to Chib Calloway. The gangster brushed past him, not even waiting for an invite.

'Nice place,' he was saying as he walked into the open-plan living area. 'Great outlook, too. Always fancied living somewhere with a view of the Castle ...'

'You didn't answer my question,' Mike said sternly.

Chib turned towards him. 'No secrets between us, Mikey. Any time you want to see my place, you only have to ask. Is that coffee I can smell?'

'I was just brewing some.'

'Milk and one sugar,' Chib told him. Mike hesitated, then headed for the kitchen.

'What did you make of Mr Hate?' Chib called out to him.

Mike was still half asleep, but adrenalin was making itself felt. What the hell was Calloway doing here?

'Have you heard from him?' he called back over his shoulder. He had a view of half the living area, but Calloway was out of sight.

'Not yet. Lot of art on your walls, Mike. I've been doing

a bit more digging on you – from what I can tell, you're absolutely minted. Makes me wonder ...'

'What?'

'Why nick paintings when you can afford to buy them?'

'Sometimes the ones you want never come on the open market.' Mike carried through two rushed mugs of coffee and saw that Chib had been busy snooping. The gangster was smiling as he gestured behind one of the room's cream leather sofas.

'Not much of a hiding place, Michael. Anyone would think you want to get caught.'

'I didn't have much time,' Mike said by way of excuse. 'They were on the sofa when you rang the bell.'

'Mind if I take a peek?' Chib didn't wait for assent. He was already easing out the paintings. 'Four?' he said.

'Two belong to Allan – I'm keeping them for him.'

'Mind if I ask why?'

'He's got a girlfriend,' Mike answered, hiding his mouth behind the coffee mug. 'Knows a bit about art, so he doesn't want her seeing them.' He was hoping Chib would accept the lie.

'So which two are yours?'

'The portrait and the landscape.'

'Glad to hear it – Allan's two look like something from playschool.' Chib studied the Monboddo and the Cadell. 'Nice,' he decided. 'Are they worth the same as mine?'

'Roughly – probably a little less, actually.'

'But then I only got the one, and here you are with four of the little beauties.'

245

'One was all you wanted.'

Chib kept nodding, still appearing to be making an appraisal of the paintings. 'The portrait looks a bit like that bird from the auctioneer's.'

'I hadn't noticed,' Mike stated. Eventually, Calloway accepted the proffered mug with a grunt of thanks.

'Definitely a resemblance,' he mused, his eyes on Beatrice, concentrating on the swell of her cleavage. 'Think she'd like me any better if she knew I own an Utterson?'

'Laura Stanton, you mean? More likely she'd turn you in.'

'True ...' Calloway gave a dismissive sniff, then took a slurp of the coffee. 'The reason I'm here is, I've been thinking about that bawbag of a copper.'

'Ransome?'

'That's the one – you heard any more from the prof?'

'Just a text to say everything's fine.' Again, Mike hid behind the mug he was holding. 'The media say it's someone called Hendricks who's in charge of the investigation ...'

'Gav Hendricks is a featherweight; it's Ransome we need to keep an eye on.' Chib had taken a step towards Mike. 'Say he takes your friend Allan in for questioning ...'

'Allan's fine.'

'He better be.'

Mike didn't want Calloway coming any closer, so made a show of wandering over towards the window, realising too late that it might make him appear nervous: hadn't Allan done the selfsame thing? He found himself staring out of the window anyway, and could make out the roof of

246

Chib's black BMW 5-Series. Two men were resting against the car, one of them smoking a cigarette, the other checking his phone for messages.

'You brought your boys,' Mike commented.

'Don't fret – they don't know it's you I'm visiting.'

'Why not?'

Chib gave a shrug. 'Not sure who to trust these days … and it's nice to keep a few secrets, isn't it?'

'I suppose so, though it didn't stop you telling Hate my name.'

'You leave Hate to me, Mike.' Chib was wagging a finger. He decided that he'd spent enough time admiring the paintings, and had started on another circuit of the room. 'It's all right for some, eh? I mean, look at you – you've got your money in the bank, art on your penthouse walls … *and* behind the sofa. You're living high on the hog, Mr Michael Mackenzie.' Calloway gave a humourless chuckle. 'Some of us still have to go out there and graft for a living. This coffee's champion, by the way. Any more of it going?'

Mike took the empty mug and headed for the kitchen. He didn't like it that Chib knew where he lived; liked it even less that his goons were stationed outside, and that Chib now knew there were four masterpieces in the apartment – not forgetting the lesser pieces exhibited on the walls. He heard a bleep from the living area and figured Chib was making a call or sending a text. He hoped it wasn't an invitation for the goons to join the party – maybe they were coffee-lovers, too …

When he returned with the replenished mug, however,

Chib was pointing towards the coffee table, on top of which sat Mike's own mobile.

'Sounds like you've got a message waiting,' the gangster explained.

'Thanks,' Mike replied, handing Calloway the coffee. He walked over to the table, but then hesitated. Hadn't his phone been sitting in the inside pocket of his jacket? The jacket that was still draped over the back of one of the chairs? He glanced towards Chib, who was studying Allan's two Coultons again, slowly shaking his head. Mike picked up the phone and glanced at its screen. Two text messages. The first was from Laura: *need to see you* was all it said. Under normal circumstances, this would have gladdened Mike's heart, but these were far from normal circumstances, as the second text demonstrated.

Westie short-changed. Another picture or 20K cash, you choose. Alice.

'Nothing urgent, I hope?' Chib was asking.

'Not really.' Mike pretended to be punching a reply into the keypad, aware of Chib's eyes drilling into him.

'So you're pretty confident about your pal Allan?'

The question caught Mike off guard. 'Of course,' he spluttered. 'Why shouldn't I be?'

'Well, because of his taste in art for one thing.'

Mike barked out something that he hoped might be construed as a laugh, Chib obliged by smiling back. He straightened his back and clasped his hands behind his head, studying the room again as if he were considering its purchase.

'Very nice,' he commented. 'Bet it cost a few bob.'

'A few,' Mike conceded.

'Owe any money on it?'

'No.'

'Didn't expect you would, man of your talents. What's that word they use about businessmen when they know what they're doing … ? Ecumen?'

'Acumen,' Mike corrected him.

'That's it.' Chib nodded slowly. 'Now do us all a favour, Mike …' He was bearing down on Mike, for all the world as though he was going to back him against the wall. 'Use some of that famed *acumen* of yours to make sure nothing goes wrong, starting with your good friend Mr Allan Cruikshank. A chain's only as strong as its weakest link, isn't that what they say?' The two men stood only inches apart, so that Mike could feel the gangster's breath on his face. He took a moment to steady himself.

'From where I'm looking,' he said eventually, 'the weakest link is that headcase Hate. If he wants to take you down, all he has to do is send the cops an anonymous tip-off.'

'But then his clients wouldn't stand a cat in hell's chance of getting what's owed them. When it comes down to it, they're business people, same as you. So don't you go worrying about that, and don't give *me* cause to worry about anything at your end.'

'A chain doesn't have an end,' Mike said quietly.

'A chain's nothing *but* ends!' Calloway snapped back. They locked eyes for a moment, and then the gangster turned away. It looked to Mike as if he was readying to leave. The replenished mug, still three quarters full, was placed on the coffee table. Chib exited into the long hall-way, Mike following.

'Maybe next time I'll get the full tour, eh?' Calloway was gesturing towards the art that lined the walls. 'And like I say, there's an open invite to mine. Not half as snazzy as yours, of course, but then it's been through the wars – a bit like its owner.'

The thing is, Mike thought to himself, *I don't know your address, while you now know mine*. The front door was open, Chib striding out on to the landing with a backwards wave of the hand. Mike pressed the door closed after him and leaned against it, as if to repel further intruders. He listened out for the sound of the lift arriving, and hazarded an eye to the spy hole. The lift doors were sliding closed. He turned and walked back to the living area, scooping his phone up and making for the window. As yet there was no sign of Calloway. Mike didn't want the gangster seeing him making a call – no telling *who* he'd think Mike was talking to – so he retreated a few steps into the room before punching Gissing's number into the keypad.

Laura wants to see me ...

Westie's girlfriend is getting greedy ...

But it was Gissing he wanted; maybe the professor could offer solace, or at least the vague reassurance that, as bad as things might seem, Mike's life was not yet ready to implode.

The call was answered. 'My boy, this is unexpected ...' The line was terrible, Gissing's voice breaking up.

'Where are you?' Mike asked.

'Keeping my head down, just as we agreed. At least, I thought that's what we'd agreed …'

'How much does Ransome know?'

'He seems to know that *I* know Charles Calloway.'

'How is that even possible?'

'Your guess is as good as mine.'

'Things are starting to unravel.' Mike heard the BMW's engine starting.

'I'm sure you're exaggerating, Michael.' Gissing sounded so calm that Mike felt it a shame to spoil things. So he came to a sudden decision: he would keep the news of Allan's paintings, Hate's collateral and Chib's visit to himself.

At least for now.

'By the way,' Mike said, 'I've told Allan about Ransome.'

'How did he take it?'

'He took it.' Mike paused. 'How did it go at the warehouse yesterday?'

'I did all that was asked of me in my usual thorough manner. They're even offering to pay me for my time.'

'Your message said Ransome is probing – what does that mean?'

'It means what it says – he's not part of the official inquiry, yet he's sniffing around it like a dog after a truffle. I happened to mention as much to DI Hendricks when I saw him. He wasn't best pleased.'

'Nicely done, Robert.'

'I thought so,' the professor purred. 'Meantime, the very best thing we can do is stay calm and keep ourselves

251

very much to ourselves, except in the direst of straits.'

These *are* the direst of straits, Mike wanted to tell him, but instead, watching the BMW retreat down the long, sloping driveway, he found himself agreeing. With a sigh, and running his free hand through his hair, he asked again for Gissing's whereabouts.

'I'm at home, keeping busy with some marking assignments. But whenever boredom strikes, I find I have one or two things I can gaze at in wonder and reverence. We are blessed, are we not, Michael?'

'Blessed,' Mike echoed, as Chib and his men finally disappeared from view.

24

Chib Calloway had fairly stalked towards his car. Johnno had flicked away his cigarette, Glenn holding open the rear door for their boss.

'Unless you want to drive ...?'

But Chib had been content in the back, looking over his shoulder as the car pulled away. No sign of anyone at the top-floor windows.

'Good meeting?'

'Never you mind,' Chib had growled, chewing on a thumbnail while he considered potential courses of action. Of course, in a sense it wasn't for him to decide. The demand had been made to Mike – twenty grand or one of the paintings. The girl called Alice, she had to be Westie's girlfriend. Chib knew about Westie, but no one had thought to mention that there was a bird in on it as well.

And now the pair of them were getting greedy. Chib found himself tutting, while at the same time admiring their bare-faced cheek. What were they going to do – run to the cops? Not likely, with the two of them being every bit as complicit as anyone else. They were testing Mike's nerve, that was all, same as Chib himself had just been doing. Problem wasn't really Mike, though – it was that wet pal of his, Allan Cruikshank. Losing his bottle. Mike's lie about the new girlfriend might have worked if he'd had time to refine it. Over the course of his professional life, Chib reckoned he'd probably heard about twenty thousand lies, the majority of them honed to near perfection. Mike's attempt hadn't been in the same league. Hadn't even been playing ballboy.

Another reason for the little visit today: Chib wanted to see exactly how rich Michael Mackenzie was. Just because he'd run a company, sold some product, it didn't mean things hadn't gone tits up along the way. Plenty of guys Chib knew had made money only to blow the whole lot on misguided shares or badly tipped nags. But Mike was living the high life, no question about it. Chib doubted the paintings on the walls were repro. Flat-screen TV must've been three or four K. As for the flat itself – not much change out of a million. Hell, the way things were in Edinburgh, maybe even a million-five, million-six.

Which was all to the good: Chib liked a man with money.

Mike could solve the Westie problem by throwing cash at it, but that didn't mean they wouldn't come back wanting more – might happen next week or next year, but it would happen. Come to think of it, Mike could solve Chib's own cash-flow problem, too, if the Vikings decided they didn't want to go with the painting. The planning ... the clandestine meetings ... car manoeuvres to lose any tail ... the handover of the shooters ... all these things had kindled something in Mike Mackenzie. He'd been growing to like it. Introducing him to Hate, however, might have been a mistake – Mike hadn't been ready for *that*. Hate had scared him good and proper, and he had yet to recover his early confidence. Still, he'd held up pretty well this morning.

How did you get this address?

Chib had to smile at that – it had been as easy as asking an estate agent. They all knew 'the Mackenzie pad', could reel off the magazines and supplements it had appeared in. Another good reason, Chib told himself, for not being flashy with your cash and your choice of residence. Didn't want every fucker knowing your business or that you might be worth a visit.

'Where to, boss?' Glenn was asking from the driver's seat.

'Home,' Chib said. The other text message had been from 'Laura'. When Chib had noted her resemblance to the portrait, Mike had been all casual – *Laura Stanton, you mean?* But the pair of them were close. She sent him texts, used only her first name, and sounded keen to see her millionaire businessman friend. Chib would have to consider the ramifications of this, too. But for now, one of his own mobiles was trilling. He recognised the number and considered not answering, then told Glenn to pull over. Chib was pushing open the door before the BMW was fully stationary. He'd taken a deep breath and flipped the phone open.

'Calloway?' came the quiet voice.

'Hiya, Edvard.' The only name Chib had for the man: Edvard. Boss Hogg of a Hell's Angels chapter in the wilds of Norway. They ran drugs from all over: Denmark to Sweden; Russia to Finland; Norway to the UK. 'Happy with the collateral?' Chib noticed that he was standing beside some railings. Behind them was a patch of churned-up grass, some kids having a kickabout.

A quarter-century back, that was me. Nobody would dare take the ball away once I had it ...

'Well,' Edvard was saying, 'that's why I wanted to talk with you.' The voice was cultured, never threatening. Chib had been informed early on in the relationship that he would never meet its owner. Probably not even Hate had got to meet Edvard ...

'I hope there's not a problem.' Chib was staring at the game without really seeing it. A dog was barking. It had been tied to one of the goalposts.

'No problems as yet – in fact, quite the contrary. You will know, of course, that collateral such as yours can make for a reliable form of currency?'

'The one you've got isn't even posted as missing.' Turning towards the car, Chib noticed that the passenger-side window was down, meaning Glenn and Johnno were listening. Of course they were. Chib knew he had to keep from saying anything meaningful. He walked further down the pavement.

'That's good, that's very good.' Edvard's voice was as soft as a lullaby. 'So then, to cut the story short, perhaps more of our business could be transacted in similar fashion in future?'

Chib doubted it.

'Sure,' he agreed, sounding enthusiastic. 'No problem

at all, Edvard. You like your art, huh? Me, too.'

'I like money better, Mr Calloway.' The voice had turned cold. 'And what I'm really passionate about just now is the money *you* still owe me.'

'It's coming, Edvard …'

'I'm happy to hear that. I'll be in touch soon about further transactions.'

The phone went dead – Edvard never stayed on too long, just in case. Chib snapped the phone shut and tapped it against his teeth. He was replaying the conversation, and winced when he got to *You like your art, huh?* To anyone listening in – on a wire-tap, say – he'd just given away the nature of the bloody collateral!

Good work, Chib … Nice fucking going …

Still, Edvard wanted to do business with him. More paintings to be swapped between gangs as security on various deals. Tap, tap, tap of the phone against his teeth. The dog howling now in frustration. The BMW drawing up alongside Chib, making him realise he'd kept on walking. He was thinking about Edvard and the people Edvard did business with, hundreds and thousands of miles away from Edinburgh. How much did they know about art? About the Glasgow Boys and the Scottish Colourists? If paintings were just collateral to them, just something to be held on to while deals were being done …

Professor Robert Gissing reckoned that this kid Westie was a master forger, and Chib began to wonder about that, too. He was still thinking as he got back into the car, thinking as they pulled away from the kerb. Westie and Alice, Alice and Westie.

Westie short-changed.

'I know how you feel, pal,' Chib said out loud.

'Boss?' Glenn asked from the driving seat.

'Nothing.'

'Who was on the phone? Was it Hate?'

Chib sat forward in his seat until his face was almost level with Glenn's. 'Any more sticking your big pointy nose in, you'll have my hands around your throat – understood?'

'Loud and clear,' Glenn said, sounding suitably chastened. 'It's just that ...' He swallowed hard, as if fearing his boss's hands. 'If you're in trouble, me and Johnno want to help.'

'What we're here for,' Johnno piped up.

'Well, isn't that touching?' Chib crooned.

'We feel maybe you don't trust us the way you used to,' Glenn persisted.

'Oh aye? And who are you going to complain to – your shop steward? Get a grip, Glenn. Some of my business you're better off *not* knowing. I'm taking more than my share of flak, just to keep you two off the radar, know what I mean?'

'Not really, boss,' Johnno eventually admitted. Chib just groaned and slouched back again. Mackenzie's coffee was giving him a headache. Had to be the coffee. Either that or brain cancer from the mobile phone. One or the other.

What else could it be?

There was a restaurant next to the auction house. It had been a bank at one time, and still boasted a rococo interior of vast fluted columns and intricate cornicing. In the morning the tables were kept empty, ready for the lunchtime rush, but breakfast could be had at one of the booths by the window. Laura was stirring a foamy cappuccino when Mike arrived. He pecked her on both cheeks and ordered water – *frizzante* – from the waiter before sliding on to the bench across from her.

'No coffee?' she asked. There was a plate in front of her, showing leftover crumbs from a croissant. Little pots of jam and pats of butter sat untouched.

'Already had my share of jolts this morning,' he explained. 'I haven't seen you since the day of the auction – how did it go?'

'Not quite record-breaking.' She was stirring her spoon slowly around the remains of her drink. 'Did you hear about the warehouse?' She seemed to be studying him as he adjusted his shirt cuffs.

'Yes,' he said, eyes widening. 'Wasn't that extraordinary?'

'Extraordinary,' she echoed.

'You probably know the people at the National Gallery – they must have had a fit.'

'I'd imagine so.'

'Bloody lucky the gang didn't get away with it.'

'Lucky, yes ...' Her voice drifted away, though her eyes stayed locked on him.

'Don't tell me,' Mike said, affecting a laugh. 'Shaving foam on my ear lobe?' He made a show of checking, but wasn't about to be rewarded with anything like a smile.

'One of the paintings was the portrait by Monboddo

of his wife, Beatrice.' She pronounced the name in the Italian style. 'I remember it from the exhibition and how you couldn't take your eyes off it ...' She waited for him to speak.

'Nice to know I was under surveillance,' was all he could think to respond.

'Allan teased me,' she went on, 'said the reason you were so keen was because she looked like me.'

'Well ... I suppose there's a certain truth in that.'

'You remember that night of the exhibition? Some of us went to a restaurant after ...?'

Mike winced. 'Don't,' he said. Too much wine at the preview, and Mike giddy at this new world he had entered, a world where people knew about art, and spoke from the heart. One too many brandies at the restaurant. He'd caught Laura's eye several times. She'd always smiled back. Then she'd gone to the ladies' and he'd followed her, barging in and trying to kiss her ...

'Do you know anyone called Ransome?' she asked suddenly, bringing Mike back to the present.

'Should I?'

'I knew him at college – he tried much the same thing with me once at a party. Followed me to the loo ...' Noting the pained look on Mike's face, she broke off the reminiscence. 'I hadn't laid eyes on him in a while,' she said instead, 'but then the day of the auction, he came to see me afterwards. He said he was interested in a local villain called Chib Calloway who'd been sitting in the front row with two of his henchmen close by.'

'I was at the back, cosying up to the dealers.'

'You didn't see this man Calloway?' She watched as he shook his head. 'But you know who he is?'

'I know the name,' Mike conceded, straining his neck to see if the waiter was on his way. 'What's any of this got to do with me?'

'I'm not supposed to tell you this, but Ransome thought maybe you'd brought Calloway to the auction.'

'Me?' Mike raised both eyebrows. 'Why would he think that?'

'He didn't say, but he managed to describe you.' She paused, her stare intensifying. 'And Allan and the professor, too. He wanted your names, and I didn't see how I could refuse ...'

'Where's my water got to?' Mike muttered, craning his neck again. His mind was racing. Ransome must have been watching Chib that day. He'd seen Mike leaving the auction house with Gissing and Allan ... probably followed Chib and his men there and was watching outside ... He'd have seen Mike, Allan and Gissing heading for the Shining Star – with Chib and his men following close after ... Had Ransome actually been in the bar and seen Mike talking with Chib? No, the place had been dead – Chib, sensitive to surveillance, would have noticed him, surely. So what had led him to connect Mike and the others to Chib? The answer seemed simple enough – he'd been at the National Gallery, and had spotted Mike and Chib in the café. More crucially, however, Ransome now had all their names ...

'And then,' Laura continued, 'after the robbery, Ransome called me. Twice, actually. It was Saturday night, so it had to be important to him, even though he made the questions sound casual ...'

'Was he after another snog?'

Laura gave a sad little smile and dropped her gaze to the contents of her cup. 'That's the wrong question, Mike. You should be asking me, who's this Ransome chap? What's he got to do with anything? But you already know, don't you?'

'I really haven't a clue what you're getting at ...'

'He works for Lothian and Borders Police, Mike, and he was asking about the professor.' She sat back, as if finished talking but ready and willing to hear anything Mike might have to say.

'No clue at all,' he stressed.

Laura sighed and folded her arms, concentrating so hard on the cappuccino now that she might have been inviting it to levitate.

'I mean ...' he blustered on. 'Well, I'm not sure what I mean.' The water was arriving on a silver salver, ice and lime in the tall, slender glass. The waiter began to pour, then asked if they needed anything else.

Yes, Mike felt like telling him, *an escape hatch*. But he just shook his head in time with Laura. They watched the young man leave. Laura unfolded her arms and rested her fingertips against the rim of the table. Such long fingers, the nails immaculate.

'I knew Ransome pretty well, back in college days,' she stated quietly. 'He was a determined sod, even then. That night at the party, I had to knee him between the legs. I'm not sure that'll work, as far as you're concerned ...' She screwed shut her eyes and Mike feared she was about to start crying. He reached across the table and covered her hands with his own.

'It's really all right, Laura. He's probably after some dirt on this guy Calloway. He sees us at the same auction and starts imagining all sorts of conspiracies. Nothing to worry about – Ransome's not even part of the team looking at the heist ...' Realising that he was thinking aloud, he broke off, but not quickly enough. Laura's eyes had reopened.

'The botched heist, you mean.'

'Sure ... yes, of course.'

'How could you possibly know?'

He knew what she was about to say and bit down on his bottom lip.

'How could you know Ransome's not part of the team?' she duly obliged.

Mike fixed her with a look. He knew there were things he should be saying, reassurances he should be giving. Her eyes gleamed and intelligence shone from her face. So much more *alive* than Lady Monboddo. Mike knew that whatever he said, she'd see through it. There would be more questions on her part, more lies on his, all of it spiralling downwards. Things he couldn't tell her, explanations and excuses he couldn't give. Instead of which he slid out of the bench, reaching into his pocket for money to place beside his tumbler. Her head was bent over the table, staring hard at its surface. He leaned over to kiss her hair, pausing with his face there, breathing in her subtle perfume. Then he straightened up and walked towards the door.

263

'Mike?' she called to him. 'Whatever it is, maybe I can help.'

He nodded slowly, hoping she would catch the gesture, even though he had his back to her now. The waiter was standing by the door. He held it open for Mike and said he hoped he'd have a nice day.

'Thank you,' Mike replied, heading out on to George Street. 'I'm not at all sure that I will ...'

Glenn Burns had been working for Chib Calloway these past four and a half years, and was certain of only two things: his boss was in trouble, and overall, in the scheme of things as it were, and with everything taken into account, *he* could do a far better job. Chib, no offence, had terrible people skills, lacked vision, and seemed to bounce from crisis to crisis. Glenn knew this because he'd been studying business textbooks in his spare time. One lesson he'd taken to heart was Always Sleep With The Enemy. Not that he'd actually climbed into bed with DI Ransome, but he'd whispered sweet nothings into the copper's ear, hoping Chib's decline and fall would prove both swift and bloodless. So far it hadn't panned out, yet here he was, meeting Ransome again, and this time the man had photos to show him.

'Yeah, I know them,' Glenn admitted. 'I mean, I don't really *know* them, but Chib put the frighteners on them one time in a bar.'

'The Shining Star?'

'That's the one. Then he insisted on going to that boring sodding auction and they were there, too. We went back to the Shining Star again and there they all were, seated in the selfsame booth as before. This one ...' Glenn tapped one of the photos. It was a cutting from a magazine. 'He's the one who went to school with Chib – or so Chib says.'

'It's true; I've checked.'

'Anyway, that day at the Shining Star, once the other two have left, the school pal comes over and has a chat with Chib.'

'What about?' Ransome was gazing at something on the other side of his windscreen. They were parked atop Calton Hill, just to the east of Princes Street. Great views of Edinburgh, if you could be bothered to look. So far all Glenn had done was climb out of his own car and into the detective's. It smelt of leather. Nothing in the ashtray till Glenn deposited a wad of gum there, nicely souring the look on Ransome's face.

'They were gassing about the auction – who was going up and down in value, who wasn't selling at all. I zoned out, to be honest – boring as all-get-out. Chib wanted to know about bidding and paying and did they take cash and this guy was telling him ... Name's Mike, right?'

'Mike Mackenzie,' Ransome confirmed. He might not have liked the gum in his ashtray, but when Glenn un- wrapped a fresh stick and offered him one, he was quick enough to take it, chewing it like it was chateaubriand flavour. 'The other two are called Gissing and Cruikshank,' he continued. 'One works at the art college, the other at First Caledonian Bank. But it's Mike your boss seems to know best, right?'

'Right. They met again another time – we picked Mike

up in the Grassmarket, just outside the Last Drop pub. But Chib kicked me and Johnno out of the car, so Christ knows where they went or what they talked about ... Who is he anyway, this Mike?'

'Just some sod who got lucky and made a fortune from computers ... lives in some swanky penthouse in Murrayfield.'

'That's a coincidence ...' Glenn furrowed his brow.

'What is?'

'We were out there first thing this morning. Some fancy address called Henderland Heights. Chib wouldn't say why ...' Glenn broke off talking, stunned into silence by something he thought he would never see.

Detective Inspector Ransome trying to grin and whistle at the same time.

Ransome knew what he should do. He should take what he knew – his suspicions, evidence and conclusions – to the Chief. But then the Chief would say, 'Why didn't you tell Hendricks any of this? *He's* the officer in charge of the case.' And it would all filter back to Hendricks anyway. *His* collar. *His* glory. Wouldn't matter that the donkey work had been done by Ransome.

He needed more.

Needed the proof that would lead to arrests for armed robbery. Mackenzie and the others, they'd conspired in some way to help Calloway pull off the heist – there was precious little doubt in Ransome's mind that Chib was behind it. He'd been scouring the city for muscle to help him – Glenn had been clear on that. Or maybe it was this character Hate, leading a team of Hell's Angels: the very people who'd have access to sawn-offs and the like. But it couldn't have happened without inside info, which was where the 'Three Musketeers' came in. Rank amateurs, probably, cajoled or threatened until they were in way over their heads. It would be easy to break them – easier by far than confronting Chib himself. And when they broke, he would have the gangster where he wanted him.

And Hendricks, too, come to that. Hendricks had given him an earful on the phone. Somehow he'd got to hear that Ransome had visited the warehouse. *Stay the fuck away*, those had been Hendricks' instructions. Ransome had come back with a few choice words of his own before ending the call and refusing to answer when Hendricks rang back. Sod him. Sod the lot of them. A bit more hard evidence was needed, that or a confession. Evidence would be difficult without search warrants, and his various hunches and titbits of surveillance were never going to secure any of those. Not even his covert source could connect Calloway to the heist in any way other than tangentially.

He really needed more.

Hard evidence or a confession …

And suddenly, Ransome knew exactly what to do. And who to do it to.

25

Tuesday morning, just gone eleven, Westie was working on his degree show. He was stuck in the basement of the College of Art, which meant no windows, no natural light. Westie's solution was a series of striplights, standing at angles against the walls so that any paintings hung nearby would throw jagged shadows across sections of the room. The problem was, it was hard to see the paintings themselves. Added to which, the floor had become treacherous, snaking coils of electrical flex leading from the lights to an overloaded junction box. He'd been told by the janitor that there were Health and Safety issues and by one of his tutors that the 'art of display' was part and parcel of the exhibition. In other words, if Westie couldn't provide proper lighting and an environment that wasn't a potential deathtrap, he might be marked down.

Not that Westie needed to worry, of course. He was whistling a happy tune – 'So What?' by Miles Davis – as he worked, safe in the knowledge that his extra-curricular activities on behalf of Professor Gissing and his friends had already secured him a high pass ... maybe even a distinction.

'Doesn't mean you can slack,' Gissing had warned him. 'Your show has to exhibit a basic level of competence, otherwise the mark's going to look overly suspicious.'

Westie reckoned he could do 'competence'. And he was proud of his seven chosen canvases, pastiches of Runciman, Nasmyth, Raeburn (twice), Wilkie, Hornel and Peploe. The Peploe was a particular favourite: a still life featuring potted plant, fruit bowl, and, at the very edge of the canvas, ketchup bottle. Gissing, a fan of Peploe, hated it, which was why it was going to be Westie's centrepiece. He wanted to hear the professor praise it to the other assessors, albeit through gritted teeth.

The fresh injection of cash into Westie's bank account had meant he could go to town on his frames – no trawling the junk shops and skips. He had bought from an architectural reclamation specialist in Leith. The frames were gilded, ornate, original, and immaculate. He'd spent some more of the money on a couple of meals out and was thinking of renting a proper studio so that Alice could have her living room back.

'That's going to eat into my film studies funding,' she had complained. 'Unless we do something about it.'

It had taken a lot of talking to persuade her not to go asking Mike for any more cash. But then she'd started saying they should sell the DeRasse and pocket what they could.

'No point us having it if it's got to be kept hidden – I'd be as happy with one of your copies anyway.'

He'd asked who they should sell it to and she'd just shrugged her shoulders. 'Got to be someone out there who'd want it, no questions asked. I'll bet we could get fifty thou easy …'

Never easy, Westie thought to himself now. She had worked hard to talk him out of including the DeRasse in his exhibition. He realised that thinking about all of this had interfered with his whistling. Back to the top, Miles … Every time he replayed the heist itself, he ended up laughing. Bloody Lavender Hill Mob and no mistake. Gissing clutching his chest like he was about to peg it – *that* would have been interesting. Allan with a waterfall of sweat running down his face from under that ridiculous wig. Mike had done okay, though – he'd been cool throughout, definitely cut out for it. That was another reason Westie didn't want to start hassling for a bigger cut: Mike had something about him. The four hoodies had been Mike's doing. You got the feeling with Mike that, despite the haircut and the hand-crafted boots, he definitely knew people. People you didn't want to know.

Could probably handle himself, too, while Westie was a fully paid-up pacifist – give peace a chance and all that …

'This is some awful dump, by the way,' a voice growled from the doorway. Westie studied the man who was lumbering into the room. Shaved head, leather coat, gold rings and neck chain. 'Don't know why you're bothering, son – nobody's going to find you down here unless you leave a trail of breadcrumbs.'

'Can I help you?' Westie asked as the stranger chuckled at his own joke.

'Course you can, Westie. I wouldn't be here otherwise.'

The man was holding out a pudgy hand. Westie could have sworn there was scar tissue on the knuckles. 'I'm Chib Calloway. Reckoned it was high time we had an actual face-to-face.'

'Chib Calloway?'

The man nodded. 'Judging by the way your jaw's grazing the floor, I'm guessing the name means something to you. That's good – saves lengthy explanations.'

'I know who you are,' Westie admitted.

'Then you know why I'm here?'

Westie felt his knees trying to buckle. 'N-no ... I've no idea w-why you're here.'

'Has nobody bothered to tell you, Mr Westwater? Dearie me ...'

'Tell me what exactly?'

Calloway chuckled again and patted him on the shoulder. Westie's knees almost went again under the pressure. 'The extra guys on your team last Saturday, did you think they maybe appeared in a puff of smoke? The shooters and the van ... who the hell did you think organised it all?'

'You?' Westie just managed to choke the question out.

'Me,' Chib Calloway confirmed. 'I'm pretty impressed, actually ... reckoned someone would have blabbed. Good that my name's kept out of the spotlight. And yet I find myself having to come here ...' The gangster started tutting as he began a tour of the studio and its contents. Westie wanted to ask what was going on, but the greater part of him really didn't want to know. Only a couple of the paintings had actually been hung, the other five resting against one of the whitewashed walls. Calloway had crouched down to flick through them, saying nothing. Eventually, he stood up again, brushing imaginary dust from his palms. 'I don't know much about art,' he apologised, 'except for the noble art, of course. Know what that is, Westie?'

'Boxing?' Westie offered.

'That's it exactly – boxing.' The gangster was walking away from Westie, heading towards the doorway. 'Closely followed by hammering, battering, kicking, gouging, slashing, hacking and stabbing.' He turned and gave a smile. 'Not quite so noble by the time it gets to that stage, of course.'

'L-look, Mr Calloway, I just did what I was told. N-nobody said you were part of the ... I mean, you've got n-nothing to worry about, not from me.'

Calloway was advancing slowly on Westie again. 'You saying it's all down to your girlfriend, then? How is Alice, by the way?'

Westie's face creased in puzzlement. 'I don't understand.'

Calloway took a deep breath. 'Your dear, sweet little Alice sent a warning to my friend Mike Mackenzie. She says you want an extra twenty K on top, either that or another painting. According to her, you feel cheated. Is that right, Westie? Do you feel hard done by?' But the student's powers of speech had deserted him.

'Now,' Calloway went on, seemingly satisfied by this reaction, 'how do you suppose she got Mike's mobile number? Want to go fifty-fifty or ask the audience? No, because she got it from *you*, Westie. She got it from you ...' A forefinger stabbed Westie in the chest. It felt like the heft of a blade, the barrel of a gun. Calloway had leaned forward from the waist so he was eye to eye with the student. 'Unless you can come up with some other highly convincing explanation.' Spittle hit Westie's face. He didn't dare wipe it away until Calloway had started another circuit of the room, taking care not to trip over the various cables. 'These are dangerous times, Pretty Boy,' he was saying. 'People get a bit frantic, a bit crazy.'

'I didn't know the silly cow had sent that text!'

'But you knew she was thinking about it, didn't you? You knew it was a *text*, even though I never mentioned the fact.' Calloway had turned and was closing in on Westie again. His hands had emerged from his pockets. They were bunched into fists. 'The pair of you talked it over, maybe tweaked the wording till you'd got it just right ...'

'We only thought ...'

The punch hit Westie in the stomach and sent him backwards until he hit the wall, either side of a framed canvas. Calloway had followed up with a hand around the student's throat.

'It's good that we're getting to know one another,' he spat, 'because you're going to do something for me. Two things, in fact. For one, persuade your bony-arsed girlfriend that nobody's getting shafted around here except *her*.'

Westie, eyes bulging, had started to nod as best he could. Calloway released his grip and the young man collapsed to his knees, coughing a string of phlegm from his mouth. Calloway crouched down in front of him, a hand resting on either shoulder.

'Is that a deal?' he asked.

'No bother, Mr Calloway,' Westie managed to gasp. 'I'm on that straight away.' He managed to swallow. 'And what's the second thing?'

'The second thing is this, Westie – we're going to be a team, you and me.' Calloway was nodding as if to reinforce the point.

'A team?' Westie's ears were ringing and his mouth felt full of sand. There was juice in a carton on the floor next to him, but he didn't think now was the right time for a refreshment break.

'Looks like those forgeries of yours did the business, young Westie,' Calloway was telling him. 'In my book, that means you know what you're up to. Quick turnaround, too, from what I'm told. So now you're going to make me a few more.'

'More copies?'

Calloway nodded again. 'Plenty more paintings in that warehouse.'

'You can't be serious.'

'Don't fret.' The gangster offered a smile. 'We're not going to turn the place over again – do I really look that thick?'

'So you want them for yourself?'

'In a manner of speaking.'

Westie felt himself relax a little. 'Sure, Mr Calloway, I can do that. After all, what's the difference between hanging a fake on your wall and owning the real thing?'

'If the fake's perfect, no difference at all.' Calloway helped Westie back up on to his feet, brushing dust from his shoulders.

274

'Do you have anything particular in mind?' Westie asked. 'Doesn't have to be from the warehouse – I can do you a *Mona Lisa* if you like.'

'No, Westie, not the *Mona Lisa*. These have to be paintings that are kept locked away from the public gaze.'

'How many are we talking about?'

'Couple of dozen should do it.'

Westie puffed out his cheeks. 'That's a lot of work.'

Calloway's face tightened. 'You're forgetting – you've a lot of making up to do after that little stunt Alice tried to pull.'

Westie raised his hands in surrender. 'No problem,' he said. 'Not for you, Mr Calloway. I'm flattered you think I'd be good enough.' Watching the gangster's features relax again, he decided it was safe to ask a question. 'By the way, which painting did you get from the raid?'

'It's by some guy called Utterson – *Dusk on Rannoch Moor*. How about you?'

'A DeRasse,' Westie was able to say, despite the sudden queasy surge in his gut.

'Never heard of him.' Calloway's hands still rested on Westie's shoulders. 'Any good, is he?'

Westie cleared his throat. 'Not bad. Experimental … style of Jasper Johns but a bit hipper … Do you want to swap?'

The gangster just laughed, as though Westie had been making a joke. Westie tried smiling back, maintaining the illusion while his brain screamed.

The Utterson! Why did it have to be the bloody Utterson?

26

Allan Cruikshank was in his office at First Caledonian Bank's HQ on the corner of George Street and St Andrew's Square. The building was becoming cramped, and being Grade I listed there was little way to renovate it to accommodate the twenty-first century. Allan's office was half its original size, subdivided by means of a partition wall. The only view from his remaining window was of a ghastly seventies office block to the rear of the building. Along with everyone else at his level, Allan worked to monthly targets. His roster of High Net Worth clients had been underperforming of late, and he should have been making a few calls, maybe arranging lunches or pre-dinner drinks, the better to talk them into sticking some more of their money the bank's way. He knew that, if asked, Mike Mackenzie would come on board as a client, but then they would cease to be just friends; the transaction would sit between them, changing everything.

But then who was Allan kidding? They were no longer 'just friends'. They'd pulled off a heist together, and Allan now had something he'd always wanted – at least theoretically. He owned two paintings that First Caledonian, despite its muscle, its own extensive portfolio of art, and its own curator, could never possess.

And he hated the fact. He didn't think it was simple cowardice that had convinced him to hand the paintings over to Mike for safe keeping. It was just that the Coultons didn't mean anything to him. He realised he'd have been as happy with Westie's reproductions. And at least he could have displayed those ... His fingers drifted over a nick on his chin. He'd been shaving this morning, not really concentrating. Hadn't slept much either, not since Saturday. He tossed and turned and imagined himself in a police cell, a courtroom, a prison.

'You were a bloody fool, Allan,' he said out loud. Not that any of it had been his idea, not really. Gissing had come up with the original notion, and Mike had fleshed it out. Without Mike as a conduit to Chib Calloway, they'd probably never have gone ahead with it. Allan's role had been secondary, negligible. Christ Almighty, he sounded as if he was explaining himself to the prosecutor.

When the alarm bell sounded, he jolted upright. But it was only the phone: the buzzer signalling an internal call. He picked it up.

'Allan Cruikshank speaking,' he said, stifling a yawn.

'Front desk, Mr Cruikshank. There's a gentleman here to see you.' Allan's appointment diary was open in front of him, empty till mid-afternoon. He knew what the receptionist was going to say, but still felt a rush of cold at her words.

'He's with the police – Detective Inspector Ransome. Shall I send him up?'

'Can you tell him I'm in the middle of a meeting?' Allan waited while his message was relayed.

'He says he's happy to wait,' the receptionist trilled, 'and he'll only need five minutes of your time.'

'Then tell him to wait there in the lobby. I'll be another quarter of an hour or so.' Allan slammed the phone down and jumped to his feet. The window looked inviting: four floors to the waiting roadway and oblivion. But he knew it only opened an inch and a half – nobody at First Caly wanted an accident. If he exited his office and walked towards the lifts, there was a stairwell for use in a fire. He didn't know where it would bring him out, though ... maybe into the very lobby where his nemesis was waiting.

'Hell and damnation,' he muttered, picking up the phone again. Mike wasn't answering at home, so Allan tried his mobile. This time he got through.

'Hello?' the voice said.

'That bloody detective's here,' Allan blurted out. 'Wants to talk to me. He knows, Mike. He *knows*. You'd better get yourself over here.'

'Who is this?'

In horror, Allan studied the display. He'd transposed two digits of Mike's number! He ended the call, squeezed shut his eyes, and felt like weeping. Eventually, he took a deep breath and tried again, making sure this time that it was Mike who answered.

'It's got to be about the heist, Mike,' he explained. 'You've got to help me.'

'By rushing over there?' Mike asked after a lengthy

pause. 'And what message would that send, Allan? You've got to brazen it out.'

'Why the hell is he here? Who's been talking?'

'He's fishing, that's all.'

'You don't know that!'

'We won't know *anything* until you've talked to him. Have you got something you can take to calm down?'

'Maybe if someone whacked me with a hammer ...' As the words left Allan's mouth, he regretted them. He didn't want Mike getting ideas, ideas he might take to his new best friend – Chib Calloway. Allan swallowed hard and took a nice deep breath. 'I'll be fine, Mike. Sorry if I overreacted.'

'Call me when you're done with him.' Mike's voice was all steel.

'Always supposing I'm allowed one phone call.'

The joke was weak, but Mike laughed anyway. 'Just be yourself, Allan. You're a deal-maker, remember that. And Ransome's not even part of the official investigation. As far as I can tell, he's been on Chib's case. He's probably sniffing around anyone who knows him.'

'But *how* does he know?'

'There's a chance he saw us at the auction, and maybe at the Shining Star afterwards.'

'So he knows we're interested in art and drinking ...'

'You can bet I'll be on his list, too. But you've barely met Chib, Allan – and that's all you need to tell him.'

'Okay,' Allan agreed. 'Thanks, Mike.'

'Call me straight after.'

'Sure,' Allan put the receiver down, then picked it

up again and spoke to his secretary, asked her to head down to reception in a couple of minutes and sign in a Mr Ransome. He didn't bother saying who Ransome was. Then again, she'd know by day's end – the receptionists and secretaries were as thick as thieves. Allan spent the time trying to compose himself. He pulled some paperwork from his drawer and spread it across the desk. Switched on the TV to the stock market screen. By the time the knock came, he was seated behind his desk, sleeves rolled up, calculator to hand, jacket draped over the back of his executive chair.

'Come in,' he called.

Ransome was younger than he'd expected, and dapper with it. He'd known HNWs with less style.

'Nice place to work,' was the detective's opening gambit. Allan had stood up long enough to shake hands across the desk. He gestured for Ransome to sit down. 'Lot of expensive-looking art on the walls,' Ransome continued. 'Down in the lobby ... all along the corridors ...'

'First Caledonian has its own curator,' Allan informed him. 'Our portfolio is worth in excess of twenty million.'

Ransome gave a whistle. 'Do they ever let the staff borrow something for a couple of nights?'

'Not at my lowly level of management.' Allan attempted a self-deprecating smile. 'What's this all about, Inspector? I admit I'm intrigued.'

'You're a hard man to track down, Mr Cruikshank. The hoops I've had to go through ...' The detective shook his head slowly. 'All I had was your name, you see. That

280

and the name of your bank … Ever had any trouble with money-laundering?'

'Certainly not – the regulations make sure of that.'

'A banker would be a useful contact, though, wouldn't he? If you *did* want to launder money.'

'Quite the opposite. As I say, we're obliged by law to report unusual levels of activity to the authorities.'

Ransome didn't seem particularly interested in any of Allan's answers. Nevertheless, the questions kept coming. 'I understand you work with High Net Worth individuals, Mr Cruikshank?'

'That's right.'

'Is Michael Mackenzie a client?'

'That comes under the heading of privileged information, Inspector. Has something happened to Mike?'

'You do know him, then?'

'We've been friends for over a year.'

'And Charles Calloway?' Ransome broke off. 'Sorry … you probably know him better as "Chib".'

'I really don't know him at all – we ran into him in a wine bar one day, but that's about it.'

'This would be the Shining Star wine bar? Just along the road from here?'

'That's right.' Allan had been expecting a flipped-open notebook and pen, maybe a hulking junior colleague standing against the door like a silent sentry. But Ransome just sat here with his fingertips pressed together, one leg crossed over the other.

'When you say "ran into him" …?'

'I mean just that. He saw us looking at him, came to the table and gave a couple of scowls and snarls.'

'He's good at that, is Calloway.'

'A professional, I'd say.'

'And this was just yourself and Mr Mackenzie …?'

'Another friend was there – Professor Robert Gissing.'

Ransome raised an eyebrow. 'I seem to know that name. Wasn't he the one called in to run an eye over those paintings from the Granton heist?'

'That's him. He's head of the College of Art.'

Ransome gave a thoughtful nod. 'So you didn't speak to Chib at the auction?'

'Which auction?'

'The one a couple of weeks back … and again – funny coincidence – just along the road from here.'

'I'd no idea Mr Calloway had an interest in auctions.' Allan leaned back in his chair and clasped his hands behind his head. Ransome just smiled and was thoughtful again. 'I'd really like to know what this is all about, Inspector.'

'You say that Calloway came over to your table and a few words were exchanged …'

'Yes?'

'So what was your friend Mackenzie doing joining Calloway at the bar, chatting and sharing a drink?'

'Must have been after I left,' Allan improvised.

'Loyalty's an admirable quality, Mr Cruikshank, when it's not misplaced. What do you think those two would have had to talk about?'

'I don't know … schooldays maybe.'

'Schooldays?'

Allan licked his parched lips. 'They were at the same school for a short time.'

The way the detective nodded to himself told Allan that this wasn't news to him. 'Might start to explain why they've been spending so much time together recently,' Ransome speculated. 'I happened to see them at the National Gallery, *and* at that auction, *and* at the Shining Star. And I know they've been taking little drives together – sure you weren't there with them, Mr Cruikshank?'

'I can assure you I wasn't.'

Ransome leaned forward. 'Well what about this, then – Calloway has been to Mr Mackenzie's home at Henderland Heights. What does that suggest to you, Mr Cruikshank?'

'It doesn't suggest anything to me.'

'Your friend Mackenzie collects art, doesn't he? Someone at the auction house told me as much. Then he takes a known criminal on a tour of our national collection, after which they attend an auction together, checking out the going rate for various artists. Doesn't that begin to suggest *anything* to you, Mr Cruikshank?'

'Nothing.' Allan entwined his hands more tightly around his head, willing himself not to leap up from his chair and grab the cop by the throat. But then that might look suspicious, mightn't it? Instead, he apologised for not offering Ransome a coffee or tea.

'Your secretary already did that, sir. I said I wouldn't be staying. But you look like you could do with a cold drink, if I might suggest.' Ransome made a gesture and Allan realised that his armpits were showing and his shirt was damp with sweat. He lowered his hands into his lap. The detective sighed and reached into his jacket pocket, lifting out a small cassette-player. 'While I remember,' he said. 'Would you take a quick listen to this?' He held the machine out in front of him at arm's length and pressed a button. Allan listened to Westie's call to the emergency services.

Strangest bloody thing … white van … dumping bodies …

As the call ended, Ransome hit the stop button. 'Does that voice ring a bell, Mr Cruikshank?'

Allan shook his head slowly and determinedly.

'Our forensic team's hanging on to the original recording,' the detective said, studying the tape-player before slipping it back into his pocket. 'Amazing what they can do these days. An engine turning over in the background … they can isolate the sound and match it to a specific brand of car. Isn't that incredible, sir?'

'Incredible,' Allan echoed, thinking of his Audi. Had its engine been running? He couldn't remember now.

'There'd be immunity, you know,' the detective was saying as he rose to his feet. 'I mean, I'm just thinking aloud here, but anyone who helped us put Chib Calloway behind bars would be a hero, pure and simple. Don't tell me you've never wanted to be a hero, Mr Cruikshank?'

'I've told you, I barely know the man.'

'But you're good friends with Michael Mackenzie – and *Mackenzie* knows him.'

'So talk to Mike.'

Ransome nodded slowly. 'Thought I'd try you first – you strike me as the rational sort, the sort who'd see sense.'

284

Ransome was halfway to the door, but he paused again. 'It wouldn't just be immunity, Mr Cruikshank – it would be anonymity, too. We're hot on that these days for people who help take the likes of Calloway off the streets.' He took a final look around the room. 'You had a break-in here, didn't you? At First Caly, I mean ... few years back now.'

'Yes.'

'Rumour at the time was, Calloway was responsible.'

'Then he's not very clever – we don't tend to keep bullion on the premises.'

'Still got away with a pretty penny, though.' Ransome sniffed and rubbed a finger along the underside of his nose. 'Another rumour at the time ... he had help.'

'Help?'

'Someone on the inside.'

'Just what exactly are you getting at?' Allan's voice had hardened.

'Nothing, Mr Cruikshank. Just that he's got previous that way – contacts, people he can scare or bribe into helping him. Good of you to take the time to see me. Funny, though ... when I asked your secretary, she said you didn't have any meetings this morning.' He gave a little bow and a smile, then tapped his watch. 'Told you I only needed five minutes ...'

And with that he was gone.

Yes, thought Allan, five minutes to shred a man's nerves and send his whole life crashing to smithereens around him. He needed some fresh air, needed to walk off some of the adrenalin, but he couldn't leave now – Ransome might be loitering. He had to call Mike, tell him everything. Mike was the one the detective was interested in. Mike could lead him straight to Calloway. There wasn't even any evidence in Allan's home – what did he have to fear?

He found himself pacing the room, then realised there was something on Ransome's chair, something that hadn't been there before. The detective's business card, with a mobile phone number scrawled along the bottom. When his own mobile rang, he answered it without thinking.

'Whoever you are,' the voice said, 'I don't take kindly to practical jokes.'

It was the man who'd answered the first time Allan had tried Mike. The wrong number. Allan muttered an apology, ended the call, and turned his phone off altogether. Mike could wait. Everything could wait.

Until he was good and ready to deal with it.

27

Mike Mackenzie was staring at his mobile, willing it to ring. He was seated in a Stockbridge café, having been for a walk along the Water of Leith. It had always been his preferred route when he had things to think about, problems to solve. But this time it had worked miraculously. He'd been wondering what to do about the threat from Westie's girlfriend. One call to his bank would see the transfer of an additional twenty K into the student's account, but Mike hadn't been quite ready to make that decision. Maybe Gissing could warn Westie off, or at least talk some sense into him, but the professor was answering neither messages nor texts. Mike's latest communication to him had warned that Ransome was closing in and would probably be knocking on both their doors. So far, there had been no reply.

But then, just as Mike was pushing open the door to the café, a text had arrived.

Sorry about Alice. Don't do anything. W.

Which was fine, just so long as Westie had the measure of his girlfriend. But at least Mike could file that particular problem in the pile marked 'pending'. The call from Allan had put him right off his goat cheese and rocket ciabatta.

Why didn't he ring now? Could Ransome really have taken him to the station for further questioning? Pockets emptied, belt, tie and shoelaces removed – was that how they did it?

Always supposing I'm allowed one phone call …

Had Allan cracked and told the detective everything? When the phone did ring, it caught Mike by surprise, so that he spluttered some of the coffee back into its cup. But when he looked at the display, it was Laura rather than Allan.

'Laura,' he said, answering. 'Look, sorry I walked out on you. It was bloody rude of me, and I've been meaning to call and apologise …'

'Never mind that,' she was saying. 'There's a full inventory under way at the warehouse.'

'A thankless task, I'd imagine.' He was trying for levity.

'Just bloody listen, will you? The rumour is, they're finding gaps.'

'Gaps?'

'In the collection – the missing paintings.'

Mike's brow furrowed. 'But the paintings were in the van …'

'Not *those* paintings! The others … the ones still missing. The ones the gang got away with.'

'Got away with?' he echoed, his head spinning. 'How many are we talking about?'

'Half a dozen so far, and they're not halfway through the stock check. A Fergusson sketchbook's gone, too. Plus another book with signed plates by Picasso.'

'Jesus.'

Laura's voice turned imploring. 'If there's *anything* you know, Mike, anything you can tell the police ...'

'What?'

'You've got to speak to them. Or you could always call Ransome – I'll act as go-between, if you like. I'm sure if the paintings could somehow be chanced upon, you know, if they were left abandoned somewhere ...'

'Nice of you to assume this has got anything to do with me.' Mike realised he was being studied by a woman at another table. She was probably wondering why he was stabbing his cooling ciabatta with a knife. He managed a smile and put the knife down.

'Has Ransome spoken to you yet?'

'I told you, Laura, he's not even working the case – it's Chib Calloway he's after, and his paranoia has extended as far as Allan and the professor and me.'

'Why Allan?'

'What?'

'Why put Allan at the top of that list?'

Mike rubbed at his temples, trying to dull the pain. There was a pharmacy next door to the café, and he decided he needed some aspirin. A couple of hundred should do it ...

'No reason,' he eventually said, knowing the preceding silence had already given the lie to this.

'If Calloway has the paintings, maybe you could talk to him,' Laura was suggesting now.

'Did he look to you like the sort of man you can reason with?'

'Are you trying to tell me he *does* have them?'

'Christ, no – I don't know anything about these missing paintings! What I'm saying is, I don't want to be the one making that accusation to Chib Calloway's face.'

'Mike ... just how involved are you?'

'Unattached at the moment, as it happens.' The sound she made was a sigh of frustration. 'I'm fine, Laura. This is all going to peter out, trust me.'

'Can I do that, though, Mike? Can I really trust you?'

It was an excellent question, Mike thought. He was wondering who *he* could trust, now that the game had changed.

Did anyone have the new rulebook to hand?

Alice was late back from the cinema. She'd been hosting another of her quiz nights in the bar. Themed this time, the subject being 'American New Wave'. Didn't seem to matter – the same team of four always won. Which probably explained why the turnout had started to drop. It was a problem, and she didn't have an answer to it as yet. As she climbed the steps to the flat's front door, she tried to remember if there was any food waiting for her. Hell with it, they could always phone out. She reckoned Mike would come across with the extra money – not all of it, obviously; there'd be some negotiating. But enough to keep her and her dreams on track. She was surprised she hadn't heard from him – maybe it was time for another text, issuing a deadline. As she started to turn her key in the lock, the door was flung open from within. Westie was bug-eyed, brandy on his breath. His clothes looked ready for the bin.

'What the hell have you done?' he shouted, hauling her inside by the arm and slamming shut the door.

'No idea,' she bristled. 'Care to give me a clue?'

'You stupid, stupid bitch.' He'd turned away from her, stalking into the living room, his hands held to his head as though to prevent it from splitting open. She'd seen him in some manic states before, but never like this.

'Look,' she said, 'all I did was ask for a bit more money – no harm in trying. I take it Mike's been on to you ...'

'Mike? Mike?' Saliva was flying from the corners of his mouth. 'If only ...' He turned to confront her. 'Remember I told you there was a sleeping partner? I'd to paint an extra fake for him? Turns out it's Chib Calloway.'

Alice looked at him blankly. 'Who's Chib Calloway?'

'He's Edinburgh's equivalent of the mafia. Not the sort of guy you want on your back.'

'So Mike's gone running to him?'

'*He's* the sleeping partner! The one who loaned us the guns, the van, the extra pairs of hands ... Calloway came to see me today at the art college. He had two messages for me. One, we don't get any extra cash. Two, he wants me to do more paintings.'

'What for?'

'Does it matter? Thing is, your hare-brained scheme has gone tits up, and *I'm* the one in the shit. How could you be so stupid?'

Alice's face had hardened. 'I was thinking of *us*, Westie – thinking of *you*. They weren't treating you right.'

'At least they were letting me live, which is more than'll

happen if I don't come good for Chib Calloway. I can't believe you'd do this to me!'

'Do what?'

'Try blackmailing Mike.'

She leaned forward so that her face was an inch from his. 'Get a grip, Westie. You could just say no to this guy – what's he going to do? If he tries anything, we go straight to the nearest cop shop.'

Westie stared at her for a moment, then slumped on to the sofa, elbows on knees, hands still wrapped around his head. 'You don't get it,' he muttered. 'You don't get it.'

'Oh, here we go.' Alice rolled her eyes. 'The tortured artist bit – like I haven't seen it before a hundred times.'

'Just leave, will you?'

'Leave?' Her voice was rising again. 'It's my bloody flat, in case you've forgotten!' He didn't move, didn't speak. 'I'll leave, all right,' she stated into the silence. 'Just you try and stop me!'

Westie heard her grab her things and go. When he finally looked up, the room was blurred with tears.

Ransome and his CHIS were in a pub on Rose Street, standing either end of the bar and communicating by mobile phone. CHIS stood for Covert Human Intelligence Source, this being the police's new favoured terminology. But Ransome knew precisely what Glenn really was – he was his grass, his nark, his snout, his snitch.

His mole in Chib Calloway's organisation.

'It'll be you running the show soon,' he was reminding the hoodlum, even though Ransome had no intention of allowing Glenn to step into Calloway's shoes. Only thing he'd be stepping into was the same prison cell as his boss ... and wouldn't that make for fun and games, once Chib knew the part his one-time lieutenant had played in his downfall? 'Chib's men all trust you,' Ransome continued. 'So all we need to do now is nail him for that art heist – more than a dozen paintings missing at the latest count. Must be tucked away somewhere.'

'I thought the thieves left them in the van ...'

'Keep up, Glenn – inventory on the warehouse keeps throwing up pictures that are no longer there.'

'So they *did* get away with some?'

'Looks like – nothing in your boss's house or the boot of his car?'

'I've not had the boot open in a while ... I could take a peek.'

'And while you're at it, make some excuse to get inside his home, too – have a rake around. Where else could he be stashing them?'

'You sure it's him in the first place?'

'Come on, Glenn ... he must have let something slip.'

'Nothing.'

'Then he didn't want you in on it. Maybe you're on the way to the subs' bench, Glenn – you and Johnno. Maybe Chib's building himself a new team ...' Ransome lifted the whisky glass to his nose, smelling seaweed and peat smoke and maybe a hint of hot road tar. The produce of a coastal distillery, somewhere far to the north and west of Edinburgh. Just the one drink, though – he had Sandra's Vietnamese duck to look forward to. He forced himself to stare straight ahead at the row of optics, rather than try for eye contact with Glenn. There were plenty of drinkers between them. 'What is it you're drinking, Glenn?' he asked.

'Smirnoff Ice. Cheers, Mr Ransome.'

'I wasn't offering to buy you one. If I go telling the barman to send a drink to the other end of the bar, it'll look like a pick-up.'

'Then why did you ask?'

'Just curious, same as I'm curious about the where-abouts of these pictures.'

'Funny thing,' Glenn said, 'but remember I told you we'd been to Henderland Heights?'

'Mike Mackenzie's flat, yes.'

'Well, on the way back, Chib got a call. Someone called Edward, but pronounced funny. And Chib said something to him about "collateral" and how it wasn't even posted as missing.'

'What did he mean by that?'

'Dunno. He realised Johnno and me were being nosy and made sure we were out of earshot for the rest.'

'He's got to have it stashed somewhere, whatever it is …'

'There's the clubs and pubs – they've all got cellars and storerooms. Plus the snooker and pool halls … dozens of places.'

'You could ask around, see if Chib's made any visits without you knowing.'

'If he gets wind of it …'

'Make sure he doesn't. Are you absolutely sure Mike Mackenzie's a recent addition to Chib's social scene?'

'I'm sure. But, Mr Ransome, maybe that means Mackenzie's hiding the paintings for Chib.'

'The thought had crossed my mind. Tough to get a search warrant, though ...' Ransome gave a loud sigh. 'Look, Glenn, it's all very simple really. If we can get your boss for the warehouse, there's no fallout. No one's going to know you played any role in it at all. Makes your accession all the easier.'

'My what?'

Ransome closed his eyes for a second. 'You taking Chib's place as the city's number one,' he explained.

'Right.'

The pub's double doors flew open as a stag party burst in. Easy enough to spot the bridegroom-to-be, reduced to his underpants, shoes and T-shirt, the latter defaced by graffiti and egg yolk. Ransome angled his phone away from the fresh wave of noise.

'Keep your eyes and your ears open, Glenn. Next day or so is going to be crucial. Believe me, Chib's empire is ready to fall. Make or break time for you, my friend. You ready to ascend your boss's throne?'

'Ready for what?' Glenn had pressed a finger to his ear, holding the phone more closely to the other. 'I didn't catch that, Mr Ransome. Too much noise. Hello? Mr Ransome?' Glenn took a few steps back, the better to see the far end of the bar. But the detective had already headed out into the night.

28

It was eight o'clock on Wednesday morning before Mike got through to Chib. They arranged to meet at ten at the disused snooker hall. Mike had been cagey on the phone, keeping it short, intent on saving his fury for the meeting itself. But then he reminded himself who – and what – Chib was, and revised his strategy accordingly.

Chib was standing behind one of the unlit tables when Mike pushed open the door. The gangster's face was in shadow as he rolled a series of reds against the opposite cushion, studying their trajectories and momentum.

'What's on your mind, Michael?' Chib asked, his voice refrigerator cold.

'I think you know.'

'Let's pretend I don't.'

Mike slid his hands into his jacket pockets. 'The warehouse is missing a few paintings, Chib. A dozen or more, as it turns out – which kind of blows our brilliant plan to smithereens. They may not have noticed the switch, but they know a robbery's happened because they're suddenly short twelve masterpieces!'

One snooker ball hit another and sent it spinning on its axis. 'I saw it on the news,' Chib intoned. 'One reason

I was off limits last night. If we'd met then, I might've been a bit hotheaded. Still can't say I'm too thrilled about it, though ...'

'If you'd thought about it for one second ... one single, solitary *second* ... you'd have realised they were bound to do a full stock check.' Mike paused. 'Or did your four bright young things just get greedy and grab the oils for themselves?'

'Sorry, Mike, I'm a bit confused ...' Calloway leaned down with his elbows on the rim of the table. His face was visible now, eyes peering up at Mike. 'Didn't you use those same four guys to cover the guards and the gatehouse? Leaving you and *your* friends to empty the vaults?'

Mike burst into an incredulous laugh. 'You've had all night to come up with a story and that's the best you can do?'

'I'm tempted to say the same thing.'

'You're not seriously suggesting *we* lifted those paintings? Are we supposed to have tucked them under our jumpers?'

'How would I know? I wasn't there – but then neither were my boys. They were keeping an eye on the hostages while you went about your business. When are they supposed to have pulled off this miracle? Did they make themselves invisible so they could get past you in the vaults without anyone noticing?'

Mike thumped a fist down hard against the green baize. A cloud of dust flew from it. 'Why the hell would we go to the bother of *stealing* paintings? We'd taken all the trouble of switching them so nobody would ever be the wiser!'

'Maybe one of you got greedy.'

'I would know if that had happened.'

'Really? You were standing over your pals the whole time as they emptied their vaults?' Chib was silent for a moment, then exhaled noisily. 'You talk a good game, Mike. I could almost use someone like you on my team.'

'This is crazy!' Mike spun away from the table, running his hands through his hair, stopping just short of tearing out a few clumps.

'I'll tell you what's crazy,' Chib stated quietly. 'Your pal Allan was paid a visit yesterday by Ransome.'

'How do you know that?'

Chib was standing upright again. His grin just showed against the shadows, much like the Cheshire Cat's. 'I had Johnno tail the bastard for a few hours, wanted to know what he's up to. Ransome paid a visit to First Caledonian Bank – I remember you telling me that's where Allan works ...'

'It's not a big deal – Allan called me at the time to tell me it was happening.'

'And?' Chib was slowly rounding the table.

'And nothing – I spoke to Allan afterwards. It was a fishing expedition, that's all.'

'You sure about that?'

'Look ... is this you laying down some smoke? Right now, it's these missing paintings I'm bothered about.'

'Who else was in the warehouse?'

'Westie and Allan.'

'Not the professor?'

'He stayed in the van – couldn't risk him being ID'd.'

298

Chib was by now face to face with Mike. 'What about afterwards?'

'How do you mean?'

Chib rubbed his jaw. He had neglected to shave for a couple of days and there was a rasping noise as his fingers crossed the greying stubble. 'I've heard of it happening – a bank gets turned over ... doesn't have to be a bank, could be a petrol station, supermarket, anywhere really ... Once the thieves have hoofed it, the staff call the cops, but then they've got that five- or ten-minute wait ... all this stuff's still lying around the place, and whatever goes walkies will be blamed on the robbers ...'

Mike's eyes narrowed. 'You're saying the guards at the warehouse ...? But wouldn't the visitors see something?' He shook his head slowly. 'No, I'm not buying that.'

'You'd rather convince yourself it was me?' Mike could feel the man's breath on his face – garlic had played some part in the previous evening's meal. There was a hint of milky tea, too – breakfast, probably. 'Only three of my guys,' he went on, 'were in the actual warehouse, meaning they must've taken – what? – four paintings apiece. What in God's name were they wearing – tents?' Chib offered a cold chuckle. 'No, my friend, this was down to your lot, and I'm sure if I ask them nicely, Westie and Allan will spill their guts – literally, if need be.'

'What about asking your own guys first?'

'I don't need to.'

'Wouldn't be the first time a small-time crook had given in to temptation ...'

Their mutual staring contest lasted twenty seconds,

Chib the first to blink as he reached into his jacket for his phone. Mike concentrated on keeping his breathing steady, his demeanour solid. Not much sleep last night – too many questions. Of course he'd been turning over some of the same suspicions Chib had just voiced. Little phrases had kept recurring ... *no such thing as the perfect crime ... honour among thieves ... traitor in the ranks* ... Chib's eyes were on him as he punched in some numbers. Mike knew he was right – no way those four had been hiding anything under their jackets, and nowhere in the back of the van to stash so many extra paintings, sketchpads and illustrated books. Mike needed to think, needed to talk to Allan and Westie. He'd decided not to call them straight away, see if either decided to call him first, as soon as they heard the news. Not a peep. On the other hand, maybe they were just following orders – Gissing's orders: lie low ...

'Glenn?' Chib was saying. 'I want you to round up Billy, Kev, Dodds and Bellboy. Get them round to the snooker hall pronto.' As he snapped shut his phone, Mike's sounded. Westie's number on the screen.

'Mind if I take this outside?' he asked Chib.

'Someone I shouldn't know about?'

'Just personal,' Mike said, hauling open the door. Outside on the pavement, he took a few deep gulps of air as he answered the call.

'Hello?' he said, wondering whether to expect Westie himself or the girlfriend, Alice.

'Mike, is that you?' Westie's voice.

'What can I do for you?' Mike asked.

'I just wanted to … I want to say sorry … I'd no idea Alice was going to send you that text. And it stands to reason she didn't really mean it. We don't … I don't want any more money. Or a painting, come to that. I'm quite happy with everything.'

He didn't sound it. 'You've got enough paintings, then?'

'I suppose so.' Westie sounded confused.

'And how many's that, Westie?'

'What do you mean? Just the DeRasse – you know that, Mike. So are we okay now, yeah?'

'I'm not sure, Westie.'

'See, I've got a favour to ask.'

Mike's shoulders tensed. The street was mid-morning quiet: a newsagent's at the corner, a second-hand shop still waiting to open. Tenements across the way, but no one at the grimy windows. 'I might not be in the mood,' he told Westie.

'I can appreciate that, Mike. But I've apologised now, so maybe you can … you know …'

'What?'

'Get Calloway off my case!' The words were just short of a scream, so that they came over in a distorted crackle.

'I wasn't aware he was *on* your case.'

'You didn't send him round here to scare me off?'

Mike's brow furrowed. 'What's he been saying, Westie?'

'He wants me to do more fakes for him – loads of them. And I'm scared, Mike – scared to say no, but scared of what'll happen if I say yes.'

301

Mike had turned round to face the windowless snooker hall. It was called Diamond Jim's, the paint peeling from its signage. Had there ever been a Diamond Jim? And if so, what had happened to him? 'Why does he want them, Westie?'

'You think I was going to ask? He's a monster, Mike, everybody knows that. He threw a guy off the Scott Monument once.'

'Threatened to,' Mike corrected him. 'Did he tell you what paintings he wants?'

'I don't think he knows yet. Says they've got to be like the ones we took – you know, unlikely to be posted missing.'

Mike found himself nodding. 'Have you seen the news, Westie?'

'Christ, no – has something happened to her?'

Mike wasn't really listening. He'd spotted a bag of rubbish in the pend that separated the two tenement blocks. It had burst open and a rat was feasting on the contents, slithering over the remains of takeaway meals and beer cans. It dawned on Mike that he was a very long way from home. Westie had called Chib a monster – hard to disagree. And after all, wasn't Edinburgh the very city that had spawned *Dr Jekyll and Mr Hyde*? Mike placed a hand against the snooker hall's dank, defaced wall, and felt it leave a thin residue all across his palm.

A hellish spot, he thought to himself.

So why go back inside? Why not run for it and try to forget that he had once known anyone called Chib Calloway? Somehow he didn't think it would be that simple. And the first to flee ... well, they would become the prime suspect, wouldn't they?

'What?' he asked into the phone. *Has something happened to her?* Westie had asked, and now he was saying something else.

'Alice,' the voice repeated, cracking with emotion. 'I don't know what I'm going to do ...'

'How do you mean?'

'I had a go at her last night ... about her sending you that text, and Calloway and everything ... She walked out, Mike. She's been gone all night.'

Mike swore under his breath and rolled his eyes heavenwards. 'You've got to go after her.' He spoke quietly and calmly into the mouthpiece, despite his pounding heart. But he noticed that he was having to hold the phone in both hands to stop it being shaken out of his grip. 'You've got to bring her back, sort things out between you, get her to see sense. She knows *everything*, Westie – and she's got less to lose than the rest of us.'

'How do you mean?'

'If she goes to the police, there's practically nothing they can charge her with.'

'She wouldn't do that.'

'And if she's feeling like you've turned against her ... well, what's to stop her trying a spot of blackmail again?'

'She won't ... not now she knows Calloway's involved.'

'She might. So here's what you have to do, Westie – you call her, text her, go knock on her friends' doors, any family, that cinema she works in – you track her down and then you drop to your knees and tell her you're sorry. She's got to come back, Westie. She's got to.'

There was silence on the line for a moment, then the sound of sniffles being wiped away. 'I'll try, Mike. What about Calloway?'

'First things first, Westie. Let me know, soon as you find her.'

'Find who?' Chib was standing in the doorway to Mike's left. Mike ended the call and thrust the phone back into his jacket.

'Nothing,' he lied, making a show of checking his watch. 'You reckon your lads will be here soon? I have other business ...'

'They won't be coming, Mike.' Chib looked up and down the street as if for witnesses. 'I changed my mind. We both know this has nothing to do with them. But from the sweat on your face and the way your hands are shaking, I'd say it *could* have something to do with that call you just took.'

'It was from Westie,' Mike confessed, rubbing at his forehead. The day was muggy. His shirt was sticking to his back.

Chib thought for a moment, then offered a smile. 'He told you about my little scheme?'

'Bit late to start replacing the missing paintings, I'd've thought.'

Chib shook his head slowly. 'You're not even close.'

'So what *are* you up to?' Mike folded his arms, trying to control the tremors.

Calloway sniffed the air as he considered his answer.

'Seems to me,' he eventually offered, 'we're all up to something, Mike – even you. That means there's going to be winners and losers. Want to take a bet which side I'll be on? Now come back indoors and we'll grab a couple of cold drinks.' Chib was holding open the door. Mike stared at it. A scene from *Goodfellas* flashed through his mind – the hero's wife, offered a fur coat by the bad guy. All she had to do was walk into the warehouse and pick one out ...

'I've got to be going.'

Chib seemed to read his thoughts. 'Of course you do, Mike,' he said quietly. 'But do me a favour, will you?'

'What's that?'

A dark smile spread across the gangster's face. 'Tell Westie I hope Alice comes home ...'

29

'Took your time,' Ransome complained into his phone. He was at his desk, doing some actual real work for a change. That was exactly how DS Ben Brewster had put it: *actual real work*. Sarky little bastard. But now Glenn had called, and he had some information for him.

'I've got good news and bad,' the voice rumbled.

'I always like the bad news first, Glenn – that way there's something to look forward to.'

'Chib had you tailed yesterday.'

Ransome's grip on the receiver tightened. 'Why didn't you warn me?'

'Johnno's just told me ...'

Ransome wondered if Johnno had been there when he'd visited First Caledonian's HQ. Had to give the man credit: Ransome hadn't spotted him.

'What time was this?'

'About eleven till three.'

Meaning Chib probably now *did* know Ransome had paid Allan Cruikshank a visit. That might work out okay, actually ... Chib turning the screws one side of the banker, Ransome the other. 'So what's the good news?' he asked.

'I've got four names for you. Chib told me he wanted to talk to them, then changed his mind. I reckon they're the ones he was recruiting.'

Glenn recited the names while Ransome jotted them down. 'So who are they? Bellboy's the only name I seem to know.'

'Same here.'

Ransome sighed loudly. 'Okay then, here's an easy one: where's Chib now?'

'Diamond Jim's in Gorgie.'

'The snooker hall?' Ransome tapped his pen against his notepad, thanked his CHIS, and ended the call. Complaints were rising into the air – someone in the crowded office had farted. Clipboards were being waved like fans; groans and pleas to try opening a window. The smell hadn't reached him yet, but if he rose to leave he knew he would get the blame, so he held his ground and studied the names on his pad.

Billy, Kev, Dodds and Bellboy. Bellboy was a hard wee bastard. The others would be pals of his; known to local coppers, no doubt. Add Mike Mackenzie and Calloway himself and you had a posse big enough to pull off the heist. 'The gang's all here,' he muttered to himself. He still wasn't sure about Allan Cruikshank and Professor Gissing. Oh, he reckoned they knew about it – knew *all* about it. Mackenzie would have taken them into his confidence, bragging, showing off.

Making them complicit.

Making them accessories.

Which meant one of them might just squeal. Ransome

307

hadn't had a proper talk with Gissing yet. From what he'd seen so far of the old man, he thought he knew the type. Probably marched against the bomb in the fifties. Liked the idea of a student riot in '68 but couldn't get anyone else in Edinburgh to agree with him. Typical trendy leftie grown old, still anti-police and unlikely to cooperate as a result.

Leaving the banker, Allan Cruikshank. Ransome intended letting him stew another day, max, before a second visit, trusting the man didn't have an aneurysm in the interim. But now that the detective had started to consider the professor, he realised there might be some fun to be had there, too. Before that, though, he had to pass these four new names around, get a minion to run a check. He'd managed to shift a further half-inch in depth from his in-tray.

'Time for a break,' he persuaded himself, tearing the page from the notebook.

Mike had spent a fruitless half-hour at the art college. Gissing's secretary wasn't around, and neither was he. The door to his outer office was open, but the inner sanctum was locked tight. There was paperwork on the secretary's desk and her phone was ringing. Mike was tempted to pick up, just in case it was Gissing himself, but instead he placed his hand against the coffee mug next to the telephone. There was some residual warmth, meaning the secretary couldn't be far off – unless she'd clocked off early. In the end, he scribbled a note and slid it under Gissing's door. Just the three words – NEED TO MEET

– and his initials. Heading back downstairs, he decided to visit Westie. The basement was labyrinthine. Plenty of students were at work, but no one had seen Westie. Eventually, a bearded and bespectacled man – somewhat older than the undergraduate norm and standing in a studio half filled with hay bales – told him that Westie was in the next room along. Except that he wasn't there. His door was ajar, and inside there were signs of recent activity. Seven paintings, framed and prepped. A couple were waiting for hooks to be hammered into the wall against which they rested. The hooks were on the floor next to them, as was a small hammer. Mike hoped that Westie was on the hunt for Alice. He hoped he wasn't hunched on the sofa in his flat, getting stoned and maudlin.

'You a dealer?' It was the beard from the next studio along. He was wiping his hands down the front of his overalls. It took Mike a moment to realise he probably meant *art* dealer rather than any other kind. Mike shook his head.

'There was a guy here yesterday,' the man continued, 'looked like a bouncer. I asked Westie afterwards who he was. Said he was a dealer. Takes all sorts, I suppose ...' The man was shuffling back towards his work.

'Excuse me,' Mike called to him. 'Is Westie's stuff any good, do you think?'

'Define "good",' the man said, moving out of view.

Mike thought about this and decided that he couldn't. He headed upstairs again and pulled open the door to the outside world. Someone else was coming in, so he took a step back. The man made to pass him with a nod of thanks, then stopped in his tracks. Mike realised who it was: Ransome. He stared at the floor, but too late.

'You're Michael Mackenzie,' the detective said.

Mike pretended to look surprised. 'That's right,' he said. 'Do we know one another?'

'Has your good friend Chib Calloway not mentioned me to you? Or Allan Cruikshank, come to that?' Ransome was holding out his hand, waiting for Mike to reciprocate. Mike shook it.

'Allan?' he asked. 'No, I don't think he has. Do you work with him?'

Ransome laughed. Some students wanted to get past, so that the two men had to move back inside the reception area. 'I'm a police officer, Mr Mackenzie. Surely Mr Cruikshank must have said something to you about me?'

'Why should he?'

'Because I'm investigating your friend Chib Calloway.'

'You keep calling him that, but I wouldn't class him a "friend".'

'What, then? An associate – would that be nearer the mark?'

'We were at school together, Tynecastle High ... bumped into one another again recently.'

'And found that you share an interest in fine art,' Ransome mused. 'Does that explain your trip here today, Mr Mackenzie?'

'I'm a bit of a collector.' Mike offered a shrug. 'Degree show's coming up and I was hoping for a sneak preview.'

Ransome nodded along with this, but looked far from

convinced. 'So you weren't just warning Professor Robert Gissing not to speak to me?'

Mike managed a laugh. 'Why in God's name would I do that?' He cut the end of the sentence off with a little cough. He'd been about to add the word 'Inspector' but couldn't remember if Ransome had identified himself as such. He'd already slipped up with Laura; couldn't have it happen again.

'You don't deny you're friends with Professor Gissing?'

'I certainly know him a damned sight better than I do Chib Calloway.'

'You'll know where I can find him, then.'

'He has an office on the top floor. I can't say for certain he'll be there.'

'Well, I'll try anyway.' Ransome smiled and made to move past Mike.

'What's this all about? First Allan Cruikshank and now Professor Gissing ... you seem to be talking to half my friends.' Mike was trying for levity, but Ransome's stare was steely.

'You can't be that short of friends, Mr Mackenzie, surely.' He seemed about to leave it at that but then paused. 'I've just been to see a man called Jimmy Allison – too much to expect that you know him, too?' Ransome watched Mike shake his head. 'He was the victim of a mugging, night before the Granton warehouse heist. You'll have heard something about *that*, Mr Mackenzie?'

'The heist? Sure,' Mike agreed.

'Well, this curator ... expert in his field ... he lives just a short hike from here, one of those newish blocks of flats by the canal.'

'Yes?'

'Only he wasn't there. His wife's up to high doh – called the police even, only no one thought to tell *me*. He's gone missing, you see. Since yesterday. She's worried he's got concussion.'

Christ, first Alice, and now this ...

'Could have fallen in the canal,' Mike eventually commented.

'Is that what you think, Mr Mackenzie?' Ransome's jaw was jutting. 'Thing about Mr Allison is, he knows Professor Gissing.'

'Half of Edinburgh knows Robert Gissing.' Mike paused. 'You can't think that the professor had anything to do with ...?'

Ransome responded with a twitch of the mouth. 'Only bit of good news I've got for you, Mr Mackenzie, is that having spoken to you, I don't think it's your voice on the tape. But pretty soon now, I'm going to know who made that call.'

'What call?'

'Ask your friend Allan.' Ransome gave a little bow as he moved away. Mike watched him disappear into the building, then made good his escape, breathing hard. Allison was missing: what the hell was *that* about? Maybe concussion was the truth of it. Poor sod *could* have ended up in the canal. A tap on the head was all that had been requested and required, but Mike should have been there to make sure.

Maybe Allan was right – maybe the best thing to do was ditch the paintings and phone in a tip-off. Problem was, Hate still had his hands on one of them. Plus the forgeries might be traceable back to Westie, once identified as such. And Mike would need to convince Westie and Gissing to give *their* paintings back.

You wanted this, Mike, he told himself …

'Oh, Christ, Gissing!' Mike slapped at his forehead. Say the secretary had returned. Say she unlocked the door. The detective would find Mike's note lying there … He slapped himself a couple more times for luck, then noticed that passing students, portfolios tucked under their arms, were staring at him.

'Performance art,' he explained, striding towards another of his favourite thinking places: the Meadows.

By six o'clock, the offices of First Caledonian were closed and Allan Cruikshank felt it safe to start answering his home telephone. Checking his messages, he discovered that the half-dozen calls he'd ignored during the course of the day had all been from his secretary, wondering where he was, asking if he was ill, telling him she was cancelling all his meetings. There was nothing from Mike or Robert Gissing, and nothing from the detective. Allan had turned off his mobile phone, and felt little compunction to switch it on again. He had the feeling that the first person he spoke to, he'd end up telling them everything. Had he been a religious man, he might have headed up Leith Walk to the Catholic cathedral, where confessionals doubtless awaited. He'd even considered Margot, but she would scold him and maybe even laugh at his plight, relieved to have rid herself of such an idiotic specimen.

Allan's stomach had been growling since mid-morning, but he lacked an appetite. He'd sipped eight or nine glasses of tap water, but still felt unquenched. Daytime TV had proved little solace. One chat show aimed at housewives had contained a lengthy discussion about the international trade in stolen art. And at the top of every hour there'd been a news update, which Allan always switched off before the heist could be mentioned. He was shaved and dressed in his work suit, having woken up from a brittle, short-lived sleep determined to go into the office as usual. His resolve had lasted as far as the front door. With his hand ready to turn the lock, he'd frozen. There was a whole terrifying world out there. This flat was his only refuge. Most of the rest of the day he'd stayed by his window, wondering if Ransome or some other authority figure would exit the police station and take the short walk to the tenement, pressing the bell marked CRUIKSHANK. There were no signs of any media interest. Patrol cars came and went. Plainclothes officers ambled outdoors for cigarettes and conversation. With his window open, ears straining, all Allan could ever hear were birds in the trees and the rumble of buses on Leith Walk.

He could take one of those buses and lose himself elsewhere. Or a train south. An aeroplane headed overseas. He had a passport, and a couple of credit cards, only one of them nearing its spending limit. What was stopping him? Did he want to get caught? Ransome's card was in his wallet, giving off some kind of weak radiation so that he was always aware of it. An eleven-digit phone number was all that stood between him and a kind of atonement. What was he so afraid of? Letting Mike and Robert Gissing down? Or the wrath of Chib Calloway? Seeing himself in the newspapers and the dock? Or slopping out with the other inmates? Seated on his living-room floor, his back to the wall, he raised his knees and wrapped his arms around them. His secretary would have left for the evening. There'd be no more phone calls from work. If he could get through the rest of the evening, maybe things would start to look a little brighter. Maybe tomorrow would be better.

Maybe things would turn out all right.

30

It was nearly eleven that night by the time Chib Calloway got home. He'd decided to have a word with his young team after all. A phone call wouldn't do it – had to be face to face. You looked someone in the eye, you pretty much knew if they were lying to you. He got the distinct feeling Mike *hadn't* been lying. Whoever had snatched the daubs, it hadn't been him. That still left plenty of suspects, but then the four kids hadn't seemed like they were lying either.

'We did just what we were told to, no more, no less,' Bellboy had stated, acting as the group's spokesman. Missing half his teeth but still eloquent. Well, compared to his comrades he was.

The rest of the day had been about meetings. There was a lap-dancing club on Lothian Road, lease expiring and current management thinking of shifting their sphere of operations elsewhere. Chib had been asked if he wanted to take the place on as a going concern. Problem was, he got the feeling the best girls would be moving on with their old employers, and it would be tough finding the talent to replace them. Plus there'd have to be a refit, and he'd been quoted seventy-five to a hundred K 'for a really outstanding job, something to get the VIPs in'. Who was kidding who? You always stuck 'VIP' on the windows and the adverts, but your clients were sleazebags and stag groups. Chib had done the clever thing, asked Johnno who the regular doormen were, then given one of them a buzz. As a result of which, he learned that the place had been dying on its feet for the past three months.

'Wouldn't touch it with a bargepole, Mr Calloway.'

End of story.

Chib had been waiting for other calls – from Hate; from Edvard. Kept checking his phone, but nothing so far. At day's end, he had dispensed with the services of Glenn and Johnno, dropping them at one of his own pubs but declining their offer of a 'swift one'. On the drive home, he'd listened to a bit of Dire Straits, always seemed to make the world a better place. He parked the BMW in the driveway – the garage belonged to the Bentley – and stood for a moment, staring up at the night sky's orange glow. He'd bought a telescope once from a place on the Royal Mile but hadn't had much success with it. Light pollution, he'd been told, all the city's streetlamps … So he'd made the shop take it back with a full refund. Turned out later, they'd given him twenty quid too much, which hadn't bothered Chib in the least.

Some of his men wondered why he chose to live on a new-build estate when he could have practically any house in Edinburgh. But those four- and five-storey Georgian piles in the New Town, they just didn't do it for him. Too finicky and formal. Nor did he want rolling acres and stables and all of that, which would have entailed leaving the city behind. He was an Edinburgh boy, born and bred. Not too many could say the same: whole streets filled with English accents, not to mention the students – tens of thousands of them. But this was still Chib's city, and sometimes he couldn't help but love it to bits.

The house – corner plot, detached, ex-show home – was in darkness. A neighbour had warned him he should keep a light burning in the upstairs hall, just to deter the thieves. Chib hadn't bothered pointing out that thieves weren't quite that stupid. Did the neighbour think they skulked around the place wondering why whole families congregated on the upstairs landing? Thinking of it now, Chib had another chuckle to himself. The neighbours were okay, though – never minded when he turned the volume up a bit or had some of the lads and a few girls round for a party. His wife, Liz … the house had been her idea. They'd hardly been there a year when the cancer had started to eat away at her. She'd always got on with the neighbours, and most of them had paid their respects at the funeral. That might have been their first inkling that Liz's husband was a man of substance. The cortege had been vast, consisting mainly of large gentlemen in dark glasses, their movements choreographed by Glenn and Johnno.

Little wonder the neighbours never complained about the noise.

He had yet another little chuckle, then walked up to the door and slid the key into the lock. Another thing about the house: ten-year warranty. And the builders had thrown in an alarm system free of charge … Not that he ever used it. Once he had closed the door behind him, he felt a sense of contentment. This was where he could relax, unwind, forget all his worries. A couple of whiskies and some trash TV. The local Indian restaurant would deliver. So would his favourite pizza place. And if he fancied fish and chips instead, well, the guy there would hop on to his moped, too – just because Chib was Chib. But tonight all he wanted was the whisky – maybe three or four of them, to be honest, just to shut out any lingering memories of Mackenzie, Ransome and Hate. It was the amateurs he was most wary of. People like Hate and Edvard – and even Ransome – they knew how the game was played. Mackenzie and his crew were another matter entirely, and that meant things could go wrong, spectacularly wrong. Of course, Chib himself had been no more than peripheral. If the cops came sniffing, what was there to find? He didn't give a toss if Mackenzie, the banker and the prof all went to jail. What skin would it be off his nose? Then again, it would be a blow, no doubt about it, if Westie went with them ...

With these thoughts running through his head, he couldn't be anything but surprised to walk into the living room, flick on the lights, and see that someone was waiting for him there – though not exactly of his own accord. The man was bruised and battered, bound and gagged. He was seated on one of Chib's dining chairs. It had been dragged away from the table and placed in such a way that it would be the first thing Chib saw when he walked through the door. The man's eyes seemed to be pleading, even though one of them was swollen shut and the other reduced to little more than a slit. There was a crust of blood below the nose, others either side of his mouth and trailing down into the top of his stained shirt from his left ear. Sweat was drying in what hair he had left to him, and his shirt and trousers were torn.

'This is Mr Allison,' Hate said, emerging from the kitchen. He was eating a banana from the fruit bowl.

'I know.'

'Of course you do. You worked him over first time round, didn't you?'

Chib stabbed a finger in Hate's direction. 'Nobody,' he said quietly, 'does this to me. Nobody comes into my house, making all sorts of mess ...'

'I don't think we've made a mess,' Hate replied calmly. He then dropped the banana skin on the floor and ground it into the carpet – Liz's carpet – with the heel of a black cowboy boot.

'You're tangling with the wrong man,' Chib warned him, breathing hard, stoking himself up. Hate ignored him, concentrating instead on Jimmy Allison. The man flinched as Hate's hands reached towards him, but all Hate did was peel the length of silver tape from his mouth.

'You know the rules, Mr Allison,' Hate reminded him. Then he turned his attention to Chib, while resting the palm of his hand against the crown of Allison's head.

'Mr Allison here, as I'm sure you're aware, is a curator at the National Gallery of Scotland. His expertise is in nineteenth- and twentieth-century Scottish art. He has a soft spot for McTaggart, so he tells me, and also Samuel Bough.' Hate bent down a little so his face was level with the curator's. 'Is my pronunciation adequate, Mr Allison?'

With eyes screwed shut in fear, Allison nodded his agreement that it was.

'It is perhaps an irony,' Hate continued, straightening up again, 'that Mr Allison should suffer such similar mishaps in so short a space of time. The perils of the World Wide Web, I'm afraid. His name materialised as someone in the area who might be able to tell me a little more about the painter Samuel Utterson. Our conversation – when we finally got round to it – was illuminating. So much so, that I decided Mr Allison should inspect *Dusk on Rannoch Moor*.'

Chib closed his own eyes for a moment. He knew what that meant – it meant the curator now knew too much. No way Hate was going to let the poor old bastard walk away from this. He started thinking of possible burial sites, and watched as Hate bent down beside Allison again, removing his hand from the man's head and running it down his face until it held him by the chin.

'Now,' Hate was crooning to his hostage, 'why don't you go ahead and share your conclusions with Mr Calloway here? Tell him what you told me, Mr Allison.'

Allison swallowed hard, as if trying to summon some saliva into his parched mouth. And when his lips parted, in the seconds before he started to speak, Chib realised pretty much exactly what the terrified man was going to say …

31

Mike had been dreaming about trouble at sea. For some reason, he had dismissed his crew and set sail alone on a long voyage, only to find himself unable to steer the craft. There were too many buttons and switches and levers. The maps made little sense, though he had marked his destination – Sydney – with a large X. Before long, he had found himself in the middle of a storm and taking on water. The spray stung his face, and he realised he was soaked to the skin. He awoke to find that his face really was wet. Someone was standing over him, holding an empty glass. He sat bolt upright and wiped at his eyes with one hand as he reached with the other for the light switch. When the bedside lamp came on, he saw that it was Chib Calloway holding the glass. Behind him stood two more men, one of whom seemed to be at the mercy of the other.

'What the hell's going on?' Mike spluttered, blinking. 'How did you get in here?'

'My friend Hate seems to have a way with locks,' Chib explained. 'Don't go thinking you're the only one it's happened to. Now get yourself dressed.'

Still disorientated, his mind a jumble of questions,

Mike swung his legs from under the duvet but didn't rise to his feet.

'A little bit of privacy?' he requested, but Chib shook his head slowly, then startled Mike further by dropping to all fours. Tutting, Chib reached beneath the bed and slid out the four paintings.

'Still haven't learned, have you? I half expected to find them behind the sofa. Christ, we could have been in and out of here with them while you were fast asleep.' Chib rose to his feet again and tossed Mike's trousers to him. 'No time for modesty, Michael,' he warned him.

With a sigh, Mike got into his denims, then reached for the T-shirt draped over the back of his chair. 'What's this all about?' he asked, pulling it over his head.

'Know who this is?' Chib asked. Mike didn't think he meant Hate, though he'd recognised him almost immediately. As for the man Hate was holding upright, the man with the pulverised face and blood-soaked shirt, well, Mike had been trying not to look at him at all. He sat back down on the bed and slipped his feet into his shoes.

'Not a clue,' he said, lifting his watch from the bedside table.

'That's nice,' Hate said, meaning the watch. 'Cartier – the Santos 100.' Even Chib turned to stare at him. 'I've got one at home,' Hate explained. Then, to Mike: 'I looked you up on the web, Mr Mackenzie. You're a wealthy man. That's lucky … means we can work something out, perhaps.'

'First things first, eh?' Chib reminded him. Then, turning to Mike: 'I was asking if you knew Hate's friend there … His name's Jimmy Allison – ring any bells?'

Mike's eyes widened. 'The specialist?'

'And now the recipient of *two* beatings, which I think you'll agree is a mite unfair.' Chib paused for effect. 'Especially when nobody's laid a hand on *you*. Now get into that fucking living room. We're going to have words, you and me.' He scooped up all four paintings and marched towards the door. Hate waited for Mike to follow, then brought up the rear with Mr Allison. Mike was still avoiding eye contact. The mugging might have been Gissing's idea, but he'd gone along with it. In fact, he'd told the professor it was 'genius'. Hard now to justify his elation – consequences had been missing almost entirely from the plot. And what the hell was Hate doing with Allison anyway? Mike didn't doubt that the answers were waiting for him in the living room, but feared what else might be there.

Hate dumped the curator on one of the chairs. The man's hands were tied behind him, his mouth covered with tape. Mike thought about pouring himself a drink, but wasn't sure his hand would be steady enough. Besides which, the parched-looking Allison might see it as yet another small torture.

'See this?' Chib was saying. He'd placed the paintings on the coffee table and was pointing towards the sofa. There was another picture displayed there.

'It's your Utterson,' Mike told him. '*Dusk on Rannoch Moor*.'

'That's right. And what did I do with it?'

'You gave it to Hate.' Mike had no idea where the conversation was going.

'And what did Hate do?'

'I don't know.'

'Well, have a think about it, shit-for-brains!'

But Hate had noticed the home cinema system. 'Pioneer,' he commented. 'Good make.'

'Jesus, will you shut up?' Chib yelled at him.

Mike wondered which was preferable: that the sound-proofing stop his neighbours downstairs hearing any of this, or that they decide to call the police to say that something bad was happening in the penthouse. Chib had turned towards him again.

'Come to any conclusions yet?'

Mike rubbed at his eyes again and slicked back his hair. 'At a guess, Hate decided he would verify the painting – despite my warnings. He went to Mr Allison here, who is an authority on the artist, and somehow Mr Allison had an accident and you came to me for help instead of head-ing for A and E.' Mike held Chib's stare for a full twenty seconds. With a growl, the gangster fetched the Utterson from the sofa and held it four inches from Mike's face.

'I'm not exactly the expert here,' he snarled, 'so maybe you'll know better. When exactly was this painted?'

'Early twentieth century …'

'Is that so? Well, maybe you're right. Take a closer look. In particular, tell me what's going on in the bottom left-hand corner.'

Mike didn't know what to expect. The artist's signature, most probably. He saw heather and long blades of grass and a bit more heather.

'Right at the very corner,' Chib suggested. And then

Mike did see it, and he screwed shut his eyes. 'Well?' the gangster prompted him.

'Looks like there's something lying in the grass, half-hidden,' Mike muttered.

'And what does it look like to you, Mike?'

'A condom … a used condom.'

'And can you enlighten us all – why exactly would a painter of Samuel Utterson's reputation have felt the need to add that particular touch?'

Mike opened his eyes again. 'It's Westie,' he stated. 'It's a sort of calling card of his. He copies famous paintings, then adds an anachronism, like an airliner or a mobile phone …'

'Or a condom,' Chib added. Mike nodded his agreement. 'See, Mike, what I can't understand here, what I'm really failing to get my head around, is why you would do this to me. You really thought I was so stupid I wouldn't notice?'

'In actual fact,' Hate interrupted, '*you* did not notice.'

'This is me talking here!' Chib yelled at him again.

'I don't know anything about this,' Mike said. 'Really I don't.'

Chib burst out laughing. 'You can do better than that, Mike!'

'I promise you I can't, because it happens to be the truth.'

'Well, we'll just go and ask Westie then, see what he has to say about it during his last few minutes of life. But before we do that, there's the small matter of my fee. What I'd like from you, Mr Michael Mackenzie, software

326

millionaire, is one hundred and seventy-five thousand pounds – payable in cash. That way, Hate here can return home, job done. The amount of grief you and your lot have caused me, I should be asking for more, but let's open proceedings at one seventy-five ...'

'One eighty,' Hate said. Chib pointed towards him.

'One eighty with the gentleman at the back. Do I hear any advance on one eighty? Shall we say two hundred, sir?' Eyes boring into Mike's. 'Going once ...'

'Just let me fetch my wallet,' Mike drawled, receiving a punch to the gut for his efforts. His knees buckled. He'd never felt anything like it. Brute strength, speed and accuracy. He reckoned he might just about get through the next minute without vomiting on his own floor. Breathing would be good, too ...

Chib had hunkered down in front of him, grabbing him by the hair and yanking his face up so they were eye to eye.

'Am I in the mood for jokes?' the gangster spat. There were flecks of white either side of his mouth.

'I don't keep cash around the house,' Mike said between gasps. 'Never know when someone might come waltzing in. And even ... even making a request to my bank ... it takes time ... time to arrange that sort of money.' He sucked in more air. 'Plus, as soon as I say "cash", alarm bells are going to ring.'

'Money-laundering,' Hate agreed. 'The banks have to inform the authorities.'

'And you're suddenly the Bank of fucking Scotland?' Chib roared at him.

327

'Look,' Mike said, having regained most of his breath. 'Those four paintings are worth a lot more than the money you're asking. Why not just take three of them? Maybe leave me one …' He nodded towards Mr Allison. 'We've got the very man here who can judge them authentic.'

Chib stared at him. 'You've got some fucking nerve, Mike.' Then, over his shoulder towards Hate: 'What do you think? Want to take your pick?'

Hate's response was to walk over to the coffee table, lift the Cadell beach scene, and stick his fist straight through it. Calmly, the huge man then lifted the Monboddo – the glorious portrait of Beatrice – and did exactly the same thing.

'Get the picture?' he said.

'I think so,' Mike answered with a fresh groan. As Chib released his hair, he started to get to his feet, checking that his knees would lock and hold him upright. The painting … Hate had dropped it back on to the table. Was it beyond repair? No way of telling. And there sat Allan's two ugly offerings, pristine and untroubled. 'So what now?' he asked to nobody in particular.

'We wait here till morning,' Chib replied. 'Then a little trip to the bank, followed by a friendly visit to our art-forger-cum-dead-man.'

Mike had picked up the portrait of Beatrice. 'They can't *all* be fakes,' he said, almost to himself.

'All that matters is, mine was,' Chib stated. 'Big mistake.'

'But not *my* mistake, Chib.'

The gangster shrugged his shoulders. 'Nevertheless, you're the one with the money.'

'Which the bank won't just hand over!'

'Ever heard of transfers, Mike? I've got accounts all over the place, in any number of names. The dough goes into one of those, I close the account pronto, and Hate here gets his share.'

Hate didn't look thrilled by this scenario. Mike guessed the man had already been kept waiting longer than he liked.

'Why do you think Westie did it?' Mike asked Chib.

'We'll soon find out.' Chib was studying Allan's two paintings, one in either hand. His own worthless Utterson lay abandoned on the floor, where anyone was welcome to step on it. Chib held one of the Coultons in front of Mr Allison. 'What do you think, Jimmy – are these the real thing for a change?' Without waiting for a reaction, he turned towards Mike. 'Maybe I'll take them with me, unless you've got any objection?'

'They're Allan's, not mine.'

'Then you can sort it out with Allan.'

Mike's eyes were on the curator. He needed a diversion, and poor Mr Allison was just about his only bet. 'I'm really sorry about this,' he said quietly, though he wasn't sure if Allison had much hearing left. 'I mean, I'm sorry for what's about to happen to you ...' The man was staring back at him now as best he could: nothing wrong with his ears. 'They need me,' Mike continued to explain, 'at least for another day or so. I've got money, you see, and they want it. But you, Mr Allison ... they're just about done with you. And Hate doesn't seem to me the type who likes loose ends. You might promise on the heads of your grandkids that you won't go running to the cops, but Hate's not about to take a risk like that.'

'Shut it!' the Scandinavian warned.

'Just thought he ought to know.' Mike turned his attention to Chib. 'I really *don't* know what Westie was playing at. Gissing checked all eight paintings ...' He broke off, starting to get the glimmer of a notion.

'What?' Chib prompted.

'Nothing.'

'Want me to set Hate on you? You've seen what he can do.'

To reinforce the point. Hate himself had taken a few steps forward. It was as much of a chance as Jimmy Allison was going to get. He was up on his feet and running. The first thing he did was shove at the door nearest him, which flew open. As he tried closing it after him, Hate made a lunge into the gap. Chib was starting to laugh, realising that the curator had stumbled into Mike's bedroom – no other exits. Mike, on the other hand, knew exactly what he was doing. He shoulder-charged the off-balance gangster and did some running of his own – down the hall towards the front door. He flung it open and bounded down the stairs, taking them three at a time. As he ran from the building, he was grateful to note that Chib hadn't thought to bring his minders with him. The BMW, however, was locked tight, so Mike flew past it, making for the boundary wall. He scrambled over it, landing in a neighbour's garden. With only moonlight to guide him, he crossed the lawn and heaved himself over into yet another garden. A couple of cats on a windowsill glowered at him, but at least there were no dogs, meaning no barking. One more wall and he was back on the roadway. It was an alley locals used as a short cut, too narrow for vehicles to get down. He took it and kept moving. He patted his trouser pockets, double-checking that he had his wallet. That meant credit cards and cash, but no phone. And no keys to the flat, always supposing he would ever dare to go back. He tried not to think about the havoc Hate and Chib might be wreaking – or how they might then vent their spleen on the hapless Mr Allison …

Mike's own options were limited. He could find a hiding place and wait there till morning, growing chilled in the process, or he could aim for a main road, where a taxi might just find him. After ten or fifteen minutes he paused to catch his breath, crouched low behind a hedge. The houses here were Victorian: three and four storeys high and semi-detached. Some were used as small hotels. For one mad second he considered a late-night check-in. But he was still too close to home.

'No rest for the wicked,' he told himself, regaining a little of his breath. Damage report: his knuckles were grazed and his shins and knees bruised. There was a stabbing pain in his chest and his lungs were aflame. He knew he should head straight to Westie's flat and warn him what was coming. Would Chib know the student's address? If so, it would be *his* first stop, too.

'You could always go to the cops,' he whispered out loud. Would that be enough to save Allison's life? But then what was he going to say? And what was the point, when Chib, Hate and Allison would be long gone from the flat? He screwed shut his stinging eyes, trying to impose some order on his thoughts.

Say Chib knew where to find Westie – Mike's best course of action would then be to head for Allan's. They could always call Westie, see if he was available to answer. Maybe he was wandering the streets, seeking Alice ... And come to think of it, why was Mike so worried? The little bastard had kicked this whole thing off in the first place!

'With a bit of help,' Mike was forced to concede.

From his hiding place, he heard the distinctive diesel chug of an approaching cab. Its brakes squealed as it stopped outside one of the hotels. A middle-aged couple got out, talking loudly, slurring their words. Mike peered over the hedge and reckoned he had a chance. He tried to seem as nonchalant as possible as he emerged from hiding and stuck his arm in the air, gesturing with his hand. The driver had just stuck his roof light back on, but turned it off again when he saw him. Mike climbed into the back, almost overcome by the cloying perfume left behind by the woman. He closed the door and slid the window down, hungry for fresh air.

'Gayfield Square,' he told the driver.

'Lucky you caught me,' the man responded. 'I'd just about made up my mind to call it a night.' He was having trouble finding his passenger in the rearview mirror. Mike had slumped as far down into his seat as he could. 'Had an evening of it, by the look of things,' the driver rattled on. 'Not that there's anything wrong with that. We've all got to let off steam sometime, haven't we? Whole country would explode otherwise.'

'I'm sure that's true.' Mike was on the lookout for a cruising BMW; either that or two hulking figures on foot. But the streets were empty.

'City's been a bit dead,' the cabbie was saying. 'Only real problem I've got with the place – nothing ever happens in Edinburgh, does it, sir?'

32

The look of horror on Allan's face did nothing but deepen as Mike told his story. The only moment of relief came when Mike started to apologise that Chib had got his hands on the Coultons.

'He's welcome to them,' Allan had said, sounding as though he honestly meant it. 'And now that we're shot of all our ill-gotten gains, let's shop Calloway to Ransome.'

'And leave the professor in the lurch? Besides, Chib wouldn't hesitate to tell the police everything, meaning you and me would still go away. Then there's Westie to consider ...'

They tried the student's mobile, but it was only his messaging service. After the beep, Mike left a warning, to which Allan added a yelled coda:

'It's your own stupid fault, you moron!'

Mike ended the call. 'I hope he's out somewhere and not just wasted or blotto.'

'If he knows what's good for him, he'll have left the country.'

'That might not be too far from the truth,' Mike mused.

'Far as I'm concerned, they can go rot, him and his

'grasping girlfriend both.' Allan had started to pace the room, loosening his tie and undoing the top button of his shirt.

'Why are you dressed?' Mike suddenly thought to ask. 'It's the middle of the night.'

Allan studied himself. 'I've not been to bed yet.'

'You wear your tie in the house?'

'Never mind all that – what are we going to do, Mike? That's the bigger question. I knew something like this would happen! I knew it would all go wrong!'

'Well, Allan, the first thing *you* can do is try calming down.' Mike wanted to add that *he* was the one whose house had been broken into. *He* was the one who'd been threatened and assaulted, who'd had to flee for his life, scared witless as he leapt from garden into garden. *He* was the one known to Chib and Hate both – the one they were blaming for *everything*.

Looking at his friend, however, he doubted any of that would help. Allan was muttering about 'all that planning' having 'gone down the drain'. So instead, Mike repeated his first instruction and watched as Allan nodded distractedly, taking off his glasses and rubbing at them with the corner of a handkerchief. Mike poured out more coffee – without offering a refill to his friend – and allowed his head a moment's rest against the back of the chair. He even let his eyelids droop for a few seconds, but the image of Chib Calloway's furious face made him open them again. There was going to be hell to pay, no doubt about it. Allan was staring at him.

'What did Westie think he was doing?' he was asking.

'Could he just not help himself, had to leave some sort of bloody signature? Or was he having a go at us because he really did see us as "the establishment"? And how come he didn't swap the forgery for the original at the warehouse? Was it maybe just a cock-up?'

'The Utterson was in *your* vault, Allan,' Mike stated quietly.

'What?'

'Chib's Utterson was one of the paintings you lifted from the warehouse.'

'Then I don't understand. Are you saying we left the original painting in the back of the van? And what about all these other paintings they're saying have gone AWOL? How many did we end up taking?'

'We need to speak to Gissing,' Mike commented. 'After Westie, he'll be the next person Chib and Hate will want a word with.'

'And then it'll be us?'

'Don't worry, Allan – I'm sure you're parked solidly at the foot of his list.'

This produced a thin smile. 'You might be sorry about that, but I can assure you *I'm* not.' The smile was enough to prise a laugh from Mike, which started Allan off, too. Shoulders heaving, Mike pinched the bridge of his nose. Allan was catching his breath and dabbing at the corners of his eyes. 'How did we ever get into this, Mike?' he asked.

Mike shook his head slowly. 'Never mind that – let's concentrate on how we're going to get out of it.'

'There's always this ...' Allan had produced something

336

from the breast pocket of his shirt. Mike took it and peered at the tiny writing. It was a business card belonging to DI Ransome, dog-eared and smudged, and complete with his mobile phone number.

'Last resort,' he said, tucking it into his wallet. 'First off, we go see Gissing.'

'What if they're waiting for us?' Allan's nerves were beginning to reassert themselves. Mike thought for a moment.

'I've got a plan,' he told his friend. 'We'll have to take your car, though, and I'll explain on the way ...'

The cabbie had been right: Edinburgh was dead. It was a perennial problem with the city. It lacked the boisterousness to be found in larger cities like Glasgow and Newcastle. Lack of traffic, meaning Allan's car would be easy to pick out. But then they did have a slight advantage – Mike knew Chib's BMW by sight, while Chib had no idea what marque Allan favoured. Added to which, Chib had only met Allan fleetingly, and Hate didn't know him at all. Which was why Mike lay flat along the back seat of the Audi, having instructed Allan to be on the lookout for Beamers. Whenever they were forced to stop at junctions and red lights, Allan's hands would tighten on the steering wheel. If a car drew up behind or alongside, his spine would stiffen, his gaze fixed on the windscreen. Mike knew what he looked like – a drunk driver, terrified of the breathalyser. He only hoped Chib and Hate would think so, too.

There were a few taxicabs on the roads, their roof lights

showing them to be still for hire, touting for customers who simply didn't exist. Mike had considered a brief detour past Westie's tenement building, just to check the lie of the land, but he didn't think Allan would be keen, and wasn't even sure it would be worth the risk. Gissing lived just outside town, and that was where they were headed. It was a large detached property in Juniper Green. Mike and Allan had been guests there at a couple of parties, where the professor had introduced them to critics, college lecturers, and a few established artists, one of whom, over dinner, had doodled all over his paper napkin, Allan slyly pocketing the result while the table was being cleared. Mike mentioned the incident now as they left the city centre behind, hoping to keep his friend's mind from other things.

'Always meant to frame it,' Allan responded with a nod. 'My big regret is not asking him to sign the bottom of the bloody thing …'

It was another mile or so before Mike told him they were getting close. 'Pull in to the kerb,' he suggested. They were still a few hundred yards shy of Gissing's house. It sat behind a low stone wall on what had become a main commuter artery into the city. At one time, the wall would have been topped with iron railings, but they had been removed during World War II for use in the manufacture of armaments. Gissing had told the story once over port and brandy.

'Load of bollocks, of course,' he had chuckled. 'They collected tons of the stuff and ended up tipping the whole lot into the Firth of Forth. No way you could use it for anything useful, but it made the civvies feel they'd done their bit for the war effort.'

Mike reminded Allan of this as Allan turned off the ignition and headlights. Allan just nodded and handed over his mobile phone. They'd agreed that if there was a callbox in the vicinity, they'd use that, but there wasn't. Mike punched in the numbers and waited for an answer, then took a deep breath.

'Somebody's breaking in next door!' he yelped. 'I heard the glass smashing. The old guy lives there on his own, so I'm really worried – I'm going to go take a look, but please send a car!' He reeled off Gissing's address, then hung up. 'And now we wait,' he said, handing the phone back.

'They'll have you on tape now,' Allan commented.

'Least of my worries.'

'Almost certainly,' Allan conceded. 'They've got a recording of Westie, too, you know – Ransome played it to me. He says they can identify the make of car from the engine noise.'

'Ransome's full of crap,' Mike retorted, hoping he sounded more confident than he felt. Having spoken with Ransome himself, the detective would have little trouble identifying his voice from a recording. But then he would know Allan's voice, too. It didn't matter. None of it mattered, not in the wider scheme …

A quiet night in the city for Lothian and Borders Police – this was a given, when it took only four or five minutes for the patrol car to arrive, its blue lights bouncing off the surrounding buildings and trees. The lights were switched off when the car came to a stop. No siren either – maybe they didn't want to scare away the felons, or it could just have been a courtesy to the sleeping neighbours. That was Edinburgh for you. Two uniformed officers got out. Neither bothered with his cap. They wore black stab vests over white short-sleeved shirts. One was holding a torch, shining it towards the professor's house. They opened the garden gate and walked down the path towards the front door. Mike waited. There were half a dozen other cars parked along the length of the road and he wanted to see if any of them suddenly sprang into life.

'Nothing,' Allan stated. The two policemen had disappeared around the far side of the house.

'Okay, then, nice and slow …'

Allan turned on ignition and headlights both and they cruised past the house, Mike staring hard from the back seat. The torch was casting huge shadows against the house next door and the garage Gissing had never used since outgrowing his sports car.

'Drive on a bit further and turn around,' Mike commanded.

'Yes, bwana.' Allan signalled into a side street, executed a three-point turn, and started back the way they'd just come. The officers were out front again, trying the doorbell, peering through the letterbox. Mike could hear the crackle of a two-way radio.

'Nobody's home,' Allan said.

'Or else they're keeping very quiet,' Mike added. Not that he believed this for a second. They parked again, opposite side of the road this time and facing away from Gissing's house. It was only a couple of minutes before the patrol car moved off. A few seconds later Allan's phone sounded.

'That'll be the police switchboard,' he reasoned, 'wondering why we're making hoax calls.'

'A good reason not to answer.'

'I wasn't planning to. I can always report the phone as stolen …'

'If you like, but I doubt you'll fool Ransome.'

'True.'

The phone stopped ringing eventually. They sat for another five minutes, just to be sure, and then Mike patted his friend's shoulder.

'Do we park outside?' Allan asked.

'Let's walk. The air will do us good.'

They got out and, still keeping their wits about them, padded quietly towards the house. No lights had come on in any of the neighbouring properties. None of the cars nearby was a BMW.

'Maybe Calloway's already snatched him,' Allan hissed.

'Maybe,' Mike said, not really believing it.

'Cops could come back at any moment.'

'Yes.'

Mike pushed open the wooden gate and headed down the garden path towards the living room's large bay window. He pressed his face to the glass, but the shutters were closed on the inside. There was another window to the left of the front door – Gissing's dining room, where Allan had pocketed the artist's napkin – but the shutters were closed there, too.

'Fingerprints,' Allan whispered in warning, and Mike realised he'd been resting his hands against the glass. He shrugged and headed to the side of the house, taking the path past the garage.

'I don't get it,' Allan said, following close behind. 'Place looks deserted – has he gone into hiding? If he misses the degree show, people will start to get suspicious …'

The rear garden was silent, the moon appearing suddenly from behind a bank of cloud, giving Mike more than enough light. The conservatory was empty – they'd sipped their port and coffee there after dinner, seated on squeaky wicker furniture. But now there was nothing. The space was completely empty. No shutters either at the kitchen window, allowing Mike to peer inside. Again, the room had been stripped.

'He's done a runner!' Allan gasped.

'Only possible explanation,' Mike agreed. He had taken a couple of steps back on to the lawn. It needed cutting, his shoes sinking into it, but one of his heels caught the edge of something more resistant. It was a cardboard sign, attached to a wooden stake. He hoisted it up, so that Allan could see for himself the words FOR SALE, across which another piece of card had been attached. There was just the single word printed there.

SOLD.

'All the way down the damned Limpopo,' Mike muttered, tossing the placard back on to the ground.

33

Dawn was breaking as Allan dropped Mike off outside the apartment block.

'You absolutely sure about this?' Allan asked from the driver's seat. Mike just nodded.

'Go to the cops or don't go to the cops … your call, Allan.'

'You don't want me to come with you?' Allan was craning his neck in the direction of the penthouse. 'In case they're still there?'

Mike shook his head. 'But I appreciate the offer.' Mike hoped he sounded confident. Inside, he was exhausted. 'Remember – whatever you do, don't go back home, not until this is finished one way or the other.'

'So how come *you're* going home?'

'Because I'm the one with the answers.' Mike reached down into the car so he could shake his friend's hand. At the same time, he pressed something into it: the card with Ransome's number. Then he closed the car door and tapped twice on the roof, watching Allan drive off. Chib Calloway's BMW was gone. That didn't mean he hadn't left his goons upstairs, but Mike headed there anyway, taking the lift rather than the stairs. It was only a few hours since he'd been bounding down these same steps, in mortal fear for his life, leaving three men in his flat. One thing he really didn't want to find was the cooling corpse of Jimmy Allison ...

When the lift doors slid open at his floor, he hesitated for a moment. His front door stood gaping, just as he'd left it. Stepping out of the lift and into his hallway, he could see that revenge had been exacted. The paintings that had lined the walls were now strewn across the floor, stomped and gouged beyond repair, as if clawed at by a wild animal. He could well imagine the thwarted gangster, teeth bared, shredding them and jumping on them and feeling so much better afterwards.

'Wonder what I'll tell the insurers,' Mike speculated aloud.

Glass crunched underfoot as he made his way to the living area. No welcoming party, but no sign of a body either. Mike released the breath he'd been holding. Dribbles of blood on the chair where Allison had been sitting, and a small pool of blood soaking into the carpet in Mike's bedroom – evidence that the curator had been punished further for his attempted escape. He wondered at the man's fate, but only for a moment. He knew that really he should be thinking about his own destiny, and how far he could influence it. But fatigue washed over him again and he flung himself on to the sofa. There was a patch of water over by the fireplace and the faintest aroma of urine. Calloway again, or perhaps Hate. The smashed TV was probably Hate's work, too. Allan's Coultons had gone, but Mike picked up the remains of the Monboddo portrait.

Beatrice smiled back at him with what remained of her face. He tried smoothing the tatters of canvas back into place, but chunks of paint flaked off in the process. She looked like a car-crash victim, her face a jigsaw of scars.

'Sorry,' he apologised, placing her beside him.

Aside from the TV and the artworks, not much damage had been done. He got up and went into the kitchen, running himself water from the tap. The TV would have made quite a bit of noise, which might have alerted both men to the fact that there were neighbours who could be wakened. He took the filled glass into his computer room, drinking as he went. Stuff had been thrown on to the floor, but it was nothing a bit of tidying couldn't fix. The keyboard was awash with whisky – the contents of a bottle he'd left on top of the filing cabinet. Okay, so both would need replacing. The cabinet itself, which contained all his bank statements and investment details, remained locked. There was a mangled kitchen knife in the wastepaper bin, which told him someone had tried forcing an entry. The key was in his bedside drawer, meaning no one had bothered to look too hard for it. Desk drawers stood open, contents disturbed or emptied on to the floor. It could all be fixed.

The inventory had given him a little bit of strength. He reckoned if he'd been in charge of ransacking someone's home, he'd have been more thorough, altogether more *professional*. This was petty and spiteful and nothing else. Calloway was forgetting the first rule of business – any business.

You couldn't allow it to become personal.

He found a spare cigarette in a packet in his bedroom and smoked it on the balcony, staring out across the city. Birds were singing, and he thought he could even hear the distant sounds of animals awakening in the city zoo on Corstorphine Hill. When the cigarette was finished, he went back inside and wandered through to the kitchen, opening a cupboard, bringing out a dustpan and brush. His cleaner came in on a Friday but he guessed this was beyond her remit. He swept up some of the glass from the TV screen, but tiredness came crashing down on him once more and he retreated to the sofa. He closed his eyes and thought back to how it had all started – with Gissing's seemingly casual remark: *Repatriation of some of those poor imprisoned works of art ... We'd be freedom fighters ...* Mike mulling over the possibility and then bumping into Chib Calloway again at the National Gallery, the gangster keen to learn about art, or at least about the profits to be made from it. Next thing, Mike was telling Gissing they should do it. He'd intended the target to be one of the city's institutions – a banking headquarters, or maybe an insurance company – but Gissing himself had other plans ...

'Of course you did,' Mike said out loud, raising his glass in a reluctant toast to Gissing's plot.

Of the three of them – Gissing, Allan and Mike – only Mike could have come close to affording the paintings they were planning to steal. So why had he agreed? And not just agreed, but seemed at times to be the chief instigator – why had he done that?

'Because you played me like a fucking Stradivarius, Professor,' he told the empty room. Gissing had been only too happy to take a back seat – less suspicious that way. A year ago, he'd planned the exact same heist, but hadn't had access to accomplices. But then Allan and Mike had come into his orbit, and he had probed at their weaknesses ... assessed their potential.

And found them just about perfect.

And all because Mike had been bored. And greedy, of course – he'd coveted the painting of Beatrice ... one thing he could never own, no matter how wealthy he became. Then there was Calloway himself, offering glimpses of a very different world. At school Mike had craved an invitation to join Calloway's gang, its pecking order dependent on heft and ruthlessness rather than brains and guile. His first year at university, he had gone off the rails. He would pick fights in the Student Union bar. At parties he was unpredictable. He probably only won half his battles, and had eventually come to his senses, had begun to conform, to fit in ...

'Jekyll and Hyde,' he muttered to himself.

One thing still niggled. Had Calloway and Gissing been in cahoots? Mike didn't think so, which meant that bumping into the gangster at the gallery really had been an accident – almost the only unplanned event of the whole scheme. Bringing Calloway into play had been Mike's idea, meaning the current mess was down to him. He was sure that was how Gissing would see it ...

His head was resting against the back of the sofa, eyes closed. During the slow drive Allan and he had taken around Edinburgh, he had explained some of it to his friend, adding his own best guesses and assumptions to the mix. Allan had had to stop the car once or twice, getting things straight in his head, asking questions, refusing – at least at first – to believe what he was hearing, then slapping the palms of his hands repeatedly against the steering wheel.

'You're a rational man, Allan,' Mike had told him. 'You know this is the only way it all makes sense.'

He'd then reminded Allan that Edinburgh had nurtured Sir Arthur Conan Doyle, and that Doyle's creation Sherlock Holmes had spoken the truth when he said that once you had eliminated everything else, whatever was left, however improbable it might seem, had to be the truth.

Mike wasn't sure whether Allan would go to the police. Maybe he, too, would return home, the better to wait out his fate. As for Mike ... well, his fate was already here, announcing itself by way of the one creaky floorboard in the hallway.

But then he heard a voice calling his name, forming it as a question and sounding concerned.

'Laura?' he called back, getting to his feet. He realised he hadn't switched on any of the lights, but none of the blinds were closed, meaning he could make her out well enough as she emerged into the room. 'Just doing a bit of redecorating,' he explained as she stood open-mouthed, arms by her sides.

'What happened?'

'A slight falling-out.'

'Who with? Godzilla?'

He managed a tired smile. 'What are you doing here?'

She had walked further into the room, negotiating her way around the shards of glass. 'I've been trying your phone – both your phones. When you didn't answer, I got scared. Mike, what have you got yourself into?' He didn't really need to answer. She'd picked up the portrait of Beatrice. 'I knew it,' she said with a sigh. 'Knew it was you behind the heist. How did you do it?'

'Switched the originals for copies.' It sounded so simple and straightforward when put like that. 'Which Gissing then verified?'

She nodded slowly. 'So he's in on it, too? But what about the missing paintings?'

He gave a shrug. 'Nothing to do with me, I'm afraid. See, all the time I thought I was part of a team, I was actually being groomed as the patsy.' He managed a dry chuckle at his own hubris. 'Can I offer you a drink?' He raised his own empty water glass.

'No.'

'Don't mind if I ...?' He made for the kitchen again, Laura following. 'Actually, I wasn't the only patsy,' he went on. 'I made the mistake of bringing an outsider on board.'

'Calloway?' she guessed.

'And it was decided that *he* would make the perfect fall guy. He's a philistine, you see, and that's what this whole thing was about – us versus them.'

'So Ransome was right all along ... you and that thug were partners?'

'Allan was in on it, too, and a student at the art college called Westie.'

'Plus Professor Gissing,' she added.

Mike drained the glass before answering. 'Above all of us, yes,' he said quietly. 'Professor Robert Gissing. He's done a runner with all the missing paintings.'

'I've never liked him. And I was never really sure what you saw in him.'

'I wish to Christ you'd tried warning me.'

She was still holding the Monboddo. 'And all for this?'

'All for that,' he conceded.

'Why is it so important, Mike?'

'I think you know the answer.'

'She looks like me, is that what you're saying?' Laura studied what was left of the portrait. 'You do realise there's something slightly creepy about that? I mean, you could just have asked me for a date instead.'

'We had a date, Laura – didn't work out too well ...'

'You give up too easily.' She was still studying the painting. 'Who did this damage?'

'Hate.'

'I'm sorry?'

He realised she didn't know about Hate. 'He's a man Calloway owes money to – it's a long story.'

Neither of them said anything for the best part of a minute. Laura broke the silence.

'You're going to go to jail, Mike.'

'Believe it or not, Laura, jail's way down my schedule of concerns right now.'

Just as Mike had done before, Laura was trying to push the canvas back into something like its original shape. 'She was lovely, wasn't she?'

'She was.' Mike agreed. Then he corrected himself: 'She still is.'

Laura was blinking back tears. Mike wanted to take her in his arms and hold her until the world evaporated around them. He turned round and placed the glass on the draining board, then gripped the edge of the sink with both hands. He could hear her putting down the painting, then her arms were wrapping themselves around him from behind, her head resting against his shoulder.

'What are you going to do, Mike?'

'Run away,' he said, only half joking. 'With you, if you like.' What were the alternatives? He could hand the money over to Calloway and Hate, as requested, but they would always have a stranglehold on him, and he doubted he would see an end to the payments until the well was dry. Then there was the curator – when he turned up dead, or merely mangled, the police would have something else to investigate. And with Ransome's input they'd soon be visiting the penthouse flat with difficult questions for its owner.

'I'll call Ransome,' Laura stated. 'You must see it's the only sensible option.'

Mike turned towards her. 'Sense hasn't played much part in this so far,' he said. Her arms stayed loosely around him. Their faces were only an inch or so apart, but there was something moving in the shadows of the living area. Mike looked over Laura's shoulder.

'Don't let us stop you,' one of Calloway's henchmen drawled, adding for his partner's benefit: 'That's twenty notes I owe you.'

The other man smiled. 'Told you, didn't I? The flat's worth checking, no matter what the boss says.' Then, to Mike: 'You going to give us any trouble, Mackenzie?'

Mike shook his head. Laura had released her grip on him and had swung round to face the two intruders. 'But she's not part of this,' Mike explained. 'Let her go, and then I'll come with you, anywhere you like.'

'Sounds reasonable.' Glenn and Johnno were in the kitchen now. 'Mr Calloway should be fronting one of those TV design shows, shouldn't he?' Johnno said. 'Renovations while you wait ...'

Both men laughed at this. Their eyes were on Laura rather than Mike. He placed a hand on her arm. 'Off you go, then,' he instructed.

'And leave you with these two animals?'

'Just go!' He gave her a little nudge in the back. She glowered at Calloway's underlings.

'I happen to be an old friend of DI Ransome's. Don't think I won't run to him if you touch so much as a hair on Mr Mackenzie's head!'

'Bad move, Laura,' Mike muttered.

'He's right, missy – means you'll be coming with us now ...'

Mike lunged at the two men, yelling for Laura to run. But Glenn brushed him to the floor while Johnno took Laura's arm and spun her round, his other hand muffling her cries. Mike was up on one knee when a foot caught him under the chin, launching him backwards to sprawl across the kitchen floor. Glenn knelt on him, and Mike felt his organs want to explode. There was a grin on the face behind the fist, and then the fist itself connected with the side of Mike's jaw. He had a moment to register that he was spinning towards unconsciousness. He wondered if his boat was waiting for him.

And also if he would ever see Laura again.

34

Ransome woke up and knew that was his lot. It was almost five – not bad for him; he'd managed four and a half hours. Mrs Thatcher, he seemed to recall, had got by on as little if not less. He left Sandra in bed and padded towards the bedroom door, leaving the landing light off as he made his way downstairs. In the living room, he turned on the lamp next to the sofa and reached for the TV remote. He knew that checking the news headlines on Teletext and Ceefax would keep him occupied for ten or fifteen minutes. After that, there was either Sky News or BBC24 on Freeview. He peered through the inch-wide gap in the curtains. The street outside was silent. Years back, whenever he woke up early he took delight in heading into town, stopping at bakeries and all-night cafés, listening to cabbies telling the story of their night's work. But Sandra had started complaining that he was waking her and their neighbours both, revving the car as he reversed out of the driveway. Not too many of his colleagues had ever met Sandra. She didn't like official functions or parties or the idea of the pub. She worked in NHS admin and had her own group of friends – women who would attend talks in bookshops and museums, or plan outings to foreign films and tea rooms. Ransome's theory was that she felt she should have done better at school, maybe gone beyond secretarial college – a university degree, perhaps. She gave off an air of quietly simmering dissatisfaction with her lot, and he had no wish to compound this with early-morning engine noise, even though none of the neighbours had actually ever complained to him about it.

The kettle might wake her, too, so he stuck to a glass of milk and a couple of indigestion tablets. The faint peeping noise in the hallway he put down to a small bird outside, but when it persisted he knew he was wrong. His jacket was hanging up behind the front door. The coat rack had been Sandra's idea, and woe betide if he draped his clothes over the end of the bannister or on the backs of chairs. His mobile was in the inside pocket. The noise wasn't because it needed charging. It was a message from the previous evening. Donny was a guy Ransome knew who worked at the Criminal Records Office. The message was succinct: PHONE ME. So, having gone back into the living room and closed the door tight, that was exactly what Ransome did.

'Donny, it's me.'

'Christ, man, what time is it?'

'I just got your message.'

'It can wait till morning.' Donny was coughing and spluttering.

'Spit it out,' Ransome commanded.

'Give me a break.'

Ransome listened as Donny got out of bed. A door opened and closed. More coughing and loud sniffles.

Another room had been reached, the rustle of papers.

'Got it here somewhere ...'

Ransome was at his own window, staring at the outside world again. A fox cantered down the middle of the road, for all the world as if it owned the place. This time of day, maybe it did at that. Ransome's street was quiet and tree-lined. The houses were from the 1930s, which kept prices low compared to the Georgian and Victorian properties only half a mile away. The area had been called Saughtonhall when Ransome and Sandra had moved in, but solicitors these days tended to say Corstorphine or even Murrayfield instead, in the hope of adding a few thousand to the price. Sandra and Ransome had even joked for a time about whether their street qualified as 'South Murrayfield' or 'South South Murrayfield'.

Any further south and we'd be on the doorstep of Saughton Prison ...

'Take your time, Donny,' Ransome muttered into the phone.

'Here we go.' A final flourishing of paperwork. 'Right nasty piece of work.'

'Who?'

'The Viking with the tattoos – you asked me to track him down, remember?'

'Of course I did; sorry, Donny.'

'His name's Arne Bodrum. Hails from Copenhagen but spends most of his time elsewhere. Served two years for what we'd probably call GBH. Ran with the Hell's Angels and is now reckoned to be an enforcer for same, specifically a chapter whose HQ is Haugesund in Norway. It's thought they make their dough running drugs into countries like Germany and France – not to mention the UK.'

'That much I already know, Donny. What else have you got?'

'More along the same lines, plus the guy's mug shots. The whole lot'll be on your desk in about three hours.' Donny paused. 'Can I go back to my pit now?'

'Sweet dreams, Donny.'

Ransome ended the call and placed the phone on the windowsill. Hate was acting as a go-between. No ... more than that ... he was *an enforcer*. Glenn had said Calloway owed money on a drug deal, the creditors being an overseas Hell's Angels chapter. It meant Chib was hurting, needing a quick injection of cash. And who did they both know had cash? Step forward, Mike Mackenzie. Or First Caly, come to that – and hello again, Allan Cruikshank. Ransome reckoned this was the sort of thing he could take to the Chief, ask again for a full-scale surveillance and maybe some of those search warrants. He wasn't stepping on Hendricks' toes – there was no need to mention the heist – so there'd be no reason to turn him down. If a budget couldn't be found, Ransome would do the whole thing by himself, gratis and for nothing.

All he needed was permission.

He had walked away from the window and now had his back to it, which was why it took him a moment to realise his phone was vibrating. Incoming call: had to be Donny with something else, maybe something crucial. But the sill was narrow and the phone fell to the floor just as Ransome was reaching out towards it. The casing went one way and the memory chip another and the thing went dead. Cursing under his breath, Ransome reassembled the phone, then had to switch it on again. The screen had suffered a fracture, but the LCD display behind it was readable. No messages. He went to last call, didn't recognise the number, but then he didn't know Donny's mobile number, did he? Hit 'callback' and pressed the phone to his ear.

'Thanks for getting back to me, Inspector. I think we were cut off ...'

It wasn't Donny's voice. Ransome couldn't place it at all. 'Sorry, who is this?' he asked.

Silence at the other end, as though options were being weighed – last chance to hang up, et cetera. And then a clearing of the throat, and when the name was announced Ransome put the face to it straight away. After all, hadn't he just been thinking about the man? Could this really be happening? Had he dozed off and this was all some bizarrely satisfying dream? First Arne Bodrum, and now this ... Ransome sat himself down and crooned his opening words into the mouthpiece.

'Something must be troubling you, Mr Cruikshank. Why don't you tell me all about it ... ?'

'Nice of you to drop by,' Chib Calloway said.

Opening his eyes, Mike knew where he was: the abandoned snooker hall. Chib was standing in front of him. Some way off, Hate was studying the positions of the balls on one of the tables. Five chairs had been arranged in a line, and Mike was seated to the far right, hands tied behind his back, feet strapped to the chair legs. He looked to his left and saw Laura next to him, similarly bound. He gave a low groan of apology in her direction, which she acknowledged with a slow blinking of the eyes. Westie was next along, his own eyes brimming with tears, then came Alice, whose sharp gaze was nothing but venom with Calloway as its target. At the furthest end of the short, unhappy row sat the hapless curator, Jimmy Allison, looking dazed and bereft, and whose only crime had been to become a recognised expert in his field.

'Wake up, dummy,' Calloway was telling Mike. 'Time to get a good smacking.'

Hate had grabbed one of the reds in his paw and was making his way towards the chairs. He tossed the ball as he walked, catching it each time with a slap of his cupped palm.

'Lots of bodies to dispose of,' he speculated.

'No shortage of resting places,' Calloway assured him. 'We've got the North Sea and the Pentland Hills, not to mention all those building sites around Granton ...' Then, to Mike: 'I've already had a fulsome apology from Westie here.' He made to pat the young man's cheek, causing Westie to flinch and screw his eyes shut in expectation of something harder. At the sight of this, Calloway gave a low chuckle and turned his attention back to Mike. 'But not much by way of explanation.'

'You expect me to fill you in?'

'Before we fill *you* in,' Hate growled.

'I hope there's no extra charge for the lousy puns,' Mike said. Hate wrapped his fingers around the snooker ball and drew back his fist.

'I told you, Hate – he's mine!' Calloway snarled, stabbing a warning finger towards the Scandinavian.

'You're not in a position to order me around,' Hate told the gangster.

'My town, my rules,' Calloway spat back. It was like watching two caged animals, feral, territorial and deadly.

Hate spat on the floor, then channelled some of his pent-up anger towards the ball, hurling it at the wall behind the chairs. When it landed – out of Mike's sight line – it failed to roll, telling him it had split in two.

Calloway leaned down so he was level with Mike's face.

'My boys tell me you were quite the Sir Galahad with your lady friend ... But how smart was it to go back to your damned flat?'

'About as smart as kicking and slashing your way through half a million quid's worth of art instead of taking it with you.'

'The old red mist descended,' Calloway explained. 'Besides which, what the fuck do I want with paintings?' He rose to his full height and walked along the line till he was in front of Westie again.

'Leave him alone!' Alice raged. 'You touch him again, I'll rip your balls off!'

Calloway gave a whoop, and even Hate offered a lop-sided grin of admiration.

'She's a tough old broiler, Westie, isn't she?' Calloway asked. 'Easy to see who wears the cock in your house ...' Then, for Mike's benefit: 'Westie here tells me it was

Gissing's idea to switch paintings on me. He doesn't seem to think you knew anything about it.'

'You've been to Gissing's house?' Mike waited for the gangster to nod. 'Then you'll have seen the evidence. I'm guessing he left town yesterday. Maybe even before that – explains why he couldn't be reached on the phone. I thought he was lying low, but actually it was more like deep cover. That house of his must've been on the market for weeks, meaning he knew exactly what he was doing.'

'And what was he doing, Mikey?'

'Let the others go and I'll tell you.'

'Nobody goes anywhere,' Hate interrupted, stabbing a finger in Mike's direction. The finger was encased in sleek black leather. A driver's glove. Hate had started to pull them on, one for each hand. Mike knew what that meant: some work – manual work – was about to be done. And no fingerprints. He focused his attention on Calloway.

'One thing you need to know – both of you. I'm not afraid of you. Maybe I was once, but not now.'

Nor was this mere bravado – almost the only thing he had left, it seemed, was a sudden and irrational lack of fear. The school bully was right there in front of him, and Mike wasn't flinching. He was aware of the others watching him as he spoke: not just Laura, Westie and Alice, but even Allison, who was leaning forward, straining against his restraints for a better view. Hate, too, hands now gloved to his satisfaction, was acting the spectator.

'You *should* be afraid,' the gangster was saying.

'I know,' Mike agreed with as much of a shrug as his bonds would allow. 'But somehow it's not working.

361

Maybe it's because of all that money you need me to get for you.'

'I can lay my hands on plenty of cash without your help!' Calloway snarled, but not even Hate looked convinced by the outburst.

'Let them go,' Mike stated calmly. 'I can tell you the whole story once they've walked out of here.'

'Not a chance,' Hate growled.

'What do I need the "whole story" for, anyway?' Calloway added. 'I know I've been cheated, and that's all that matters.' He straightened up and started rolling his shoulders, limbering up for the task ahead. 'Which one do you want to kill first, Hate?'

'The strongest,' came the answer. 'Always leave the weakest until last.'

'Wise words,' Calloway conceded. 'Probably means we should start with Westie's little ball-breaker.'

'Bring it on,' Alice said, baring her teeth.

'With pleasure, sweetheart.'

Mike realised that he had to start telling the story – it was the only thing that might postpone all their ends.

'You're not the only one who's been conned,' he blurted out to Calloway. 'We all have – in as much as we've been set up for a fall. Gissing planted a seed in my head, then watered it by coming up with the notion of switching paintings. The plan was so well conceived, he'd obviously been thinking about it for a long time. In fact, he said as much. But suddenly he had an absolute need to put it into action, and that meant finding allies – allies who'd then take the fall on his behalf.'

'You and your flaky friend Cruikshank? Don't go think-ing I've forgotten about him, by the way.'

Mike nodded, then wished he hadn't. When Glenn had thumped him, he'd done a sterling job.

'Me and Allan,' he said, swallowing back the nausea. 'Gissing already had his eye on Westie for the role of forger. He was wary of *you* becoming involved, though – it raised the stakes, I suppose. But he soon changed his mind. At the time, I thought it had been too easy to persuade him, but now I can see his thinking – out of all of us, you were the perfect fall guy, someone the police would love to nail. But then you went and asked for a painting ... Well, as far as he was concerned you were one of the great unwashed. He couldn't let you have a precious original – that would have been sacrilege. At the same time, he doubted you'd ever spot a fake, so he made Westie here prepare an extra copy without the rest of us knowing.'

Westie was nodding. He picked up the story. 'The pro-fessor came to see me. He told me he needed an extra copy of the Utterson, and no one was to know about it. I asked him why and he told me I was better off staying ignorant. That "ignorant" rankled – I knew it was the way he'd always thought of *me*.'

'So you added one of your little secret flourishes to the finished article?' Mike guessed.

Westie nodded some more. 'We made the switch while you and Allan were back in the warehouse doing the final check. The professor hid the real Utterson inside the back of one of the paintings he'd chosen for himself – it was a nice snug fit.' And then, for Calloway's benefit: 'Honest,

363

Mr Calloway, if I'd known it was meant for you, I'd never have agreed.'

Mike watched the gangster pat Westie's cheek again. He was thinking of all the other clues, clues he should have spotted: the plans Gissing had drawn up, with so much thought and detail having gone into them, and the professor's own comment when Mike had said that the plan itself seemed perfect – *most plans do, when you first think of them* ... Yes, Gissing had had the heist in mind for some considerable time, but not just so as to steal some paintings – he'd been doing that for years without anybody noticing. Sneaking the occasional small masterpiece out with him when he visited the warehouse on one of his many 'research' trips. But then he must have learned of the upcoming inventory – *a full and thorough inventory* – the first one in years. He'd realised then that the missing paintings would not be overlooked. So he had brought forward his retirement without telling anyone outside the college. His house had been placed on the market. And then he'd gone fishing for companion plotters. When he'd first laid out the plan, he'd made sure to tempt Mike with the Monboddo and Allan with the prized Coultons – appealing to their avarice ... When the inventory's discrepancies were noted, the police investigation would zero in on these dupes – after all, hadn't they just pulled off a heist? Stood to reason they'd be the ones with the missing paintings, leaving Gissing himself tucked away somewhere out of sight. Somewhere abroad was Mike's guess. It wouldn't be anywhere the professor had discussed; would be some secret place that he held dear. He'd mentioned Spain, then

364

changed his mind and said the west coast of Scotland – one of his very few slip-ups, and Mike should have realised at the time what it meant.

'I'm getting bored with this,' Hate complained into the silence. 'Time to do some killing.'

'Gissing's the one you want,' Mike stressed, eyes boring into Calloway's. 'When you're finished with me, promise you'll not forget that.'

'I'll remember,' the gangster allowed. 'But as of this moment, I'm inclined to agree with Mr Hate here – there's been far too much talking.'

'About time,' Hate stated, punching his fist into the palm of his other hand. Mike turned his head towards Laura. He was almost close enough to kiss her goodbye.

'Sorry I got you into this.'

'You should be.' There was plenty of iron left in her voice. 'So the least you can do now is save the day.'

His eyes stayed locked on hers, and eventually he gave a slow nod, pain pounding through his brain. The nodding appeared confident and the eye contact was good. His senses seemed heightened, just as in the immediate aftermath of the heist itself, and he was with the woman he loved. This is living, he thought. Shame about the rest of it ... Save the day, Laura had demanded. Who was he to argue?

In fact, the only thing he lacked was a plan.

Any sort of plan.

35

Johnno and Glenn stood guard on the pavement outside the snooker hall. Johnno was smoking, looking twitchy.

'What's up?' Glenn asked.

'Why are we stuck out here?'

'Might work better for us – we can't be called as witnesses.'

'You think Chib's going to top every single one of them?' Johnno's eyes had widened, but only a little.

'Seems likely.'

'And what the hell's Hate doing here? I still owe him for what he did to my arm.'

'Some wars you just have to walk away from, Johnno.'

Johnno stared at him. 'Walk away?'

Glenn shrugged. 'Whatever the mess in there ends up being, guess whose job it'll be to mop things up after?'

'Ours,' Johnno agreed, flicking the remains of his cigarette on to the roadway. 'What's it all about, anyway? Have you figured it out yet?'

'I've got an inkling – but like I say, best *not* to know.'

Johnno cupped the front of his trousers. 'I'm bursting. Reckon I can ...?' He nodded towards the door of the snooker hall. There was a toilet in there, but he'd have to walk past everyone to reach it. Glenn shook his head slowly.

'If I were you,' he said, 'I'd try over there.' He gestured towards the pend on the other side of the street.

'Fair enough.'

Glenn watched Johnno cross the road, watched as he headed down the lane and disappeared behind a row of communal bins. He'd already retrieved his phone from his pocket. Once Johnno was out of sight, he flipped it open and started punching numbers.

Mike wasn't at all ready to die, and if he was going to live, so was Laura. It was his fault she was here. She'd only come looking for him because she'd been worried, which meant she cared about him. Least he could do in return was save her life, or (more likely, admittedly) perish in the attempt.

The air in the snooker hall felt electric. Hate had taken a step forward, and Chib Calloway didn't look like doing anything other than aiding and abetting. Alice had just stopped cursing the pair of them out, having received a slap for her efforts. Westie had bitten his lip, saying nothing, so she'd vented her spleen on him for another half-minute or so. At the far end of the row, Jimmy Allison looked beaten by life and accepting of his fate. It seemed to Mike that he'd lost some dignity and control of his bodily functions to go with the blood on his shirt front.

'I've been in this goddamned country too long,' Hate was saying. 'All I want to do is go home – whether I get my client's money or not.' He'd turned towards Calloway, a sudden sneer making his face even uglier. 'I know Edvard will be keen to hear about the fake you were going to try to fool him with.'

'I've told you a dozen times, I didn't know it was a fake!' Calloway growled. But then his own face lost some of its tension as he realised what Hate had just said.

'You haven't told him?' he asked with ominous calm.

'Just get me the money and he need never know.'

'But I'm already in negotiations,' Calloway was saying. Mike saw that the gangster was looking towards Westie. Yes ... because the Hell's Angels back in Scandinavia did a lot of international trading, and fine art made for useful collateral. On Calloway's instructions, Westie was going to make more fakes with which to dupe Hate's employers ... and those same employers didn't know as yet that they'd been tricked with the Utterson ...

Mike was impressed. He could see Calloway calculating all the possibilities and permutations in an instant. And when he made his move, it was lightning fast, too. Hate had turned away from him to face the line of hostages again, trying to decide who would be first to die. He didn't hear the snooker cue being lifted from the table, didn't feel the change in air pressure as it was swung at the back of his head. The force of contact snapped the wood in half with a crack, splinters falling into Mike's lap. Alice screamed, and Laura gave a little yelp. The giant stumbled and almost fell on top of Mike, but he didn't go down, not quite. Calloway started raining blows from behind, yelling for his henchmen to come and help him. The door opened and one man ran in.

'Johnno!' Chib commanded. 'Whack him hard!'

'About fucking time,' Johnno snarled, joining the fray. He got a good kick at the doubled-over Hate, blood spurting from the giant's nose. But Hate was already fighting back, heaving Calloway halfway across the room with a shoulder charge. Mike realised that Alice was screaming again, but not in horror at the events unfolding right there in front of her – she was shouting for help, struggling against her bonds. Mike saw why: she was staring wide-eyed at the open door, beyond which lay the outside world, so reassuringly unchanged and unthreatening. A pavement, a lamp-post, the roadway ... Anyone passing would be bound to notice and fetch help. Maybe a passenger in a car, or a cruising cab-driver ... It had dawned on Westie, too. He wrestled with his chair until it tipped over. He started wriggling, using any purchase he could find, slithering and jerking his way towards anywhere that wasn't here.

'Don't leave me!' Alice yelled at him.

'I'll get help,' he gasped, the heel of one shoe squeaking against the floor. As he moved, he left a slight trail in his wake and Mike was reminded – suddenly and absurdly – of a snail beginning some epically slow journey. He turned his head to check on Laura, but her eyes were on the wrestling match in front of her. There were flecks of blood on her cheeks, nose and forehead – Hate's blood.

As for Jimmy Allison ... his shoulders were heaving with a crazed species of laughter at the unfolding spectacle as Johnno launched himself on to Hate's back, one arm around his throat. Calloway was upright again and

369

preparing to charge. Mike was still impressed by the fluidity of the man's thinking. An ally had become an enemy in the blink of an eye. He couldn't be sure, though, whether Hate's demise would necessarily lead to the group's salvation, which was why he started working away at his own bonds. Westie was halfway to the door now, and Alice was still crying out for help. Calloway had a question for Johnno.

'Where the hell's Glenn?'

'Thought he was right behind me.' The reply came from between gritted teeth, as Johnno continued to squeeze the life from Hate. But then the giant powered himself backwards into one of the tables. Mike thought he could hear a sharp cracking sound – not dissimilar to the snapping of the cue – as Johnno's spine connected with the table's wooden rim. The arm fell from around Hate's neck, and as Hate stepped away, Johnno slumped to the floor, face twisted in pain. Calloway meantime had aimed a kick where it hurts most, reminding Mike of school playground tactics. But it seemed to have little effect, and Hate swiped his gloved fist hard across the gangster's jaw. The follow-up punch felled Calloway, knocking him unconscious to the floor. Hate took only a couple of moments to gather himself. Bubbles of blood appeared at both nostrils and his breathing was ragged. His face was near puce from the attempted strangulation. He staggered towards the door and slammed it shut, then bent down to drag Westie away from all hope of freedom. Westie screamed in agony as he was pulled along the floor by his hair. Hate hauled the chair upright again between Laura and Alice.

A clump of Westie's hair fell from his gloved hand as he removed it. Alice was yelling obscenities at the giant, but he ignored her. Instead, he reeled back towards Calloway and Johnno, assessing any level of threat they might still present. Satisfied, he turned his attention towards Mike and the others.

'I'm going to kill you all,' he spat, his voice hoarse. 'And then I'm going home.'

'Your employers won't like it,' Mike said coolly, 'if you don't take them their money. Remember – I'm the guy who can deliver it.'

But Hate was shaking his head. 'A photograph of the corpses will suffice.'

'You don't think the police will show an interest?'

'I'll be long gone.' He looked around him again. 'Calloway has to die, and there can't be witnesses.' Hate pointed towards Mike. 'I'll be saving you till last, my friend.'

'Does that make me the weakest?'

'You're *all* weak! This whole city is weak!' Hate threw his head back ceilingwards and gave a little groan – not, it seemed to Mike, of pain, but rather of dismay at the blunt stupidity encountered so far on his adventure. 'Someone like Calloway … he's an idiot, and yet somehow he gets to be in charge? You're fools, the lot of you.'

'You might have a point.'

'Oh, I do.' A grin spread across the blood-smeared face as Hate reached behind him, into the collar of his shirt. Slowly he pulled out a slender, gleaming knife and started to survey his kingdom. Calloway, unconscious on the floor, blood trickling from one ear. Johnno in a heap, conscious

371

but wishing otherwise, moaning in agony. And the five trussed figures in their chairs.

'Best thing you can do,' Mike stated, 'is walk away from here before Glenn comes back with the cavalry.'

'Glenn?'

'Calloway has *two* bodyguards, remember? You might not have much time.'

'He'll find his boss dead, along with the rest of you.'

Mike came to the conclusion that at long last he had run out of options. His only hope was to charge at the man, try ramming his head into his stomach. He knew it was hopeless, but what else was there? Hate himself seemed to realise this and gave a soft chuckle. Mike turned towards Laura. She was trying hard to hold back the tears.

'Not exactly how I'd hoped things might work out for the two of us,' he apologised.

'As second dates go, I'll admit I've had better.'

Westie, who'd started struggling against his bonds again, had keeled over on to the floor for a second time. Alice wasn't far off joining him. Allison was still chuckling to himself, eyes screwed shut, sanity evaporating. And all of this for a few paintings, Mike thought. All because I was bored, pampered, infatuated, and greedy.

And tricked by the greater villain – Professor Robert Gissing.

It galled him to think that Gissing was dodging all of this, enjoying his retirement surrounded by however many masterpieces. Cocktails on the patio and lazy days in the sun …

'One last thing,' he said, gaining the murderous giant's

irritated attention. 'I've told Calloway and now I'm telling you – Robert Gissing is the man who conned all of us. Find Gissing and you'll have your hands on an art collection worth millions. Remember to tell your client that when you get home.'

Hate thought for a moment, then nodded slowly. 'Thanks for the tip,' he said. 'And to return the favour, I'll make this quick – not painless, maybe, but quick ...'

He placed himself in front of Laura, leaned down a little towards her, and drew back the knife. Laura's scream drilled into Mike's ears. He squeezed shut his eyes, straining one last time at his bonds. But then there was another sound, that of a door being kicked in. He opened his eyes to the sight of figures streaming through the doorway, dressed in black stab vests and some of them wearing visored helmets. On each chest, the word POLICE was picked out in white lettering. The officer at the front had dropped to one knee, and Mike realised he was pointing a pistol at Hate. Hate froze for a moment, the knife poised. Laura's mouth was still gaping, though her screams had been silenced by the arrival of the cops. Hate turned his head so his eyes met Mike's. The look was worth a thousand words. The officers were barking out a repeated order and eventually the giant complied. The knife fell to the floor with a clatter and he raised his arms above his head, kneeling down as instructed, sliding his hands slowly around to the back of his head, awaiting the restraints.

The officers fell on him. The pistol was reholstered only after the handcuffs had been securely fastened.

'We were told there are firearms,' one of the faces behind a visor stated.

'I've not seen any,' Mike told him.

'Get me out of this bloody chair!' Alice yelped.

Mike was looking towards the doorway. Glenn, the missing henchman, was standing there. So was Detective Inspector Ransome. Ransome was whistling a little tune, hands in trouser pockets, as he stepped inside. He stared down at Calloway, then crouched down in front of him and checked his neck for a pulse. Satisfied, rubbing a little of Calloway's blood between thumb and forefinger, he stood up again and headed for the row of chairs.

'Anybody hurt?' he asked. For some reason, the question made Laura laugh.

'Use your eyes, Ransome,' she said. 'The guy at the end is barely breathing!'

Ransome ordered two officers to get the curator into an ambulance, then stopped to pick up Hate's knife, checking it for blood. When he saw it hadn't been used, he sliced through the tape with it, so that Laura's hands were free. Despite Alice's pleas, Mike was next. Ransome handed the knife to Laura and asked her to do the honours. She looked towards Hate and then at the knife, but Ransome tutted.

'Enough drama for one day,' he chided her. 'Leave Mr Bodrum to us.'

'He might be Bodrum to you,' Mike commented, 'but he'll always be Hate to me.'

As Laura began cutting Alice and Westie free – the latter complaining that he'd broken his arm when he fell

– Ransome helped Mike rid himself of the ties around his ankles, then had to help him to his feet.

'Better?' the detective asked.

Mike nodded his agreement. He felt light-headed and his headache was intensifying. 'How did you find us?' he managed to ask.

'Glenn Burns. But to be honest, we were already on your trail ...' The detective turned his head towards the doorway, Mike following suit. Allan was standing there, looking slightly sheepish. When Mike smiled and nodded, he came inside, taking in as much as he could.

'Christ, Mike,' he said, wrapping his arms around him. Mike whispered into his ear.

'How much have you told him?'

When the embrace was finished, the look in Allan's eyes was clear.

Everything.

'Sorry,' he said.

'Don't be,' Mike answered.

'I hope it was all worth it,' Ransome mused.

'Ports and airports,' Mike said, grabbing the detective by the arm. 'You've got to stop Robert Gissing leaving the country.'

'Might be a bit late for that, Mr Mackenzie. Besides, it's not your little Ladykillers gang that concerns me – a DI called Hendricks will be wanting to speak to you about all that.' Ransome nodded in Calloway's direction. 'There's the prize I was after ... so I suppose really I should be thanking you for delivering it.' With a smile, he moved off, just as the paramedics arrived. Hate was on his feet and, flanked by policemen, about to be escorted outside.

'Looks like you won't be going home just yet,' Mike called out to him.

'I'm not the only one,' the giant spat back.

'There's something in that,' Laura conceded.

36

'You *will* testify against Calloway?' Ransome asked.

Mike was being led towards a waiting police van, Allan next to him. Handcuffs had not been thought necessary. The DI called Hendricks had turned up, looking grumpy. Mike had watched Ransome explain the situation to him, which had done little to lighten his colleague's mood but had given an extra spring to Ransome's own step afterwards.

Mike shrugged now. It was a good question, after all. 'Should really be the other way round,' he told Ransome. 'After all, *I'm* the one who dragged him into it.'

'But you *will* testify.' It sounded like a statement of fact rather than any kind of question. 'If you do, it'll go easier for you.'

'Meaning what?'

Ransome shrugged. 'Six years instead of eight. You'd be out of jail inside three. I'm sure you can afford the best lawyers in the land, Mr Mackenzie, and it shouldn't be too hard for them to paint a picture of you in court as a naïve playboy who got in with the wrong crowd. Maybe a friendly psychoanalyst can plead diminished responsibility.'

'Meaning I'm not in my right mind?'

'Not at the time, no.'

'How about me?' Allan asked. 'Where do I figure in this?'

'Same goes, but with the added factor that you did the right thing and turned yourself in, and in the process helped save five people from being tortured and killed.'

'Seven, actually,' Mike corrected the detective. 'Hate wasn't about to leave Chib and Johnno alive.'

'See?' Ransome told Allan. 'You're practically a hero.'

An ambulance was parked next to the police van, and Jimmy Allison was being stretchered into it, an oxygen mask tied to his face. Another stretcher would be needed for Johnno. One man required a blood transfusion and some stitches, plus a potential lifetime of psychological counselling.

The other needed a new spine.

Mike wondered again at the sheer nerve of Robert Gissing: stealing paintings for years, never detected but about to be undone by something as straightforward as an inventory. Gissing, railing against the storing from view of so many important and beautiful works, making the same argument to practically everyone he met ... in order to seek out a few gullible souls who might be duped into doing something about it. Then seeing to it that Allison was attacked so that he himself would be on hand to verify a series of fakes.

It was sublime, but so much could have gone wrong. Nevertheless, it was the only roll of the dice left to Gissing. And against all the odds, it had worked. And now Mike would go to jail and Allan would go to jail and Westie would go to jail. Allan looked devastated, but Westie didn't seem too bothered. Mike had heard him inside the snooker hall, explaining to Alice that prisoners got to do art classes and everything.

'Might well make the Westie brand even more valuable when I come out. Notoriety is something you can't just buy off the shelf ...'

Maybe he had a point at that, but it hadn't stopped Alice from giving him a solid punch to his damaged arm, so that he'd howled and doubled over while she turned and walked away.

She would be taken in for questioning. They would all be questioned, especially Hate, who even now was struggling against his restraints and his captors both. He was like a force of nature, and Mike was thankful the giant was being afforded a van of his very own.

'If we all go to jail,' Mike asked Ransome, 'will we be in the same wing as Calloway and Hate?'

'I doubt it. We'll find you the softest option possible.'

'Even so, Calloway's bound to have friends on the inside.'

Ransome gave a little chuckle. 'I think you're overestimating him, Mr Mackenzie. Chib's got more enemies than friends behind bars. You'll be fine, trust me.'

There was a shout from nearby. It was Glenn Burns. He was being led in handcuffs to a waiting patrol car.

'You fucking well owe me, Ransome! You owe me *everything*!'

Ransome ignored the outburst and concentrated on

Mike instead. The van doors stood wide open. They led to an inner cage with two bench seats.

'So Gissing's got all the missing paintings?' Ransome asked.

Mike nodded. 'Calloway's got a couple of the ones we swapped, if he hasn't already trashed them.'

Ransome nodded. 'Mr Cruikshank here told me all about them. And Westwater and his girlfriend have another?'

'A DeRasse.'

'And what exactly are *you* left with, Mr Mackenzie?'

Mike considered this. 'I've got my health, I suppose. And a story to tell the grandkids.' He watched as Laura was brought out of the snooker hall. 'Incidentally, Laura's got nothing to do with any of it. I know she's a friend of yours ...'

'She'll have to give us a statement,' Ransome said. 'After that, I'll see she gets home.'

'Thanks.' Mike stared at the inside of the van.

'Not easy, is it, sir?' Ransome asked.

'What?'

'Being a criminal mastermind.'

'You'll have to ask Robert Gissing that.'

Laura had spotted them and was heading their way. She touched Ransome on his forearm. 'Any chance of a word with the prisoner?'

Ransome seemed reluctant, but her eyes won him over and he noticed that Chib Calloway was being led out of the hall in handcuffs, having woken up to find himself surrounded by Lothian and Borders' finest.

'I'll just be a minute,' Ransome warned as he headed

off in Calloway's dazed direction. Laura leaned in towards Mike and pecked him on the cheek.

'I asked you to save the day,' she told him, 'and you duly obliged.'

'You might not have noticed,' he reminded her, 'but really it didn't have much to do with me.'

'Actually,' Allan piped up, 'if we're discussing life-savers ...'

Laura beamed a smile at him and gave him a hug and a kiss, before turning back to Mike. This time when they kissed it was on the lips. Allan made a show of turning away, so they had at least the semblance of privacy. She wrapped her arms around Mike and he felt warmth flowing through him.

'Will you be in prison for a long time?' she asked.

'Will you be waiting for me?'

'I asked first.'

'Ransome reckons three years. He also says I should get the best legal team money can buy, and a psychiatrist who'll vouch for my insanity.'

'So you'll probably end up a pauper?'

'And a lunatic – is that going to affect our relationship, do you think?'

She gave a little laugh. 'Let's wait and see.'

Mike was thoughtful for a moment. 'I'll have to find out how often I'm allowed visitors ...'

'Don't count your chickens, Mackenzie – will jail be smelly and full of leering sex maniacs?'

'Probably – and that's just Allan.'

A couple of uniformed officers were approaching, ready

to usher Allan and Mike into the van. Laura and Mike embraced again and shared a final, lingering kiss.

'If I'd known,' Mike mused, 'that this was all a fellow had to do to win you over ...'

'Break it up now,' one of the uniforms said.

'One more thing,' Mike told Laura as they were separated. 'When you visit, I'll need you to bring me stuff. Maybe I can give you a shopping list?'

'What sort of stuff?'

He pretended to be thinking. 'Atlases,' he said at last. 'World atlases ...' He was halfway into the back of the van. 'Plus travel books, art books, list of museums and galleries of renown.'

'You're going to better yourself, is that it?'

He decided that the best thing to do was nod his agreement. She didn't get it, not just yet. Allan did, though, and gave him a glance that said as much.

Said there was someone Mike needed to find, just as soon as they let him out ...

Epilogue

Professor Robert Gissing was in the study of his white-washed home in the centre of Tangier. His reverie had just been broken by the sound of a motorbike misfiring. The windows had been thrown wide open, and the sun was high overhead in a clear blue sky. He could hear the varied noises of business wafting up towards him from the market downstairs. Bartering and general gossip, plus the diesel clatter of antiquated vans and lorries. They never really disturbed him, and now the motorbike's surly engine had been switched off, too. He could sometimes smell spices and coffee in the air, and cardamom, citrus fruits and incense. They all added to the sensations of a life being lived to the full in a world rich in everyday wonder. He was happy here, with his books and a glass of infused mint. There were fine rugs overlapping on the floor and fine paintings covering a good deal of the available space on the walls. He had no telephone and he received no mail. He had access to the internet, thanks to the café at the end of the street, but only used it once or twice a month to catch up on the news from Britain. He would do a word search, entering names such as Mackenzie and Calloway, Westwater and Ransome. He didn't know enough about computers to be completely confident that he wasn't leaving a trail of some kind by doing this – he remembered reading an article once about how the FBI would monitor people's borrowings from libraries, names being flagged up if they were taking out items such as *Mein Kampf* and the *Anarchist Cookbook*. He didn't suppose the internet would be very different, but all the same felt it a risk worth taking. Know your enemy and all that.

Of course, it was entirely possible that he'd been forgotten about, dismissed by the police as untraceable. And if *they* couldn't catch him, what chance did amateurs like Mike and Calloway have? Okay, so Mike had some knowledge of computers, but Gissing doubted this extended to covert tracking and the like.

For the first couple of years, however, he hadn't stayed anywhere for too long. Fake passports had been provided in a variety of names, costing him thousands but worth every penny, euro and dollar. One of the paintings that had come into his possession happened to be by an artist coveted by a Saudi businessman. Gissing had known as much when he'd taken it. The collector had paid Gissing half what the piece was worth on the open market, on the understanding that it would remain in his private gallery.

'For both our sakes,' Gissing had warned him, 'but especially yours.'

The gentleman had understood and had been delighted with the purchase. That deal alone had allowed Gissing to travel in some style: France, Spain, Italy and Greece, then Africa. He had now been in Tangier for four months, but had moved his things here from storage only once he was confident that he would be staying. At the local cafés he was known as 'the Englishman', a misapprehension he had done nothing to correct. He had grown a beard and often wore a panama hat and sunglasses. He had also fought hard to lose three and a half stones in weight. Only on a few occasions had he wondered if it had all been worth it. He was, after all, a fugitive. He could never return to Scotland, could never see friends again or drink whisky with them in a decent pub while the drizzle fell outside. But then he would spend a while gazing at his paintings, and a slowly spreading smile would replace any lingering doubts.

The CD he had been listening to stopped abruptly at the end of its final track. Bach, played by Glenn Gould. He was working his way through the classical repertoire. The same thing went for books – he had vowed to try Proust again, and to reread Tolstoy. There was even a plan to study Latin and Greek. He reckoned he had another fifteen or twenty years in him, plenty of time to savour each morsel, each sip, each musical note, word, and stroke of the brush. Tangier was similar to Edinburgh in some ways – a village masquerading as a city. He was no longer a stranger to his neighbours and the market traders. The owner of the internet café had invited him to dine with his family. Street children liked to tease him. They tugged on his beard and pointed at the bow ties he'd taken to wearing. He would sit at outdoor tables, picking at his dinner and sometimes wafting air across his face with the brim of his hat.

It was, he had concluded, neither better nor worse than the life he'd once had in Edinburgh – it was different, that was all. He regretted the involvement of Michael and Allan, naturally he did. But Calloway had been Mike's idea, and a very bad idea at that, though in retrospect almost perfect for Gissing's own purposes. Of course, it hadn't worked precisely to plan. Michael and Allan, not to mention Calloway, had been able to persuade the authorities that the missing artefacts had nothing to do with them. Gissing's photo had been published in a great many newspapers across the globe, hence his nomadic existence. But all that was in the past now, and he could start to relax a little. The book containing the Picasso lithographs was written in Spanish – some folk tale or other. He'd vowed to teach himself Spanish also, so as to savour it all the more. His favourite painting, however, was a Peploe still life, full of glassy realism and romance. He wasn't sure now about the one Wilkie portrait in his collection. If he ever needed additional funds, it would probably be the least painful to part with. The Saudi had said he would be interested, should future negotiations prove possible. For now, though, Gissing was quite content.

The doorbell sounded, followed by a knocking. He didn't get up immediately, but when the knock was repeated, curiosity got the better of him. He rose with a little effort to his feet and padded barefoot across the floor. Was he expecting someone?

The answer was yes. Yes, and always. It was a couple of weeks since his last search of the internet. Anything could have happened in the interim. People could have been released from jail. All the same, once freed from custody, they would still have a job on their hands to track him down ...

Before he had quite reached it, the door began to open.

'Hello? Is anyone home?' The voice was accented, but he couldn't quite place it.

'Can I help you?' Gissing was saying as he went to meet his visitor.

If you enjoyed

Doors Open

Don't miss

THE IMPOSSIBLE DEAD

The new thrilling novel from Ian Rankin

Coming soon in Orion hardback

ISBN: 978-0-7528-8953-5
Price £18.99

Day One

1

'He's not here,' the Desk Sergeant said.

'So where is he?'

'Out on a call.'

Fox stared hard at the man, knowing it wouldn't do any good. The Sergeant was one of those old-timers who reckoned they'd seen it all and faced most of it down. Fox glanced at the next name on his list.

'Haldane?'

'Sick leave.'

'Michaelson?'

'Out on the call with DI Scholes.'

Tony Kaye was standing just behind Fox's left shoulder. An instant before the words were out of his mouth, Fox knew what his colleague was going to say.

'This is taking the piss.'

Fox turned to give Kaye a look. News would now travel through the station: job done. The Complaints had come to town, found no one home and had let their annoyance show. The Desk Sergeant shifted his weight from one foot to the other, trying not to seem too satisfied at this turn of events.

Fox took a moment to study his surroundings. The notices pinned to the walls were the usual stuff. It was a modern police station, meaning it could just as easily have been the reception area of a doctors' surgery or DSS office, as long as you disregarded the sign warning that the Alert Status had been lifted from LOW to MODERATE. Nothing to do with Fox and his men: there'd been reports of a blast in woodland outside Lockerbie. Kids, probably, and a good long way from Kirkcaldy. Nevertheless, every police station in the country would have been notified.

The button on the counter had a hand-written sign next to it saying Press For Attention – which was what Fox had done three or four minutes ago. There was a two-way mirror behind the counter, and the Desk Sergeant had almost certainly been watching the three arrivals – Inspector Malcolm Fox, Sergeant Tony Kaye and Constable Joe Naysmith. The station had been told they were coming. Interviews had been arranged with DI Scholes, and DSs Haldane and Michaelson.

'Think this is the first time we've had this stunt pulled on us?' Kaye was asking the Desk Sergeant. 'Maybe we'll start the interviews with you instead.'

Fox flipped to the second sheet of paper in his folder. 'How about your boss – Superintendent Pitkethly?'

'She's not in yet.'

Kaye made show of checking his watch.

'Meeting at HQ,' the Desk Sergeant explained. Joe Naysmith, standing to Fox's right, seemed more interested in the leaflets on the counter. Fox liked that: it spoke of easy confidence, the confidence that these officers *would* be interviewed, that delaying tactics were nothing new to The Complaints.

The Complaints: the term was already outdated, even though Fox and his team couldn't help using it, at least among themselves. Complaints and Conduct had been their official title until recently. Now they were supposed to be Professional Ethics and Standards. Next year they'd be

6

something else again: the name Standards and Values had been mooted, to nobody's liking. They were The Complaints, the cops who investigated other cops. Which was why those other cops were never happy to see them.

And seldom entirely cooperative.

'HQ means Glenrothes?' Fox checked with the Desk Sergeant.

'That's right.'

'How long to drive there – twenty minutes?'

'Provided you don't get lost.'

The phone on the desk behind the Desk Sergeant started to ring. 'You can always wait,' he said, turning to lift the receiver, keeping his back to Fox as he started a muffled conversation.

Joe Naysmith was holding a pamphlet about home security. He plonked himself on one of the chairs by the window and started reading. Fox and Kaye shared a look.

'What do you reckon?' Kaye asked at last. 'Whole town's out there waiting to be explored . . .'

Kirkcaldy: a coastal town in Fife. Kaye had driven them there in his car. Forty minutes from Edinburgh, most of them spent in the outside lane. As they had crossed the Forth Road Bridge, they'd discussed the long queue of traffic on the opposite carriageway, heading into the capital at the start of another working day.

'Coming over here, stealing our jobs,' Kaye had joked, sounding his horn and giving a wave. Naysmith seemed to be the one with the local knowledge.

'Linoleum,' he'd said. 'Used to be what Kirkcaldy was famous for. And Adam Smith.'

'Who did he play for?' Kaye had asked.

'He was an economist.'

7

'What about Gordon Brown?' Fox had added.

'Kirkcaldy,' Naysmith had confirmed, nodding slowly.

Now, standing in the police station's reception area, Fox weighed up his options. They could sit and wait, growing restless. Or he could phone his boss in Edinburgh with a complaint of his own. His boss would then call Fife HQ and eventually something would happen – the equivalent of a wee boy running to his daddy when the big kid's done something.

Or . . .

Fox looked at Kaye again. Kaye smiled and batted Naysmith's leaflet with the back of his hand.

'Break out the pith-helmets, young Joe,' he said. 'We're heading into the wild.'

They parked the car on the seafront and stood for a few moments, staring out across the Firth of Forth towards Edinburgh.

'Looks sunny over there,' Kaye complained, buttoning his coat. 'Bet you wish you'd worn more than a donkey jacket.'

Joe Naysmith had become inured to comments about his latest designer buy, but he did turn the collar up. There was a fierce wind blowing in from the North Sea. The water was choppy and puddles along the promenade offered evidence that the tide was prone to break over the sea-wall. The gulls overhead looked to be working hard at staying airborne. There was something odd about the design of this waterfront: almost no use had been made of it. Buildings tended to face away from the view and towards the town centre. Fox had noted this elsewhere in Scotland: from Fort William to Dundee, the planners seemed to deny the existence of any shoreline. He'd never understood it, but doubted Kaye and

Naysmith would be able to help.

Joe Naysmith's suggestion had been a beach-walk, but Tony Kaye was already heading for one of the wynds leading uphill towards Kirkcaldy's shops and cafes, leaving Naysmith to dig out eighty-five pence in change for the parking. The narrow main street had roadworks on it. Kaye crossed to the other side and kept climbing.

'Where's he going?' Naysmith complained.

'Tony has a nose,' Fox explained. 'Not just any old café will do.'

Kaye had stopped at a doorway, made sure they could see him, then headed inside. The Pancake Place was light and spacious and not too busy. They took a corner table and tried to look like regulars. Fox often wondered if it was true that cops the world over tended to act the same. He liked corner tables, where he could see everything that was happening or might be about to happen. Naysmith hadn't quite learned that lesson yet and seemed happy enough to sit with his back to the door. Fox had squeezed in next to Kaye, eyes scanning the room, finding only women intent on their conversations, past being interested in the three new arrivals. They studied their menus in silence, placed an order and waited a few minutes for the waitress to return with a tray.

'Good-looking scone,' Naysmith commented, getting to work with his knife and the pat of low-fat spread.

Fox had brought the folder with him. 'Don't want you getting too comfortable,' he said, emptying its contents on to the table. 'While the tea's cooling, you can be refreshing your memories.'

'Is it worth the risk?' Tony Kaye asked.

'What risk?'

'A smear of butter on the cover-sheet. Won't look exactly

9

professional when we're doing the interviews.'

'I'm feeling reckless today,' Fox countered. 'I'll take a chance . . .'

With a sigh from Kaye, the three men started reading.

Paul Carter was the reason they'd come to Fife. Carter held the rank of Detective Constable and had been a cop for fifteen years. He was thirty-eight years old and came from a family of cops – both his father and an uncle had served in Fife Constabulary. The uncle, Alan Carter, had actually made the original complaint against his nephew. It involved a drug addict, sexual favours and turning a blind eye. Two other women then came forward to say that Paul Carter had arrested them for drunken behaviour, but offered to drop any charges if they would be 'accommodating'.

'Does anybody actually ever say "accommodating"?' Kaye muttered, halfway down a page.

'Courtroom and newspapers,' Naysmith replied, brushing crumbs from his own copy of the case-notes.

Malcolm Fox had some of those newspaper reports in front of him. There were photos of Paul Carter leaving court at the end of a day's testimony. Pudding-bowl haircut; face pitted by acne. Giving the photographer a hard stare.

It was four days since the guilty verdict had been delivered, along with the Sheriff's comment that Detective Constable Carter's own colleagues seemed 'either wilfully stupid or wilfully complicit'. Meaning: they'd known for years Carter was a bad cop, but they'd protected him, lied for him, maybe even attempted to falsify witness statements and put pressure on witnesses not to come forward.

All of which had brought The Complaints to town. Fife Constabulary needed to know, and in order to reassure the public (and, more importantly, the media)

10

that the investigation would be rigorous, they had asked a neighbouring force to run the inquiry. Fox had been given a copy of Fife Constabulary's Suspension Policy and Suspension Process Considerations, along with the Chief Constable's written report outlining why the three officers under investigation were still at work, this being 'in the best interests of the force'.

Fox took a sip of tea and skimmed another page of notes. Almost every sentence had been underlined or highlighted. The margins were filled with his own scribbled queries, concerns and exclamation marks. He knew most of it by heart, could stand up and recite it to the café's customers. Maybe they were gossiping about it anyway. In a town this size, sides would have been taken, opinions rigidly formed. Carter was a slimeball, a sleazebag, a predator. Or he'd been stitched up by a low-life junkie and a couple of cheap dates. Where was the harm in anything he'd done? And what had he done anyway?

Not much, except bring his police force into disrepute.

'Reminds me a bit of Colin Balfour,' Tony Kaye said. 'Remember him?'

Fox nodded. Edinburgh cop who liked to visit the cells if women were being held overnight. The prosecution against him had faltered, but an internal inquiry had seen him kicked off the force anyway.

'Interesting that the uncle's the one who spoke up,' Naysmith commented, drawing them back to the current case.

'But only after he retired from the force,' Fox added.

'Even so . . . Must have stirred up the family a bit.'

'Could be some history there,' Kaye offered. 'Bad blood.'

'Could be,' Naysmith agreed.

11

Kaye slapped a hand down on the pile of papers in front of him. 'So where does any of this get us? How many days are we going to be shuttling backwards and forwards?'

'As many as it takes. Might only be a week or two.'

Kaye rolled his eyes. 'Just so Fife Constabulary can say they've got one bad apple and not a whole cider factory?'

'Do they make cider in factories?' Naysmith asked.

'Where do you think they make it?'

Fox didn't bother joining in. He was wondering again about the main player, Paul Carter. There was no use trying to interview the man, even though he was available. He'd been found guilty, held in custody, but had yet to receive a sentence. The Sheriff was 'deliberating'. Fox reckoned Carter would go to jail. Couple of years and maybe a listing on the Sex Offenders Register. He was almost certainly talking to his lawyers about an appeal.

Yes, he'd talk to his legal team, but not to The Complaints. The man had nothing to gain by grassing up his mates at the station, the ones who'd stood by him. Fox couldn't offer him any kind of deal. The most they could hope for was that he would let something slip. If he talked at all.

Which he wouldn't.

Fox doubted anyone would talk. Or rather, they'd talk but say nothing worth hearing. They'd had plenty of warning this day was coming. Scholes. Haldane. Michaelson. The Sheriff had singled them out for their conflicting or confused testimony, their muddying of the water, their memory lapses. Their immediate boss in CID, Detective Chief Inspector Laird, had escaped criticism, as had a Detective Constable called Forrester.

'Forrester's the one we should be talking to,' Kaye said suddenly, breaking off from his argument with Naysmith.

12

'Why?'

'Because her first name's Cheryl. My years of experience tell me, that makes her a woman.'

'And?'

'And if one of her colleagues was a sex pest, surely she'd have had an inkling. Surrounded by blokes circling the wagons when the rumours start flying . . . She's got to know something.' Kaye rose to his feet. 'Who's for a refill?'

'Let me check first.' Fox took out his phone and found the number for the station. 'Maybe Scholes is back from his wee jaunt.' He punched in the number and waited, while Kaye flicked the back of Naysmith's head with a finger and offered his services as a barber.

'Hello?' It was a woman's voice.

'DI Scholes, please.'

'Who's calling?'

Fox looked around the café. 'I'm from the Pancake Place. He was in earlier and we think he left something.'

'Hold on, I'll put you through.'

'Thank you.' Fox ended the call and started gathering up all the paperwork.

'Nicely played,' Tony Kaye said. Then, to Naysmith: 'Back into your donkey jacket, Joe. Let's get that jack-hammer started . . .'